## Praise for Owen Hill

"*The Giveaway* tetralogy is a nasty, rat-a-tat-tat twenty-first-century noir, cynical as hell, which is where most of these characters live, or try to. Nobody is happy or satisfied, adrift as they are in their squirrelly, self-contained universe, having given away the Big Chance without realizing it. Sometime detective Clay Blackburn is one of them but he's squirming to escape, and like the fatalist crime writer David Goodis, Owen Hill is wise to the perverse pleasures derived from watching people squirm."
—Barry Gifford, author and poet

"Subtle and evocative, the compelling mysteries contained in *The Giveaway: The Clay Blackburn Story* feature a gumshoe-poet's keenly observed forays behind the fabled facade of the Bay Area. A journey of reveals only a transplanted Southern Californian like Owen Hill, wry insider and outsider, could pull off."
—Gary Phillips, author of *Ash Dark as Night*

"The mystery is real, the stakes are high; some people make it through while others ... well, let's just say they're compromised. Here we have the essence of noir, a sense of life lived at the edges, which is, come to think of it, a pretty good description of Clay's world."
—David Ulin, *Los Angeles Times*, on *The Incredible Double*

"Very well written, well paced, well timelined, and well charactered. I chuckled seeing so many of my poetic acquaintances mentioned in the text."
—Ed Sanders, on *The Incredible Double*

"Is this Berkeley noir? I'd call it lustily readable. And such reading set me to thinking about tone and that to get it right is a saintly gift (which Owen Hill has) of hearing and lavishly staying on one wiggly and implausible note throughout passages of poetic lore, pretty hot sex, action (of all things!), and multimusings on 'the life' of book writing, book selling, and humbly accepting oneself as condemned to love the many leaves we turn with aimless passion before we ourselves rattle and blow away down these raunchy beloved streets."
—Eileen Myles, author of *The Importance of Being Iceland*, on *The Incredible Double*

# The Giveaway
## The Clay Blackburn Story

Owen Hill

*The Giveaway: The Clay Blackburn Story*
© 2025 Owen Hill
This edition © 2025 PM Press

This book is a work of fiction. Any references to historical events, real people, or real places are used fictitiously. Other names, characters, places, and events are products of the author's imagination, and any resemblance to actual events or places or persons, living or dead, is entirely coincidental.

All rights reserved. No part of this book may be transmitted by any means without permission in writing from the publisher.

*The Chandler Apartments* was previously published by Creative Arts Book Company, 2002. *Righteous Kill* previously appeared in *Berkeley Noir*, published by Akashic Books, 2020. *The Incredible Double* has been previously published by PM Press, 2009.

ISBN: 979-8-88744-103-0 (paperback)
ISBN: 979-8-88744-113-9 (ebook)
LCCN: 2024943086

Cover design by John Yates/www.stealworks.com
Interior design by briandesign

10 9 8 7 6 5 4 3 2 1

PM Press
PO Box 23912
Oakland, CA 94623
www.pmpress.org

Printed in the USA.

*The Chandler Apartments*
2002
For the Poets

*Righteous Kill*
2020
For Jerry Thompson (Thompson)

*The Incredible Double*
2009
For Liz Leger

*Mayakovsky's Bugatti*
2025
For Noah Ross

# Contents

FOREWORD  The Blackburn Files *by Jonathan Lethem*  ix

The Chandler Apartments  1

Righteous Kill  105

The Incredible Double  113

Mayakovsky's Bugatti  201

ACKNOWLEDGMENTS  331

ABOUT THE AUTHORS  333

FOREWORD
# The Blackburn Files
*Jonathan Lethem*

Close to the climax of the action in *The Chandler Apartments*, the first of Owen Hill's three Clay Blackburn adventures, the poet/book scout/detective is forced to dive out onto the highway to escape his own intentional, deceptive wrecking of one of his cherished tiny sports cars, a Miata. Blackburn is rescued, given shelter and solace, by a couple of rustic, pot-growing off-the-grid hippies, who take him in and tend his wounds. "They brought out some of their products and we smoked," Blackburn tells the reader. "They treated me to their homemade dark ale. I found their singsong voices relaxing. I'm an old punk. I shaved my head in the late '70s, took lots of meth, listened to the hardest and fastest music I could find. Hated hippies. Too old to care about those differences now. Anybody who stands outside the mainstream is okay by me."

By the time we get to know him, Blackburn is more of a normcore than a punk. His chosen music is mostly squeaky hard bop jazz and moody, late-night Van Morrison albums, while meth has been replaced with his beloved signature cocktail, the Negroni. Drink, though, is hardly Blackburn's sole vice. In fact, so far as vices are concerned, he's something of a collector of them: poetry, rare book editions, impulsive sex—which, due to his switch-hitting, he's eligible to indulge in with the whole of the wild roster of humans who populate his adventures—and rich foods; these are just the most prominent. Blackburn is, above all, addicted to his own luxuriantly wandering eye, his own curiosity, and to the trouble into which it leads him—he's a connoisseur of weirdos and weird scenes, attractive interior design, lazy seductions, and unprecedented intoxicants. Blackburn's short haircut and outwardly mild temperament enable him to blend easily into a panoply of milieus, which may prove helpful in all three of his forms of "professional" engagement: the book scouting, the detective work, and the poet garnering voices and texture from the scenes he drifts through.

Yet the more we get to know him, the more we're persuaded Blackburn is a Pure Product of Berkeley. He's not only queer, but a queer sort of all else he declares himself to be: a queer sort of detective, a queer sort of communist or anarchist, and beyond—a queer sort of gourmet, ethical thinker, cat owner, and—for certain—a queer sort of narrator. Not that he's incapable of giving it to us straight: Blackburn's tartly honest as he tabulates his preferences in food and drink, in literature and fucking, as he is when he declares in favor of the kind of people "who stay outside the mainstream." The difficulty comes, though, in how the zero-sum depredations of money, gentrification, and greed and their accompanying slick ideologies tend to warp and corrupt the systems of affiliations and attractions that Hill explores in his fictions.

That's to say: These flippant, jubilant, and gently (but increasingly) surreal tales about an amoral poet-detective are also at their root truly dedicated in their study of the city of Berkeley, which, though it may fancy itself seceded into a "People's Republic" of its own, is nevertheless both a funhouse mirror reflection and a microcosmic facet of the Great American Nightmare we all inhabit. Written surprisingly slowly—the three books and one short story covering almost a quarter century—they capture a sense we urbanists all feel, of living in the past, present, and future of our cities simultaneously, a thing that may drive us slowly insane. As Blackburn runs his circuit of beloved touchstone locales and facades through the stories again and again—Le Bateau Ivre, Moe's, Brennan's, the various cafés with their Italian names, and his beloved Chandler Apartments—we feel they have become a string of rosary beads which he fingers obsessively, just to be certain they're still there. The penultimate time he mentions Fred's Market, it is accompanied by a desolate parenthetical: "(now gone)."

This functionally means that Hill has to fudge the dates and ages in his sequence, since Clay Blackburn stays youngish, or early-middle-aged, even as the Berkeley around him slides, in its trapped-in-amber bubble, toward the dystopian present. Blackburn is a bit like a *Peanuts* character, then, a Linus still dragging his philosophical blanket around while the world ages—matures? curdles?—around him, over a period of decades. Of course, the "knight-errant" is the entrenched role of the detective in hard-boiled stories, as is well established in Raymond Chandler and Ross Macdonald. Fundamentally, he's a man out of time. If Hill has injected the *Black Mask* detective archetype with some of the ingredients of its opposite, a kind of amoral, indolent, epicene, and hedonistic flair that suggests Patricia Highsmith's Tom Ripley character, he's nevertheless isolated the essential time-lost quality that gives all such hard-boiled narrators their bittersweet Proustian undertone of remorse.

When I say that Hill studies "systems of affiliation," those systems are, of course, made, like Soylent Green, out of people. Unlike books or a trusted cocktail or meal or cup of espresso, people are unreliable by their nature: Can't live with 'em, can't kill 'em. Nor can Blackburn always trust himself not to be corrupted, although his form of being "on the take" turns out, heartbreakingly by the end of the sequence, to be the lover's weakness. Without giving anything away, the great *object petit a*—aka, the unattainable—Dino Centro forms a desublimated counterpart to the Terry Lennox character in Raymond Chandler's masterpiece, *The Long Goodbye*. More than just the one who got away, Centro, like Lennox, is the one who breaks the heart you thought couldn't anymore be broken, who steals the innocence you no longer thought you harbored. If Chandler's detective's long quest is fundamentally how to hold to the standards of chivalry while drowning in corrupt modernity, Hill's is more a matter of what it is to retain one's queer dissident posture when a stylized obedience to capital turns all the countercultural havens into pod-people enactments. Is Robin Hood corrupted the minute he lays a hand on the dough? Is hedonism a sufficient compass to lead one through the dark maze? Read the Clay Blackburn stories and find out!

# The Chandler Apartments

# 1.

Once I had a wife, and she liked cute little cars. A little out of character for her (she was the solid career type), but charming. She looked great in convertibles, so we bought one even though Berkeley is usually a little too cool for them. Paid cash, thanks to my Uncle Deke, who died with a savings account and no heirs. When we parted she bought herself a vintage Triumph, found (I swear) a Brit boyfriend, and made no claim on the Miata.

It's a dumb car, especially for me. I'm a book scout. That is, I go to estate sales, postal auctions, the homes of the widows of college profs, the Goodwill, anyplace where there might be a sellable book. Then I take said books to various booksellers, starting with rare book dealers and quality used bookstores, then down the line of dusty little shops, internet sellers, and finally a dealer from Manila who sends anything in English to ... who knows where.

My silly little Miata (bright red ... God help me) does impose a certain amount of self-discipline, which is a good thing for any book hound. I can only fit six or seven shopping bags (bags, not boxes—easier to handle) per haul, so I go for the cream. If I score on a bigger library, I have to prevail upon Marvin and his old Econoline, which means making him dinner, anything he likes. He likes expensive. When we got the Meltzer library (well, not the whole thing, Moe's Books got there first) he wanted Chilean sea bass ($17.99 a pound) and two bottles of Sattui chardonnay. Throw in several Negronis and a few shots of Laphroaig, and I could have gone to Bekins. Marv looks like an old hippie, but his tastes are yuppie all the way.

I have no off-street parking, so the Miata takes a beating. Telegraph Avenue, world-famous open-air asylum, is hell on parked cars. If you can find a space at all. I moved to the neighborhood after the breakup, six years ago. The Chandler Apartments. A beautifully restored '20s building overlooking a sea of kooks. Its denizens are split down the middle, half rich-kid students and half rent-control survivors. I pay the rent-board-dictated price of $453.35 a month for a large, airy studio on the fourth floor. Four big windows with a view of Oakland and the hills. The grad student down the hall pays $809.94. The owner, a New York/Berkeley lefty, is surprisingly nice about the situation. For the first couple of years the noise from Telegraph drove me nuts, but now I find it comforting. Call it a sense of community. Even the craziest street person knows my face, and for a few quarters a month they treat me as a friend. There's a sense of adventure, of movement, on the Avenue. That's a scarce commodity in late capitalist California (America? the industrialized world?). The bongos, the Krishnas, the cries of imaginary friends have stopped disturbing me now. Actually, they drive all thoughts of loneliness from my mind. Though I've never been especially prone to loneliness.

Scouting isn't making me rich. Actually, if it weren't for cheap rent, the wolf would be camping on the front stoop. Old Uncle Deke helps a little. Just under $20,000, now in a CD. Mad money. And an occasional adventure takes me out of the state, or the country. Last splurge was a trip to Paris with an old friend, recently released from an ugly relationship. She needed to do something dramatic, and I was handy. I guess I have a knight-in-shining-armor complex. Well, no guessing about it. Kind of embarrassing in pre-post-feminist Berkeley. It gets me into scrapes, but I enjoy playing Good Samaritan, especially to a certain kind of person, lithe and flip, with underlying vulnerability and a great kiss. Maybe I'm a cad. After the Paris trip the Miata got keyed, and when I innocently asked her ex about the wound, I had to duck a wild flail, kick him in the knee, and beat it back to the Chandler. I'm too small (five foot eight, 142 pounds) to win most fair fights, so I've learned how to hit and run.

## 2.

Peggy Denby is, like me, a small-press poet. That is, we write poetry with no hope of being published by a major house. My books have been published by the likes of Angry Dog Press and Thumbscrew Press, and in mags like *Gas*, *Bluebook*, and *Twatsdelight*, which is Peggy's. *Twat* is best described as irreverent post-post-punk pseudo cute. You know the look. Fake leopard skin and kitty glasses. The *Twatsdelight* logo features a martini glass. And that is Peggy's look too.

Her message had said, "Meet me at the place where you always go," and I dutifully entered Le Bateau Ivre at the right time, scoring an outside table under a tree on a beautiful May Monday afternoon. The Drunken Boat has one real waiter and a bunch of kids. Real Waiter took my table, so I ordered a Negroni. I didn't order for Peggy, because I hadn't seen her in at least two years. Last time I ordered for someone I hadn't seen in a while it was a mistake. He'd become a twelve-stepper, and I had no choice but to drink his stout for him. Sound advice: Never drink a Negroni with a stout chaser.

The wise waiter brought me the perfectly chilled drink. I took a nibbling sip, tasting the bitter Campari on the tip of my tongue, the part that better detects sweet things, then I smelled for the gin, which was, thankfully, there. Then I took a slightly bigger sip and treated the rest of my tongue to the flavors. The third sip was really more of a slug. I tried to collect my thoughts. I've had a crush on Peggy for ten years, and five years ago we had what I guess could be called an affair (we slept together more than once). Despite being intimate we were never close, really. We had some nice talks, but they were mostly about poetry or art, nothing too personal. I would have pushed it further. Like I said, I have a crush on her. But she wouldn't let it go that way. For one thing, she wanted a real husband, and I pride myself on not being a real anything. Well, I like to think I'm real, as in honest, but I can't fit the role. Any role. I can't even fit the role of the misfit, a role that may have intrigued her. I work too hard, always pay my bills, keep my (many) bad habits in check.

When Peggy met Thomas we stopped seeing each other. I still appeared in her mag, and I once featured her in my (now defunct) mag, *Blind Date*. But I think I made Thomas uncomfortable, or the both of them, or something. I saw her a couple of years ago before they went off to England for Thomas's unofficial sabbatical. He's up at Cal, a lecturer in English lit. Or should I say, was. He died a couple of months ago. I sent Peggy a card and kind of expected a call. It didn't come until yesterday.

She was only a few minutes late. She looked astonishingly beautiful. What is a man supposed to say when a woman loses weight? Or, to put a finer point on it, what is a man in Berkeley supposed to say? She was one of those women who could pull off being chunky, but now she wasn't chunky. She looked like an athlete. The '80s nerd look had always worked for her, I guess, but now anything would work. The blonde hair was very short now, and the black glasses seemed bigger on her smaller face. Her skin didn't seem as white as before. She must be exercising outside, I thought. She kissed me full on the lips, but it wasn't a sexy kiss. Our deft waiter appeared, and she ordered straight Beefeater, ice, no lime, and after he left said, "I'd have ordered more, but it seems weird to order a double in a garden." She was right. The Drunken Boat is more a café. I usually have my second drink at home.

"I missed you, Peggy."

"Missed you too. My life's a mess. Do you still like to give aid and comfort to lonely women?"

"I suppose it's a fault. And most of the women I know would probably do better without me."

"Don't be so modest."

Then we got off the subject for a while, talking about her new book. Experimental short stories, "kind of languagey." I tried to steer things back to her messy life, partly for the sake of gossip, but also because I sensed that she really did need help. She was slippery, though, only half referring to being depressed, to having "big problems." Finally I got bored and asked her outright. "All right, I'll tell you more, but not here. Come with me back to my place."

And so we got into her Volvo, not the new kind, but one of the classic old ones that artsy women so often drive, and went to her place on Lake Merritt.

She lived on the tenth floor of a newish condo, down near Fairyland. The living room faced San Francisco, the kitchen looked out across the lake. The big tinted windows didn't seem to open. I thought of a hotel where I'd once stayed in Waikiki, my memory jogged by the Hawaiiana that filled the apartment. Bobble-headed dolls and leis littered the end tables. Mylar-framed Don Ho record covers, fake flowers, funny ashtrays. I often feel confused in places like these, because I actually like this junk. My grandmother and my dear great-aunt Dinah decorated this way; it brings back nice memories. But I understand that I'm supposed to feel some sense of irony. I don't. Too much Robert Lowell, I guess. The lowest-common-denominator type is lost on me.

I sat on the futon, which was covered in a material that, in my surfer youth, we called "jams." Sky-blue background with a white floral design. My first love wore a skirt like that. Peggy offered me a drink. I opted for bubbly water. The situation seemed serious. I wanted a clear head. She went into the kitchen and made us drinks. I assumed that hers was alcoholic.

"What's the problem, Peggy?"

She sat on the floor in front of the couch, a hideous driftwoody coffee table between us.

"It's still difficult to talk about anything having to do with Thomas. I'm still grieving. But something's terribly wrong. When he discovered that he was sick, he wanted to travel. He called the trip a sabbatical because he didn't want people to know. He just wasn't ready to talk about it. We thought he had at least a year. But by the time we got to Rome he was pretty sick. He insisted on taking the train down to Calabria, and then on to Sicily. I got him to a hospital in Palermo, and he got a little stronger. One day I returned to the hotel after sightseeing to find that he'd been taken back to the hospital. He was dead by the time I got there. Less than a month after the initial diagnosis.

"In Rome we stayed at the Margutta, on the Piazza del Popolo. We went down to one of the cafés the first morning. He pulled some papers from his book bag. There was a bankbook, a regular passbook, and a couple of bank statements in envelopes. The passbook had a balance of $27,503 and change. The statements were for CDs and a mutual fund, each worth over fifty thousand. I was shocked that he had so much money, considering the way he spent. He always kept those things separate, and we didn't talk about it much. He had more than me, of course, but I do all right with the tech writing and various temp things. He paid three-quarters of the rent and helped out on vacations. But we never talked about the specifics. He said it would be easy enough for me to get the money, even though we weren't legally married. As Thomas always said, 'Why bother?' He'd made a will. But when he died and it was time to straighten these things out, I found that the money wasn't there. Large chunks of the accounts had been withdrawn, every few days, and deposited into his checking account. Almost a half a mil was drawn from that account, mostly by checks made out to cash."

"Do you have a contact at the bank?"

"Yes, Dean. Dean Centro. He said that it would be easy enough to do. The checks were cashed at various banks, and there were lots of ATM withdrawals."

"But Thomas was pretty ill. How'd he do it?"

"We don't know, although he was up and around at least part of the time."

"Does his son know about this?" I knew Thomas's son, Hart Opffer, a little from the literary world.

"Yes, although he doesn't know the amount. He suspects that I did it. There's a daughter too, Stephanie. A spoiled little dot-commer. She also assumes that I took the money. They both hate me, the way that kids often hate young second wives. I'm thirty-one, two years older then Stephie, and three years younger than Hart. And I was to be left a larger cut, half, with the children splitting the other half. Also, I got the apartment. But I'll have to sell. I can't afford these payments."

"Have you talked to the police?"

"Yes, but there's been no crime. They aren't too interested."

"I'll talk to some people, but I'm no detective."

"I've heard that you've done some work like that."

"A little, once or twice, kind of by accident. Maybe you should call Sam Truitt. He makes a living at this sort of thing."

"Oh yeah, Sam Truitt, poet-detective. Problem is, he's teaching at Naropa this summer. To be frank, he was my first choice."

"Thanks. You could, you know, call a non-artsy detective. A pro."

"I couldn't do that. Too painful. What I really need is a friend. But, if by chance you do find some of this money, I'll give you some. Say, twenty thousand, if you recover it all?"

"I'll talk to some people. And on those other jobs I got some expense money. Just gas and lunch, and plane fare if I need it. Or you could pay this month's rent and I'll devote full-time to it."

She went into the drawer of an end table and pulled out an envelope. Counted out six one-hundred-dollar bills.

"Do you always have that much cash on hand?"

"Drug money. They still don't take cards."

## 3.

Marvin is my best friend, and, in a way, my landlord. He owns the garage where I store my books. It's a small one, attached to his old bungalow-style house in North Berkeley. He bought the place in the mid-'70s, before Chez Panisse, the Cheese Board, and Black Oak Books made the neighborhood upscale. He's "old Berkeley," meaning that his politics are to the left of Mao but that this doesn't stop him from appreciating the better things in life: Niman Ranch beef, good wine, trips to Cuba. He drives his old van down to Silicon Valley a couple of times a week, where he makes a ton of money doing something that I'll never understand. When people ask him what he does he says, "I'm kind of a programmer, I guess." He looks and dresses like Neil Young. He refuses to tell me his age, but I'd guess he's in his late forties, about ten years older than me.

Once a week I make him dinner, rent on the garage. This week I made shrimp ravioli, and I got off cheap with a pinot grigio. Dinner conversations revolved around SUVs and the types who drive them. He drives a gas-guzzling monster too, but at least his has some style. The Peggy situation didn't come up until I started serving the ricotta cake and the grappa.

"So," he asked, "is this what you're doing for a living now?"

"This?"

"Helping people, mostly women. Getting expense money, and a little something after the job. It is more profitable than scouting."

"I'm not *doing* anything. There was one job, then another. Now this. Word of mouth. I won't be printing business cards. After all, I don't really know what I'm doing. I can't use a gun, can't really fight. I was never a cop."

"You're a pretty good street fighter. And, like any book bum, you're a good con man and a good liar. But your best qualification for the job is that people don't take you seriously. You're no threat until you kick 'em in the balls and run."

"You can write my résumé."

"Clay Blackburn, PI. Sounds like a TV show. That masculine name had to come in handy someday." He punctuated this remark by downing his grappa. Signaled for another.

"Also featuring Marvin Clarke, marginal character, nerdy sidekick, sometime computer whiz."

"Fuck you. Okay, so there's Peggy the widow, and some missing money. And it's worth twenty grand if you find it. Where do you go from here?"

"There's a son and a daughter. And there's Peggy. I'll start asking questions and see how it plays. And I could talk to somebody at the bank."

"I could get his records easily enough."

"Really?"

"If it's on a computer, it can be found. You'll owe me some dinners, though."

Deal.

# 4.

Marvin called me the next morning, asking for Thomas's mother's maiden name, which of course I didn't have. Called back a few minutes later to say he didn't need it, he had the info, and he'd give me the lowdown "at dinner." I hung up and the phone rang. Now Peggy wanted to take me to dinner. She had things to talk about. I called Marvin back, got a quick summary, and rescheduled him for the following night. I didn't want anything getting in the way of an intimate dinner with Peggy Denby.

The lowdown wasn't really low, though. Thomas had been draining the accounts of cash for months, a little at a time. He'd probably shown Peggy old statements, because by the time they hit Calabria they were pretty well drained—by check, ATM, and phone transfer to anther checking account. I'd suspected that. I wondered where that money went. I figured he'd spent it on something fun, in his last months on earth. Drugs or something. Why not? Anyway, I didn't think I had much chance of recovering it. Cash doesn't stay cash for very long. I'd have dinner with her and hear her out, but the $600 and a nice dinner was the best I could hope for.

Oliveto has a place in local culinary history now, and it has upgraded along with the neighborhood. But I still remember it as friendly and unpretentious. I used to eat breakfast downstairs a lot when I lived in Rockridge. When my second chapbook came out, the management let me do a reading in one corner of the café. Now the downstairs has tablecloths and service, and breakfast would be a splurge.

I waved the waitress away and wound my way through the crowded room and back to the bar. No hard liquor downstairs, which meant no Negroni. I ordered a Punt e Mes with soda. The bartender had a starched white shirt, just like Paris. She also had about fifteen pieces of jewelry pierced through various parts of her, which is probably just like Paris too. I wanted to make conversation, but the place was too crowded. They were playing (I swear!) the Gypsy Kings on the stereo, which is just like somewhere ... somewhere in Europe. To match the blotchy spongy paint job, the arched doorways, the tile floor. Euroland. I wondered if the Gypsy Kings were camp yet, and not knowing made me feel old. The bartender brought me some pistachios and two olives, compliments of the house, and accidentally (?) brushed my hand, which made me smile. I said, with a frown, "Do you like this music?"

"No, the management makes us play this bullcrap."

I liked her style. The other bartender was a taut little guy, a mystery-eth of the type that grows hereabouts. From where? Who cares. Whatever. His T-shirt was shortish, like what you'd expect a young girl to wear, but he wore it well. He bumped into my server, and she put one arm around him and giggled. I felt ancient, although I've only got about ten years on them. I'd sell my soul to watch them fuck, I was thinking, as Peggy Denby came into the café.

There's a woman who works at a certain bookstore in Santa Monica, a store that specializes in art books. Since the mid-'80s, she's been wearing the same uniform to work: a very short black dress, heavy black glasses, Doc Martens. Short blonde hair, LA beach tan. Severe facial expressions, then a slow smile. She is on my short list of reasons to live. We've never had a conversation, but I've heard her speak. She has a deep voice, like Lauren Bacall. In the fifteen years that I've "known" her she has grown more beautiful. Our relationship is, for me, the only marriage that could work. And now here was Peggy Denby, same outfit. A little gawkier than my Beatrice, perhaps. And she put her hand on my shoulder, and leaned down, and in a voice an octave lower than I remember, said, "Ready to come upstairs?" And I climbed the stairs with my arm around her, hand on the hip.

Upstairs at Oliveto there was an air of excitement. The yuppies and amateur restaurant reviewers were waiting to be entertained. We got a good table, looking out at College Avenue. I have to admit that I was excited too. Great food with a beautiful woman. Reminded myself that she's recently widowed, probably not ready for anything too heavy. Tried to think of something I liked about Thomas. Couldn't.

The appetizers were ridiculous, but they tasted good. Tiny pieces of prosciutto and artichokes were strewn around a huge platter. A couple of olives. I looked around at the other diners. They nibbled, rolled their eyes to the ceiling, sipped some wine. Looked down at their tables, as if deciphering some ancient code. Nodded their approval.

Peggy ordered the wine, and it was perfect. The faux rustic food arrived, spit-roasted meats, Swiss chard. We still hadn't said much.

Finally, "There's more to all of this than I've told you."

"I figured as much, Peggy."

"Something went on in Italy. Thomas gave me the slip a few times. Lots of phone calls at the hotel. He had these sidelines."

"Sidelines?"

"Stuff. African stuff. Greek stuff."

"Peggy, I don't know if I can help you. I'm no pro. But you trusted me enough to pay me the six hundred. Why don't you just tell me what you know, think, and want. If I think I'm in over my head, I'll return the money. And you know I'll be discreet. For starters, what do you mean by stuff?"

"Artifacts. He was, in his words, kind of an archaeologist. He loved to travel, and he'd pick things up. After a while he got a reputation, and people, dealers, I guess, would come to him. Sometimes he'd represent collectors. He never used the term 'black market,' but he'd buy, say, a little piece of folk art, a trinket, as he called them, and he'd leave it in the hotel room. We'd come back, and then it would be gone. Then, weeks after getting home, someone would deliver it to the apartment. Then it would disappear again."

"Weren't you curious?"

"Of course. And I loved looking at the artwork. But when I asked about it all he'd make a joke, or he'd say, 'Don't worry, there's no real risk.' It didn't seem like such a big deal. After all, who in this town hasn't done a little smuggling? When I was twenty I lived for a summer off some hash that I bought in Amsterdam. If Thomas was buying and selling a few trinkets, no big deal."

"But now you're starting to worry?"

"Well, there's the missing money. And he did die suddenly."

"I thought he was ill."

"Yes, but he was supposed to have some time left. And I wasn't there when he was taken from the hotel. I was told that a maid discovered him and called an ambulance."

"Peggy, I can try and find the money for you, but I want no part in anything deeper. If you think somebody killed him, we'll call the cops."

"The cops would laugh. Anyway, I don't expect you to find a murderer. But I think he was into something deep, involving lots of money. More than he let on. And I'm legal heir to half of it, according to the will. Well, 'legal' is probably the wrong term, considering where it came from. But if you can help me, we could split my part."

"How much? And where might it be?"

"I don't know, but he hinted that he'd come across some 'special trinkets.' He kept using that phrase."

I didn't give her a definitive answer. She ordered a half bottle of dessert wine, then a glob of chocolate something, then coffee. Visions of Roman statuary danced in my head, along with Fra Angelico, Leonardo, other crazy stuff. My poet side was giving in to the romance of it all—and to Peggy, who was leaning close, talking about other things, personal stuff, old times ... pale blue eyes can be a problem for me, and a certain type of deep voice, with a certain timbre, the right mix of breath in the vowels, can talk me into anything. Sometimes I fight it for a while, sometimes I don't, but at some point I just let go.

## 5.

I had visions of a sexy weekend in Hawaii world, but it didn't turn out that way. The should we/shouldn't we dance seems to be part of my karmic makeup. I just bring it out in people. She had one vodka (no mixer), her eyes glazed over, and she began thinking and feeling out loud. Life-story time. And I was drawn into it, and she heard my story, or at least the sitting-on-the-floor-with-a-woman-late-at-night version, and then we were closer friends than we'd anticipated. The situation had some weight. I've slept with friends, and I've had it be good. Actually, come to think of it, I've slept with most of my friends, although with some we really did just sleep. It's a tricky situation, which is what makes it delicious. In order to make it work you need just the right amount of time and space. Outside interests help. They keep the focus from getting too sharp. But the key is this: an almost Zen-like lack of expectations. Being a poet, I think of it as a kind of negative capability. You dive into the sex-friendship, see where it goes, hope for the best. Let the currents carry you toward the non-shore, the non-goal. And remember to enjoy the water. Because if the thing doesn't work out (whatever "work out" means), you're both going to sink like bricks.

And so the voice of experience whispered, Take it slow. And I sensed that she was hearing the same voice. Wasn't always like that for me. But as the big poet said, I have had to learn the simplest things last. Which made for difficulties.

She went into the kitchen, after two a.m. I guessed, and came out with one tumbler about a quarter full of a very smooth Scotch, and we shared it standing by the window, looking out at the lake and the skyline. A good kiss, then a better one. A few more. I'm tired, me too, you shouldn't drive, you shouldn't either. I'll take the couch. No, you take it. Is this okay? Yeah. But then we sat on the couch and talked some more. At some point she got up and went to bed.

Next morning she came out wearing a goofy short robe. Another Hawaiian print. Went outside and got a *Chronicle*. Started some coffee. There was nothing studied about her. She bumped into things, her hair fell into her eyes. Her robe was barely fastened, in a way that should have been coy. But I don't think she was capable of coy. You rarely meet a beautiful person, of either sex, who isn't on some level aware of their beauty, or at least of the attention they attract. Here was an exception. The great haircut just happened to be comfortable for her. She got a tan because the sun relaxed on her. Exercise made her feel healthy. Vanity had little to do with these matters. I liked that a lot. She lit a cigarette, which surprised me.

"I didn't know you smoked."

"Once in a while. It's nice having you here. Sorry I wasn't ready to go all the way. God, what a silly phrase. I feel like I'm in high school. Do you ever get flustered, Clay? I'm flustered. I'm probably too old to be flustered, but I am. I'm a widow. Imagine. A widow." Her voice broke.

"I'm almost always flustered. A constant state. You won't know me when you finally see me calm."

"Now? You're flustered now?" Her voice was strong again. I had pulled her out of it.

"Of course I am. I've been attracted to you for years, and last night we got this close. Don't apologize. It's okay. It just worked out that way. But my pulse is weird. I feel fuzzy. I can't hold a thought. Flustered."

"Flustered." She smiled as if we'd invented the word. First word of our own personal language. "Clay, I lost my husband, and now I'm into some weird shit that I can't understand. This isn't my life. I write experimental verse! I'm most comfortable when I'm swimming in words. I've always pulled away from life. My heroines are Emily Dickinson and Leslie Scalapino. I don't trust my senses. My friends are mostly academics. You fascinate me. I mean the way you live. The apartment on Telegraph, digging for old books. All the nuts you hang out with. But I don't know how close I'd want to be to that."

"You came to me, dear."

"For help, because you're out in the world more."

"Don't you think you're overdoing this a little? You do live in Oakland. Look outside your window, isn't there a shooting or a drug deal happening out on the lake?"

"Just help me out, Clay."

I said I would.

And then she surprised me again, by going into the kitchen and making breakfast. "My habit has always been to cook for my lovers." Lovers?

We talked like a couple till the eggs came, and they were just plain scrambled eggs, but they were good.

This became our pattern for the next few weeks. I didn't doubt that eventually I'd move off the couch and into the bedroom. I knew the attraction went both ways. I felt a little frustrated at times, but I enjoyed her company enough to endure. When she had a reading in LA I was entrusted with a key. I came in twice a day for the three days and fed her cat, Gertrude Stein. I began to worry about the situation. I've been told by various people that I fear commitment. Actually, fear has nothing to do with it. I am completely (sometimes masochistically) committed to my friends, my lovers, my work, my art. I just happen to think that traditional marriage is a dismal, dreary way to live. When I was young and stupid, I shrugged, said, Try anything once! and tied the knot. Like I said, once I had a wife. Waste of time. There's one simple thing I learned early.

I wasn't entirely sure how Peggy Denby felt on the subject. Oh well, my head was still above water. Negative capability.

# 6.

Marvin found out about some math books in San Jose. We took the van down. The books were good. Fifteen bags of graduate texts published in Germany. The nerd who owned them was moving to a new place in Aptos. Seems he struck it rich in some high-tech way, and he just wanted to lighten his load before moving to a huge house by the sea. He took about a dollar a book. Worth at least ten apiece at Moe's.

I felt a little giddy as we loaded the Econoline. I suggested that we go to Santa Cruz and stay in a motel by the boardwalk. There's a Mexican dive restaurant I really liked down there, Tampico. I had a vision of waking up, fuzzy from tequila, then clearing my head by jumping into the waves. Of course Marvin was all for it. Marvin's up for anything that can be consumed. After he agreed, I added that I'd like to swing by Natural Bridges and talk to Hart Opffer. He groaned but said okay.

We knew Hart from here and there. He was an artist, poet, lecturer, café intellectual. Dabbler. For a time he owned a bookstore in San Francisco that didn't go. Lately he'd been a sort of literary entrepreneur, booking readings and chauffeuring famous writers around. He had a show on KPFA and on KZSC, the Santa Cruz college station. He'd bought a house by the beach when houses there were cheap. It was the kind of '70s beach box that surfers used to share. Probably worth three-quarters of a mil now.

Hart seemed happy when I called, but he didn't invite me up to his place. We met in a bar downtown. The Red Room, or that's what everybody's called it since I lived there in the mid-'70s. It was a dive back when I was a regular. Then it became retro, and popular with students. Judging from the lack of happy-hour customers, it had fallen out of favor with the cocktail generation. Hart is a good-looking man with long brown hair and New Agey, too-clear grayish eyes. He announced that he was just back from Cuba and that it was wonderful, but also a little sad. He shook his head, didn't quite cluck his tongue. I felt Marvin tense up. Marvin goes down there a couple of times a year. His mission is to spend as much American money as possible in a communist country. He fully supports Castro, and I suspect he's done some kind of work for the Cuban government. I have the normal, Berkeleyite liberal soft spot for Castro, Che, and co., but I can't support Castro's cutthroat ways. But then I don't support any political leader. As Marvin has pointed out, many times, brutality is part of being a head of state, anywhere. Marvin sees Castro as our asshole, an asshole for the downtrodden.

Marvin sensed, and later conversation proved, that Hart went down for cheap rum, cheap boys, cheap girls, cheap whatever. All the things Santa Cruz had to offer before the earthquake. Well, subtract rum and add cheap pot. After the town was leveled in '89 the chamber of commerce types took over, and now the place looks and feels like Santa Barbara. Another victory for the shopping mall that took over California.

"Yes," sighed Hart, "the poverty is really sad. But when I'm there I feel such a sense of the authentic. The place is poor yet unspoiled. You look at the children there, and their faces are so open!"

Marvin was gearing up for a speech. If I didn't do something soon, he'd be banging the café table, quoting Marx. I decided to get right to another sore point. At least Marvin had a little stake in this one.

"I've been seeing a lot of your stepmom."

"Don't call her that. Dad must have been temporarily insane. Why are you seeing her?"

"We seem to be traveling in the same circles. Did you know she's having trouble with the estate?"

"Of course. But the answer is simple. She took the money, at some point, or talked him out of it. And now it's spent and she wants more. She's getting around to blaming me for it. Me or Stephie. And she's got Dean Centro on her side. That creep. I hate banker types."

Marvin was getting ready to pounce. I kicked him under the table. I pointed out that Peggy is an artist type.

"My stepmother, as you call her, is a fake. Her poetry stinks. Double-bubble lingo-babble."

"Not authentic like yours, eh, Hart? Plumbed from the depths of the working classes?" This from Marvin, who was just getting started. "How much did you pay your employees when you owned that crummy bookstore?"

I couldn't afford to let him get rolling. I needed information. I listed the questions in my mind: Did Hart know how much money was involved? About his father's love of trinkets? Did he notice a change in his father's spending habits?

Sometimes fate throws one a fish. Marvin got up to go to the toilet. He asked me to order him another drink. I didn't. I had five minutes to talk to Hart. He claimed he didn't know how much was involved. He shared his father's love of collecting; they spoke about it often. But he didn't know his father's sources. I didn't buy that one. I nudged things in the direction of Thomas's spending habits, but he dummied up.

Marvin returned with a killer look in his eyes. Hart looked otherworldly. Too much time in the hot tub, I guessed. I paid the bartender, shook hands with Hart, got Marvin the hell out of there.

Tampico was a fiesta. End-of-semester party time. Our table was by the kitchen, but relatively quiet. Every so often we would hear a shriek coming from the direction of the bar, followed by laughter and applause. I faced a huge trophy fish, the kind that Hemingway might have caught.

This inspired me, so I ordered a seafood plate and extra tortillas. Pacificos, with shots of tequila on the side. Life is good in Santa Cruz, especially if you don't have to live there. Marvin drank his first shot in one gulp, not his usual style. He was pissed.

"That lingo-babble line is mine! I used it in a review in *Poetry Flash*. Rich bastard. How did he get so rich?"

"Story is that he sold his part in the store to his partner. Bought a couple of houses. Land rich, with lots of debt. A postmodern success story."

"He probably stole Peggy's money."

"How? There's no proof." I tasted my tequila. We'd ordered the high-end stuff. If the richest gold bullion could be turned into a drink, it would taste like this. I decided to let the Hart subject drop. Marvin is very persuasive. I needed to keep my mind open. I couldn't make up my mind until it was time to make up my mind. I sank into myself, said, Clay, just poke around. See how it plays. There's no deadline. After all it's only money. Nobody's going to die or starve if it isn't found. And, there's this new thing, Peggy. That's the most interesting part of all of this.

Talk of politics, poetry. Relationship war stories, travel plans. Nothing having to do with the book business. That subject is off-limits when we're having fun. The food was perfect. Spicy and greasy in all the right places. Marvin ordered flan as an excuse to sit a little longer. Finally we decided to stand at the bar and have one last shot of the good stuff before heading on to the motel.

The bar was a scene. Young, beautiful amateur drinkers were talking too loudly and bumping into each other. A too-new jukebox was playing great Mexican music. Lots of accordions and horns, and high sad voices that immediately grabbed me and dragged me down about a thousand miles to La Paz and a certain group of expats that almost ruined my life, but in a good way. I looked over at Marvin and his eyes were glazed over, no doubt reliving some adventure south of the border. He had gone to school in San Miguel de Allende, then hung around for a year, then spent some time in Central America doing who knows what for the right (left) side.

I noticed a woman at the other end of the bar. Not as young or beautiful as the students. But sexy. She was sitting, facing away from the bar, talking to a clump of coeds. They moved on, and she swung back to face the bartender and order another beer. I knew I'd seen her, but I was a little fuzzy on where. She caught my eye and came over. We were halfway into a hug before I remembered. Stevie, a buyer at Logo's Books and Records. A second later, I heard Marvin, almost at a yell, say, "*Stevie O'Hara!* How the *hell* ... ?" and I remembered that they'd had something, a fling? Or was it more serious? Couldn't remember.

People from the other California have a thick drawl. I mean people from Stockton, Salinas, Palmdale, Merced ... anyplace but LA and San Francisco. Once, a twerpy little grad student at Cal confided to me that he'd had a difficult time losing his accent. He'd grown up about a hundred miles from the Bay Area. Stevie wore the accent very well. She seemed proud to be a hick. No cowboy hat, but I remembered seeing her wearing one. She looked like a country singer, before country singers started looking Hollywood, an Emmylou Harris type.

"You guys havin' fun down here? You know you coulda called."

"I didn't know you still liked me." Marvin was half standing, swaying a little, wearing a goofy smile.

"Sheeyit, Marvin. I still love ya." Big smacking kiss. "You guys bring me any good books?"

I didn't want Marvin to spill the beans. She'd want those math books, but I knew I'd make more money in Berkeley. As Marvin took a breath to speak I jumped in: "No, Stevie, just a pleasure trip."

She was wearing a white T-shirt with the sleeves ripped off. I was noticing this, and the dark auburn hair that fell on her shoulders, when I also noticed Hart enter the bar, flanked by a couple of frat boy types. Kids like that didn't use to come to Santa Cruz. These guys looked like Nazis. How is it that you can tell the punk buzzcuts from the fascists? Must be the pleated khakis. Hart saw me and pretended not to. I think. They went to a table in the back, Hart's back to me. One of the kids came to the bar and ordered. Marvin was too excited by Stevie and the Tres Mujeres to notice much. I ordered another round and waited for Marvin to go empty his rather weak bladder.

"Hart Opffer's here. Do you see him around much, Stevie?"

"Fuckin' bastard's sellin' me books like a sonofabitch, every two or three days."

"Getting ready to move?"

"He won't say. Good stuff, though. Hard to deal with. Thinks he knows more'n me about books. If he's so good, why doesn't he get back in the business?"

Hart and his friends downed their drinks and beat it fast. Marvin came back, none the wiser. No bar fight tonight. I decided to excuse myself and let Marvin and Stevie catch up on each other's lives.

The sea/mountain air felt great as I walked back to the boardwalk area. I went down to the amusement park. Nothing's quite as creepy as a closed carnival. There was some phosphorous in the waves, and a full moon. Full-on spooky. The ancient roller coaster was lit by floodlights, as was the log ride, a generic amusement where tourists ride big "logs" into the "river." A little thrill in the groin, a splash of water. Not a bad idea.

The motel had a balcony that faced another balcony, but by moving all the way to the right and sitting on the railing I could see the ocean, and a little of the southern tip of Monterey Bay. I went inside, leaving the sliding door open. I got comfortable on the bed, then I took a long shower. A little thrill in the groin, a splash of water, and then to sleep.

Marvin called me at four to tell me he'd be staying at Stevie's and that he'd pick me up at the motel at checkout time. Thank you, Marvin. I got back to sleep for a couple of hours, then I was up for the day. I did a mental hangover check and came up healthy: no migraine, not squeamish, no signs of dehydration. I felt a little regretful. Not as wild as I used to be. I went outside in a bathing suit and T-shirt. Down to the boardwalk again, then a little north to the city beach. The realtors haven't gotten around to gussying up this part of the waterfront. The tacky big hotel at the north end of the beach is an imposing reminder that humanity is eating up the world at an alarming rate. But the pier is still kind of shack-like, and the Coconut Grove, a '30s dance hall, still stands proudly. There's an old interesting mix of lowlife types: punks, trailer trash, old hippies. Soon someone will decide to clean up the area. See: Santa Barbara.

It was getting light, the beginning of a very warm day. Still, I knew the water would be cold. Always is in Northern California. I felt grateful that the surf was flat. I'm only a fair swimmer. I jumped into the freeze without testing the water. A couple of crazies applauded, and I got up and bowed. It was too cold for a real swim. I got out, winded, feeling on top of the world. "Hey, I'm in love," I said aloud. And I wondered if Peggy had been thinking of me.

I was back and dressed just in time for checkout. Marvin drove up, looking very bright-eyed. He had the robust, healthy look of the just-been-laid. We exchanged knowing looks.

"I don't suppose you and Stevie talked about Hart."

"Actually, he was mentioned. We smoked some pot that she got from him. Seems he's still a pothead. Can't go a day without it. Grows it in his backyard. He gave her some as a semi-bribe. She still turned down most of his books."

We drove home in silence, except for Marvin's occasional humming.

## 7.

Sunday afternoon on the Southside of Berkeley on a very warm day in late spring. There was a celebration in and around People's Park, the anniversary of some riot, in which someone was brained by a club or shot, but his/her death was not in vain as the forces of scruffiness held on to this empty lot, keeping it out of the hands of the evil board of regents. Oh well. The War of the Roses was probably a tawdry affair too. Holidays and festivals are probably the only good legacy of war. And on this glorious day South Berkeley was putting on a great, goofy party.

I waded through the park and over to Haste Street to watch the skaters. Boys in their late teens, shirts off, rolling up a ramp and falling back. Seeking that feeling in the groin. And, in the audience, little girls and lecherous old guys like me, seeking the same thing. A punk band took the stage behind me and started to play. They looked kind of silly in the sunlight, all in black sweatshirts, but they had good sneers and the music was just bad/good enough to show that they got it. On the lawn a few crazies were speaking to their imaginary friends. Old hippies were dancing the same dance they've danced for thirty-five years.

When the forces of boredom won for good, a few losers moved from the hinterlands to the City. Then San Francisco got too expensive and they moved to Berkeley/Oakland. Something like that probably happened in parts of NYC. And Amsterdam. Anyplace else? If you appreciate lost causes, you can fall in love with this place. Casablanca in the '40s couldn't have been much more interesting and diverse. Sadly, if you listen closely, that mainstream steamroller can be heard, crossing the Bay Bridge. Soon Berkeley will be a conquered province. What will become of us?

I walked down Haste Street, past Amoeba Music and the tattoo places. Thought about stopping for coffee at Caffe Med, but didn't. Too anxious to get home. Entered the Chandler with a smile on my face. Through the lobby, well-preserved 1920s, with a big mirror and wallpaper, dark wood. Ride the caged elevator to the fourth floor. Big, light studio lined with books. Windows facing southwest, with the view of Oakland almost hidden by tall trees. The street noise that used to keep me awake. Home. There was a message from Peggy:

Hey. Are you back yet? Didn't know if you were spending the night (pause). I'd like to talk. It's probably time to come clean (laughs).

Checked my email. Also from Peggy: Call me as soon as you get in. And I did, but she wasn't there. Phone tag.

I decided to call Dean Centro. Searched my desk, found the card that Peggy had given me. It still took a good ten minutes to get a real voice. Ms. Real Voice then put me through to Mr. Centro. I noticed an Italian accent, but barely. No, he wasn't officially handling Peggy's affairs. He'd been a friend of Thomas's. He was just helping out. At this point instinct told me to go into my dumb poet routine.

"Actually, I'm calling because Peggy says she trusts you. I have this CD, and it isn't making much, and I don't know what to do with it. I'm a poet and you know how we can be with money."

"We have people who can handle that for you. They make it pretty simple."

"That stuff is never simple to a poet."

"Okay. Any friend of Peggy's ... but I'm off soon. Why don't you meet me at Café Roma, around five thirty? You can tell me what you've got, and what you expect to make. I'll bring some information for you."

Roma is very crowded at that hour, and there's no full bar. I got an espresso and found a table in the back room. People use that area as office space. Laptops and cell phones. At least it's quiet. I was a bit early. I had a strategy meeting with that con-man part of my brain. I would continue to play dumb. Only mention trinkets if absolutely necessary. At this point in the game nobody knew I was involved. I could safely assume that Peggy got my name from the pomo lit crowd. Some connection to that job I did for Stephen Rodefer's friend. The poetry world is pretty insular, and there are worlds within that world. The pomo poets have little truck with the beats, and they don't speak to the academics. God help the detective who tries to get straight info out of that little subculture. Hart Opffer, for instance, would have no idea that I do these little jobs.

Dean Centro would be wearing a white dress shirt and khakis. I spotted him and waved. I noticed that there were no pleats in the pants. They were, however, quite obviously pressed. He was an amazing specimen. About five foot ten, olive skin, hair bleached by the sun (sunlamp?). The kind of body awareness that borders on arrogant. He ordered a single espresso and carried it over in one hand. Like they do in Milano, or so it seemed. We shook, and our hands fit together like a glove. Suddenly I was in a foreign movie. He had green eyes. Sad, questioning, Giancarlo Giannini expression. We sat down and he put his soft briefcase on the desk. Pulled out a few pamphlets.

"All these funds are rather vanilla. You won't make a huge return. But the risk is fairly low. I assume this is for retirement?"

I sensed an angle. I could say yes, and that would be that. I decided to push things a little, see what he was selling. "Mr. Centro, I have about twenty thousand to invest. If I could double that in a few months, I'd do it. I'm ready to take some risks."

He smiled, and the pamphlets were returned to the briefcase. "How well did you know Thomas?"

"I was closer to Peggy. But we got along well."

"Did you know about his collecting?"

"A little. It was mentioned. But I never saw the art pieces. Is that what they were?"

"Not quite. Well, some could be called art. He called them trinkets. And they were, so to speak, this and that."

"I don't understand."

"There were, for example, the strigils."

"The ... ?"

"Strigils. After working out at the public baths, an ancient Roman would smear olive oil on his body." Centro smiled, leaned closer. I felt myself blushing.

"Go on, Mr. Centro."

"Please. Dean. Or even Dino."

"Go on, Dino."

"As I said, this ancient Roman would cover his body with oil. Then he would scrape the oil, dirt, and sweat from his skin with his trusty strigil, a thin, shoehorn-shaped bronze blade. A good collection of strigils can command a handsome price."

It was my turn to lean forward. "Do you think I should invest in strigils?"

"Not exclusively. For example, there are unguentaria."

"Do tell, Dino." Dino's eyes were dilated. He was sexy as hell, and I wanted to think that he was getting off by flirting with me. But I knew it had more to do with Roman beauty products.

"An unguentarium is a little bottle. It's where the Romans kept their perfumed oils. And there are the Etruscan treasures. Little statues that fit in your hand. And jewelry and surgical tools."

"Is it legal to buy and sell these things?"

"Quasi-legal at best." He shrugged. He looked me up and down. "You're a poet, so I thought this would interest you. Poets take risks, right?"

"That's the stereotype. We're also terrible businesspeople. And I'd hate to end up in jail."

"Have you ever been in jail, Clay Blackburn?"

"A few times. Civil disobedience type stuff. I trashed a police car during the Gulf War."

"Perhaps you learned, in your journey through the legal system, that prosecutors give certain crimes low priority. Even if you were caught investing in this, um, scheme, you wouldn't go to jail for long."

"Why not?"

He lifted his hand to his dress shirt and pulled on his white collar. "I'm European, from a good family. Italian-Swiss. I'd get you a good lawyer." Then he brought the hand down and placed it carefully over mine, his pinkie brushing the lip of my espresso cup. He turned my hand over and playfully slapped my wrist. Shrugged again.

I told him that I was interested but that I needed more information before I gave up my money. He was vague. Some things were coming on the market, and he needed capital to acquire them. He could sell them for a three hundred percent markup, within a few weeks. If I chose, I could take my payback in trinkets. Or, better for me, he would handle the buy and the resale and pay me $40,000 on my twenty.

I was told that I had a couple of days to think on it. He'd call me. We walked out together. He hugged me goodbye, and as he did he kissed my neck. If I'd had the money with me, I'd have waved it in his face until he promised to follow me home. Sadly, I knew that his flirtations were part of the con.

## 8.

No messages from Peggy. I called again and again. Got the machine. Modern life. Fred's Market for a Pacifico, Bongo Burger for a Persian

Burger. A crazy that said, no, Jerry Garcia is not dead. This news flash is worth a quarter and two nickels. Decided to eat dinner on the roof of the Chandler. Postcard view of the Golden Gate, starting to fog over. Gray skyline. Pleasant breeze off the bay. Nice place to live. Wondered where I was going with the Peggy thing. The money hunt seemed silly. Either the money was spent or I was in over my head and would never find it. I supposed there could be some trinkets floating around. What do I know about trinkets? When I finally got to talk to Peggy I was going to back out. She could talk to a real detective. Shouldn't mix romance and business. And for me romance always comes first.

I finished the Persian Burger as the fog was getting uncomfortably cool. Went back to the apartment. Peggy's key right there on the desk. Then into my pocket. I tried to call one last time. No answer. Maybe she's on the computer. Maybe I'll just go over and check on the cat ...

By the time I reached the lake it was getting pretty cool. I knocked, then again, then louder. Used the key. Cold inside too. All the windows were open, to my surprise. No meow. The cat must have been hiding in the closet again.

Before I did these jobs I had little everyday involvement with death. At estate sales, I would have to speak with the bereaved. Affect a serious countenance, shake hands, make my offer. I'd lost my share of friends and relatives, but they were off camera, so to speak. They say that homicide detectives are completely hardened to death. Smoke a cigarette, drink a Coke, check out the scene, break for lunch. I'm not quite that hard. Not yet. And this was Peggy.

She was lying on her stomach, head twisted to one side. An unnatural pose. I touched her, and she was cold. A different type of cold. Only the dead feel like the dead. I had a childhood memory of kissing a very old relative goodbye, as she slept in an open coffin. Like kissing dry ice, or metal so cold that your lips could stick. The dead have touched me in a few places now. Once I had occasion to cut a man down from a tree. He'd been hanging for at least a day. As he fell, his shoulder touched my forearm. Another time, I pulled a bloated body from the ocean, near San Pedro. Much later we found that it was a woman. Since them, my hands always seemed too cold. I bent down and kissed Peggy. Dead Peggy. Peggy's corpse. Then I went over to the couch, put my face in my hands, and caved in.

For a while. Sort of half asleep. I shook myself, then paced around the apartment, but away from the windows. There was lots of traffic on the street. Had anybody noticed me? Doubtful. Thousands of cars, people hurrying home from work, talking on their cell phones, thinking about other things. I hadn't noticed any pedestrians. Or neighbors. I checked out the apartment. There had been a struggle. Blood in strange places. The closets had been emptied onto the floor. Drawers were open. The cops would call it a robbery, do a routine investigation. I could call and play good citizen. What good would it do? It would be a great risk for me. I'm getting pretty good at my new job. The secret to my success comes from being a fly on the wall. Nobody would dream that I'm a ... whatever the hell I am. American poets have two things in common: We are anonymous, and we are useless. I've learned that there's a kind of power in that. The *I, Claudius* factor. Lose that and I lose my new source of income.

I didn't worry about the fingerprints. Mine would be everywhere. Yes, officer, we were old friends. I visited once in a while. These investigations never go too far anyway. I was sure that the real motive had something to do with empty bank accounts and Italian trinkets. But the overworked Oakland police wouldn't dig that deep. Just another robbery/murder on the lake.

Gertrude the cat came out of the closet and went over to Peggy. Sniffed. I felt a wave of emotion, then I did something stupid. I scooped up the cat and wrapped her in my jacket. She didn't fight much. I walked out of the apartment, where, even in daylight in a heavily populated area, nobody would notice a man leaving a murder scene, carrying a cat in his jacket. I got in the Miata, told Gertrude to ride shotgun, and drove down to Emeryville. I drove past the Watergate Apartments, past the Chinese restaurant, down to the water. I didn't want to have to explain having a key. And I didn't want Dean, or Stephie, or Hart to know that I was so close to Peggy. Needed to stay anonymous. I left Gertrude in the car and walked out onto the pier, and I dropped Peggy Denby's key into the bay.

I stayed at the Chandler for a week or so. Marvin sold the math books to Moe's, and I had some cash left over from Peggy's six hundred. I could afford to hide out. I turned off the phone. Didn't check the mail. I shuffled from the roof to the studio to the laundry room. Ate delivery food.

On the eighth day I woke up and went down to the Miata and took Highway 1 as far as Cambria. It was dangerously foggy around Big Sur, but I drove fast. The Miata is a dumb car, but it steers well. Death was just beyond the passenger side, a few hundred feet, straight down to the Pacific. I came close to going over on one of the bridges. Slippery road. I pulled in at Nepenthe and had two overpriced Negronis to make the drive more challenging. Came close again, then pulled over at Lucia and put the top down. By the time I reached San Simeon I was soaked from the fog spritz. I found a motel near the ocean. Checked in, called Marvin so that he'd know where to reach me, walked the beach. Sea otters were clanking mussels together, opening them up and feasting. A thick marine layer kept everything cool and gray. I walked until I got hungry, then had seafood at a seaside bar/restaurant. Watched TV, walked the beach again, went to sleep. The next morning I ran the beach until exhausted. Training. For four days I ran, walked, did sit-ups and push-ups, watched TV, ate fish. And made plans.

On the fifth morning Marvin called with the information I needed. Some names and addresses. I checked out of the hotel. I drove to a little toy store in Watsonville and bought a couple of Mexican wrestler's masks and a toy gun. Then I drove to the Capitola Mall, where I found a suburban sex shop. I bought some leather cuffs in various sizes. I put it all in a daypack and drove to Seabright Beach. A few people know my face in Santa Cruz, but I wasn't likely to see anybody out at Seabright. It was midafternoon and the June fog had just cleared. I parked the Miata a couple of blocks from the beach. I stopped at a deli and got a turkey sandwich and an Orangina to go. I ate on the steps that lead down to the beach. Lots of tourists, but Seabright never seems too crowded. I walked down to the water line and found a nice piece of driftwood. About the size of a club. I put it in my daypack. I looked south to the yacht harbor and watched the boats come and go. I took the bus to downtown Santa Cruz, because a red Miata is a dead giveaway. The transit center was a minor risk. Clay! What are you doing here? Just checking on some books, that's all, nice to see you ... but I didn't see any familiar faces. After a short wait I caught the Felton bus. Out through the east side of town and into a dense rainforest. Beautiful, strange country. Hiding place for old hippies, drug dealers, mass murderers. And now, or so I'd heard, second home for tech yuppies.

His name was Trak. He was a rich-kid type who attended UCSC, off and on. Stevie had told Marvin that the merchants didn't like him much. A little too rowdy. He often hung around with Hart, which seemed kind of strange. Hart's boys are usually artsy and fey. Trak could play a Nazi in a WWII movie. A strapping blond.

His place was across the San Lorenzo River, by a small bridge, and near the banks. The house was familiar. I'd attended parties on this street twenty, twenty-five years ago. Back then the houses were rickety, populated by a strange mix of river-rat hippie and punk. Everybody grew and consumed lots of pot, so the style was very relaxed. Secondhand sofas on the porch, lots of dogs. The houses smelled of mildew, mixed with various types of exotic smoke.

The town had indeed changed. The houses had new windows, new paint, Ikea lawn furniture. The place stank of tech money. I found the address and went around to the back. I wasn't sure what I was going to do on this visit. I might just case the place. I might break in and search for ... evidence? Trinkets? My hunch was he and/or one of his friends was involved in the strigil trade. My ultimate goal was to scare him into spilling some information, maybe even pointing me to the killer. I checked out the windows and the doors. If I found him home, I'd do it by force. Otherwise I'd have to gaslight him somehow.

As luck would have it, he was in his backyard, facing the river, sitting on a lawn chair, drinking a Beck's. I spotted him as I came around one side of the house, about a hundred yards away. I slowly, quietly unzipped the daypack and pulled out a wrestler's mask. This one was white with silver trim. Then I pulled out the other and put it in my back pocket, along with a handkerchief, the kind that Labrador retrievers wear. I pulled out the driftwood and put the pack back on my shoulder. I walked, slowly and quietly, up to him. He didn't turn. I hit him, very hard, just at the base of the skull. He turned toward me with a funny smile. I hit him again. I'd aimed for the temple, but I shot low and got him in the ear. I felt myself cringe. That must have really hurt. He slumped over, and I came around and kicked over the flimsy chair. He fell hard. He looked half out, eyes not quite focused. Once upon a time I had boxed. Not pro. Golden Gloves. When you see that look in your opponent's eyes you know you've won. Unfortunately, I also know how it feels to be that far gone. I wasn't the greatest boxer. I slipped the second wrestler's mask over his head, backward. I cuffed his hands behind his back. Cuffed his left leg to the picnic table. I hit his right kneecap a good shot with the driftwood. He wouldn't kick me with a broken leg. I sat down in his newly vacated chair and finished his beer and waited for him to come to. After a while he started to stir. I'd decided to do my Truman Capote Key West queer imitation.

"Thank you for the beer, sir. A few questions and I'll leave you be."

"Fuck you."

I felt a little sick inside. He was going to be feisty. I began to hate myself for doing this. I pushed those feelings down. He had to be really frightened, scared out of his wits. That was my only chance of getting information. I stuck the barrel of the toy gun into the bleeding wound on the back of his head. Pushed hard. "I'm going to kill you if you don't answer a few simple questions. I know how, and I don't like you."

I heard the beginning of a whimper, or something. A terrible sound. He cracked.

"Okay. Anything you want."

"Who killed Peggy Denby, and why?"

"She got herself killed."

"How so, sir?" I was laying the Capote act on thick.

"She came at us. We were supposed to get the strigils, that's all. We didn't think she'd be home. She came at us! Screaming. She threw things. She whomped Weldon with a tiki torch. He was bleeding like a stuck pig. It became a free-for-all. I didn't know she was dead until Hart called yesterday."

"Who's Weldon?"

"My partner. But he's gone. Left town. You can kill me, I won't tell you where."

I decided to let that one go. "Did Hart hire you?"

"Yes."

I heard voices upriver. Hikers. I needed to learn more, but I had to beat it fast. I tied the handkerchief around his head, covering his mouth. Only a semi-effective gag, but it would have to do. I packed my things and left, back to the bus stop, back downtown, back to Seabright. I deposited the daypack and its contents in the beach dumpster, after smudging any possible prints. Not that it mattered. Mr. Trak wouldn't be going to the police.

A little more than an hour later I was hunting for parking in Berkeley traffic. I found a semi-legal place on Regent Street, close to home. When I entered my apartment Gertrude ran up to me like a dog. I fed her, then made myself a Negroni. My hands were shaking. I'd risked killing somebody to satisfy a hunch. What if I'd been wrong? Too late to think about that. I wasn't wrong. Unfortunately, circumstances hadn't allowed me to get all the information I needed. Halfway through the drink I allowed myself to feel a sense of satisfaction. I'm not a very nice person, I guess. I enjoyed bruising that strapping young man. Even a broken leg doesn't mean much to someone so young. And he didn't even get a glimpse of me.

I checked my messages and my email. There was a memorial reading for Peggy planned for Sunday at the Small Press Distribution warehouse. That's not as strange as it seems. SPD is a nonprofit. They distribute (or try to distribute) our chapbooks and our magazines. Nobody else would. In effect, the SPD warehouse is where our poetry goes to die. A perfect place for a poet's funeral.

I went to Andronico's for steak and red wine. I owed Marvin many good dinners. I didn't have the energy to do something elaborate, but I knew he'd appreciate a New York, very rare. He'd come into the kitchen, see the steak warming to room temperature on the counter, say, "That's not very Berkeley of us," and smile.

And so he did. And then he took his place in the dining room, the one with the best view of the hills. I brought out the steak, salad, bread.

"Do you think you broke his leg?"

"Not really, although the adrenaline was flowing. I probably hit him pretty hard."

"The wrestling mask is usually reserved for surer cases. You didn't really have much to go on. I'm surprised you didn't just talk to him."

"I'm pissed off. And I don't like the idea of frat boys in Felton."

"Still …"

"Let's change the subject. Who is Weldon?"

"According to Stevie he runs with Hart and company. Helps him schlep books, does work around the house. I don't think you should waste too much energy on him. Let him go, unless you want revenge. If your mind is on strigils, or getting to Hart, Weldon would just be a waste of time."

"Where do I go from here?"

"Depends on what you want."

"I want to fuck with Hart."

"Kill him?"

"You know that's not my style. I'd like to get the strigils. Maybe find the evidence to put him away. That is, if I can do it and stay anonymous. I don't want him or the cops to know I'm involved. After this adventure I'm going back to full-time book scouting."

"I've heard that before."

## 9.

The SPD warehouse is down on Seventh Street, in an area that was once an industrial wasteland. You know how it works: Artists move into a depressing industrial area to take advantage of cheap loft space. The artists need a café. The café draws student "bohemian" types. A nice restaurant opens. Soon there is a full-scale yuppie attack, and the artists are priced out. At this writing the neighborhood is about halfway ruined. There's still a nice junkyard, and there's enough violent crime to keep the place honest. But not for long.

As I approached the warehouse I noticed little clumps of poets, grouped by school. There's a group without a name, mostly from the Mission District in San Francisco. They were smoking cigarettes out by the gutter. A couple of old surrealists were holding court near the front door, dressed in Salvation Army suits. The Language poets, our turn-of-the-century avant-garde, stood silently off to the side. They were well dressed, in a scholarly way.

I entered the building. There's a little reception room up front, lined with small-press books. I looked for one of mine, found a copy of *Selected Poems 1984-90* (Hardball Press), and smiled to myself. The room was crowded with people, and a little too warm. I hugged Gloria Frym and waved hi to Ishmael Reed. Then I pushed my way to the warehouse area. It's a bright, clean space. Shelves had been moved and chairs had been set up. A good-sized crowd was milling about. Tragedy brings out the poets. Especially an early death. We eat it up. Until the age of thirty we pray that we'll die young. Most of us push the issue, in various ways. After thirty we feel regret. An untimely death is the poet's best chance at fame. Immortality is the driving force for us.

It was surprisingly stuffy, given the high ceilings. I saw Marvin come in, talking to Stephen Ronan. Then right behind them Hart, with his sister, Stephanie. I remembered seeing her somewhere, but I couldn't place where. She looked unhappy and out of place. I sympathized. Not that I really felt out of place. But I would have liked to. These poetry gatherings are like family reunions. I look around and say, I'm not like these people. Then I say it again, and again. And then I cut the crap. When I stop resisting, I realize that, like it or not, I'm at home with these folks. I share the jealousies and the marginalization and the self-hatred that surfaces when you realize that you are not a useful member of society. But I also share their sense of defiance. Poets are a pissed-off bunch. I like that.

It took a long time to get us to come to order. I found a seat next to Michael McClure, behind Hart and Stephie. Jack Foley emceed. One by one, Peggy Denby's friends read their poems. They were earnest and sincere in their delivery. But the poems seemed hollow. Double-bubble lingo-babble. Poetry has become either overly sentimental (Maya Angelou) or maddeningly abstract (Ashbery). There should be a contemporary poem for every wedding and funeral. This is our work. But we've chosen to give humanity short shrift. I closed my eyes and thought of Peggy, and the words became a blur. In softer focus, the poems seemed more helpful. The human voice can be soothing, regardless of content. The voices washed over me and I thought of sitting on her floor and talking all night. I thought of all the possibilities. She was the one, I thought. Or at least one of the ones. We would have stayed in each other's lives for a long time. For a time I tried to imagine that all the voices were hers. I came/became conscious of the readers again as Michael Price came to the podium. Rather than read a poem of his own he quoted Ed Dorn, and I was reminded of the greatness of his verse:

> And so you are mortal
> after all said I
> No mortal, you describe
> yourself
> I die, he said
> which is not
> the same as Mortality

And the lights went up, and there was a low murmur. Stephanie turned to me with a "Do I know you?" smirk. She had sensibly short brown hair. She was tall. She was wearing expensive clothes, the kind that come from online catalogues. There was a beautiful leather jacket slung over her seat. Her eyes were brown and almond shaped. She had a perfumy scent, rare in Berkeley, where perfume is considered an affront to those with allergies. Hart introduced us and she shook hands in a businesslike way. She was definitely not my type. We'd have different values, nothing to talk about. I wanted to fuck her. In fact, I would have cut off any given finger with a chef's knife for the chance to fuck her. This was not the appropriate time to be feeling these things. Which made the feeling stronger. I was sweating, and my eyes were probably dilated. People were shaking hands and saying hi. People who I hadn't seen in years, people who I care about. They annoyed and distracted me.

I followed them outside and tried to make small talk. They said they were in a hurry. Hart turned to say hello to Lyn Hejinian, and as he did Stephie slipped me her business card.

It was late Sunday afternoon. I circled my apartment for nearly an hour, with post-memorial tears in my eyes. Finally I took a place near Shattuck Avenue, many blocks from the Chandler. On the walk to my apartment I bought a *Street Spirit*, the newspaper of the Bay Area homeless, from a woman with two teeth. When I was out of her sight range I threw it in a dumpster. Sometimes I read the *Spirit*. Often I can't. If I read every issue I'd eventually become a terrorist, which would be a good thing for the world at large. Not so good for me.

I stopped at my apartment to feed the cat, then went straight to the roof. It was clear in the East Bay. San Francisco was fogging in again, in that postcard way. I decided to try to remember as much as I could about Peggy. Every reading, every party. Every late night that we spent drinking Macallan or Glenfiddich, discussing everything. I drifted for a long time. After a while I thought about the strigil situation. Decided to give it all up, then decided to stay with it. Too curious. And I knew that Hart had a hand in it. I didn't think Trak was lying about that. There had to be some justice. Or revenge. Or something.

I still had Stephie's card in my top pocket. I told myself that she might have some information. That I should call her. After a few seconds I stopped lying to myself about the reason.

"Well, well. Clay Blackburn. Are you asking me on a date?"

"I suppose so. You did give me your card."

"So I did. Can you come this afternoon? We could have coffee somewhere over here."

She gave me an address in Montclair. I have a good sense of direction, and I know the East Bay. Still I got lost. The house was up a few hills and behind a few trees. You couldn't quite call the driveway a private road, or maybe you could. There was an LA-style lawn and a porch the size of my apartment. I remembered hearing somewhere, probably from Hart, that there had been a rich husband. Hearn somebody. No. Somebody Hearn. Stephanie Hearn. I think she used his name. I couldn't remember his name because I kept getting stuck on Lafcadio. Probably no relation.

She was wearing a fuzzy white sweater. The kind that you don't see in Berkeley. Short dark-green shirt. Khaki, but upscale khaki. No pleats. If I sold the Miata, I could probably buy her a pair of shoes. Expensive shoes stand out in an obvious way. I once bought a pair in Rome. I wear them when I need to look like a rich person. Doesn't matter what I wear with them. Stephie's shoes were dark and plain, but the heels were built to make all the muscles in her legs behave in a sexual way. They were well-exercised legs, but they hadn't seen a lot of sun. Milky Irish skin. A strange match with the almond eyes.

She met my gaze. I remembered Hart has those eyes. Yet in Hart's face they look too small and beady. What a difference a head makes. She ushered me in and we were silent for a while. It seemed like a long time. To break the ice I asked her about her work. I'd remembered something about her and computers. She went into a long monologue about e-tailing. First she started a company that sold exercise videos on the web. They'd take a profile, then they'd pair the customer with the best video. They raised enough capital to make a good start and then they were bought by a bigger company. She took her earnings (her word) and founded (her word) a company that sold chocolate made by a small Belgian factory. They were bought out by Whitman's and will soon be part of the Kmart website. Then she bought into ...

"Before we go on with the resumé, perhaps we could go out for a drink?"

"I'll make you something here. But I won't join you yet. I have a hard and fast rule: Never drink before sundown. If you do, run straight to AA."

"Whatever you do, don't summer in Stockholm." She didn't acknowledge the joke. I think, on some level, she did understand that she was in the presence of another human being. But I'm not entirely sure. Not everyone has a soul.

We went into the kitchen. Hanging copper pots, huge cutting table in the middle of the room. Restaurant-quality stove. But no bar area. Elegant houses used to have bars. The world is going to hell in a handbasket.

"What would you like?"

"Do you have Campari?"

She opened the cupboard. A bottle of Campari peeked out from behind a bottle of Sapphire gin. Fitting.

"I'll have a Negroni."

"What's that?"

"I figured you'd know, since you have the Campari."

"Once a year I go to Bevmo and buy a few cases of everything. For the Christmas party. I'm not even sure what I have. For myself, I just pour some vodka in a big glass and top it off with tonic."

"Aren't you from that new cocktail generation?"

"I don't think so. I'm too old. When I was in college we drank rum and fruit juice. I go to the new bars after work sometimes. But I don't pay much attention."

She was boring, plodding, without subtlety. They all are. Too much screen time. Computers have turned us all into lab rats, pressing the right button to elicit the proper response. That's what passes for interactive. Was my attraction to her sadistic or masochistic? Probably it was beyond psychology. It had more to do with scent, although her scent was rather bland. Maybe it was a class thing. Like *Swept Away*. But that sort of thing didn't usually appeal to me. Oh well, she had given me an opening.

"I could teach you how to make the perfect Negroni. Would you like that?"

"Is that something I should know?" When she asked she almost sounded sincere.

"A good Negroni is life's second-best sensual pleasure." And thank god she didn't ask what's first.

"All right. You teach me. I'll have one too. It's nearly sundown. I guess I can cheat by a few minutes."

I started by slicing the lime that I found in her oversized reefer. I found a great martini set and put it on the cutting table. Bought, she said, on eBay, '40s vintage. Simple pitcher, long glass stirrer, oversized glasses. Clear. First rule: No tinted glass. Ruins the color. I found the vermouth and put half a shot in each glass. She came behind me and looked over my shoulder. She was just a little shorter than me. Her chin touched the back of my neck. I swirled the vermouth, then poured it in the sink. That's all you need of the vermouth. Made her smell a glass. I poured a shot of Campari into the bottom of the pitcher. I filled the pitcher with ice. I poured three shots of the good gin over the ice, slowly. Swirled the ingredients until cold. Poured them into the glasses. Added a small squeeze of lime and dropped a wedge in each glass.

She was delighted by the color. She took a sip and made a face. "Strong."

"That's the point. It's sort of like drinking a single espresso. A strong shot of flavor, and a condensed version of the drug."

She shrugged and gulped. We moved to a living room area, to a big couch. The kind of couch you see advertised in *SF Weekly*. SoMa sofas. I sat down and I wanted to move in. The white leather was cool and then warm. She put on some music. A sound that I took to be the Dave Mathews Band. Although it could have been somebody else. That kind of music bores me. We finished our drinks and she volunteered to make another.

"What if I make them stronger?"

"They won't taste right. But we'll get drunker."

She dumped an extra shot in the pitcher. We took the drinks back to the huge white couch. We drank, and she spoke of many things. None were of much interest. IPOs, stock options, new economic opportunities. The language of this particular California gold rush. She told me that the house was part of the divorce settlement. He owned three, and an apartment in Vienna. It was an amicable split. He still stops by when he's in town. He's mostly in eastern Europe, finding new markets. For what, I don't know. Didn't seem worth asking. I didn't mention the strigil situation, or Peggy. Couldn't find an opening.

There was another round, and then we were horizontal on the couch. She was on top, and I felt like I was swimming in leather and skin. She was, to my surprise, very good. Better than I am, if you want to look at things that way. I was surprised that it had been so easy. And that I was so attracted to someone that I really didn't like. It took a while to hear that certain click that I hear when the rational part of the brain goes dead and nature takes over. But eventually I did hear the click, and we stayed on the couch for a long time.

She asked me if I wanted another drink. I took this as an invitation to spend the night and said yes. We took the last drink into the bedroom. Beige and black Ikea. Not as obviously expensive as the living areas. A framed Thiebaud print over an oversized bed. A little like a hotel room in Sonoma. I wasn't really listening to what she was saying but her voice was sounding more pleasant. I still didn't like her, but I was taking her more personally.

## 10.

I spent less and less time at the Chandler. I'd put in some quality time with the cat, make some calls, and go out searching for books. Marvin suggested that I disguise Gertrude by fattening her up. She was kind of sleek when I took her from Peggy's apartment three weeks ago. I put her on a diet of Yoplait, Ben and Jerry's, and cheese omelets. She gained a couple of pounds. He also suggested a funny collar, to throw people off track. I decided on zebra stripes, with a green name tag: Emily. Emily the indoor cat. My friends loved her. Stephie tolerated her. If by chance Hart were to come over, Emily would go in the walk-in.

Marvin also suggested that I stop seeing Yuppie Girl, as he dubbed her. I didn't, although my only real reason was lust. But then, is there a better reason for anything? I'd pretty much ruled her out as a suspect. I would occasionally try to nudge the conversation into strigil territory, but she didn't seem to know much. She was aware that brother Hart was some kind of collector, but it was all very vague.

In the weeks that followed we fell into a pattern. I would go over there. She seldom came by the Chandler. I would cook a nice dinner in her perfect pots, on her perfect stove. We'd go out on the second-floor terrace and look at the bay, and I'd hear about her stocks, and nod, and wait. Sometimes she'd tell me about something that had happened at the office. Usually it involved a field trip of some kind. Intrigue at the brewpub, or the billiards place, having to do with what people used to call office politics. The actual work didn't seem to matter. This seemed strange and sad. She confided to me that she had once been very depressed but that antidepressants had helped a lot. I felt a speech welling in my throat. Of course you're depressed, your life is depressingly drab. Those feelings are the only sane reaction to the world that you have made. But I let that speech stick in my craw. None of my business, I told myself.

After getting some air we would go to the big white couch. She called her couch Pablo, her bed Eileen. She said they were named after people she'd always wanted to sleep with. We would get comfortable on Pablo and I would sink into a physical rhythm that I have rarely known. It had nothing to do with two souls touching. That romantic conceit has, sadly, been ripped from my heart. Still, there were times when I thought I was falling for her. Time proved otherwise. It was purely physical. But that's not something to complain about. I'm not really a spiritual being. I'll leave that to the Dalai Lama. For me, consciousness is at its highest at the point of orgasm. Other times come close: staring at a Franz Kline painting, listening to Chopin's nocturnes, reading "Song of Myself." But they don't add up to those times when I was on Pablo with a rather blandly beautiful woman named Stephie and then a moment later I wasn't with anyone. I was just a piece of meat attached to another piece of meat, and I closed my eyes and saw colors you don't expect to see in nature, and we floated like there was no gravity, beyond identity, or personality.

Eventually we would start to drift off and she'd say, "Time to visit Eileen." And we'd get into her very large bed, between sheets with astronomical thread counts, and under a comforter that cost more than I make in a month. I'd get myself into a position to smell her hair, and I'd fall asleep with my right hand between her legs, at the thighs. She said that boys' hands always seem to rest there when they sleep.

Marvin was getting jealous. I was spending most nights over there. He wasn't getting as many dinners. He doesn't understand these romantic/sexual obsessions. He has people who he sees. That's how he puts it. Men and women, mostly people he's known for a while. Some are single, others are married. They drift in and out. There always seems to be someone when he needs company. He doesn't appear to worry about it much. His romantic notions involve the failure of communism. I've seen him in tears over Lenin's death. I try not to mention the Spanish Civil War. I agree with him that the failure of international socialism was the great tragedy of the twentieth century. But it doesn't touch me in the same way.

I had to make Marvin a great dinner, or he'd guilt me all summer. I dug out the pasta machine and made noodles tossed with yellow tomatoes from a friend's garden. It's a nice first course. Then I took the Weber up to the roof and smoked a pork loin. Braved the lines at Berkeley Bowl for some nice greens. Bought a large chunk of very good chocolate and a bottle of grappa. His favorite dessert.

He came in and I opened one of the two bottles of Tavel that Alice Notley had brought me from Paris. He beamed from ear to ear. We ate a long, slow dinner and drank more than usual. He told me one of those promise-not-to-tell-anybody stories, about how a few days earlier he'd been cut off by an SUV and had followed it at a safe distance. It parked at Andronico's in North Berkeley. And there, in broad daylight, he dragged his key down the side of the car. Then, satisfied that nobody was watching, he keyed the other side. He took a short walk and came back. The SUV was still there. There were people in the lot, but nobody seemed to be paying attention. So he took out his Swiss Army knife and punctured a tire.

"I could have lit the car and myself on fire. Nobody'd notice. We live in a strange world. People can't see outside themselves."

"The guy who owns the SUV probably noticed something."

"Yeah, but it was no big deal. He probably called AAA on the cell phone and went on his way."

And so we traded hell-in-a-handbasket stories for a while. Finally he got onto the subject of Stephie. How I disappoint him, going out with a capitalist slug. I pointed out that she isn't a slug, that she works very hard.

"Hard work? Going to theme restaurants with investors? And I hear from some of my friends in that world that she isn't very good at it. She's more in debt than Amazon. Everything's in hock. People keep pouring money into her companies, because that's what people do. But she needs a winning streak soon, or it'll all dry up. I think you should question her more closely about the strigil caper. Anyone who is financially vulnerable is a suspect."

Marvin had made his point. He was a little smug about it, but I didn't even try to shoot him down. I'd been thinking with my dick. Usually that isn't so bad. I mean, why not? The brain is overrated. It second-guesses, it frets, it hides the little childhood traumas, it gives itself headaches. The penis points to love, warmth, affection. Most of the time, and for most people, that's just fine. But in this new line of work I have to find a balance between the two. Thinking with my dick could get me killed.

## 11.

It was my waiter's day off so I ordered a Glenfiddich, straight. Can't ruin it. You just pick up the bottle and pour it in a glass. The student waiter took my order, disappeared for twenty minutes, then brought me the drink. I was sitting outside on the patio, facing away from Telegraph Avenue. From that angle I could pretend to be in the South of France. Trees and an old brick house.

It was time to have a strategy session with myself. Okay. I had fallen for a woman, a poet, kind of nerdy. Marvin would call her a double-bubble lingo-babble poet. But she was cute. And I liked her. We could talk. Smart and funny. She told me half of a story about some money that was missing from her late husband's estate. Mentioned his love of "trinkets." Then somebody killed her in her apartment. A hunch told me that it wasn't a random crime, so I used a little force and found that Hart Opffer, son of the late husband, was party to the murder. Trinkets figure into this somewhere. I'd been asked to get involved in some scheme to acquire more.

Berkeley is a small city surrounded by big cities. South Berkeley is a village. So it wasn't much of a coincidence when Dino Centro came out to the patio.

"May I join you?"

"Sit down, Dino."

"You were lost in thought."

"I was thinking about Peggy Denby. I miss her."

"I understand you were close."

"We were good friends."

"More than that?"

"No." I was ready to blow my cover and grab him by the collar, make him tell me what he knew. But, as I've said, anonymity is my best defense. I sank back into myself. Remember, Clay, one side of my head said to the other, negative capability. I decided to nibble at him.

"I haven't had time to think about that investment."

"I assumed you were out of town, since I didn't hear from you."

"Did Peggy have anything invested?"

He started to say something, then didn't. He sat for a while.

"No. Well, through her husband. She didn't talk about it much. Our friendship was more personal. We gossiped, talked about local politics, things like that. I like contemporary art too, and she was a great date at openings. Why do you ask?"

"This strigil business is, as you said, quasi-legal. Could there be a connection to her murder?"

He looked suitably nervous. Didn't mean anything. Murder makes everybody nervous.

"The people I deal with aren't like that. We're businesspeople. We aren't criminals. I mean, we do break laws. Everyone breaks the law. But these laws are more subtle, and so are we. I've never been party to any violence."

"But there must be lots of people involved. If someone found out that Peggy had a good cache of trinkets in her apartment, wouldn't that be a motive for, at the very least, a burglary? Breaking and entering is risky business. Maybe things got screwed up, and violence turned out to be plan B."

"You haven't talked to the police?"

"I never talk to the police. And you know the cops aren't going to look too deeply into this one. Unless they know about the trinkets."

## 12.

He was one hard question away from losing his cool. I let him stew for a few minutes, then a couple minutes more. I looked for the waiter. Ordered two Scotches.

"Peggy was our friend. I'd like to know who was responsible. Wouldn't you?"

"Of course, of course. But I don't know. I have no idea who killed her. There may have been some items in the apartment. I'm not sure."

The drinks came quickly, to my surprise. He took a healthy gulp.

"If I tell you what I know, you will go to the police."

"As I said, I never talk to cops. I'd just like to satisfy my own curiosity."

"Are you a detective or something?"

"Of course I'm not a fucking detective."

"The last cache of artifacts is missing. If you come across it, I'll split it with you."

"Missing since when?"

"Thomas inspected them in Italy. Soon after that they vanished. A mix of things, from a dealer in Livorno. Included were an exquisite Etruscan figurine, a few strigils, some Roman kitchen utensils, some surgical tools. Our richest load."

"Worth?"

"About ten years' salary at the bank. I'm from a good family, but they've cut me off. A few indiscretions." A look of beatitude came over his face. "Imagine," he said, "a spatula that was used to sauté onions and peppers at the Forum!"

"Dino, you devil."

He sucked at his drink. "If we get to be friends, I could tell you stories." He leaned forward. Some people are sexier when ruffled. Not Dino. He looked puffy and sad.

"I doubt that I'll ever come across your strigils," I said. "I'm going to back away from that. I only asked you about Peggy because, as I said, I'm curious."

"I think you're more involved than you let on, Clay."

"Why?"

"I was on Solano Avenue the other night. I saw you coming out of Ajanta with Stephie. Holding hands." He flashed a comic lurid smile.

"What's Stephie got to do with this?"

"She's heavily involved in the trinket trade. Big ticket items too. All over the globe." Dino was obviously loving this.

"I had no idea, Dino."

"I almost believe you."

"Really, Dino. The trinket trade is beyond me. And I never discuss money with Stephie."

He laughed. "But money is all she'll discuss! It's all she knows. She isn't like me. Money is my business, but it's just a job. I'm interested in what it will buy. I'm a sensualist, and that gets expensive. Money is a necessary bore."

"Filthy lucre?" I was having fun too.

"Clean, dirty, neutral. No matter to me. They don't ask when you pay the bill at Chez Panisse. And now it's time for me to get back to the bank and shuffle dollars. Maybe some will stick to me before the end of the day. Remember, if you happen on some trinkets, you bring them to me. I know where to go with them. And I'm discreet."

He leaned forward again and looked me in the eye. His eyes looked kind of buggy. I think he was trying to flirt. But I was charmed by his silliness. I felt myself blush.

"I've heard about you, Clay."

For a second I thought he was referring to some of my bisexual adventures. Then it dawned on me. He'd heard about my little jobs. Blown cover.

"And who else knows?"

"Don't worry, Clay. I heard from Nanos Valaoritis at the Greek Festival."

"Aren't you Italian?"

"But I love moussaka! Nanos says that you once found some Cavafy manuscripts that were stolen from a rare book dealer. I think most of the poets in town know your game."

"Luckily nobody listens to poets."

"Lucky for you, yes. Because Hart probably hasn't gotten wind of it. You make him nervous as it is."

"Hart hangs out with poets."

"But they don't like him much. To a poet, every non-poet is a philistine. Publishers, translators, editors, the UPS guy ... all philistines."

"What about you? How does a banker gain entrée into this netherworld?"

"I once lived with Harold Norse. He is a great gossip. And, I am told, a great poet. I don't read poetry myself. Harold introduced me to everyone. You're a fascinating lot."

I vaguely remembered that Harold had lived with a young Milanese businessman. I think, maybe. Keeping track of Harold's lovers would be a full-time job.

Dean Centro stood up, rather abruptly. "Time to get back to the bank." We shook, and his hand lingered in mine. He'd calmed down a bit, and the buggy-eyed look softened to a classic Latin-lover narrowing of the eyes and a whispered, "You have my number."

I ordered a single espresso, just to linger. Stephie was involved, Peggy was possibly involved. Hart and Trak are murderers, as is somebody named Weldon. Dean Centro is a crook. And I am a dubious character. I turned my chair around to look at the Avenue. Pale sunlight. The kind that comes right after the fog fades back. Across the street, three exquisite college students were heading toward Bison Brewery. I couldn't make out their tattoos, but they had them, and long dreads. And as the dark-haired woman kissed the blond man, her girlfriend, who I took to be East Indian, leaned on her, back to back, and I tried to freeze the moment. I didn't want to move into the future just yet. But the moment wouldn't freeze.

## 13.

Saturday morning I hit the garage sales. I hate them, but my stock was getting low. I needed fodder. Fodder is pocketbooks, popular novels, dictionaries. Normal stuff that I can use for quick cash at the trashier used bookstores. I put together three bags of stuff, possibly a day's pay. On the way to Half Price Books I spotted a yard sale on Regent Street. And there, under some Ian Fleming pulp, in perfect condition was a copy of Campion's works, edited by Percival Vivian, Oxford University Press, 1909 edition. Not a large book, but hefty. Type so beautiful that I had to blink back tears. I've only seen a few of these. I already own one, so there was no temptation to keep it. I walked over to Ho Chi Minh Park, sat in the cool morning sun, and spent some time with Thomas before taking him to Moe's Books: *Fain'd love charmed so my delight / That still I doted on her sight.*

I made enough to last a couple of days without raiding the savings account. I stopped at the Chandler, changed, and walked up Dwight to the track to do a little running. Then I came home and hit the heavy bag. One corner of the studio is my mini boxing gym. Heavy bag, light weights, jumping rope. Very heavy padding on the floor, to keep the downstairs neighbor from complaining. When I was twelve I boxed Golden Gloves. That first year I lost most of my fights. No punch. Couldn't take a punch either. I'd score well, because I had fast hands. But about midway through the fight the other guy would hit me hard, and I'd go down. I had some courage (stupidity?), so I'd usually get up for my second (or third) knockdown. Then one day Archie Moore came into the gym in Long Beach. He had come up from San Diego to raise funds for his youth group. He saw me take some good shots during a sparring match. It made him laugh. Maybe his plane was delayed, or maybe he was bored, but for some reason he took me aside and worked with me. He didn't teach me how to punch. He said that I was hopeless in that area. But he taught me how to slip punches, how to stay out of range, how to block punches with my arms and hands.

I had reached that age when you realize that adults are a corrupt lot and that the rest of your life isn't going to be a great deal of fun. I was full of adolescent bitterness. I had no heroes. But I had to listen to Archie Moore. It wasn't that he was the ex-light heavyweight champion. I couldn't give a fuck about that, at the time. It was his cadence and the timbre of his voice. It was his diction, and his strange word choices. He quoted Shakespeare, Keats, Muhammad Ali, FDR. He made up rhymes as he went along, teaching me to duck and move. He said, "You are one proud white boy, but you probably haven't heard of Jean-Paul Sartre, let alone Kierkegaard. You're probably Irish, but you haven't even read Yeats! Not like that, fake to the right, chump!"

Archie Moore's poetry was pretty powerful. I listened to his instructions. I still didn't win many fights, but I rarely went home in pain.

I worked up a good sweat, showered, ordered a Persian Burger from Bongo. Took it back to the Chandler. I was feeling dramatic so I put on some Liszt. Loud. Gertrude/Emily joined me for a fry. After dinner I opened a second Pacifico and went to the computer to work on a poem. My daily dose of sanity. I had been at work for a couple of hours when the phone rang. It was Stephie. We spent the latter part of the evening on Pablo and Eileen.

I was starting my second espresso when Hart came in. Stephie had warned me that he might come by for breakfast. He gave me a warm hello but we didn't shake hands. He went into the big, perfect kitchen and got himself a demitasse. He was wearing a lemon-yellow golf shirt and black jeans. I understood the shirt to be an ironic gesture, like wearing an aloha shirt at a South of Market café. He poured a cup of coffee and drank it standing, next to Stephie. I was amazed at the resemblance and that he could seem so ugly to me, and she so alluring. My gaze shifted from his almost comically beady gray almond eyes to her strange, mysterious, exotic-looking brown pair.

Hart was jovial in a phony way. It's always a little strange, meeting your sibling's lover. At least he was trying to be nice. We were nicey-nice, back and forth, and then he started to feel me out.

"In Santa Cruz you were asking me about Peggy's financial situation. Did you find anything interesting?"

It struck me for the first time that Hart and Stephie were Peggy's heirs. But there couldn't have been much of an estate, what with the missing money.

"Actually I didn't look that hard. None of my business."

"But you brought it up."

"Because Peggy was upset about it. Now that she's gone I've forgotten about it. Too many other things on my mind."

"Like?"

"Like mourning for a dead friend. And book scouting. Writing poetry. The usual."

"I assume that Peggy just spent it. But if you hear anything, I'd like to know."

Stephie seemed unnerved. "Hart, let's get off the subject of Peggy."

And we did. But there were more questions about my life, my living, about Marvin. Hart was fishing. Instinct told me that he didn't know a thing about my other job. I wasn't sure why he was asking so many questions, but I didn't call attention to that. I decided to just flow with the conversation and play dumb.

Finally talk turned to his career, and I suffered through his résumé. A family trait? He'd designed covers for a couple of Creeley books. Very tasteful, in his words. And he was organizing a writers' retreat down in Cabo. Philip Levine would be there, as would Jorie Graham. And they were trying to convince Pinsky to come down. When he said Pinsky's name he looked skyward and sighed.

"Why would you want to subject that poor country to Pinsky? Doesn't Mexico have troubles of its own?"

"Very funny. Pinsky's poetry is high art. You and your Mission District, Telegraph Avenue scuzzy poets wouldn't understand that. I've got things to do. Nice seeing you."

But before he left he straightened out the pleats in his khakis.

My work day consisted of going up to the garage and pulling out twenty Loeb classics that I'd been sitting on for almost a year. They are an instant sell. I drove down to Moe's Books and sold them for six dollars each. I wanted to have some scratch so that I wouldn't have to scout for a couple of days. I'd decided to get myself some of that strigil money, if only to keep Hart from getting it all. High art, my ass.

I called Dean Centro and he said he'd meet me, this time at Oliveto, downstairs. My Loeb money wouldn't last long there, even downstairs. But I went along with it. I arrived early, as is my habit. Punt e Mes at the bar, same star-quality bartenders. Dean arrived in (I swear) seersucker. I looked deep into his eyes and told him that I was almost ready to invest. Couldn't he tell me more? It's a lot of money.

"Well, not here." He looked around the bar.

As far as I could tell nobody was paying attention. I laughed.

"You laugh. But we have to be careful. As you said, there is a lot of money at stake. My apartment is close by. Finish your drink and we'll go there."

And I did. The apartment was directly across College Avenue and upstairs, above a used clothing store. It was the kind of sweatbox that would have gone for two hundred a month before the techno gold rush. A matchbox of a studio with a view of the BART tracks. But it was expensively furnished. This is a new phenomenon in the Bay Area. There was a double bed with a low modern Italian headboard. Little black end tables that looked antique. The Chinese vase was from a specific period of history that you would know if you were an expert in Chinese history. The tapestry was Indonesian. Even the hot plate was the expensive kind. I've seen them in Sur La Table. I was taken with the rug. It was a saffron color and showed no signs of wear.

"I have some good beer."

"Yes."

And he pulled two from Belgium from the hotel-style reefer. We sat for a while. I let him think. Finally he nodded to himself.

"If you get me twenty thousand before next week, and a little traveling money, I can double, or perhaps triple, your investment within, say, another week."

"Where will you be going?"

He hesitated some more. He downed the beer the way you'd drink a Bud on a hot day. Got himself another. "Why do you need to know?"

"It's my whole bank account. I'd like to know where it's going."

"Mexico."

"I thought strigils were Italian."

"People will be there."

"What kind of people?"

"People from all over, with treasures from everywhere. A kind of convention. There's a fishing village not far from the Cabos. Santa Catarina. Well, it's even outside of there. There's a hotel on the beach. Caters to the sportfishing trade. It's been booked by people who share my interest. People can come in by boat. The authorities assure us that there will be little or no customs check-in. Those who drive or fly in may have more trouble. But most of these people are seasoned smugglers."

"Strigil people?"

"Whatever you want to call us. Seekers of treasure."

"The treasures of the gray market. A kind of *Antiques Roadshow*."

"Gray, black, whatever. You won't see this stuff on PBS."

"So you'll go down there and do some buying."

"And selling, and trading. And there will be a yacht there that will take a few of us over to Mazatlán, where there will be some smaller sessions. From there I'll go to Mexico City, and with any luck I'll come home with a fortune. I have some good product. But I need spending money. And I may want to buy and sell something while I'm there. This is a tightly knit group. It's good form to buy a few things. Primes the pump."

"I have a week to think about this?"

"Say, two days. I have other investors, so either way I can make the trip. But I'd be lying if I said I didn't need your money. I'm a little cash strapped. And cash on hand is always important when traveling to corrupt countries. I've bought my way out of trouble a few times."

"I'm beginning to feel like a loan shark."

"You can triple your money. Who cares?"

"Let me sleep on this."

When I said the word his eyes got wider. He smiled in a flirtatious way. Somehow people know that I will do almost anything for sex. Almost anything. Dino was cute, but not twenty thousand cute. Still, it occurred to me that I could possibly come out of this with a few blow jobs. I leaned in his direction. Our faces moved closer. We stopped for a fraction of a second, so as not to collide before the first kiss. But at the end of that fraction he moved back, just an inch.

"How sad that I have another appointment!"

The bastard was teasing me. He wanted his money.

I got back in time to make Marvin dinner. Lots of people were milling on the Avenue. There was a scheduled demonstration. Berkeley's still good for several a year. Usually they're pretty pathetic. Once in a while there's a corker. We pushed the dinner table closer to the window. I made some burgers and we got ready to watch the fun. We finished dinner and still nothing had happened. Some punks were drinking out on Dwight Way. And, of course, there were lots of cops. They usually outnumber the demonstrators. We decided to take our wine up on the roof, to get a better view. It was a pretty warm night. On the way out the door I grabbed a chocolate bar. We climbed down to a fire escape, split the chocolate, and settled in to watch the show.

And a great show it was. Marvin had heard that the theme was the automobile. The demonstrators were against them. I imagined that there would be a Critical Mass–style bike-a-thon. Those can be fun. It started to get dark. The cops looked a little nervous. These things usually end before dusk. In recent years the cheap, inadequate streetlamps have been aided by white Christmas lights, just like Paris. The lights gave the trees and the stores a nice glow. There was an ominous silence. Marvin looked at me and nodded happily. I remembered an old-timer telling the story of how Paul Goodman once tried to give a speech from a Chandler fire escape. He was interrupted by tear gas. I hoped that the young anarchists who now organize these things would give the cops hell. Our side hadn't won in a long time.

It was now flat-out dark and still nothing. A few of my neighbors joined us on the roof. We began clapping in unison and yelling, "Rock 'n' roll!" Some of the cops gave us tough looks. Other smiled. They know their parts.

A couple of the punks started hopping up and down, punching the air with their fists. There was a roar, like when someone hits a home run. A mob came down Dwight and turned onto Telegraph. It was a substantial crowd. The cops retreated, giving the mob some space in front of Shakespeare & Co. They backed off more, to allow traffic to flow up Dwight, but it didn't. The cops looked pissed. This wasn't part of the script. Someone on my roof said that they were supposed to rally at People's Park, then come down Haste Street, which was closed for this purpose. The cops had been outflanked. Clubs were drawn, but not raised. The Berkeley police are good at this. They herded the crowd into the middle of the street, in front of Caffe Med. A crusty bunch of regulars drank espresso at the sidewalk tables. Seen it all before.

An old Toyota came around the corner, pushed and pulled by a half dozen people, all dressed in black hooded sweatshirts. They were quite solemn. The crowd began a chant that I couldn't understand. They produced cans of lighter fluid and doused the car. Some of the cops laughed, which clued us in. The car was a prop. Otherwise, batons would have been raised.

The car went up in flames. It was wimpy, it was staged, but it was a beautiful sight. It burned slowly, evenly. They must have drained the gas tank. A tow truck appeared a couple of blocks away. It got warm down on the streets. People peeled off their sweatshirts, their shirts. Public nudity is often a part of these. People started beating on things: trash cans, the sides of buildings. Tribal sounds. I felt bad for a couple of the less-stable homeless people. They looked scared. Probably didn't realize it was just a show.

Marvin threw his arms around me, and we both had a good laugh. We've destroyed two cars in our time. Both police cars. And it wasn't sanctioned by the local government. We turned one completely over on the night Dan White got away with murder. Then one of our cohorts lit it up. Full tank of gas. Boom! During the Gulf War we beat the shit out of another one with a policeman's abandoned baton. I went to jail for that. They caught me running away. But they didn't want to bother to prosecute. Cars are easy to replace.

We went back in and took the stairs down to the street. There was a fine racket, and lots of pretty young anarchists were jumping around in various states of excitement. There was a frat boy contingent, as usual. There would be fights later in the evening. I noticed a familiar face. Trak. I wondered what he was doing in Berkeley. Could that be Weldon with him? He looked familiar. Had I seen him in Tampico? I couldn't trust my memory. I moved closer, but it didn't help. Weldon, if it was Weldon, was a small man of about twenty-five. Short, bleached hair, square jaw, solid arms. They milled around for a while, apparently got bored, and walked off in the direction of campus.

The street took on the look of a big cocktail party. People laughed and talked in small clumps. The police were more relaxed. A guy in a Mohawk brought coffees to go to a couple of the cops. The show was over, except for the cleanup. I walked Marvin to his truck and returned to the Chandler.

## 14.

My neighbors were hanging out in the lobby and on the stairs. There was lots of imported beer. I absentmindedly counted the different brands. Singha, Amstel, Sierra Nevada, something with a green frog on the label. Two rich students were drinking malt liquor. Slumming. Eight types of beer and one bottle of white wine. A woman with a crew cut was smoking a turquoise cigarette, which reminded me (fondly) of high school. I'm getting old for this, I thought, but then what else would I do? I reached the fourth floor and stepped over Mariem and Joanne, who told me, mid-kiss, that there was a party at John and Dina's. Their door was open so I went in to say hello. Somebody handed me a too-full lowball glass. Jack Daniel's. Another fond memory from high school. Most of the guests were crowded around the windows that face Telegraph Avenue. At street level two punks were having a half-hearted fistfight in front of the remains of a bonfire, setting up a nice visual. I'm the only poet in the building. My neighbors, at least the nonstudents, are painters, photographers, video artists, or conceptual/installation types. The guests were mesmerized. All those artsy brains were twisting the experience into who knows what, dreaming up projects that would make them famous, or at least keep them occupied. And, this being Berkeley, they were playing a kind of intellectual game of connect the dots. How does this relate to Adorno? Jung? Emma Goldman? Meher Baba? Johnny Lydon?

One of the punks took a punch just as the low flame turned to toxic smoke. One of the guests hooted. The punk got up, dazed and smiling. I recognized him, noting that his nickname is Smiley. Teresa the painter sidled up to me and we clinked our lowball glasses.

"So, Clay. Tell me. What the hell is a strigil?"

"I hear that the ancients used to scrape their bodies with them."

"Hmm. Maybe this guy isn't as boring as he seems."

"Who?"

"He's in the kitchen. Dino something. Says he's a friend of yours. And when he says it, he raises one eyebrow. Like this."

And she deftly raised one eyebrow, looking sideways over her shoulder for effect.

"Teresa, I told you. I only sleep with boys in even-numbered years. That means no men for seven months."

"So you dated him last year?"

"We haven't known each other that long."

"Should be one helluva New Year's Eve. Tell me, Clay, do you sleep with women in even-numbered years, or do you give them up for boys?"

She laughed and drifted off. I made my way to the kitchen, but not before Dina refilled my glass from a bottle of Jack Daniel's that was bigger than her head, even if you include about five pounds of red hair.

Dino was leaning against the kitchen counter, talking to Tom Clark.

"Dig it, Dino, Dante came before pasta, before bistecca alla fiorentina! And you mean to say you haven't read him?"

"Well, maybe a little, in school."

Dino saw me and gave me a long hug. Flattering.

"Can we go back to your place? I need to talk to you."

I let him in and turned on a lamp. I turned, and the gun was about a foot from my solar plexus. My first reaction was a laugh. Then I shuddered, then I caught myself and tried to act cool. I noticed that he was trembling.

"Dino, what are you doing?"

"I need that money. Now. I know you deal mostly in cash. I need some of it."

"Cut the Peter Lorre routine. I told you I'm interested in investing."

"New facts have come to light."

"Like?"

"There's a certain figurine. It's been missing for years. Today a friend called to tell me that it will resurface in Mexico. I need another fifteen thousand, give or take, to join the consortium that will buy it. They have a buyer. Six. Enough to make me, uh, us, rich. But I have to get to Baja with the money soon. Before the seller shows up. We have to make plans."

"Tell me more about the figure."

"It was first found in Vinci in the nineteenth century. It was in a villa near Livorno for years. Then it was lost, or stolen."

"And somehow Thomas got hold of it?"

"Yes. Unfortunately he died before he could sell."

"Murdered?"

"I don't know. My information is secondhand. And, after all, he was ill. Anyway, it was presumed lost."

"Could it have been in Peggy Denby's apartment?"

"How would I know? I knew nothing until yesterday! But I do know that it will turn up in a little village in Baja within the week. And if I get enough cash I can be part owner. I have a soft spot for Buenos Aires. It's an expensive place to live, but the sale of the figure could buy me a few years there."

His eyes unfocused as he dreamed, presumably, of the cafés of Buenos Aires. I suppressed the temptation to hum a tango. The gun dropped a couple of inches as his mind drifted. I hit the top of his hand as hard as I could. The gun flew to the bed. I jumped on it and held it on him. But I could tell by its heft that it wasn't loaded.

"You hurt my hand!"

"Sorry, Mr. Lorre. Does the figure have a romantic name? Like in the movies?"

"No, *stronzo*. This isn't a movie. I could have tripled your money. But you dilly-dallied. I was trying to help you."

"Let's give it a name. How about Leonardo, since it's from Vinci."

"That's silly. Leonardo was from another period. And the figure is a woman. Possibly a fertility goddess."

"Breasts?"

"Yes, but rather small, for an Italian." He was smiling, getting into the spirit of naming the figure. Another kook.

"How about Beatrice?"

"Too obvious, Clay. All right, I will play your game. But only if you promise not to throw me out the window."

"Done."

"We will call her Oriana Fallaci, after the journalist."

"Why?"

"Another Italian woman who does a little traveling."

"Well done, Dino."

"Now, there is the matter of the twenty thousand."

"Sorry, Dino. I just don't have it to give."

"But you said ..."

"A little white lie."

"Luckily I have another, uh, investor. Can I have my gun back?"

I handed him the empty gun. Our eyes met. Blond Italians are a problem for me. Can't stay away from them. Even when it's inappropriate. Especially when it's inappropriate!

"I can put some ice on that hand, if you have the time."

"Thank you. Do you have a drink?"

I brought out the Villa Massari grappa. It's a southern drink, but I didn't think this Milanese would mind. He was delighted.

He put off his other appointment till morning. And this an odd-numbered year. Rules are made to be broken.

## 15.

We slept late the next morning. He took his gun and left around noon. I spent the day reading Cavafy on the roof. I rest on Sundays, Mondays, and Tuesdays. If I leave the Chandler it's to take a walk to the downtown YMCA for a little exercise. At dusk there was the call to prayer from the little storefront mosque on Dwight, sung through a tinny PA system. It was quite warm. Not just warm for Berkeley. Real heat. I closed my eyes and imagined that I was in Egypt. Noise, bad air, the sounds of the Koran. This could be Cairo, or Alexandria. I needed a change of scenery. After this job, a long vacation.

I went into the kitchen and turned the oven up high. Opened every window in the apartment and turned on a fan. Rolled out some pizza dough. Marvin arrived as I was putting the pizza in the oven. He was tired. He'd done tech work all day. I chided him for working on a weekend, calling him a capitalist lackey. He, in turn, was merciless concerning my night with Dino Centro. I had to take it. No defense, really.

"Centro's only concern is money. He'll sell you out. I hope you didn't tell him any secrets."

"We barely said a word."

"His entire value system is based on money, you know, and—"

Here I chimed in, and we said Marvin's favorite line in unison: "AND MONEY ISN'T A VALUE."

"But I don't really agree, Marv. He's a sensualist. Money's just a means to an end."

"Hairsplitting. There's no morality in there."

"Sort of like your average American."

And it went on like this until we finished the pizza, along with a fair bottle of wine from Abruzzo.

It was the eve of Bastille Day. Marvin was going down to Santa

Cruz to spend it with some friends. I was invited but declined. A date with Stephie. This was met with more eye-rolling and a final chorus of MONEY ISN'T A VALUE. He left, and I was alone quite early. I brushed Emily, who was looking quite fat. She had been acting kind of blasé as of late. I wondered if too much ice cream could hurt a cat. Made a note to take her to the vet soon. I had no idea if she'd had her shots.

## 16.

It was with much male pride that I purchased a big box of condoms at the Chimes Pharmacy. It had been a physical summer. From Chimes I sauntered down the block to Vino for a bottle of La Commanderie de Queyret Bordeaux Supérieur. A Frank O'Hara poem was just outside the reach of my memory, something about Bastille Day, and another that takes place three days after. I hopped into the Miata, top down, and drove up to the classy part of town.

To my surprise Hart was at Stephie's. She must have seen my look of disappointment. She stood behind him and made a gesture that I took to mean, Don't worry, he's leaving soon.

He was drinking Fischer beer. "We're all French today," he said, and he raised his glass. He seemed a little drunk.

"You seem to be celebrating."

"We got Pinsky."

"Huh? Oh, for poetry fantasy camp."

"You're just jealous. Nobody would ask you to teach anywhere."

I didn't answer. There was something to what he said.

"Or maybe somebody would, Clay. I'd like to do this full-time. If that happens, maybe I can have you down for a reading or something. With a little capital, I could found a school. Fuck Naropa and New College. I could put those beatniks out of business. Get Adrienne Rich to come down. And Levine. Sky's the limit."

When he said the word "capital" I happened to be watching Stephie. A nervous look crossed her face. She caught herself and smiled blankly. I got the idea that Hart was talking too much.

"Hart, I thought you were going over to the City, to Café Bastille."

"Okay, sis, I'm out of here. I'll leave you to your fuck buddy."

She shooed him out the door. "Sorry, Clay. He's a bad drunk. I hope he takes the BART."

He'd left half a bottle of Fischer. I got a clean glass and poured myself the rest. There were, as promised, two steaks in the oversized reefer. And a shallot, a baguette, salad makings. I fried the shallot in butter and added a little wine. Arranged and tossed the salad, grilled the steaks on her indoor grill. There was also, as requested, a chunk of blue cheese. The ten-minute French bistro dinner.

After dinner she brought out some Armagnac. It was very good. She was learning how to drink like the yuppie that she was. Lucky me. Unfortunately, the drinks were more interesting than the conversation. Until she got to the subject of her brother.

"He's frustrated. He just hasn't found himself. I mean, he has his books, and the poetry. But that isn't a serious life." After saying this she covered her mouth, embarrassed.

"It's okay, dear. I've never wanted a serious life."

She took the cue. "Yes, that's right, you're happy with that life. But Hart wants, um, well, not exactly more, exactly."

"More's the word. This just happens to be enough for me."

"Right, right. Hart wants some security. That doesn't seem to be an issue with you."

It's more complicated than that, I thought. But I let it pass. How do I explain? I don't understand why I do what I do. But it does feel right. The look of embarrassment left her, and she smiled sweetly. I was growing fond of her. It happens when you sleep with somebody more than once. Partly out of a need to justify the continuing sexual union. But there's another reason too. Intimacy softens us a little. At least for a while. The old anarchists were right. If we could somehow be capable of free love, the world would be a wonderful place. It is generally agreed that human nature won't allow for this. And yet, and yet...

She seemed to sense my contemplative mood and she put on an old Brian Eno CD, one I hadn't heard in a long time. She decided that we should smoke some pot. I don't do that much, but this time I went along. And we floated along on Pablo for hours. It was very strong stuff, I was barely in touch. It crossed my mind that maybe she'd slipped me a Mickey. Who cares, I thought. We slept, or at least I did. Then she woke me up and walked me back to the bedroom.

Much later I was lying on my back, trying to remember if I'd just made love. And it came to me that I had, and I dropped off again.

I slept till ten. She had coffee ready. I needed it.

"Did you have a nice Bastille Day?"

"*Vive la France.* I have a bit of a headache. I'm not used to pot."

"Good stuff. I feel foggy too."

We had a long, slow breakfast. I showered and shaved, got ready to go. She walked me out to the car, hanging close in a white terry robe. She smelled great. When we reached the street my heart sank. The Miata had been munched. Sideswiped. Worse than sideswiped. The passenger side door was almost gone.

"Clay, why didn't you park in the drive?"

"Hart's SUV was in the way. Shit. This is going to be expensive. Shit." I got in the car and examined the door from the inside. A mess.

"Come in the house, and we'll have it towed."

I got inside and fumbled for my insurance card.

She touched my hand, said, "I know somebody who's really good. He's an old friend of Hart's. He'll do it for cost, for me."

"Really?"

"Don't worry. Your AAA card will cover his towing service. I got the number right here, somewhere. Here."

I took the card and picked up the phone. I had to restrain myself from laughing and saying, "Something's hinky here, Stephie, what's going on?"

She saw me hesitate. She reached around me from behind and said, "It's okay, Clay. I'll get it fixed for you cheap. Weldon's a great body guy."

## 17.

Weldon was in fact Weldon, the Weldon that Trak had mentioned under duress. Weldon the murderer, according to Trak. He was waiting in the office of the San Pablo Garage, a nondescript place on a block with futon shops, ethnic markets, and a Taco Bell. It was a long tow from Montclair. I hoped my insurance would cover it. I hadn't questioned Stephie about using her friend's body shop. I wondered if she found that strange. Probably not. People tend to be dazed when these things happen. Open to suggestion. I wondered if some kind of fix was in. Couldn't imagine what the angle might be.

Weldon's look was working class. Lots of tattoos and a haircut that looked like it had been done by a Portuguese immigrant in 1945, too short at the sides and greasy on top. His forearms looked like Popeye's. His hands were too small for those arms. I tried to dredge up memories of my working-class past. I always do in these places, makes it easier to communicate with the help. But that strategy was wrong here. Weldon was another type. Remember the hippies who left the city to become farmers? A simpler life, pastoral bliss, blah blah blah? Weldon was, in a way, their kindred spirit. One look told me that he had probably been a grad student at Cal. Tattoos, American cars, Bettie Page. His interests in these things started with a strong sense of irony. After a while, he began to long for the old days that never were. Decided to work with his hands.

My romantic fantasy is the exact opposite. I spent my first years out of high school in a Sears warehouse, hefting baby furniture into a delivery truck. Then I was a janitor, a hotel clerk, whatever. My coworkers were ignorant, ugly, slovenly, illiterate. As I toiled beside them I dreamed of cafés, French cigarettes, women dressed in black. As a bona fide prole, I have no respect for proles. And I put class tourists like Weldon in the same category as ecotourists. They are creeps.

This only begins to explain our mutual hatred. There was something chemical, elemental, whatever. I wanted to pick up a wrench, brain him with it, and be done with it. I'm sure he thought the same. We stood close and eyed each other.

"You need a new door. I can order one today and have it back in a couple of days."

"How much?"

"I'll write up an estimate. Have a seat and I'll be back in a minute."

Weldon returned with an estimate that was much too low. I wanted to let him know that I knew, but that would blow everything. I was supposed to think that Stephie had fixed it. Well, she had fixed something. I wasn't sure why. Weldon was smiling, above it all. Must have learned that in grad school. Fierce pride welled up inside me. I know it's a trick, you idiot. But said nothing. Playing dumb is hard sometimes.

"Thank you, Weldon. This is more than fair. Are you sure it's okay?"

"Stephie is an old friend. Any friend of Stephie's. In fact, I can have it for you tonight, if you like."

I didn't need the car, this being Monday. But he seemed to want me to have it. Deciding it was part of the con, I went along.

"We can rent you a loaner, or call you a cab."

"That's okay, Weldon. I feel like walking."

It's a pretty long walk, maybe three miles. North on San Pablo to Good Vibrations, corner of Dwight. I wanted to go in but I couldn't think of an excuse. I was all stocked up on condoms, and, alas, I wasn't involved with anyone kinky. With Stephie it was all still quicksilver, melting into each other, and losing identity, and feeling exhausted. I thought of Dino Centro. I laughed, narrowed my eyes, and thought some more. I went inside and bought some nice oil, just for luck. For next time, or for the next person, or something. I walked up a poor section of Dwight. Some of the last unkempt Victorians in Northern California. I took in the beauty of peeling paint, uncut lawns, the ripe scent of trash uncollected. A couple was selling old bicycles on their lawn. They looked to be out of the Great Depression. A note on the lawns: None of them were green. Nothing, in fact, had color. The sidewalk wasn't white, it was gray. The houses were in shades of faded brown. The people also seemed gray. The white people were a little dark, the Black people looked faded. It was a far cry from Telegraph Avenue, where everything seemed to be in primary colors. I found it all refreshing. It was like ducking into an urban museum and discovering some early Renaissance painting. A sudden quiet.

Soon the class tourists would discover this place, and they would lift it up. There would be a Starbucks and a chain video store, and fat little children on their way to soccer practice. May they burn in hell.

A few blocks later Dwight got more boho, tattoo parlors and Asian restaurants. Thankfully, it's still a little shabby at the edges. I peeked into Industrial Tattoo, to see if Lorine was there. She did mine: just three words, block letters. A poem by Giuseppe Ungaretti titled "Matina," translated by me, from an old signed edition of one of his books, found in Shakespeare & Co. in the early '80s: ENORMITY ILLUMINES ME. Down the inside of my right arm. Lorine was in the back taking a break. She had shaved her head, showing a tattoo that looked like the top of a (her?) skull.

"Hi, Lorine. I like your skull."

"Great, huh. If I get sick of it, I just let my hair grow back. No tattoo. Except for the nineteen others." She was wearing a T-shirt with the sleeves torn off. I could see that a short-sleeved shirt would conceal the dragons, spiders, and panthers that covered her square, sturdy body. I liked that. There are times when looking normal is the best revenge. Element of surprise.

"This guy named Weldon is doing some body work on my car. Lots of tattoos. Do you know him?"

"Be careful with him. He has a temper. Reed did some stuff for him. He didn't like it and he had a hissy fit. He comes on all intellectual, then he wants to fight. Psycho."

I walked up to Fred's Market and got Lorine a Coke. She started in on her girlfriend problems. I tried to follow but it was hard to put names to faces. And there were lots of names. So I nodded a lot and tried to look understanding. Finally we finished our Cokes and I made my way back to the Chandler.

The cat looked fine but I decided to take her to the vet the next day. She probably needed her shots. I called the body shop. Somebody said the car would be finished in a couple of hours. Record time for body work. Jobs like this can take a few days. Something was up. Perhaps they wanted me to stay home? No, doesn't make sense. Lack of a car doesn't ensure that in the Bay Area. There's still BART and AC Transit. Perhaps they wanted to plant something on me. But it would be tough to frame me for Peggy's murder. No motive.

I went up to the roof to get some sun. I was struck with a memory. Early in my friendship (affair? whatever) with Peggy we came upstairs on a blustery day. Nothing special happened. But I remembered her hair being ruffled by the wind, and the way she leaned over the fire escape to look at the garden that fronts the sushi place down below. Had Peggy died of natural causes this would have been a wistful, sad memory. The fact that she was murdered made these feelings unbearable. There would be sleepless nights for many years to come. Lots of nightmares. No therapist can help with this type of grief. I went back downstairs and waited in my room.

I wanted to read the old poets. I read some Thomas Carew and some Richard Lovelace. Finally I decided on an old anthology of troubadour poetry. Poems from the days when poets could beat people up. And did. I had a feeling that I'd have to defend myself soon. Dark thoughts.

The time came to pick up my car. I decided to call Friendly Cab. The service is terrible. Often the bus is faster. But I wanted to be alone in the back seat of a car. The turbaned driver rang my bell and we sped down Haste Street until we hit rush hour traffic at Shattuck. The driver had a foul mouth for a Sikh. I found that amusing, but he felt obligated to apologize for every "fuck," addressing me as "boss."

The body shop was an anticlimax. Weldon wasn't even there. The door looked great. My next step would be a visit to Earl Scheib for a paint job. I wrote a check and drove back to the Chandler. I did notice that the door felt different, but I guess that was to be expected. It was a little heavier, and the window was easier to work.

## 18.

I decided to finish the day with some errands. First the cat. I parked in the loading zone and put Emily in the cardboard case that I'd picked up a few days before. It was decorated to look like a circus cage. I made jokes about taking her to the circus to see the lions. Emily didn't appreciate the joke. She gave me a good scratch as I loaded her into the carrier.

By the time I got to the car she'd practically destroyed her new circus cage. She was also screaming loudly and hurling her body from one side of the cage to the other. The car door was a struggle. I fumbled with my keys as the carrier swayed with her weight. I was approached by Bruce, one of the local crazies. Remember that bald guy who was in all the John Ford movies? The one who talked real slow and had a sincere look in his eyes, even when muttering non sequiturs. I think his name was Arthur Shields. Bruce is Arthur Shields reincarnated. He stood close and stared.

"Hi, Bruce." Very long pause.
"Would you like some help?"
"Yes."
"Five dollars?"

"One dollar."

"Okay."

He helped me get Emily into the passenger seat. I fished a dollar out of my pocket.

"I said five."

"I said one." Long pause.

"Okay."

I got into the driver's side. Bruce slammed the door. Too hard. It made a weird double clunk. Something in the bowels of the door had fallen over. I didn't pay too much attention.

As I put the Miata into gear Emily popped out of the carrier and bounded into the back seat. Luckily the top was up. Otherwise she'd have joined the walking wounded at the corner of Telegraph and Dwight. Another Berkeley runaway. I threw the useless cage into the back seat and drove up to College, then right toward the Claremont Pet Hospital. I knew they'd administer the shots without an appointment and give her a quick look-see. Emily screamed and jumped from seat to seat until we were almost there. At some point she became fixated on a strange bulge that had appeared in the upholstery of my new door. It was a hard little edge. Emily batted at it, then rubbed her lip on it, leaving a trail of cat drool. When I pulled in at the cat hospital I reached over and felt at the lump in the door. Something hard.

When we got into the waiting room Emily attacked a border collie, who then peed on the floor. I was warned against bringing her in unpacked. I promised to get a regulation cat carrier before my next visit. She was pronounced in good health and we were sent on our way. There was more screeching on the ride home. Finally I deposited her at the Chandler, where she happily ate about a pound of kibble.

I called Marvin to make sure he was home. He was, so I got back in the Miata, which was parked in a yellow zone, and drove back to North Berkeley. He was in his garage when I arrived. We poked at the door. Loose part? What part would a door have? Marvin suggested that I take it back to Weldon, but I declined. There was something funny going on.

I became too curious. I had to see what was inside the door. I knocked at and around it. Hollow. But aren't these doors kind of hollow anyway? I noticed differences in the doors. The new door was heavier. I slammed them both. The new door didn't sound right. I felt a wave of frustration. Something was inside that door.

Keats said that a poet's life is one of continual allegory. I am a poet. I'm not at the level of Keats or Stein or even Tim Dlugos, but I walk the same path. And I believe that my life is a kind of symbolic narration that holds clues to the secret meanings of things. Most people choose not to pick up on these clues. Bully for them. But those who take the time to study the lives of the poets can learn something valuable.

People often ask me if I've studied Zen. I haven't. But I must have that way about me. I am, up to a point, a very patient man. Marvin says that I have the longest, slowest fuse of anyone he's ever met. Often, I'm so caught up in being amused and/or bemused that I don't notice I'm irritated. At least not for a long, long time.

I sat on a stool in Marvin's garage. It's the kind of black rolling stool that you see in bookstores. The staff at Moe's gave it to him when they bought some new ones. It's pretty scuffed up. I stared at the car and I thought about the door. And I thought about Maria, my ex-wife, and the rides we'd take in the Miata when it was new. In the summer we'd go down the coast almost every weekend. I thought of Maria's long, blue-black hair. Thought of her olive skin, how it became more olive as summer wore on. I remembered driving all the way to Zuma Beach one Sunday without a plan, sleeping in the car, then driving back.

Marvin went into the house and came back with two Bohemia beers.

"What are you going to do?"

"There's something inside that door."

"I know, Clay. I could probably find somebody who knows how to take the door off, or how to remove the upholstery without ruining anything."

I didn't hear him, really. I walked over to the corner that holds the tools. There aren't many. Most of the garage is used for book storage. There was a mallet, a handsaw, a small shovel, and a huge pair of shears. All a little rusty. Marvin isn't much of a gardener. He lets things grow over till the neighbors complain. Then he hires somebody to cut it all back.

But there they were. The pair of oversized shears. I opened the door. I inserted the open end of the shears into the edge of the fake leather, then I ripped open the inside of the door. I cut, sawed, and chopped. After a long, thoughtful silence, I had allowed my frustration to get the better of me. I'd become rash and destructive. I had made a mess. Life as allegory.

Marvin is addicted to spectacle, especially if it involves the destruction of property. He whooped and laughed. He slammed his fist on the hood of the car. This egged me on. I tore through a couple of layers of fabric. It wasn't easy. The shears were dull and the cloth was tough. Finally I ripped away the final layer, exposing a hollowed-out door containing three brown bags tied with twine. Marvin came around to see. We stared for a few seconds at the bags. Then I grabbed one and he grabbed two. We gently put them on the hood of the car. I opened the first. Foil, then plastic, then cash. We quickly counted the bundles. One hundred hundreds, and a thousand more in smaller bills. The second bag was well padded. Bubble wrap, then a Wells Fargo check box. Weird stuff inside. Old knives and two-pronged forks. Trinkets. Something scythe-like. A strigil? But I'd imagined those to be bigger. The third package was even more padded, with bubble wrap and old newspapers. Layer after layer. Then a cheap metal box, no lock. More padding, then Dino's ultimate trinket. The Oriana Fallaci, as we'd dubbed it. About a foot tall. Smooth to the touch. Wearing a long dress and a pointed cap. Facial features smoothed by time, but there. Deep-set eyes and a pointy nose. Her thin arms spread wide, like a lounge singer holding that final sentimental note.

"She's probably worth something. If you can find a fence."

"Maybe Dino will help me."

"You trust that jerk?"

We brought the stuff into Marvin's house and called Pizza Rustica. I felt strange paying with one of the twenties from the door but that didn't stop me. I was determined to keep that money. Better me than Weldon and co.

Marvin cleared the table of the usual clutter and opened a bottle of Sangiovese. Oriana was standing next to the pizza, gesturing, as if to say, *"Mangia, mangia!"* He was a little too happy to mention that Stephie Hearn had set me up. Hart had parked in her driveway so that I would park on the street. Weldon, or Trak, or somebody had sideswiped the Miata in the middle of the night.

"I smoked pot. I never smoke pot. I don't remember a thing."

"Probably more than pot. The bitch probably slipped you a Mickey Finn, as they say in the gangster movies."

"Maybe. I was still groggy the next morning."

"And open to suggestion. You went straight to her body guy, and he loaded the car with loot. What now?"

"According to Dino the statue is to be sold in Mexico in a few days. One possibility is that Weldon, or somebody, will try and steal the Miata tonight. They know my habit of not driving much early in the week. They could take it to Mexico and dump it before anybody notices. Or perhaps they were going to try and talk me into taking a drive down there myself. Given the right incentive, say, a library in San Diego and a night partying on the beach, I'd be up for it. And if they offered me expenses and a fee, I'd gladly drive farther south. If the stuff was discovered in my car, they could play dumb."

"Who all do you think they are?"

"Hart, Weldon, Stephie, Trak. I don't think Peggy was involved."

"You don't want to."

"I'd rather not. Although she probably had possession of Oriana. That's what got her killed. But I don't think she knew what it's worth."

"What is it worth?"

"Lots, according to Dino."

"Dino and Hart could be in cahoots."

"Instincts tell me otherwise."

"We all get sentimental toward those we've fucked. Human nature. We don't want to believe that we were intimate with someone who is evil. Why do you think people go back to abusive losers?"

"I'm just not that sentimental."

"Uh-huh."

## 19.

I have a place where I can hide things. A strange little false closet below one of the kitchen cabinets. I discovered it when I moved in. I was lining the shelves and the floor felt kind of hollow. Trap door.

When covered with pots, pans, and whatever it's perfectly safe. Down went Oriana, the trinkets, and some of the money. I checked my messages. Two from Hart. Would I like to go down to Mexico with him, expenses paid? My hunches had been right.

I had parked the Miata a couple of miles away. I didn't want it stolen while I was stashing the loot. I walked down past Shattuck Avenue and got in. The car was a mess. We'd ripped up most of the upholstery, hoping to find something else, or maybe a clue. No luck. I drove to Alameda. It was too early to do what I needed to do. I went to a Creole place called the Commodore that overlooks the yacht harbor. I ordered the Satchmo Special, red beans and rice with sausage and a Rolling Rock. I silently toasted my ex-wife, Maria, now living in New Orleans. I ate very slowly, watching the boats come and go in the early evening. It occurred to me that I might have been followed, but I pushed that worry out of my brain. I'd done enough to cover my tracks. Hart's phone messages seemed to indicate that he was clueless. I wondered if they were planning to kill me once they got the loot over the border.

I ordered peach cobbler and coffee and sat for another hour or so, watching the boats. The chef, one Frank Faté, ambled over and asked me if the food was okay. I gave him my compliments and asked for more coffee. The dinner crowd was dwindling, except for a table of eight across the room, a birthday party. They were ordering more Hennessys as I got up to go. It was about ten.

It was warm so I put the top down. I wanted to enjoy every mile of this ride. My little Miata's last stand. I got on the freeway, over the bridge, and out to Highway 1. I wanted to do the whole drive down the coast. I remembered the day we bought the car. I was skeptical and made jokes about it all, but Maria was so excited that I couldn't help feeling excited too. We went out for rides every night. We weren't embarrassed to be so in love with such a silly car. It wasn't, after all, a Triumph or a Sunbeam. It was a fake facsimile of those great cars of the '60s. Still, it was fun to drive. We'd put the top down, even when it was too cold. We'd go up to Grizzly Peak or into Tilden Park and make love, Maria straddling me in the passenger seat. The high point of our short marriage.

My generation loves toys. We've sold out for them. And I'm guilty too. For our love of toys we will someday devour the world.

It's a terrible addiction with no way out. If we stop buying them now, the economy will crash. If we continue, we will use up our energy sources and foul the air and water. These thoughts went through my head as I shifted into fifth and stepped on the gas. A nice sexy feeling.

For once it wasn't foggy as I approached Santa Cruz. I stopped at a café downtown for an espresso. I walked around to stretch my legs, then I got back on the highway. Monterey was also pretty warm. The air smelled salty, and it had that midsummer feel. It was around midnight and there wasn't much traffic at all. I breezed through Carmel, then entered the Big Sur area. I felt that fun scary feeling, like the first dip in a roller coaster. I drove fast, but not too fast. If by chance there was a witness, I wanted them to say that I was driving a little too fast. Not erratic, like a drunk driver, just a little fast. I hit a little patch of fog. Visibility went down near zero. I stepped on the gas. Plowed through the mist and hit the warm air again, almost missing a turn. That might have been the end. Mr. Poet's Wild Ride!

I came to one of those postcard bridges. Stopped mid-bridge to look at the moon. Nobody on the road for miles, full moon, crash of the waves way down below. I wondered where Lawrence Ferlinghetti's cabin might be. Thought of Henry Miller and Jack Kerouac. Who doesn't when in Big Sur? I thought about giving up on this plan and going to Nepenthe for a couple of Negronis. But that wouldn't do. I had to get rid of the car. Had to destroy it, actually. I didn't want somebody like Weldon inspecting the remains.

Into the car and on to the next bridge, which was the right bridge. There was a little service road just to the right of the bridge named Pacific Street. Street sign and everything. Between the turnoff and the bridge some missing railing. Just enough room for a Miata to go over the side and fly. A long, dark drop. I wasn't sure if the car would hit ocean or rock. Either would do. The tank was half full. Hopefully that gas would blow.

I drove up to the turnoff, pulled over, and inspected the site. The piece of railing had been missing for all of the twenty years that I'd been doing the drive. I looked up and down the street. No cars. I walked out to the middle of the bridge. No traffic for a couple of miles, at least. I looked at the drop. Was that water down there? Too dark to tell. Fear came over me. I shivered and got back into the car. I made one pass, but I didn't have the angle right. I made a three-point turn, got back into position, and tried again. Couldn't do it that time either. Lost my nerve. C'mon, Clay. They do it in the movies. You'll have plenty of time to jump out.

I sat in the car for a good fifteen minutes. Still no traffic. I needed to get it over with. I'd left a couple of tapes in the car for the trip down. I found an old Clash tape and I turned it up so loud that it distorted. I gunned the engine a few times and put it into gear. As I approached the spot I opened the door. I hit it a little too fast. I jumped and rolled, like you're supposed to, but I missed the soft sand that I'd chosen as a target. My left arm and leg hit asphalt. Hurt like shit, even through leather jacket and jeans. I heard crash sounds. Adrenaline forced me back up into a standing position. I ran to the railing with a terrific pain in my side. The car had taken a beautiful, long fall. I listened for motor sounds, but it was too far down. I imagined that I heard the Clash tape. Did I? Doubt it. I strained my eyes but I couldn't see too much. Then, after a few minutes, there was an explosion, but far away. I saw a little toy flame engulf a Matchbox car, way down on the rocks.

I sat propped against the railing and took a physical inventory. My jeans were ripped but there wasn't much blood. My ribs felt a little bruised but not broken. I could move my arm. The mission had been a success.

My rescue came more quickly than I expected. A young man shone a flashlight in my eyes, then apologized. He was with a woman. Turn-of-this-century versions of Big Sur hippies. Ash-blond dreads and baggy clothes. Strong scent of herb. I could do worse, I thought.

"Where'd you guys come from?"

"We live down on Pac Street. Are you okay?"

"I'm not sure. I lost control of my car."

"It's gone now, brother. Hope it was insured. Can you walk?"

I got up, a little unsteady. Hippie Girl helped me stay up. Strong kid. She hid her hand inside her sweatshirt, then used it to wipe some dirt from my face. She had big pothead eyes. Life is good, I thought.

They led me down the road to their cabin. It was surprisingly tidy, especially considering the many dogs and cats that came to greet me, one by one. Russ and Gail introduced me to their menagerie. Some of the animals had biblical names, which I attributed to some Rastafarian influence. Others had names that, I suppose, sound good to the hippie ear. Zafari, Aziz, Rosalia.

They gave me some herb concoction for my various scrapes and bruises. I was informed that I could stay with them until I got better, or I could call a friend. But I was not to call the cops. I figured they were somehow involved in the pot industry. "Fine with me," I said. I suggested that I spend the night, then hitch a ride to the nearest pay phone. I'd tell the cops that I spent the night by the side of the road, then walked to a phone. Worked for Teddy Kennedy, why not me?

I got comfortable on the couch and heard their life story. They had made it through high school in the Midwest, then came out together to escape Babylon. Five blissful years in the cabin, with occasional "business" trips. Not a bad life.

They brought out some of their products and we smoked. They treated me to their homemade dark ale. I found their singsong voices relaxing. I'm an old punk. I shaved my head in the late '70s, took lots of meth, listened to the hardest and fastest music I could find. Hated hippies. Too old to care about those differences now. Anybody who stands outside the mainstream is okay by me.

The ale and the drug took hold and I got sleepy. They brought me a sleeping bag and I fell asleep on the floor, flanked by a huge mongrel and two black cats.

## 20.

It went okay with the cops. I guess I was going a little too fast, officer. I lost control. One beer, officer, but it was a couple of hours before I got in the car. It went through my mind that they might want to do a blood alcohol test. They didn't, thank goodness. Russ and Gail had been generous with the dark ale and pot. I was a little hung over. After a morning of filling out reports and making calls, they took me to Nepenthe, where I called Marvin. He told me that it would be at least three hours. Again, fine with me. The place is expensive, but the food is good and the view is perfect. I sat on their back patio, facing the Pacific Ocean. Warm, clear day. I won't even try to describe the beauty of that stretch of coast. I treated myself to a rare morning Bloody Mary followed by a big breakfast.

I eavesdropped on the couple who had just been to some Esalen workshops. I feel this, I feel that. I hear you, yes. I hear what you are saying. Eventually my attention was diverted by two German women. They were kissing and feeding each other sips of Ramos gin fizz. I wanted to listen, but they were speaking German, so all I caught was German German haha German German Ramos jeen fiss! Followed by a long, tonguey kiss.

My thoughts turned to the caper. I had to convince Stephie and co. that I'd gone on a little midnight ride and accidentally put the Miata in the wide blue Pacific. They had to believe that the Oriana and the loot had gone up in flames. I needed to pull off the *I, Claudius* of all time. And I had to trust that Dino Centro wasn't in cahoots with them. I needed Dino to complete my plan.

I finished my breakfast and took a stroll around the gift shop. Lots of redwood burl, individualized coffee mugs, funny cards. I walked over to the observation deck and found a seat away from the ocean. The land was that California gold color, the color of dead weeds. Pretty, though. I ordered a house coffee and took in the sun until Marvin arrived.

"How'd it go?"

"I wrecked the car."

"As planned."

"It was more of an obstacle course than I'd remembered. I couldn't just roll it over the side. I had to drive and steer, and take it up over the sidewalk, and then jump out."

"You should have hired a stunt man. Did it hurt?"

"Scrapes."

"No more Miata. The last souvenir. Think you'll ever see Maria again?"

I said no but I thought yes. I always see everybody again. Some karmic law, I guess. Someday when I least expect it Maria will appear. Hopefully not this year.

I slept for most of the drive up. Needed it. Marvin took me home to change and feed the cat, then over to a car rental place on Oxford Street. They put me in a sky-blue Neon. I followed him back to his place and told him my exciting story. We tinkered a little with my plan and we ate lunch. He wished me luck with a bear hug, and I got into a very clean car.

I drove slowly up to Montclair but not by choice. The Neon had very little pickup. Big black SUVs flew by or tailgated. Some honked.

I couldn't do much about it. I chugged along at fifty-five, then fifty, just for spite. I wasn't in a hurry to play my scene at Stephie's. I put on the radio and got some punk on KALX. I turned it up, then slowed down to forty-five. I never thought going slow could be such an act of rebellion. I moved over to the fast lane. More honking and lots of red faces. I started to worry about being pulled over, or shot, so I zagged back to the slow lane. But it was fun while it lasted.

There was an old Mustang in the driveway, and behind that was Hart's monster SUV. They were all there. I'd have to walk into the gang headquarters and lie my head off. I collected my thoughts, walked up the long drive. I felt a cold sweat coming on. I could use that to good effect. I knocked.

Stephie answered the door and I made my entrance like Scarlett O'Hara. I found the big white couch and I collapsed. I put my arm over my face and faked a sob.

"Clay! What's wrong?"

"I wrecked the Miata."

There was a long pause. I heard the others come in. I looked up to see Hart, Weldon, and Trak. I could have guessed that the Mustang belonged to Weldon. I felt a wave of anger. These assholes wanted to use me as a mule, then kill me. I tried to use the emotion the way any good actor would. I let out another good sob. Tears came to my eyes.

"You know how I like to drive down Highway 1. I went down last night. Somehow I lost control and put it over one of the big bridges. I don't know how I managed to jump out before it went. I spent the night by the side of the road. I think I'm still in shock or something."

I took my arm away from my eyes and I gave Stephie a long, soulful look. She tried to return it, but she couldn't pull it off. The color had gone out of her face. She mumbled something like, "That's terrible, Clay," but there was nothing behind it. I gave her a puzzled look, and she looked away. I knew I had the upper hand, but I couldn't let that show. She got up and went to the kitchen. Came back with a glass of water. She was doing her best to keep up the con.

"Are you hurt?"

"Scrapes and bruises. Nothing much. But the car is gone. It hit the rocks and it blew up. Must have burned for hours. There's nothing left. I can't believe it happened. I'm so used to that road. Maybe the steering went. I just lost control."

I sat up and looked at them. Hart's a lousy actor. He shifted around and tried to avoid my eyes. Weldon was directing disgusted looks at Hart. Loading up my car must have been Hart's idea. I got up and walked over to a window.

"I'm still pretty shaky. Can I stay here for a while?"

This struck a nerve with Weldon, as I thought it would. My hunch was that he was fucking Stephie. I had to get my digs in. Looking back, that was a dumb thing to do. But as I said, I had this visceral hatred of the man. I wanted to fuck with him in the worst way.

He stepped toward me, then turned on his heels and went into the kitchen. I tried to look innocent and dumb. He came out with a beer, looking sullen. I looked over at Stephie with big cow eyes. I didn't think she'd want me around. I wanted to see how she'd get out of it.

"It's a bad time, Clay. We've got some business things we're discussing."

"I won't be any trouble. I'm just so upset. Can't you spare me a beer?" I was probably pushing it now. I asked myself how I'd really act if this hadn't been a setup. If it'd all been an accident and these really were my friends. Of course I'd want to stay and have some company.

She turned to Weldon, said, "Weldon, get him a beer." She was a little short.

Weldon gave her a look that could kill, then, without softening, looked at me. But he did get me the beer. He handed the beer over and I came very close to blowing it. He wasn't really any more hateful than the rest. But that deep chemical hatred filled me with adrenaline. I wanted to grab the bottle, beat him to death with it, and get it all over with. I searched my brain for an image that would calm me. And all I came up with was the last scene in *The Wild Bunch*, that beautiful moment when the Bunch, though outnumbered, start the shooting. I replayed the scene, and it felt like delicious temptation. But I also saw it as a cautionary tale. I wasn't ready to make that suicidal move.

I slowly drank my beer. I told them to go on with their business, that it wouldn't bother me. Hart made something up about his poetry fantasy camp. The conversation kept dwindling. I asked him about Pinsky. He said that Pinsky had dropped out but that he could get Creeley, if he could come up with some money. He had Wanda Coleman, Dorianne Laux, and David Bromige. He just needed one big star to bring students down. As he spoke his voice trailed away, mid-sentence. Everybody looked in opposite directions and waited for a chance to go. Like small talk at a funeral.

I decided to go and leave them to discuss my fate. My sense was that they had believed me. I suppose, if they didn't, they could have killed me then and there. But they didn't make a move. Stephie gave me a cold hug, the best she could manage. I held on to her for a couple of extra seconds, then kissed her on the lips. Looked over her shoulder at Weldon. He looked away.

Out to the Neon and then down to Berkeley Bowl for a piece of salmon. I owed Marvin a good dinner. Berkeley Bowl was pandemonium. I noticed, standing in line, that I had the most normal hairstyle in the store. Mine is brown and short. Theirs was green, bleached white, stringy, shaved, sticking straight up. You don't see hair like theirs on the evening news. With a hairdo like that, I thought, looking at a late-'70s-style Mohawk, you can't run for Congress. Every so often I'm reminded that Berkeley is rather strange. It makes my day.

The traffic, alas, was also typically Berkeley. I circled People's Park eight times, going west as far as Shattuck, turning left, then heading up Dwight toward the hills. Finally a tiny place opened up on Haste, in front of a free box. A grizzled wino type was standing in the middle of the pile, shopping for a shirt. He tried on a pink one with a V-neck, but that didn't do. The frilly white blouse was too small. He decided on a steel-blue T that loudly advertised Merrill Lynch, then waded out of the pile and thrust both fists upward in a victory salute.

I had barely finished slicing the tomatoes and mozzarella when Marvin arrived. In honor of the warm weather I made a pitcher of lemonade, spiked with vodka. Marvin tore into the bread and tomatoes with barely a hello.

"They're going to come after you."

"No. I don't think so. I think I snowed 'em."

"Don't be surprised if your apartment gets turned upside down."

"No, no. Really. They believed me." Marvin had a way of eroding my confidence.

"Okay. They believed you. Where do you go from here?"

I unveiled my plan as we ate a long, slow dinner. I was careful to offer him a good cut of the loot. I slowly increased his cut whenever he registered a complaint. By the end of the evening he was on board at fifty-fifty.

## 21.

I went over to Bongo Burger and ordered a Persian Burger. While I was waiting I set up a dummy email account at Streetspace, one of those email stations that have appeared in public spaces. Username: makedinorich. I emailed Dino and told him that I had something he would be interested in. He could probably track me down through some electronic means that I don't understand. But it didn't matter much. I really wanted to give him plausible deniability in the event that Hart and the gang questioned him. It did occur to me that he might be loyal to them, but I decided to take a chance that he wasn't. He'd want the loot for himself.

I was a little anxious. I checked my email from home after dinner. Nothing. I went down to Moe's to browse. I hadn't been buying and selling many books lately. I found an old out-of-print book by Harold Norse. I had a trade slip in my wallet somewhere. Moe's issues trade for books, as well as paying cash. I usually keep a trade tab going. I searched my wallet, but I couldn't find it. I had one of the found hundreds in my pocket so I broke it. This loot wasn't going to last. I wondered if the cash could be traced directly back to Thomas. The missing cash that got me into this mess. Oh well, money is money.

Moe's has a free email machine, identical to the one in Bongo Burger. It's located in the critical theory section. I decided to try my luck. I stood at the machine, which resembles something that you might see in the Starship Enterprise. Most contemporary design is based on *Star Trek,* or some other bad TV show. We're the generation that couldn't grow up. As I logged on I became aware that the works of Theodor Adorno and Walter Benjamin were looking over my shoulder. Sorry, guys. The screen treated me to a series of ads. It played some space-age music (Adorno had a problem with jazz. What would he think of this?) and then it allowed me to see my mail. Dino had also set up a dummy account, under the username figaro. I wondered if he was up at Bongo Burger, picking up a Persian Burger. More likely he was at Café Roma. Our stupid lives. His was a simple message: Show me some proof and I'll get back to you.

I went back to the Chandler. I opened a Bohemia and leafed through the Norse book:

> I was made to be a hero
> but there were no causes
> & besides I was too short.

I pulled the stuff out of the false-bottomed cupboard. I selected a trinket. I didn't know what it was. A butter knife with a hole cut out of the blade. A bottle opener, before the days of screw tops? Something for cake decoration? Funny, Clay. I'll probably never know. It fit nicely into a small-size manila envelope. On the envelope I scrawled I'VE GOT THE STATUE. I slipped it into a Moe's bag along with a book for ballast. I left Oriana out on the kitchen table while I drank and read poetry. She was beautiful, really. That ancient, quiet feeling came over me, like what you feel when you visit the Colosseum or the Parthenon. I had one of those when-this-is-all-over thoughts. When this is all over, I'll go to Rome for a month or two. I've got a good pile of money, with possibly more to come. I dreamed of Italy. I looked Oriana in her buggy eyes. Are you going to lead me to an apartment on the Spanish Steps? I wondered why anyone would want her so badly. *If I may look for you without offense / I beg you, darling, where's your hiding place?* Except that her hunter(s) had committed great offense.

I finished the Bohemia and took the stuff over to Shakespeare & Co. They know me so they don't ask me to check my bag at the door. I went back to the literature section and located a copy of Mann's *Joseph the Provider*. You will find a copy in every used bookstore in the English-speaking world. And probably in Germany too, come to think of it. It is also a book that never sells. I took the book off the shelf, and I pulled the artifact out of the bag. I leaned it against the back of the case and replaced the Thomas Mann. At some point, Harvey, the owner, will sell the store. Perhaps then, during a remodel, someone might disturb *Joseph the Provider*. My package was safe.

I walked back home and emailed figaro/Dino. I went to the YMCA and got a little exercise, then I did some writing, ate dinner, watched the news. Checked my inbox around eleven. No answer.

There was a message the next morning. The piece was authentic. He wanted to see "the girl." There was only one buyer. This person had a sentimental attachment to her, and he would consider paying a quarter of a million, which was many thousands more than the market price. He offered me a cut of one hundred thousand. And he wanted a thousand up front for expenses. I decided not to dicker. Fifty thousand to me, fifty to Marvin. Add that to the money I found in the Miata. Not a bad caper.

Arranging a drop-off was difficult. Dino kept rejecting my suggestions. Finally it was decided that I would go to Amoeba Music on a Saturday afternoon and check a backpack at the security counter. I would take the claim check upstairs to the classical room and leave it in the Bartók section at two o'clock sharp. He would give me five minutes to get out, then he would retrieve the claim check and leave with the girl. The security people wouldn't know the difference. Saturdays are busy. They wouldn't remember a face.

I entered the record store with several customers and drifted into the Saturday crowd. It was like being at a too-crowded party. I had trouble wading through the crowd to the classical section. I was getting behind schedule. I made my way upstairs to where it was less crowded. I deposited the chit in the right place. It took most of the allotted time for me to get downstairs and through the jazz section. When I hit rock 'n' roll I couldn't move. I saw figaro/Dino coming through the crowd. I'd taken too long. Should I play dumb?

"Hello, Dino. Doing some shopping?"

"Yes. Pablo Casals. I've been looking for a certain performance."

Long pause with lots of rippling possibilities. Did he know that I knew that he knew? I decided to let it drop. Plausible deniability.

## 22.

I knew that I was taking a chance by letting Oriana out of my sight. It would be easy enough for Dino to disappear. I wouldn't have the resources or the inclination to hunt him down. But I wasn't too worried. I had lots of cash, more than I'd ever expected to make from this job. And he had possession of the statue. Let them tear up my apartment. They wouldn't find a thing.

I felt light and easy and it was a beautiful day. I thought I'd go up to Tilden Park and do a little hiking, or maybe BART out to the Mission to watch the young new bohemians eat fussy food and smoke imported cigarettes. The Bay Area is rich in cheap entertainment.

I thought about it awhile, then I had a second cup of coffee. A ragged group of Hare Krishnas stopped their parade just below my window. I moved my chair over to the window to get a better look. It was a subdued group at first. Then one member, a tall, gangly young man with a skull-like head, caught the spirit, or whatever it is they catch. He had a beautiful chanting voice, and he whirled like a dervish. He lost his bearings and caromed off of a trash can and into Dwight Way, where his saffron robe caught the spokes of a student's bike. The student, a punkish guy in Seattle anarchy gear (big boots, baggy pants, black sweatshirt, shaved head) went down hard, but he bounced up like a fighter who'd been stunned by a left hook. The two men looked each other up and down, standing dumbly in the right-hand lane. There was an apology, and Mr. Krishna resumed his chanting, dancing around the damaged bike. This caused the student to laugh hysterically. Meanwhile, traffic was backing up on Dwight Way and horns were blowing. A crusty old homeless man, known as Pops, was annoyed by this. He attacked a classic yellow Karmann Ghia and had to be pulled off the hood of the car by a couple of the regular denizens of the street. A few gawkers gathered. The student punk tried to shoo them away. A pushing match ensued. It was time to call the cops, but nobody called the cops. The scene just kind of played itself out. The gawkers moved away, and Pops stumbled down Telegraph, yelling "Fuck you" over his shoulder. The Krishnas started up their chant. It was as if someone said, Fight's over, turn up the music.

Several times a day I see a small version of the last scene of *The Day of the Locust*. I'm thankful for that. Normal folks are still a little wary of my neighborhood. Those nuts are all that stand between me and gentrification. I poured myself another cup. Perhaps I'd stay home today and watch the world outside my window.

I put the three Rachmaninoff symphonies on the CD player and turned it up loud. They added nicely to the mood. Car horns, drums in the park, strings too romantic to be taken seriously, but then you take them seriously because life is just that overwhelming and corny.

If you aren't living through holy hell or dizzying highs, you aren't doing it right. A murdered friend, stolen goods, a few betrayals, three affairs. What a summer! I sat down to write a poem and things made sense, at least for the duration of writing the poem. *Oh now is it that all this music tumbles round me which was once considered muddy.*

I was sitting at my desk when Marvin called. It was getting dark. He reminded me that Creeley was reading at the University that night. I decided to go. I liked some of his early books, and it would be an interesting scene.

I had a couple of hours to kill. I made myself a Campari and orange juice and I read a little Creeley, then a little Cid Corman. Marvin came up and I made him a drink, and we walked to the UC campus.

The reading was in the Maude Fife room, on the third floor of the Wheeler Auditorium. It's a dreary building, but I believe it has some historical significance. Like much of the University it is poorly kept. I always get lost on my way to Maude Fife, but Marvin knows the way through the drab halls and stairways.

When we got there a few people were congregating in the hallway. It was a good mix of local poets and their students. Clark Coolidge was there, and Gloria Frym. I noticed Michael Palmer and Ishmael Reed. The lighting was bad. Institutional. But I've always loved the chairs. They have a faux antique look. Louis the something. But I suspect that they were bought in the '70s and repainted in the '80s. The country's premier poets have read in this room. Ashbery, Rich, Dorn. Upstairs and in the back. Most people don't even know about the series. There's very little publicity. Such is poetry in America.

We took our seats, in the middle of the room. The entrance was up near the stage so we could watch people enter. Stephie Hearn entered. Alone. I was surprised to see her at a reading. She didn't see me or pretended that she didn't. I wondered how I should play this little scene. I looked over at Marvin. He was wearing a sly smile.

And then she did see me, and I stood up and hugged her, and we sat together. Another game of "Does she know that I know what she knows?"

"I didn't expect to see you here."

"But I expected to see you. I've been worried about you since the crash. Are you doing okay?"

"I guess. I miss my car. And I've had a few of those classic falling nightmares."

She paused for a while before she asked, "Were they able to recover the car?"

"No. Burned to a crisp. At some point they'll clear away the carcass. But they don't seem to be in a hurry. That's between AAA and the city."

Robert Hass stepped up to the mic, wearing a Mr. Rogers sweater and a New Agey grin. He happy-talked an intro to the opening act, a third-generation Language poet and a grad student at the University. She looked like the book clerk Bogey flirted with in *The Big Sleep*. Blonde hair in a bun and a sensible dress. She would set up each poem with a breathy, giggly intro that was sly and funny. Then she'd switch into her poetry voice: serious, plodding, awful. The strings of pointless words put me into a semi-stupor. Marvin started to giggle. He leaned over and said, "Not a decent ... ," which is one of our inside jokes, a reference to a William S. Burroughs line from the '60s: "Not a decent fuck in the entire generation."

She had the presence of mind to cut it short. She knew she was only the opening act. Smattering of applause. Hass came out and announced that there'd be no break. My heart sank. I knew that several bottles of good wine were waiting in the classroom that doubles as a reception space. I was hoping to grab a glass between the acts. I don't remember a word of the intro to Creeley, but I do recall that Hass's eyes glistened with tears of sincerity.

Creeley sounded beautiful, and he read enough of his old poems to make me feel nostalgic, and to remind me why I took up poetry. His late work is too warm and fuzzy, even if it does deal with death. He's much loved, which is deadly to anyone in the arts. Still, who doesn't long to be loved? Can't hardly blame him. Some poets age well (Harold Norse, Barbara Guest, Carl Rakosi), others get cute. It occurred to me that a Robert Creeley reading is like a Moody Blues concert. You go to hear the hits.

He finished his reading to loud, long applause and was mobbed as he left the podium. Hass announced the number of the wine room. Marvin bolted for the door. I hoped he'd score me a glass of red. Stephie said she'd come to the reception. She wanted to tell Creeley that Hart said hello.

"Where is Hart?"

"Down in Mexico with Weldon. They're still trying to put together the workshop."

"Is Creeley going down?"

"Yes, but not for the whole six weeks. He'll do a reading and a one-day workshop. Hart had to cut down on expenses."

"Who else did he get?"

"Jack Gilbert, possibly Carolyn Kizer."

Definitely second-tier poets, I thought. Hart must be having a cash flow problem about now. I started to feel a little pissed that he didn't invite me, even though I'm really about a fourth-tier poet. Then I remembered the situation.

We waded though the hallway with the crowd. There was much hobnobbing and handshaking. In that close quarters I was reminded that poets often smell gamey. Too preoccupied to bathe?

The party room had the drab, uneducated look that we associate with Soviet communism. The cork bulletin boards were bare. A long table, a type that you'd remember from elementary school, was loaded with mid-priced California wines, crackers, cheese, and fruit. Another table displayed some of Creeley's books. I was taken by the gray sameness of the covers.

I became very aware of Stephie's presence as the only sexual entity in the room. Well, except Marvin, who isn't my type. The young Language poet who opened the show seemed too stiff and lifeless to ever bother with anything physical. I saw her talking to an editor from UC Press, wearing a frozen smile, like someone at a wedding reception. I knew instinctively that her only concern was her career. Everyone else was busy chasing prizes or publication, or a few minutes with the star. If I walked around the room and pricked each of them with a needle, would they bleed? Poets are supposed to bleed.

I was standing next to Stephie, then she turned to speak to somebody. I turned in the other direction, to say hello to somebody else. We were back to back, then our backs touched. I started to lean away, but she leaned back. Our elbows touched, and we turned our heads until our cheeks almost touched. I felt a little lightheaded. Reminded myself, again, of the situation. She possibly conspired to kill Peggy Denby. And then there was the car. Were they planning to leave me for dead on the road, once Oriana was over the border?

I couldn't sleep with her under these circumstances. Could I? She would only sleep with me for reasons of manipulation. Perhaps she wanted to make sure that I didn't have the loot. Trick me into saying the wrong thing. The thought of that only heightened my sexual tension. Sick fuck!

I knew she wanted me. I knew from our past encounters that she was attracted to me. The sexiest lover is a willing lover. And she liked it. Most people don't. Oh, they like it once in a while, or at the beginning of a relationship. But after that it becomes messy and troublesome. Or, for some, it's like taking a shit. Necessary to good health. For me, it is a third of my personal holy trinity: Sex, Poetry, Travel. We wouldn't agree on the other two, although she liked traveling well enough. But we both treated sex as a first priority. No, not just that. A sacred thing.

## 23.

We left Marvin at the party. He interrupted his diatribe on politics and poetry long enough to give me a look that could kill. I shrugged, and we went out into the night, up Telegraph toward my apartment. It was a warm, noisy September evening. Students and homeless people stood in clumps, blocking our path. Food, wrappers, and an occasional supine body littered the Avenue. The younger ones hadn't yet learned to clean up after themselves.

We entered the Chandler and took the elevator to the fourth floor. Emily greeted me with a cry for food. Stephie was indifferent toward her. But the sight of Peggy's cat made me feel creepy. I decided that I'd betray my religion that night.

"Can I have one of your famous Negronis?"

"Of course." I went into the kitchen and started to arrange drinks. She followed me in and stood very close. She bumped me once, then again. She sighed the word "Warm," wiped her brow, then took off her shirt, revealing a men's black sleeveless T, cut very short. She looked a little boyish, with her short hair and muscled shoulders. She was naturally beautiful, and she was rich enough to enhance that beauty: personal trainers, beauty products, great clothes. A walking airbrushed model. I shouldn't be attracted to this type, but I am. I don't like them. They're barely human, put on this earth to consume, which keeps our economy afloat. Over the years they have made their way as ad executives, agents, personal finance consultants, magazine editors, realtors. These days there are the e-people, buying and selling junk text and bad graphics through high-speed phone lines.

She had the finest lines I've ever seen on a woman. It occurred to me that Dino Centro had the finest lines of any man. I'd been living in a sexual Xanadu all summer long. Had that corrupted me? I tried to focus on that thought. Why were these unscrupulous people so interesting? Marvin, with his puritanical streak, would see the failure of communism in this. I remembered a story about Mayakovsky buying an expensive car (a Bugatti?) when he was sent to Paris in the '20s, angering the stuffy party types.

It occurred to me that I was aroused by her possible involvement in the murder. This thought put my brain into one of those repulsion/attraction spins that can, at times, heighten awareness very much like an amphetamine high. I gulped my drink and tried to pull myself together.

She finished her Negroni, then poured the rest of the pitcher into her glass. The bartender in me winced. Negronis should be made one at a time. The dregs are too watery. I pointed this out.

"I don't give a fuck. I'm lushing it up tonight." She pulled a chair from the kitchen table, swung it around backward, and sat that way, her legs spread in tight jeans. It was a corny move, coquettish in a bad movie way. I loved it. "Tell me what happened when your car went over the cliff," she said. "It must have been a thrill, in a way. I mean, since everything turned out all right. Don't you think back on it as kind of exciting?"

"No, I was too scared." I made a quick mental review of my story. I couldn't afford to get caught in a lie.

"Did you see the car fall? Like in the movies?"

"I was too stunned. But I did hear explosions. The car hit the beach instead of the water. It burned to a crisp on the sand."

She waved her glass, demanding a refill. "Did the cops find you?"

I refilled the pitcher with new ice and stirred a new drink. "No, Stephie, didn't I tell you? I passed out for a few hours, then I walked back to the police station." I wondered if she caught my nervousness. I'm a good liar, but I'm not psychotic. I feel uneasy when I'm fibbing.

She got up and grabbed the pitcher from me, and she poured me a huge one. Hers was slightly smaller. She tried to make it seem like an accident. But I knew the game. She was trying to fill me full of truth serum. Refusing the drink would arouse suspicion. I had to keep my head, while losing it. Or perhaps drink her under the table. An interesting challenge. I felt a perverse excitement rise into my already fuzzy brain.

To her credit she never came on with the old, Clay, I love you, I've always loved you. She probably knew that wouldn't wash. She used her best assets. She leaned on me hard as I poured her third (fourth?) drink. She paraphrased Dorothy Parker, fake slurring: "I like Negronis, two at the most, three I'm under the table, four I'm under the host." She zigzagged to the stereo, put on the Magnetic Fields CD that I'd been saving for another seduction, and flopped on my bed, which doubles as a couch. I naturally moved toward her, but she slowed things down with a little small talk. Something about the office, something about software. She was manipulating me, but on some level she also took this software talk seriously. I think it turned her on. Many people find the information highway, stock options, and websites sexy. It's probably a class thing. These people get off on the scent of money. It gives them their sexual thrust.

She must have noticed my glazed look. She leaned forward and kissed me, then she backed off again. She sipped her drink and talked some more. She brought up a new TV show that was stirring up some controversy. Contestants were asked to do various degrading things. Those that refused had to leave the show. On the thirteenth week the two finalists were taken to a beautiful home in Hollywood Hills. In the backyard, with a view of the Capitol Records building, a '30s-style swimming pool was filled with beef blood, cat urine, and dog shit. The first contestant to lap the pool won the deed to the house.

"Did you watch it last night?"

"I missed it, somehow."

"It was great! Constance won!"

"Which one was she? I only watched it a couple of times."

"Clay, you goof! How could you miss it. Constance was the lesbian therapist. Remember? She cried because the show was taking quality time away from her and her daughter."

"What about the guy with testicular cancer? I kind of liked him."

"He was a jerk. Negative and gruff. He got thrown off because he wouldn't do the naked bungee jump."

This went on for a while. The diversions of the so-called middle class. Bored with all but the most inane trivialities, they fill up their time with this fluff. Well, me too. I know the plots of every *Rocky and Bullwinkle* episode, the lyrics to every Beach Boys song. Western culture really is decadent and destructive. But we're already hopelessly ruined. Perhaps we should be exterminated.

"Clay, are you listening?"

"Yes, of course. I think the Negronis stunned me."

"You haven't been the same since the accident. Why don't you talk about it?" As she said this she got up and went to the kitchen, returning with a tumbler of ice and the gin. We were getting serious.

I needed to get specific, to make the lie more plausible. "I didn't tell the cops this, Stephie, but I was reaching for a tape when I lost control of the car. I was getting a little tired. It wasn't the Miata's fault. I guess after that I panicked. The top was down, and I bailed. Man overboard! I hit a patch of gravelly dirt, then I rolled back onto the pavement. I crawled around for a while, then I propped myself up on the handrail in time to hear the explosions. I blacked out, and woke up hours later on a dirt path that leads into the woods. I tried to hitch a ride. No luck, so I walked to the station. End of story."

"Was the car driving okay?" Her voice was a little too sharp, and she knew it.

"Yes, everything seemed fine."

She seemed agitated. She poured more gin into her half-finished drink, then took a healthy gulp. "It seems strange to me that you were just riding along, minding your own business, and the car went into the drink."

"Actually it smashed on the rocks and sand. These things happen."

Her face took on a demonic look. I found that comical, so I laughed. She took another gulp.

"Something's funny, Clay. The car must have veered to the right, or something."

"No. It didn't veer at all until I lost control."

She stood up with some effort. She went into the bathroom, muttering to herself. She stayed a long time. When she came out I noticed that she'd splashed water on her face. She poured more gin into the icy water.

"Stephie, you're ruining that good gin. Would you like some fresh ice?"

More of that comical demonic look. She slowly and deliberately stood up, the tumbler in her hand. I assumed she was getting the ice. Then, with shocking force, she hurled the heavy glass at the wall, hitting my Franz Kline print (bought at MOMA during a trip to NYC) square in the middle of the blackest part. The glass didn't shatter. It broke into two or three pieces, far as I could tell. I wondered if the solid walls of the Chandler Apartments could be damaged. Probably not.

"You fucking piece of shit! You knew it was in there! They didn't want to tell me. They were trying to fuck me over. But I overheard so they cut me in. You pulled her out with your grubby little hands, then you drove off the bridge. And you hid her before you went to the cops. You idiot, you stole that story from Ted Kennedy! It was you and Marvin, that skulking piece of commie dogshit." She grabbed the gin and took a long slug from the bottle. "I need that money. My investors are getting nervous. I have a mortgage, an office, two cars, and a couple of credit cards. I have to show profit somewhere. I just have to."

She hung her head. It looked for a second like she was winding down. I began to search my addled brain for strategies. I expected her to melt into tears, but she didn't. She swung the near-empty bottle of Sapphire gin. I moved in the right direction, but I was a little slow, due to the cocktails. The bottle caught me upside the head. It was only a glancing blow, but it stung. I had that feeling that you have when you're under the influence and something painful happens. I thought, Ouch, that would have hurt.

For the next several minutes she was an uncaged banshee. The gin bottle went through the living room window. I heard the crash below and scurried over to look. Luckily there wasn't much traffic on Dwight Way at that hour. I'd have to pay for the window, but that's all. She toppled the stereo speakers and a bookshelf. I did my best to stay out of the way. I had no choice but to let her rave until exhausted. I was surprised that someone on Prozac could work up so much passion. She went after the cat, but I scooped Emily up and threw her in the closet. For this I caught a palm on the ear. My hearing went funny.

"Where is she? I want the statue! They don't think you're smart enough, but I know you better, you walking bag of shit!"

We know clichés are based on a nut of truth. You're beautiful when you're angry, dear. I didn't say that out loud, but I wanted to fuck her in the worst way. It was one of those horrible moments that feminist men run into, when postmodern attitudes come up against a thousand years of conditioning (natural history?). *The Taming of the Shrew*.

She grabbed my copy of Lorine Niedecker's *Collected Poems* and tore the slim volume in two. But her eyes glazed over as she dropped both halves at the same time. She was losing her interest in inanimate objects. I sensed that I was in trouble.

She put her arms out like two battering rams and rushed me. I took one hand in the solar plexus, the other in the chin. I went down hard, but I managed to roll to the side. I looked up as she grabbed a pair of scissors, a rather rusty old pair that I keep on my desk for no particular reason. She dropped on me, knees first, like TV wrestlers do. She held the scissors with both hands, ready to plunge. I was a beaten man.

"Where is she?"

"I don't know what you're talking about, Stephie. You're having a bad reaction to the gin. Maybe it doesn't mix well with antidepressants."

She looked a little confused. If I could just keep up the lie for a little longer without getting killed, I could find some sort of opening.

"Then who has her?"

"I don't know. I don't know who 'she' is, or what I have to do with it. Why don't you let me up and tell me about it? Maybe I could help."

"No. You're a motherfucker. A dickweed. A walking piece of shit."

She was working herself up into an even higher form of hysteria. To my relief, she threw the scissors away. They hit a bookshelf with a thunk. She straddled me, and she lowered her middle onto mine. She pulled off her shirt. She was dripping with sweat.

Although aroused, I was also understandably confused. I said, "Are we going to fuck now?" and she laughed.

"We're going to do whatever I like!"

She got up and went into the kitchen. Oh god, not more booze, I thought. I felt the fear that you feel around the truly insane. Fear mixed with fascination. She came back with a chef's knife, actually my best one. She stood topless in jeans, glistening, butch haircut, crazed look in her eyes. She held the knife like she knew how to use it.

"I want to know where the statue is. My financial life depends on it. If you tell me, we can split the take. If you don't, I'll cut off your cock and feed it to Peggy's cat. Either way you're going to fuck me first, because I'm hot as hell. This is Peggy's cat, isn't it?"

"Did you kill Peggy?"

"No. Hart's boys did."

"Then you haven't killed anybody yet. Why start now?"

"Who said I haven't killed anybody?"

Even in times of great danger I'm pretty cool, so I didn't say "uh-oh" out loud. But I thought it. She told me to stand, so of course I did. My ribs felt bruised and my left ear was throbbing. She wrapped her arms around me, holding the knife upright behind my back. I could feel the tip through my cotton T-shirt. When she kissed me she put her tongue in my mouth. I liked that, I don't always have to lead the dance. She pushed me back a little, and the knife tip gave me a good prick. I realized that this fuck could be my last. Imagine the performance anxiety! She backed off, took off her jeans, and got on the bed. No underwear. My, how boys like that. She motioned me over with the knife, and pointed. I went down on her with the flat of the knife on the back of my head. If I moved wrong, the tip would scratch the nape of my neck. She got more excited and threw her hands back over her head, still holding the knife. I thought it was an opening, and stopped for a second. But I was too slow. I looked up to see the knife an inch from my nose.

"Back to work, asshole!"

After a long while she flipped over onto her stomach. Again she was holding the knife over her head, completely stretched out. I was embarrassed to be so aroused by the situation, but at least I was aroused. I entered her from behind. As we fucked, I ran one hand up her arm to the hand that held the knife. Every muscle in her body tightened.

"Pathetic piece of shit. Don't even try. And you keep that fuck-stick fully inflated!"

She wanted me to finish with her on top, so I did, looking into her half-crazed eyes. Then she got up and sauntered into the kitchen for a glass of water. She stood in front of the window and drank. At that moment she was the most amazingly beautiful woman that I'd ever seen.

"Sorry about the window. I'll pay for it. Now, are we partners, or are you dead?"

She turned toward the window and looked through the broken panes. It was as if she was giving me a few minutes of privacy in which to decide my fate.

I had a second, or less, to act. I lunged at her, using the edge of the bed as a starting block. The knife clanked on the floor. She gave me a surprised look as I pushed her through what was left of the glass. There happened to be an SUV speeding up Dwight Way. She hit the ground and seconds later the car hit her.

I'd have a lot of explaining to do. But it was better than getting skewered.

## 24.

I've done more than my share of the police interview shuck and jive. I just don't know, officer. We only had two drinks, and without reason she grabbed a knife and came at me. We struggled, and she fell.

They didn't believe me at first. I waived my right to a lawyer and told my story, over and over. Then, for reasons that I didn't understand, they let me go. I'd expected to spend the night. And I'd fully expected to be booked for manslaughter, probably the next day. But the cops let me off with a stern look and a "Don't leave town." Of course, that didn't mean they wouldn't book me later.

I got home at first light. A crew was still examining the scene of the crime. I called my lawyer. He made some joke about the things that happen in the sleazy quarters of the city. He said that a manslaughter trial was a possibility but that he doubted it. There was no glory in prosecuting a case like this. We made an appointment for the following day.

I hadn't eaten but I didn't have an appetite. I waited for the last of them to leave, then I took a shower and put on some clean clothes. I went up to the roof. It was warm but autumn was coming on. The breeze from the bay had a cool bite. It was foggy in Marin. I couldn't see Mount Tam. But San Francisco was clear and the water was a beautiful blue.

I didn't try to fight the numbness that I was feeling. Shock was the proper reaction. It keeps us from cracking up. I sat in the rusty lawn chair and stared and stared. I thought about my part-time job. It had started out as a few favors for troubled friends. Then I got hooked on the danger. I came up with some phony theories about my place in this subculture. Underground detective, protector of the weak. Mensch. Can a killer be a mensch? Can a killer be a book scout? I've killed a handful of people now. Not as many as my great-uncle Eric, who flew a bomber in the Pacific. Not as many as my friends who fought in Vietnam. Not as many as Castro, Mao, LBJ, George Bush, and co. Do numbers matter?

As I rationalized, sitting on the rusty chair, the clouds came in over the city and the water turned from blue to gray. With great effort I switched mental gears. Things were messier now. What of Weldon, Hart, and Trak? I needed to make them go away. Or slither away myself.

I went down to the basement and found some cardboard to cover the window. Took the elevator back because my legs were shaky. I'd have to call the manager soon. I'm sure he knew what had happened. All the other neighbors too. And my street friends, and the buyers at Moe's. They probably wouldn't bring it up. But everyone in South Berkeley would identify me as the guy who threw a naked woman out of his window.

## 25.

I finished the patch job and cleaned up some of the mess. Pulled out the espresso maker and started some coffee. There was a knock on the door and I went into a fighter's stance, like a punch-drunk boxer. It was Nellie Miles from the third floor. She's one of the really young ones who, for some reason, take me into their confidence. They seem to think I'm safe. I guess I am. I listen to their boyfriend problems. I give them beers. I guess they think I'm a nice old guy. I actually do lust after them, especially Nellie. But vanity keeps me from making advances. I imagine them saying, "Oh gross! You're too old!" That's when I get up and take a deep breath, or wash my face, or open another beer.

Nellie was, I think, nineteen. A pretty girl with shiny light-brown hair. I don't use the word "girl" in a derogatory way. You just wouldn't call her a woman.

She looked kind of sheepish. She giggled, then she produced a pipe. "I'm sorry about what happened. Do you need to smoke some pot?"

"Maybe a little." I appreciated the act of friendship. It was pretty courageous, considering what I'd just done.

She sat on the bed and we passed the pipe. I gave it the old President Clinton, not wanting to get too high. I had work to do.

"A reporter came around and talked to us. We said you were nice."

"He interviewed all of you?"

"A bunch of us. We were down in the lobby."

"Oh. I didn't notice. Too upset."

"You don't have to talk about it." She was giving me the once-over twice. I tried to imagine how she felt. She'd told me her life story, trusted me, and now this. Like most her age, she would find a way to turn it into her own personal tragedy.

"I probably shouldn't say much. You know, lawyers and all. But I'm not a murderer."

"Everybody's sure it was an accident. We like you. I like you. You're a good friend." She lit the pipe again. Then she sat for a few minutes, looking uncomfortable. "Should I go now? I don't want to get in the way."

"You probably should. But I appreciate you stopping by."

She stood up and put her hands behind her back. She reached her head up and kissed me on the cheek. Tears came to my eyes.

"Call me."

"I will."

She walked down the hall. I watched her for a few seconds before shutting the door. I went back inside and I noticed that she'd left the pipe on the nightstand.

## 26.

I washed the dishes from the night before. There was a lipstick smudge on the tumbler. She took a sip from the tumbler, she said something to me, she looked out the window, then I killed her. I washed the glass. Then I washed the martini pitcher and the other glasses, and finally the chef's knife. It looked clean, but there had to be traces of blood. She'd pricked me pretty good. I'd thrown on a clean shirt before going downstairs, and I guess it didn't bleed through. Good. I didn't tell the cops about our dangerous game.

I put on one of Beethoven's late string quartets. My first instinct was to try to relax, get some sleep. But I couldn't do that. I needed to jump into all this craziness until the job, whatever that might be, was finished. So I turned the music up loud. It's complex and scary. A swan dive into the void.

My thoughts began to race and I felt twitchy. Was I up to this? I convinced myself that I was. Into the void, become the void, love the void, make the void my own. Negative capability. My mind filled with plans and alternative plans.

There was a knock on the door. Probably Nellie, back for her pipe. I didn't bother to turn down the music.

"Mr. Blackburn?"

"Yes." I'd opened the door wide. A stupid thing to do. She was a mystery-eth. Pacific Islands Anglo? African Filipina? Couldn't tell. She was quite tall. I noticed a tattoo peeking from her sleeve. If Queequeg were a woman ... She was wearing pleated khakis, a Gap shirt, and a red scarf, badly tied. Her countenance told me she was some kind of cop.

"I'm Agent Bailey Dao, FBI."

I decided to let her in. There was nothing in the apartment that could incriminate me. Except the pipe, which I'd momentarily forgotten.

She strode in, to the middle of the room. They like to let themselves all the way in. She was square and stiff. Whatever her ethnic background, she had an Irish jaw. I've only seen jaws like that in Ireland, and then only in the rural counties. Big, scary farmer jaws. Somehow, a dairy farmer in Tipperary had gained entry into this stew of genes. So fitting for a cop.

"I told the Berkeley police everything I could. Who called the FBI?"

"We're investigating a federal crime."

I shut my mouth and half closed my eyes. I couldn't allow myself to be a wise guy. I told myself that she was feeding me these easy lines, hoping for me to bite. I smiled and nodded.

"Do you know the whereabouts of Hart Opffer?"

"I believe he's in Mexico."

"Where in Mexico?"

"Santa Catarina, I think?"

"And Weldon Key?"

"I'd guess he's down there too."

She sat on the bed, trying to look casual. She looked around the room. Her eyes landed on my VOTA COMUNISTA! poster, taken from a lamppost in Pisa. She chuckled, nodded, chuckled again. I know this act. I expected her to tell me that she was once a bohemian too, in college.

"So far, Mr. Blackburn, you haven't told me anything I don't already know."

"I'd like to cooperate. But I don't know what you want."

"We'd like to speak to Hart Opffer. But we're not sure where he is."

"He runs a school for poets down there."

"We know that. He left his school days ago. Do you know about the antique scams?"

I decided to play dumb. Or maybe I wasn't playing. "Antiques?"

"Seems Hart, and possibly his sister, were fencing various stolen items."

"Is that a federal offense?"

"Why are you so interested in jurisdictional matters? Illegal monies were moved from state to state. Also stolen goods. Satisfied?"

"I guess I'm surprised that you guys would bother."

"We can pretty much do what we want, you know. Some of the stolen items were owned by the rich and the powerful. Somebody donates to a campaign, somebody gets robbed, somebody says, have them put their best agent on this one."

"I'm not sure how I can help you."

"Look, this is a dumb case. We've got more important things to do. We need a patsy. We don't really need a conviction, just an arrest. I could find a way to stick you with it. After all, you did just kill Stephie Hearn. You're in real trouble! If we come in and find one little antique, say an earring or a brooch, you're the fall guy. But if I can get to Hart, I may be able to recover some of the loot. Mr. Rich Donor would love that."

I sat, silent. The ways of law enforcement are far over my head. Agent Dao sat on my bed, looking smug. The phone rang.

"Aren't you going to get that?"

"It's okay. I've got voicemail."

"I'm going to want to wrap this up in a couple of days. And I'm going to make it easy on you. Just a good solid lead. I want to find Hart."

"What if he's still in Mexico?"

"It doesn't matter. We have connections down there."

"I don't know where he is."

"You see what you can do. Like I said, a good solid lead. You do that for us and you won't be charged with murder."

"Just like that?"

She looked me straight in the eye. It was the sincere look of a really good politician. Agent Dao was on her way up the ladder. She'd be attorney general someday. "I can guess what happened, Mr. Blackburn. Stephie had a reputation before this came up. She probably had you wrapped around her little finger. And you did something she didn't like and she went off. Right?"

"Yes."

"You're not the first. You just got lucky."

"Lucky?"

"Lucky you weren't standing next to the window." Agent Dao stood up and went over to my desk. Wrote a number on the back of her card. "You can call this number, you say it's a message for me, and you leave the information on the voicemail. I'll regard it as an anonymous tip. You wait three, four days. If you don't get booked for murder, you can consider it my doing. I'm sure your lead will be good. I hear you do a little detective work on the side."

She shook my hand. Before she left she pointed at the pipe and chuckled. Said, "You should be more careful."

The phone message was from Dean Centro. Check your email! I went down to Moe's to use the public email machine. I got grave, embarrassed hellos from the clerks. They'd obviously heard about

Stephie's fall. I logged on to my dummy account, which was probably being monitored by the FBI. I wondered if they'd let me have the loot from Oriana, or if they had set me up. I decided to go through the motions. What else could I do? My life was in the hands of the corporate dictatorship. As always. But today was a big reminder of the fact.

The email said, Roma, Friday morning coffee. Find a noisy table.

I had two days to wait.

## 27.

Marvin came over, straight from a "business trip" to the Balkans. He asked me not to ask about it, so I didn't. Somehow he'd already head about Stephie. It didn't even occur to me to ask how. He arrived with a grocery bag full of goodies. He decided that I needed a long, heavy dinner with lots to drink.

Marvin's not a great cook, but he has a few good recipes. And he buys great ingredients. He made a risotto with a very rich stock, bought at some gourmet store. It tasted as if they'd stewed a dozen chickens and a bushel of onions in premium white wine for six months. Said risotto was fortified with Gorgonzola and prosciutto. This was served with a heavy Barolo, the kind of red wine that you can chew. With our second bottle of Barolo we had thick veal chops and kale with balsamic vinegar. After dinner he produced a tall, skinny bottle of grappa. I recognized the label. He'd bought it in Naples a few years back. This was possibly his last bottle. I told my long, sad story, finishing about halfway through my chop. He lifted his glass and toasted me, referring to our victory dinner. I took offense.

"C'mon, Marvin. It was self-defense, I know. I can live with it. But it wasn't a blow for international socialism. Actually, it was kind of tawdry."

"Bullshit. One less SUV, one less dot-commer. You said yourself that she admitted to being a killer. She wasn't killing fascists. She had it coming. The world is a little cleaner now."

I couldn't accept that, but I was too beat to argue. I shifted subjects. "How do I get out of this one, Marv?"

"Simple. Weldon and Trak. Give 'em to the FBI. They'll talk."

"Aren't they out of the country too?"

"Trak's been hanging around Santa Cruz. Don't ask me how I know. Haven't heard about Weldon. Trak should be enough."

"Trak once told me that Weldon killed Peggy."

"And maybe he did. But right now you need to get Bailey Dao off your tail. You just lead Agent Dao to Trak, and he'll talk. He probably knows. I assume he's up here tying up loose ends for Hart. Then it's off to Uruguay, or Panama, or some other place where you can change your name and live like a king off the sale of a few antiques."

"He'll probably have to give up the poetry fantasy camp."

"That was probably a scam too. Get full payment out of the students. Disappear."

"Creeley will be pretty pissed. I wouldn't want to be on his bad side."

And we both chuckled at the thought of a pissed-off Robert Creeley.

## 28.

I woke up early. A late-summer heat wave had hit the Bay Area. I put on jeans and a T-shirt, then switched to a white dress shirt. Wanted to look good for old Dino. I went to a rental place on Oxford. I rented another Neon, a green bubble with a scooter-sized engine. I drove over to College Avenue and circled for parking. Got lucky and found a space across the street from Roma.

Dino knew from our sleepovers that I take my first dose of coffee at eight thirty. I found a noisy table in the middle of the front room, in front of the espresso line. People in various work uniforms were ordering their coffee to go, fuel for the walk to the BART station. I felt sorry for them. And they were the lucky ones! The average commuter's day starts at about six thirty. I dumped sugar in my single espresso, in a real cup, not a paper one with a lid. People who drink their coffee Seattle-style simply lack class. Can't trust 'em. I gave my coffee a slow stir with my cute little spoon. I moved my chair so that I could better see the door. No Dino.

Baldwin Mrabet approached my table. He's a retired teacher. In the '50s he was blacklisted, although racism probably would have kept him out of academia anyway. During the wars of the '60s he shot a cop in Oakland. I know this for a fact, although he never got caught. Miraculously, he wasn't framed or chased out of the country like most of his friends. He moved in with his mother in St. Louis until things cooled off. In the late '70s he emerged as a memoirist. Affirmative action helped him get a job as a lecturer at Hayward State. Now retired, he's nearing eighty. I'm usually happy to see him, but I had other things on my mind.

"You look nervous, Holmes."

"I think I'm in the process of being stood up."

"Man or woman?"

"Guy."

"I won't ask."

"But you'd like to."

"No, no. Gossip doesn't interest me that much. I'm going to join you because all the other tables are full. If your date comes, I'll leave."

He had a normal cup of coffee in a mug. He sat down, and as he leaned forward, into his drink, he winced.

"Back problem?"

"I took a good shot in the ribs during one of my, um, adventures. Never healed. This was years ago."

"Sounds like a story."

"I won't bore you with it now. Except to say this. We were tough!"

I'd heard this before, but I liked it. I nodded respectfully and waited for more.

"In the '40s and '50s, if you were a red, your heroes were Hemingway, Sartre, Debs, Paul Robeson. Those guys kicked ass. We never backed away from a bar fight. And the women! Emma Goldman was the prototype. She could have kicked both of our butts, right into her seventies. Even in the '60s there was Angela Davis, and a few like her that you've never heard of. Who do girls look up to now? Oprah Winfrey? Alice Walker? Martha Stewart? Shit. I see these kids in Philly and Seattle, and they just lie down. They got to learn how to shoot to kill."

The espresso hit me as he finished his little speech. I felt awake and alive, and happy to be in Berkeley. Baldwin downed his coffee, shook my hand, and strode out of the café on the legs of a younger man.

Still no Dino.

I got myself another, this time decaf. I didn't want to be too jittery.

Lots to do today. I sat back down at the same table and dosed my coffee with sugar. Then, at last, Dino Centro. Looking very nervous.

He gave me a broad, phony smile and shook my hand. Didn't sit down. He leaned over and spoke softly. "Let's pretend it's a chance meeting. I can feel the heat closing in."

"I know, Dino. They're out there making their moves. It's my fault."

"What should we do?"

"We'll just do what we do and hope they don't care too much. I think they're looking for bigger fish. Sit down. And don't lose it. It'll only make things worse. They may think we're hiding more than we are."

He took off his seersucker jacket and sat down. Maybe, some warm day, I will find the courage that it takes to wear seersucker. Dino carried it off beautifully.

"Do you want me to just sit here and talk about it?"

"Sure, why not?" Over Dino's shoulder I could see one of Bailey Dao's boys in the espresso line. Young, good-looking, crew cut, clothes too obviously casual. A little too bemused by all the characters. I silenced Dino by putting a finger on my lips. Mr. Agent got his coffee and found a table, out of earshot.

"It's okay now. What's up?"

"I made the sale and I have your cut. And I want to get the cash out of my place." His eyes got bright, then narrowed into that silly Latin-lover look. "Clay, I hope we'll have some time to say a proper goodbye, but if we don't, I want to tell you that it was great. Perhaps our paths will cross again."

I met his gaze with my own smoky look. I wondered if it was as comical. "You're a great lay, dear Dino. And I like you a lot. I hope we do meet again. Now, where's that money!"

"Still at my place."

"Leaving it there was a risk."

"Stupid of me. I'm too nervous to think. I'm in over my head. I just want to get this over with and go to Buenos Aires. Will you come to see me? We could take tango lessons."

"I'll be happy to. If the Man lets us pull this off."

"I don't know what I'm doing. You do the thinking for both of us."

"I intend to. Just follow me in my rental car."

We drove to Dino's, a couple of miles down College Ave. Found parking close by. A good omen. We went up to his little studio. I went over to the window. Down below in the BART parking lot Efram Zimbalist Jr. was leaning on the hood of his black Buick. Ray-Bans, dress shoes, head big and square. Storm trooper. I waved but he didn't acknowledge me. No sense of humor.

Dino went into his closet and dug around. Came out with a gym bag. Pulled out a T-shirt and some shorts. Dumped the money on the bed. It made an impressive pile. He produced a piece of legal-sized paper. It was a list of his expenses. I accepted them with a nod. I took it for granted that they were hinky. A bite here, a bite there. My personal expenses come to about $22,000 a year. There was enough to last about four years. Okay by me.

"Do you want to count it?"

"I'm going to trust you, Dino." I repacked the gym bag.

"So this is goodbye."

"Until I decide to take tango lessons."

He hung his head. "You'll never come."

"Life is long, Dino. We'll meet again."

"Hope so." This time his look was sincere. Or at least convincing.

I walked him over to the window. He didn't like that idea at first, but he loosened up when I kissed him. He tried to waltz me back to the bed, but I knew what I wanted. I pushed him back to the window. Over his shoulder I could see Agent Square Head. It was a nice big double window, almost ceiling to almost floor. Dino leaned against the partition that separated the panes as I kissed him again. I unzipped his tight Euro jeans. He flopped out, half hard. I stroked the shaft with my slightly sweaty palm. Success. I slid down to my knees and I blew him like a symphony. I stood up, knees a little wobbly. I stepped to the left and looked out the window at the agent. Opened my mouth and stuck my tongue out, to prove that I'd swallowed. He looked away.

I positioned myself so that the shithead could see all of me in profile. "Hey, Dino Centro, it's my turn."

"Right there? Clay, you're a very kinky man."

Dino was very, very good. Hmm. Tango lessons. He finished, then he kissed me. The taste of my come on his tongue. Nothing like it.

Shithead shifted around, then got in the car. Sex is politics, fucker. I flipped him off as he drove away.

"Who was that for?"

"Somebody was watching us."

"You don't say! A pervert!"

One last laugh, and one more kiss, and we were on our way.

## 29.

I threw the loot in the trunk of the car and headed for the freeway. Down 880 to the dreaded Highway 17, the quickest way to Santa Cruz. The Neon did okay over the mountain road. But I still missed the Miata. I probably wouldn't bother to buy another one. I'd use my insurance money to get an older Japanese pickup. Better for scouting books.

There was no sign of the black Buick as I entered downtown Santa Cruz. I had lunch at a Chinese noodle place on the Pacific Garden Mall. I expected to see my agent voyeur, but he didn't show. I downed a Tsingtao to steel my nerves for the final detail.

I parked the Neon in downtown Felton. Took the strigil out of the glove compartment and put it in a canvas book bag. I had saved it to have as a souvenir. Now I would put it to good use. I walked up the deserted streets to Trak's house. Better to do this midday, when all the techies would be at their jobs in Silicon Valley. If Trak was home, I'd go back to Santa Cruz, find a hotel, and try again late at night.

There was no car in the garage. I went around to the back. All I had to do was place the strigil in a semi-obvious hiding place. Call Bailey Dao and make my anonymous tip.

There was some shrubbery. Who would put it there? Under the mattress of the chaise longue? That wouldn't work either. I decided to go into the house. I got in through an open bathroom window. There was a nice old desk in one of the bedrooms. Another stolen antique? I hid the strigil under some papers just as I heard a car pull into the drive. I decided, too late, that breaking into the house was a stupid thing to do. Or maybe the old subconscious wanted me to be there. Can't resist fucking with a yuppie.

As he came in the door I hit him with a good straight shot to the side of the face. My hand would be swollen for days. He went down, then he started to get up. I kicked him hard in the same place. He was out for a while. I looked around the house. He had one of those clawfoot bathtubs. I dragged him into the bathroom. He started to come to, so I kicked him again, harder. I went into the laundry room and found some rope and some rags. I tied one leg to the clawfoot tub, tied his hands together, and gagged him. He had a cell phone on his belt. I picked it up, dropped it, and stepped on it. On the way out I grabbed his home phone and took it with me. Smashed it on the front of the porch.

As I left I realized that my fingerprints were everywhere. Then I laughed. If the cops wanted me, they could have me. The FBI would either protect me or hand me over. It was all up to Bailey Dao.

I decided to take Highway 1 back home. A little slower, but the coast would calm my nerves. I stopped at a Safeway on the north side of Santa Cruz. I found a pay phone and called the number on Dao's card.

"Bailey Dao."

"I thought this was your voicemail?"

"I just happened to be by the phone."

"It's Clay."

"I know. Let's pretend I don't."

"How do I know I can trust you?"

"Doesn't matter. Somebody saw the whole thing."

"I didn't notice."

"He's pretty good."

"Did he change cars?"

"Agent Lovelace handed things off to somebody in the Santa Cruz office. He didn't like your little performance."

"Just having a little fun."

"Dangerous fun. But you got us what we need, so I'll go along with the deal. You did get us a lead. Right?"

"There's a strigil in Trak's desk. It's probably stolen."

"A what?"

"Look it up. You can use it as a bargaining chip. Tell Trak you'll send him up for grand theft strigil if he doesn't lead you to Hart. He knows where Hart is. I don't know if you're interested, but you might also ask him about Peggy Denby. I think they killed her."

"We might get around to that at some point."

"How do I know if I can trust you?"

"Don't worry. The fix is in. You won't be bothered. Enjoy the money."

"You can let me go, just like that? Hart must have really gotten into something big."

"Stay out of it. And don't talk about this. We can still arrest you if we feel like it. We do pretty much what we want."

## 30.

Roasting a chicken should be easy but it isn't. Little things matter. The chicken has to be thoroughly dried after washing. Then I pull up the skin of the breast and fill it with herbs and garlic. I like to stuff with it quartered oranges and onions. Keeps it from drying out. I have a great roasting pan that I got at Sur La Table. Cost me a week's pay, but worth it. I like to roast root vegetables in the same pan. Parsnip is good, and yams. And of course potatoes. A couple of different types, if possible. The oven has to be preheated to high heat. I drop the heat when I put the chicken in the oven.

Marvin arrived as the bird was beginning to brown. He pulled two bottles of Tavel from his book bag. Tavel is a wonderful pink wine. They drink it like water in France, but it doesn't get exported. They keep it for themselves.

"Where'd you get those? Alice Notley in town?"

"I spent two days in Paris. Just got off the plane."

"Marvin! When are you going to start telling me about your international adventures?"

"You may well be ready to hear about them, m'boy."

But he only told me what he ate for dinner and what poets he ran into. The first night he had couscous with William Talcott and Jim Nisbet. Lunched with Summer Brenner on the second day.

"For poor folks, poets sure do get around," I said.

"And now we can afford to, too. What are we going to do with that loot?"

"We?"

Sly smile. We both knew I owed him something for his help on the, uh, case.

"Any suggestions?"

"I have some work to do, south of the border. How about if we fly down to La Paz and swim in the Sea of Cortez."

"I was eighty-sixed from La Paz, remember?"

"I can fix that. All we have to do is take a little side trip to Chiapas."

"Sounds mysterious."

"It is. But I'm ready to let you in on some of my little secrets."

"As far as I know they haven't picked up Hart. He could still be down there."

"If he is, we'll beat the holy shit out of him and leave his bones in the desert. You're a rich man now, Clay. We could bribe the authorities, and the world would be none the wiser."

"And what of Weldon?"

"For all we know he's at the bottom of the San Francisco Bay. But if he turns up down there, we'll kill him too."

"Maybe we can get Robert Creeley to pay us some bounty."

"Creeley can do it himself. He's tougher than the both of us. And, from all accounts, he's armed to the teeth."

We finished the chicken and both bottles, then he went back to his bag and returned with some very good Armagnac. We discussed our future trip. We changed destinations a couple of times, from Mexico to Thailand to North Africa. But Marvin kept steering me toward La Paz. At morning's light we shook on it. I took a nap, called a cat sitter, and packed my bag. Onward to the Sea of Cortez.

# Righteous Kill

The Gilman District, newly named, was mostly industrial a few years ago. You'd go there for Urban Ore if you needed a broke-down couch to replace your more broke-down couch. There was a body shop and a good Mexican restaurant, perhaps too good, because over the years it brought in too many urban pioneers on the hunt for good manchamanteles. From famous red mole to the Gilman District. There goes the neighborhood.

I had been coming to West Berkeley since the aughts, yes, for the mole, but also for the books. SPD for the poetry, and Jeff Maser's place for used, rare modern firsts, just to browse and occasionally to sell something. I do a little book scouting, although not full-time like in the old days. It just doesn't pay, and I get a little freelance work as, believe it, an unlicensed detective, something I sort of backed into that now pays the bill at Berkeley Bowl and for the rent-controlled studio Southside.

I finished my enchiladas and the imported Coke, went by SPD, and for Marvin some Kevin Killian and for Dino *The Collages of Helen Adam*, because he wouldn't have heard of her but he would appreciate the way beauty recognizes itself, and he would love the captions: "Remember how I warned you when you're praying too late." I don't usually show up bearing gifts but Marvin had said, "It's kind of a party," and I knew Dino would be there, Dino Centro. O Dino Centro.

Walked a little farther, down to Tenth Street where Marvin had bought that house, cheap, when nobody really lived down there. The neighborhood wasn't especially dangerous, but dark, away from stuff, desolate as a staircase. Barely six figures at the time Marvin bought the house, just back from Central America. The money came from "somewhere" but "wasn't much." Marvin, the most Marxist of my Marxist friends, moving within and without radical subsets, dropping hints like, "I was in Athens and this crazy guy I know planted a bomb in a police station. I almost didn't get through customs!" Marvin, homeowner. Lovable guy. Best friend.

I knocked, door open, walked in the house that smelled a little like a cat box. Furniture that recalled places where you'd lived in your college years. It was a nice house nonetheless, '40s vintage, what they call Arts and Crafts, though I think that's a wider definition now than it was. Urban Ore and Ikea furnished, nice walls though, because for some reason Marvin liked to paint. This time the walls were very light with a bluish tint. I once asked Marvin what color it was and he answered, inexplicably, vanilla hots.

The "party" was mostly on the couch, blue Naugahyde, or, in the case of Dino, on the floor up against a matching ottoman. They were in black, awash in blue walls and furniture, except Dino, as usual, in seersucker. It was always seersucker or white linen, any season, with a gray sweater under the jacket in cold weather. It wasn't cold, so it was a blue oxford button-down. Just Dino, Marvin, and Patti O'Hara. I hadn't seen her in a couple of years.

My first impression, after that couple of years, was that she had been working out. Muscles bulging from a black wifebeater. "Still boxing, Patti?" and she went into her stance because she did, in fact, do some boxing. So, my best friend and the two people in the world I would most like to sleep with. Okay, a party, I guess.

Marvin hadn't yet read the Killian and so was suitably impressed. Dino: "I am astounded, dear Clay," and then a wet kiss. Life is good sometimes.

Dino went into the kitchen and came out with a shaker. Negronis, my favorite drink, not really Marvin's, though. He favors bourbon-based cocktails. I wondered about the occasion. Was I the guest of honor? Decided to let that one go. Why argue with Boodles and Campari, and why interrupt Dino Centro mid-shake?

Cheese Board snacks and smart talk. Conversation turned to the high cost of living, everybody leaving Berkeley. Where do we go? Bay Area out, East Coast also too expensive, flyover states opioid- and Trump-soaked. Emigrate? Marvin suggested Montevideo but not yet. Too many friends still here, and there are "battles to be won and lost." Marvin, soldier for the revolution even when there isn't one.

And then, third drinks in hand, talk about the neighborhood, those cheap-rent war stories. You could get a whole house for a few hundred! I paid a hundred bucks, down the street, for a walk-in closet in a house full of commies! True civilization starts with cheap rent and ends with gentrification. I wasn't aware that the CEO of TalkLike had moved into the neighborhood. This set off a Negroni-infused discussion of "the pig down the street" at high volume. "You have to see this place! From warehouse to palace! An oppressor workspace in Berkeley. Fuck Berkeley." This from Patti O'Hara, leaning a little too close to my ear.

Marvin suggested that we all "go for a stumble" and have a look at the CEO's "bunker." We helped each other off the couch, Dino's scent mingling with Patti's in the warm late afternoon. And one has eaten and one walks, past SPD and in a roundabout way toward 924 Gilman. The gourmet burgers, the free-trade coffee, the vegan joint, the Whole Foods. Chunky guys with beards, buried in their devices.

It was looming, almost as big as the Whole Foods down the street. Truly bunker-like although too tall, maybe three stories. Military-style brushed chrome, brick facade, blackout windows. There was still a loading-dock entrance in keeping with the industrial chic. A place to house the Tesla, perhaps. Workers used to sweat in places like this. Now they're luxury homes. Where are the sweaty workers? I wondered what it was like inside, curious, but also a little queasy, that way the hoi polloi view the aristocracy. *And the poor love it / and think it's crazy*. We looked up at the thing like apes before a monolith, then walked silently back to Marvin's place.

Plopped on the couch between Marvin and Patti, the mingling scents a little stronger, feeling sleepy but a little excited. Marvin in the kitchen making coffee, humming, then, "Well, we could blow it up," followed by, "You can't blow up all of capitalism," from Dino, who has a smidgen of the capitalist left in him. Dino almost asleep on my shoulder, oxford shirt unbuttoned, Patti lying head in my lap, legs over the couch arm. Dino, "A little graffiti wouldn't hurt," then Marvin, booming from the other room, "A bullet in the head would send a better message," and Patti, "Well, we all have guns."

Coffee, kisses goodbye, and I returned Southside, back to the Chandler Apartments, corner of Telegraph and Dwight. Feed the cat, work at some poetry. A perfect Sunday.

Following Wednesday, I was out buying books and the phone buzzed. Dinner at Marvin's. Got into the old Honda Civic and headed out to the Gilman District. Happy to find that it's the same group. Marvin cooking pasta. Eggs on the counter, so I guessed carbonara.

He's pouring an Italian white, kind of thin but in a good way. We start downing it like water. There's some music on and Dino and Patti are dancing. A nice group. Pasta and lots of jokes. Some pot with a silly name, something like Purple Urkel, but maybe I have it wrong. We're on the couch again, sides touching sides, and I'm thinking about the different ways you can melt into somebody's flesh, how the luckiest accident of birth is to be bisexual.

My brain came up for air. Marvin back in the kitchen making coffee. Said something about a neighborhood association, but not an official group. They would like us to talk to the CEO, a sort of delegation. I spaced out again since I don't live in the neighborhood. My corner of Southside is still scruffy. Gentrification is months away. When I zeroed back in they were talking about fleets of luxury cars and drones flown from the roof. The kind of thing you'd expect from techie CEO types. I was beginning to get bored, but then they asked me to go along because he had a bodyguard and an extra presence could help. I used to box Golden Gloves and I stay in shape, and occasionally I need to defend myself when doing my "detective" work, but I don't look like a bouncer either.

I was feeling a little floaty and thinking that the walk would do me good. The Gilman District isn't pretty. I guess somehow that's part of its charm, or always was, but now it's different. Couples making mid-six figures or more sucking up the urban experience, then spitting it out cleaned up and with a "get off my lawn" mentality. Live-work castles full of toys. For some reason we were walking close together, lots of touching. At some point I turned in to Dino, kissed him, and all at once everybody giggled. I felt something hard in his pants, not the thing I was looking for, though. A handgun. Dino lives, um, outside the law, so no surprise, but I was hoping for something sweeter.

And again to this palace that rose gleaming from the squalor yet somehow was uglier than the street where it lived. Patti stepped back and faced a security camera, announced us. Gilman District neighborhood watch. The warehouse-style door opened slowly, old-fashioned pulley, and it seemed that someone had called central casting and found a goon. Square jaw, shaved head, you know ...

Patti sucker punched him, then kicked him going down. Great pair of boots! I wondered where she found them. The action seemed very stylized, or does now in retrospect, like a scene in a Melville policier. Her short hair shook just right and I zeroed in on the back of her neck. I wanted to fuck her.

They seemed to know the way upstairs. Recognizance? Looking back, I'm surprised that I went along. I've been through cases and capers with these people but I didn't even know the circumstances. I knew he owned TalkLike. Tried to remember his name. Something vaguely Swedish.

No need to describe the enemy. "You're either at war or you're not," Marvin told me later.

The guy had no idea. They played with him for a while, doing up the neighborhood association drag. We'd like you to turn down the security lights, we'd like to see you at the meetings. He smiled and clichéd for a while, then was "tired" and would like us to go.

I turned to go, then looked back and Patti was Ingemar Johansson, Hammer of Thor. She had donned a single black leather glove, left hand. Solar plexus, then again a kick to the head. Dino pulled out the handgun. Three shots. Who would hear shots in a bunker? Who hadn't heard shots in this neighborhood?

I felt some panic. I had touched the desk, possibly something else. Thought about DNA and started to sweat.

"Shall we go?" This from Marvin, and so we did, but not before Dino hit the bodyguard with a couple to the head. Did it kill him? Wouldn't it have to?

We go, but not fast. Just walking. I shoot Marvin a puzzled look.

"Don't look so worried. A fixer will be along soon to clean up our mess, and, yes, they'll break the cameras. It's all set." And then, walking ahead a little, "We piss on them from a higher place."

It isn't easy to get to Marvin's roof, not like mine. You have to crawl out a window and lift yourself on a makeshift ladder, and after all that the view isn't much, just a bunch of buildings, the view of the bay blocked long ago by upscale rental properties. We did it anyway. It was a warm night, rare for Berkeley, and we needed a little air. We didn't talk about what happened, we just sat there close until it got cooler, then went downstairs and showered. When there's shooting and fighting, you need to wash it off. Marvin disappeared into the kitchen and I bathed with Patti and Dino. This was our after-party, skin and soap.

Came home late, fed the cat, looked out my window at the traffic triangle where Telegraph meets Dwight then runs south into Oakland. The usual scene, homeless guy playing conversational solitaire, a couple of sleeping dogs, a couple of lumps under ratty sleeping bags. I reflected a little on the day's "work," if that was what it was. Revolutionary fervor would have carried Patti and Melvin, but Dino must have been paid. My motivation was a mystery even to me. Sometimes you just go on your nerve.

I didn't have occasion to see Marvin for a couple of weeks. When I did it was to do a book buy in Concord, art books and a few decent novels. After we did the deal we stopped at a nondescript brewpub. "Okay, Marvin, what was up with the home invasion."

A shrug, then, "It's a small step away from your other adventures, but we wanted to take you there. It isn't your first righteous kill and it won't be your last. You wanted it, based on the guy's style and his toys. You got the gestalt and went along. If we weren't old pals, I'd say this is the beginning of a beautiful friendship. We will piss on them from a higher place."

We finished our burgers and beer, got back in his van, and headed back to the Gilman District.

# The Incredible Double

# 1.

My '87 Tercel is in great shape, only a hundred thousand miles and new almost everything, but it does have trouble with the Bay Area hills. Coming out of the tunnel on 24, leaving Berkeley, heading toward the suburbs, I was losing speed and the SUVs were losing patience. I shifted it down into second and wagged my middle finger. My best friend, Marvin, says that driving slow in a small car is a revolutionary act. Maybe he's right. A woman in a Hummer, no lie, who probably weighs in at ninety-seven pounds, half of it hair, gave me a look that could kill and waved her phone at me. When you think of spoiled little brats in military vehicles careening through the 'burbs, you know how rotten the twenty-first century will be.

First insult that came out of my mouth was "Gas-eating pig!" Way too soft, lame, actually. I floored the Tercel, and through some miracle, I caught up. I had a half-drunk can of Mr. Pibb in my nifty little cup holder, the only extra on a stripped-down car. I grabbed the can, tossed it at the Hummer. Got more on it than one would expect. Testosterone? In a perfect world I would have sped up and left her in the dust. Not enough horsepower for that, so I let off the gas and dropped back, soon to be passed by Rangers, Rams, Escalades ... sweet revenge.

Tercels aren't equipped with OnStar, so I unfolded the map, doing about fifty in the right-hand lane. More honks. Next time out this way, a six-pack of Mr. Pibb. Two off-ramps later I was in beautiful Snorinda. Six-bedroom houses, big lawns. Ghetto for the overtaxed middle class. I pulled over and looked at the directions. 233 Merwin Place. A few quick turns and I was there. Big house with a tract-home look. Nothing special. Lots of parking out front. I like that. I made a mental note to get rich and move out of South Berkeley. Maybe next year.

The house was on a slight hill, not enough to make it look stately. Still, I'd never lived this well. The landscaping was hometown America, a carpet-length lawn and some well-trimmed bushes. Old Glory waved proudly, the pole bolted to what looked like a detached garage. I walked up the sloped driveway to the front door. Gave the doorbell a nice long press, didn't hear anything. Knocked. A Haystacks Calhoun type answered the door. He was even wearing overalls. This didn't seem right.

"Are you Jerry Wally?"

"I'm a member of the staff. What can I do for you?" The lug spoke with a proper Brit accent. A walking mixed metaphor.

"Somebody named Jerome Wally asked me to come out. Said he couldn't come to me. I'm Clay Blackburn."

"Yes. The detective."

I nodded. I barely qualify. I don't have a license, don't carry a gun. I'm a book scout. But sometimes I take these jobs.

He took me through a cream-colored living room, all light and airy, that middle-class beige look. Sexy, in a twisted way. Fantasies of coming on the couch, making a mess.

We went through a yuppie-style kitchen, lots of hanging pots that didn't look used. Then through a back door to a well-trimmed little courtyard. A few feet back there was a large, square building that looked like a Motel 6. I was surprised that it couldn't be seen from the street. Hidden by trees and the front house, I guess. Jeeves/Jethro unlocked the ugly red door and let me in. To the left was a large room with a conference table. Parquet floors, a huge Franz Kline to die for, and an open staircase. I was led up the stairs to a large, open office/living space. My eyes were drawn to the Dean Martin–era wet bar. I was getting the picture. Somebody was worth a bundle.

He came down another open staircase. He didn't look like Dino. He looked like Ross Perot, but with hair. Hair for the ages! Soap opera hair, silver and sprayed. Made Bill Clinton's hair look flat. Perhaps he was a TV preacher.

He crossed the room and gave me a *Win Friends and Influence People* smile. Smarmy as all hell. A microsecond handshake, like he didn't want to touch me, and I thought, Likewise, I'm sure.

"So this is the detective! Such exciting work! I'm Jerry. So good of you to come."

"Actually I'm not a licensed detective. You should know that up front."

"We know all of that. We do our research here." He motioned me to the couch. Thoughts of making an orgasm mess left my brain like the Japanese fled Godzilla. He sat down and crossed his legs in a way that was rather limp-wristed. I hoped he was gay and not bi. Didn't want to count him among my kind.

"Do you know who I am, Mr. Blackburn?"

I'd done a little research too. "You're Jerry Wally, founder of Jerry's Drugs and More."

Another smarmy smile. "You must be wondering why I'm here."

Among other things, I thought. "You're based in Oklahoma, aren't you?"

"My home state, yes. But with hundreds of stores around the globe, I've become a citizen of the world. I'm based here for now because we've finally cracked the Bay Area market. We're opening fourteen stores in the coming months."

Except in Berkeley, where the city council gave him the bum's rush. Decided not to mention that. Just nodded and smiled. The old shuck and jive.

"I'll be doing some speaking engagements, overseeing construction, things like that. I was planning on staying in San Francisco, out by the Marina, but I was told by my security staff that this place would be safer." He gave the room a sour look. Low-class digs.

"What can I do for you?" I was getting antsy and wanted to cut to the chase.

"Apparently this place isn't completely safe. My whereabouts aren't as secret as we thought. I've been getting threats."

"Why not move?"

"Well, let me tell you, Mr. Blackburn. I don't like being bullied. I didn't build a financial empire by letting people push me around. Bad enough that Berkeley shut us out. Of course that's temporary, but it still stings. We have hundreds of stores the world over. We keep prices low. We do things right. Drugs and More stores provide a center, a public meeting place for the communities that they serve."

I had to shut him up, or hit him. Decided instead to cover my ears and sing. "Which Side Are You On," the first song that came to mind. Clay Blackburn fights absurdity with absurdity.

It didn't work. The fucker sang along with me.

"Bravo. Yes. The rights of the workers are my concern too! That's why we pay a full dollar over the minimum wage. We're like a big family..."

"What do you want from me?"

"I'm getting death threats. Somebody in Berkeley."

"You have a security staff. You could also call the police, if you haven't already."

"I'm going to level with you, Clay, because we're both men of the world. The police are useless in these cases. Not that I don't admire, no, revere them, for doing their all to keep America safe. But they are, between us, rather clunky. And as for my own staff, they're good. Really good. Gleaned from the Special Forces, mostly. They beat communism, these men. They captured Saddam, for heaven's sake! But Berkeley isn't Iraq. Berkeley is, well, really foreign to them. I had one of them, ex-CIA, I swear, tell me that Berkeley gives 'behind enemy lines' new meaning."

I sat up straight. Civic pride is a beautiful thing. "How do you know this person's from Berkeley?"

"Person. Not guy, person. So Berkeley. So quaint. Have I told you how much trouble we had opening a store in Madison? Had to Clarence Thomas 'em. Got a Black politician to take up the cause. But more of that later. The letters are postmarked Berkeley, and he signs himself T'Graph T. We figure he's some local nut. With all due respect, Clay, it takes one to know one. You could run him down and we'd be done with him."

Normally I'd get up and leave at this point. But a hungry wolf was camping on my doorstep. Book scouting was at its lowest point, what with Amazon selling used books for two cents plus postage. Only a couple of the big used bookstores could compete, and the competition to sell to them was furious. I was barely making rent.

"What's your fee, Clay?"

I work on a sliding scale. In my mind, I slid the scale as high as it would go. "My regular fee is seven-fifty a day plus expenses, and another five hundred a day when I employ my partner."

"I'll make it a straight twelve hundred a day and you can use him as you like. Or, as the natives say, use this person as you like."

A fair amount of scratch. If I could stay on the payroll for a month, I could spend serious time on the beach in Baja. I rarely have to address the issue of selling out, since, as the poet said, nobody is buying. Poetry, used books, low-rent detecting ... a recipe for a life of near-poverty. Marvin, my own personal Jiminy Cricket, would be pissed. He's an unrepentant communist. But it's easier for him. He owns his house. I was conflicted, but it didn't feel so bad. I was, as they say, born in the USA, where money is love. I was flattered that somebody cared to the tune of 1,200 clams a day.

"Okay, Wally ..."

"Jerry. Please call me Jerry."

"Here's how I work. I'll take a thousand up front. I'll poke around for a couple of days and see what I can see. If I can't do anything for you, that's that. If I think I can, the time clock starts ticking."

"Splendid. I'll write the check myself." As if that was some kind of favor.

## 2.

Jerry Wally had to rush off to a meeting, but one of his minions explained that there had been repeated short calls to Wally's cell, a number that only a few were supposed to be privy to. Nothing was recorded. Two words, raspy voice: Kill you.

This being Sunday, I stayed in Snorinda and headed to a yard sale that I'd seen advertised on Craigslist. It was a very nice yard fronting a very nice house on a street that was, well, nice. The books didn't really fit the house, or the owners, who were so bland and forgettable that I'd be hard put to pick them out of a lineup. And me a detective.

Somebody there liked movie star books. I rescued a hardback copy of *Miss Tallulah Bankhead*, a great old Hollywood bio with lots of gossip column appeal. I knew I'd never be able to sell the thing, but I needed something to read anyway and it was in perfect condition. Had a vague thought that I would write a sequence of poems based on the life of that famous bisexual tippler.

I crossed the lawn with my new find, threw it into the back seat of the very warm Tercel. September is the best month in the Bay Area. Almost too warm (for once), and in Berkeley the new students are on parade, practically sans clothes. They get younger every year, but that doesn't bother me. After all, Mohammed married a nine-year-old girl. I seem to lust after anything over seventeen. I'm almost above board.

Highway 24 was light of traffic, and soon I was parking next to People's Park, then walking down Dwight to the Chandler

Apartments, semi-subtly ogling the youngsters as they walked to class. The old lobby was cool and dark. I took the stairs for the sake of exercise, up to the fourth floor where my cat, Emily, was waiting. Turned on the fans and got myself a Bohemia beer. Put on an old Violent Femmes CD and left a message at Marvin's. I needed his input on this new job. Knew what he'd say, but I wanted to hear him say it.

I walked down to Andronico's. It's overpriced but close to home. Walking up Telegraph Avenue I encountered Bruce, my favorite street nomad. He was sitting, kind of lopsided, propped up against the wall of Eclair Bakery.

"Hi, Bruce. Kind of in a hurry."

Bruce rubbed his shaved head. He has a permanent knot, right side. Looks like a horn. "I have a sad story that I'll tell later. Do you have ten dollars?"

I gave him a dollar and rushed along.

Scouting hasn't been paying off in steaks lately, but now I could afford to splurge. Picked out a large, well-marbled New York, salad makings, and a loaf of Acme bread. Not very Berkeley of me, Marvin would say. But he'd love the steak.

## 3.

And he did. I had two bottles of Rombauer cabernet left over from better times. Opened them both. No cocktails tonight. River of red wine. And then some port. Marvin barely spoke at first, savoring the wine and the meat. He was, as usual, wearing sweats and a sweatshirt. Today it was a Moe's Books hoodie. His hair was limp and medium long. Was he trying to look like Neil Young? Why would anybody do that, I thought. But I didn't mention it. Hadn't brought up his appearance in all the years I'd known him.

"God, I love cow."

"Welcome to the food chain."

"Been there awhile. Not going to leave."

He poured himself a glass of the Rombauer, swirled, and smelled. Strong look of approval.

I put the steaks on the stovetop grill for a few short minutes.

Tossed the salad, removed the oven fries. Easiest meal on earth, unless you screw it up. This time it was perfect.

"Ever heard of Jerome Wally?"

"The rich guy?"

"Have you been in one of his stores?"

"A couple. You can't avoid them in America." To Marvin, anything east of Oakland and west of New York was America, another country. "I was doing some work in Oklahoma and I needed some stuff. They have those lunch counters, real retro. Good grilled cheese, though."

"He thinks somebody's trying to kill him. He wants me to do some snitching."

"He called you? Why? He must have a huge security force."

"Wants me to scope out the local color. His guys are too obvious."

"And you can walk the mean streets, the dive bars, the opium dens, the underbelly of South Berkeley."

"Something like that."

"The guy's a pig. Undercuts the competition, beats the unions. Middle America loves him, though. He's been born again, and he gives 'em cheap Twinkies."

"I've read the articles."

"I'm rooting for the killer."

"I thought you would. But I need the bucks. And I'm not normally pro-murder."

Marvin does something with computers that makes money. That's all I know. He's also an old lefty, and very active. After a few Negronis he's usually good for a story involving torching a cop car or destroying a Hummer. I'm not sure how deep he's in, but if there's an underground out there, he's heard of it. I asked him to get me some info and he shook his head. He wasn't going to help me protect this guy.

"C'mon, Marvin. I'm not asking you to vote Republican. I just want some background."

"Okay, I'll get you some info on the capitalist, but I'm not going to help you snitch. That guy deserves to have the shit scared out of him."

I accepted that and went deep into the kitchen cabinet. Pulled out a nice bottle of cognac. Marvin beamed, and I changed the subject.

## 4.

Thanks to Mr. Drugstore I could afford to coast. I had been living, barely, off of Ted Berrigan. Years before, I had bought a run of Berrigan books from the ex-boyfriend of a poet. She had left him flat to live in Spain with another poet who, I swear, went by the name of Sappho. The books had flowery inscriptions, like, "To Lucy in the Grand Piano ... you are beautiful ... take off that shirt!" The books occupied a sacred space on my shelf for a time, but at bottom I'm an unsentimental money-grubber, as are all book scouts. When things got tough I sold the books to Jeff Maser, a rare book dealer in West Berkeley, for a good price. Before buying them he raised an eyebrow, said, "Are you sure these aren't Bob Dark forgeries?" A reference to a famous dirty dealer in the trade. I assured him that they were real, though I wasn't sure myself. Jeff nodded, thought about it, paid off in cash.

The Berrigan fund was nearly depleted when I got my detective's advance. And so it was that I strolled into César with no debt, a fistful of dollars, money in the bank. It was going to be a liquid summer. Bring on the dancing girls! Boys too, for that matter.

I was wearing my favorite pair of black jeans and an SPD T-shirt. The sleeves were pretty short, just enough to show the bottom of my tattoo, a bright orange sun surrounded by the words of Giuseppe Ungaretti: ENORMITY ILLUMINES ME. I'm looking ten years younger than my age, I thought. It's like that when you're bucks up.

There were three open stools, a rarity at César. The tables were full. The tapas crowd was eating small food, possibly in anticipation of dinner at Chez Panisse, next door. Berkeleyites love to eat. Their love of food rivals the Italians. I took the middle stool and ordered a Negroni from my favorite bartender, a French guy with a shaved head. He iced the glass, mixed, and shook with just the right dose of panache. I sipped and tasted, as I always do, savoring the ingredients: gin, Campari, a little vermouth. Perfect. The second sip was closer to a gulp. Heaven. I ordered some high-end fries, pulled the Bankhead biography out of my book bag. Life was good.

I was reading about a meeting with Libby Holman in a Rolls equipped with a Victrola and Bing Crosby records, thinking, I just wasn't made for these times, when I noticed her, out of the corner of my eye, the way you do in bars. Dark hair with a hint of henna, scent of cigarettes and perfume. That's a rare scent in Berkeley. I was intrigued but I didn't look at first. Waited for her to order. The voice got me. Almost too deep, and smoky. A drag queen? Oh well, wouldn't be the first time. But that's another story. She ordered Oban, rocks. A yuppie? I'd prefer a drag queen; they're more fun in bed. A yuppie drag queen? Never met one of those.

I was looking toward the window, my back almost to her. I felt her lean in, smelled the perfume. Hairs stood up on the back of my neck.

"Just a good, healthy American girl with a husky voice and the strength of a horse."

Green eyes, short hair. Louise Brooks nose, long neck. Going for a '20s look, except for the fully tattooed left arm. The arm closest to me. Here comes trouble, I thought. About time. Not much had happened since my last breakup. I caught her Bankhead reference but I couldn't think of a comeback. I just looked and looked. The bartender brought the Oban. She opened her used-clothing-store purse but I reached over and closed it. Pulled out a bill and threw it on the bar.

"You sure? This stuff isn't cheap."

"I know. If you'd ordered Macallan, I wouldn't have paid. I can afford Oban."

"Oban's better, no matter what they say. You come here often?" From her it didn't sound cliché.

"Only when I'm flush."

She smiled and, I swear, licked her lips. She was a bundle of clichés, but again, I wasn't noticing. Or maybe it's that in Berkeley we live with a different set of clichés. Here she was fresh. I looked her up and down and I wasn't too subtle. I usually go for healthier women, but I decided then and there that I needed a little decadence. A fairly short dress, pumps, 1930s body, no hint of a tan. We clinked glasses and she took a hearty slug, and I did too. I leaned back about six inches and thought to myself, Well, here we go.

Another Oban and more conversation, movies and books, life in Berkeley. She'd done the hipster circuit, Brooklyn, Silver Lake, a stint in New Orleans. Mission District till the yuppies moved in. Then a run in the upper Midwest. Currently living in the forties, off Broadway, near Mama's. North Oakland, but not the dreaded Rockridge. Just enough violent crime to keep things interesting. The bar was getting crowded so we had to lean close. Her lips tickled my ear. No more music but ears in lips and no more wit but tongues in ears. As the poet said.

She turned to face me, spread her arms wide. "So, what was your first impression?"

"Sexy as hell. But probably a fag hag."

"True on both counts. Guess I dress the part. Do you have anything against fag hags?"

"It can be difficult if there's an attraction."

A laugh, consisting of a single *ha*. "I'm not exclusively a fag hag. That would mean giving up sex. Do you know what Reich said about celibacy?"

"I can guess."

She put her glass down, touching mine. Put her hands on my knees, leaned heavy. "I don't take you for queer."

"A little of both and everything in between."

"A man of experience."

"I like to try things."

## 5.

The lover and the loved, the seducer and the seducee, I can play either end. I don't have strong sexual prejudices, it's all sex and I'll sink into any role that gets me there. Usually, though, I require more time. I like to savor the persona that I've chosen, or rather, that the situation has called for. It takes some time to get past psychology, to get comfortable, to get to that place where it's all taste, smell, and feel. It's all very Zen, I guess. But I hate that Buddhist crap.

It seems Grace liked picking 'em up in upscale bars and taking 'em home for a quick fuck. Getting comfortable wasn't an issue with her. She lived in one of those charming old places where nothing works, hallways that smell like old cologne and cigarettes, threadbare carpets. Her studio apartment was fixed up nice, orange-umberish walls, Egon Schiele prints, a couple of photos of nude young boys in Sicily a hundred years ago. Fag hag. Heavy drapes. Everything brown, gold, and muted orange. I sat on a striped couch, Ikea, but nice Ikea. She went into the kitchen, a separate room off the living area. Appeared with a bottle of Scotch. Something called Lagavulin.

"Don't worry. It's good."

It was good. Smooth and a little sweet, not much smoke.

She made one of those pre-sex visits to the bathroom. I scanned the two small bookshelves. Jackie Susann and some movie bios. But also Terry Southern, Gore Vidal, Susan Sontag. No McSweeney's, no Paul Auster. I felt relieved. The only poetry was by Bertolt Brecht. Not bad.

It was a good ten minutes. I picked through *Blue Movie* looking for the raunchy parts, which was easy since most of the book is raunchy. There was a sentence about a perfect ass, then she came out of the bathroom wearing a robe that fit her style and the surroundings. Silk, I think. Bought in Tokyo. Did I like it? And she did a twirl, and I said, "Yes, very much."

She sat on the couch and we talked and kissed. Maybe it wasn't going to be the usual bang-bang-after-the-bar encounter. She put Billie Holiday on the boom box. No rock 'n' roll tonight. Fine with me. She moved away, a few inches. I pulled her toward me and her robe fell open. She seemed to like that. She had a smaller waist than I'd imagined, and smaller breasts. The boyish figure didn't go with the outfits, I'd expected a fuller look. Okay by me. She went limp and girly and I got the picture. She wanted manly. Bogie and Gary Cooper. I pulled and pushed and held her down by the shoulders. She didn't seem to want a lot of foreplay. Wanted to be taken. We'd come back around to one-night-stand sex.

A good healthy fuck and another Scotch. More talk, mostly, thankfully, of things. Art and politics. She was smart and funny, had been around, was older than I'd thought, but not by much. Thirtyish. The great joy of the zipless fuck. Do people still use that term? Well, they should. I wasn't invited to spend the night. No hard feelings about that. I had a cup of coffee, let the Scotch die down. Drove through North Oakland and back to the Chandler Apartments.

## 6.

Two strong cups of coffee and a little research on the screen. Jerry was born in Oklahoma City, raised by hard-working, God-fearing folks (aren't they all?). Dad was a plumber, but he died when Jerry Wally was in high school. He worked in a soda fountain to help make ends meet, bought the store, blah blah blah. Hard work. Praise the Lord and pass the homilies. Now employs over a hundred thousand workers, blah blah. I skipped the phony bio and found a couple of anti-Jerry sites, also the usual. Stiffs his employees, constantly being sued, buys politicians. None of the anti sites seemed especially nutty. I decided that the best way to serve old Drugstore Wally was to hit the streets, mingle with the people.

I drove the trusty Tercel down to Caffe Trieste, San Pablo and Dwight. It's a newish place, an East Bay version of the old North Beach poetry haunt. Second-best espresso in town. I noticed a few local celebrities as I waited to place my order. Maser and White, the rare book dealers, were parked at a back table. Probably discussing a deal. A couple of people from Good Vibrations, the dildo and lube emporium next door. Screeching pink hair and big belts. Nice to be in civilization, far from the suburbs.

I ordered a single espresso, known in the book trade as a pinkie lifter. Sat by the window. Not much to look at on San Pablo. A liquor store, a junk shop. Some might think it quaint. I put on my detective face. Discreetly insouciant. Nothing happening. Not a clue in the house. I was about to get up when I saw a familiar face. Suit and tie, unkempt hair. Knew him from somewhere.

"Hello, Clay. Care if I join you?" Jocko Belladonna. At least that's the name he goes by. Sometime scout. Rumor has it that he worked for the IRS as an investigator. Or was it the FBI? I don't see him at library sales. He has some other sources. Gets good books, I hear. I nodded. He went for his pastry and a latte.

"I hear you're doing the private eye thing."

"Word gets around."

"What's the job?"

I figured he knew, but I decided to keep some semblance of a cover. "Sort of a bodyguarding job."

A big guffaw from Jocko. Laughed so hard that his Allen Ginsberg–style hair flared out at the sides, like Bozo. "How much do you weigh? One forty? I hope you have a big gun."

"Somebody thought I could do the job. It pays the rent." A reference to scouting, which isn't paying well for any of us.

"Who do you work for?"

"That's classified for now."

"If you're working for a rich guy who is being harassed by a crazy Berkeleyite, I may have something for you."

"For a price?"

"You get good books, Clay. Maybe we can do a library together sometime. Or something. I'll think of something."

Jocko's a little smarmy, but he's congenial. Sharing a library didn't seem so bad. I nodded.

"That guy Bruce, Crazy Bruce."

"I know him."

"Well, this is third-hand. But I heard from Bruce that the crazy guy with the big white van—"

"Sasway?" I asked. Larry Sasway had a theory that came to him in a dream. It was Norman Mailer who killed the Kennedys, with help from Gore Vidal. A conspiracy of liberal quality lit authors. I couldn't remember the motive offhand, but everybody in town has seen his big white van, decorated with pictures of Vidal, Mailer, Sontag, and James Baldwin wielding AK-47s.

"Yeah, Sasway. Bruce says that Sasway's got a new friend who has a thing for entrepreneurs."

"What made you think I'd be interested?"

"Berkeley's a small town, Clay."

Jocko finished his pastry and downed the last of the coffee. "Remember that library. And make it a good one."

I nodded and he left.

## 7.

I had a little bag of books, enough for lunch money, sitting by the door. I felt like socializing, and I was, after all, on a case. I took them down to Moe's.

I entered the store and dumped my books on the buy counter. Someone came around behind me and looked at me out of the corner of his eye. He'd been in the Trieste. Tall and lanky. Mystery-eth. Black hair with a little artificial red. He went up to the second floor, pretending to browse. I was being followed.

Robert was the buyer. He takes his time, but the offers are pretty good. And he's good for a chat. A familiar face for twenty years or so. We talked about scouts past. We've been putting together a sort of hall of fame. Most of the stars are dead or getting too old for the game. Richie Favarito, the painter, hadn't been seen in a while. Came up from Santa Cruz with box after box. Wore the best shirts! Designed, I believe, by his wife. Banana Box Bill, another scout who went for bulk. Two vanloads a week, much of it junk. But when you hit pay dirt! All of them were full of stories, first editions that paid for trips to Vegas. The good ones can walk into a sale, go straight to the sellable book (do they smell them?), buy it cheap, and get out. Most of them read the books too. Rogue intellectuals. A dying breed.

Robert took about half of the books and paid me enough for a light snack. I left the rejects behind the counter and went upstairs to find my shadow. He was looking at anthropology books, up by the front window. When he noticed me, he picked out a book. Obviously an amateur. Must be, if I could spot him. I haven't been doing this very long. Start to think: Maybe all these crook types are obvious. Maybe I'm king of the detectives. I exited Moe's, slowly, so that he wouldn't lose me. Right on Dwight, up the stoop of the Chandler Apartments, home sweet home. I hid under the overhang till he came around, then threw a right, aiming for his Adam's apple. A good target. He turned and ducked just in time and I caught forehead. Never underestimate the criminal element. He made the mistake of trying a kung fu stance. Didn't set up right and I dug him under the ribs with my good hand. Hurt him but he didn't go down. We circled for a time, doing the old testosterone rag. Marvin came up behind him, on his way to cadge a free drink from the rich detective. He got down on all fours and we did the old Three Stooges thing, I pushed hard and he hit the pavement hard, leading with his head. There were some oglers, but they all seemed too crazy to really care. I'm sure that worse things happen on their various home planets.

We dragged him upstairs and sat him in a chair. He was woozy but not quite on Queer Street. We got him some ice and asked some questions.

He gave his name as Wilmer and said that he would never squeal.

Used that word too. Marvin gave me a wink, said, "Horst Buchholz," meaning young and green. I went to the window and checked around for cops. The coast was clear.

"I'm told that a fall from six stories will kill you. I live on the fourth floor, but there's traffic. Four floors to the pavement, then an SUV."

Horst/Wilmer shifted in his chair. Gave me a hard look. Shrugged.

I scooped up the cat and put her in the closet. She's a little window-dumb. Then I opened the window wide and pulled in the screen. Wilmer seemed pretty cool. Or maybe he was too dumb to know what was coming. Woozy? Marvin and I got on either side and lifted him out of the chair. He squirmed but he didn't really fight. He was wiry. Didn't weight much. We dangled him out of the window, holding his legs. A homeless person gave us the peace sign. You can get away with almost anything in South Berkeley.

"Who do you work for, Slim?" Marvin was having fun with this.

"He gave his name as Cabot."

"Doesn't help us much. What's he look like? Where's he live?"

"C'mon, guys." Guys?

"Hey, Wilmer, here comes a Golf. Do you think a compact would kill you? Or should we wait for something that's Ram Tough?"

"Don't tell the cops. I'm three strikes."

"Do we look like cops?" Come to think of it, I could probably pass. But Wilmer lets that go.

"Pull me up first? I'm dizzy."

We pulled him in and dumped him on the couch. "He's a big guy with a British accent. That's all I know. All I had to do was keep an eye on you."

Seems Jerry was keeping an eye on his investment. Cabot?

I was ready to let him go, but I was curious. "Wilmer, with all due respect, you don't seem like a hardened criminal. What were those other strikes?"

"Theft. I hit a register at a bookstore in Santa Cruz."

"And offense number two?"

"There are lots of registers."

Marvin smiled, wide and slow. "Hey, Wilmer, we're in the book business too."

## 8.

"Grace to be born and live as variously as possible." This from Marvin, said between quaffs of Bandol rosé. I'd been telling him about Grace, a little at a time. Grilled chicken over greens and a loaf of potato rosemary bread. His countenance grew dark and cloudy, as Conrad might say, and he looked at me with one-and-a-half-bottle eyes. "Have you done the double?"

The fountain of youth, the myth of paradise, pie in the sky, the incredible double fuck. Easier now, with all the drugs. But I hadn't gotten around to those yet. I was still doing it on the natch, as was Marvin. To hear him tell it. Ten years my senior!

"Not yet, Marvin, but I think we'll get around to it."

He let out a hoot worthy of a frat boy on Coors. Poured another glass of that beautiful pink wine. "Keep me posted."

## 9.

I fell asleep with thoughts of Grace, slept well, and called her first thing in the morning. I left a message for the whiskey-and-cigarette voice. See me soon? Got dressed and walked down to the YMCA.

Two guys in the locker room were talking about gutting the president with a fishing knife. Jolly about it though. Berkeley. Went upstairs to do my workout but the yoga people were having quiet time, and I like to sweat and grunt. Found a rowing machine away from the fray, or the lack of fray, and tried not to sweat too loudly. Decided to do some steam. There's a huge African American guy with cornrows. Sits in the back. Practically lives there. I remember that Kerouac poem that goes, "Charlie Parker looked like Buddha." This guy looks like Charlie Parker looking like Buddha. He was talking to a scrawny little guy wearing glasses. In the steam room. Nerd city. Says, "They put in some drugstore that looks like Pontiac Stadium and I'm going for my gun, son. Don't doubt me." The nerd nodded so hard that the glasses slid down his nose.

## 10.

Out on Shattuck Avenue, clean and healthy and the sun is shining, no sign of fog. Bruce was sitting in front of the movie theater, cup in hand.

"Hi, Bruce. Anything you can tell me?"

"I had something to tell you."

"Remember what it was?"

"Ten dollars." He held out his hand and I gave him a five.

"That guy with the van gave me some good pot. I'm sleepy."

"That's not what you wanted to tell me." Legend has it that Bruce was a chemistry major at Cal in the '60s and got a little creative with the chemicals. But this is a story you hear a lot around Berkeley.

"Larry says that Terry says that the guy isn't real."

"Could you give me a little more, Bruce."

"Pot's better than crack. I feel pretty good."

"A little more. Who's Terry?"

"He's real old school. He's a Marxist-Leninist."

I hadn't heard that in a while. Bruce pronounced the names slowly, with reverence.

"And who is the guy?"

"Drugstore Wally. We're a gang, Clay."

The failure of communism, right here on Shattuck Avenue. "Drugstore Wally is a phony?"

"That's what I'm saying."

## 11.

Bruce fell into a stupor before I could ask about Cabot. I decided to head home. Fed the cat (again) and checked my messages. Marvin, accepting my dinner invitation for that night. Then Haystacks—or was it Cabot?—sounding just like Sebastian Cabot, would I call him as soon as possible, or better still, come out to Orinda and see him at once.

I made myself a cup of coffee and took my time drinking. I'm not used to being ordered around. They pay the big bucks, they expect a slave. I thought about not showing at all. Then I said goodbye to the cat and found the Tercel.

Blasting hot in the suburbs. It wasn't a long ride, but it wasn't fun. I was sweating a lot by the time I got there. The porch was nicely shaded. I leaned my head against the wall before ringing the doorbell. I was enjoying the coolness of the prickly stucco when the door opened, a gush of AC. Haystacks. I wondered if maybe he was a soccer thug. They must have day jobs. Soccer thug/butler. There's an interesting life.

Haystacks was sweating as much as me, AC notwithstanding. He led me into the office. Drugstore Wally was standing in front of his desk, leaning back. In a white suit, all silvery and backlit. In his manner, he put out his hand and pulled it back fast.

"I said I'd poke around for a couple of days. That gives me another half day."

"Maybe I misunderstood. Have you found anything?"

"A street person thinks you're two-faced, and if the Buddha sees you out on the road, he'll shoot you. And you may have something to do with Susan Sontag's part in the Kennedy murders. Aside from that I'm coming up short."

He threw back his head and had a good laugh. The light played beautifully on his gray mane. Hair that rivals Michael McClure! "Well, you certainly do associate with a colorful bunch. You know, I was once a bohemian myself, in my college days. Unfortunately, I had to work for a living, and that gets in the way of all that. Then there are the drugs. Of course, I disapprove of that."

I was hit with a wave of editorial comments but I dummied up. This guy was paying my rent, for now.

"Let's cut to the chase, Mr. Blackburn. Do you have any real leads?"

Real leads mean real dollars. "I'm keeping a close eye on a couple of the local nutcases. Could turn into something."

"Does this mean you're in my employ?"

I swallowed hard and said yes. I felt a pang of longing for my days as a book scout. Damn you, Amazon. We made payment arrangements. He didn't seem to mind that I wanted half in cash as a tax dodge.

He offered me a drink, to celebrate. Decided to take him up on it. Maybe I'd learn something. He brought out a bottle of Cutty Sark. Cheap bastard. He did, however, have ice tongs. I like ice tongs.

"Detective Blackburn, tell me about some of your more colorful cases. You must have stories enough to fill a book."

I took a gulp of the so-so whiskey. I could feel the surliness rising up my spine. My neck muscles got tight, my head ached. "Gee, Mr. Wally, let me see. I once watched a capitalist bitch fall out my window, only to be run down by an SUV."

"And what part did you play in this little adventure?"

"I stepped aside when she came at me with a Ginsu knife."

"Did you do time for that?"

"Nope. Self-defense." Something sounded wrong. My poet's ears detected something. It was the way he said "time," referring of course to prison time. He didn't say it in quotes. There's a way that people use that phrase when they've actually done the time. Heavy, eyes down. Was Drugstore Wally an ex-con?

"What got you into the drug trade, Jerry? Does it go back to your bohemian days?"

"Not at all. It was the lunch counter. I love those places. The scent of grilled cheese, the coffee ..."

"What about the drugs?"

"Highly profitable. The country's getting older, Clay. I can sum up the future with one word. One word that will make the wise man rich. Do you know what that word is?"

"Plastics?"

He laughed and nodded knowingly. I guess he got the reference. "No, Clay. The word is"—big stage whisper—"*Lipitor*."

## 12.

I fed the cat again and took a long, hot post-suburb shower. It was foggy and cool in Berkeley. I went up to the roof half wet and felt the breeze. Grilled cheese and Lipitor. I was completely at sea. Over my head. But the checks were cashing. The poet side of my brain wasn't screaming yet. Working up to it, though. This guy drank bad whiskey! How could I protect someone like that. And that stupid hairdo. God. The sun was low, and of the bright orange ball variety. I sat on a rusty lawn chair and let my poet's brain go its own way.

I was on a stakeout once. No, really. Me and Marvin and a thermos of coffee, laced with Presidente brandy. We talked all night, fogging the windows of a rental car. I often drift back to those conversations. An hour or so before dawn we hatched a theory that most presidential elections have been decided on the issue of hair. Best hair wins, beginning with Wendell Willkie. Willkie had wings. Just couldn't plaster down the sides, and it looked real funny. Lost votes. Ike and Adlai were a toss-up, and in the event of a tie you look to the shape of the head. Stevenson's head was too round. It wasn't the debate that put JFK over. He beat Nixon, well, by a hair. Goldwater also suffered from those wings. No amount of Brylcreem could keep his hair from flapping. Hubert Humphrey had the worst hair in American politics. Never had a chance. McGovern-Nixon was a festival of bad hair. Voter turnout must have been low that year. Jimmy Carter had some of the best hair since the days of Andrew Jackson. Still, he couldn't best Reagan's shoe polish job. Mondale tried to out-Reagan Reagan, but he couldn't get the thickness. Dukakis broke the string. I'll never understand how he lost to Bush. I'd have bet my house on that sprayed black mass. With a coif like that I could rule the world. Clinton, always the smart politician, went for a slightly puffier Billy Graham look, and it served him well. Bush's hair isn't great, but Gore has wings of his own and Kerry's is too obvious. Palookas, both of them.

It was dark when a cool breeze brought me out of my reverie. I thought about Jerry Wally again. His hair. Something was wrong with his hair. I played our meetings over in my mind. The hairline was wrong. A rug? Possibly, but a good one. The breeze turned to wind and I went back downstairs, thinking deeply on hairdos.

## 13.

I was sitting at my desk and reading a Fielding Dawson short story. Stopped to rest my eyes. Out the window and across the street, above Shark's Used Clothing, they were at it again. For nearly a year I'd had a Jimmy Stewart's eye view of the couple. She was kind of big, but not unpleasantly so. Lots of dark hair. Black Irish? He was kind of wiry. They would start in the shower, the window on the left. I could only see heads and shoulders there. Soon they would move to the bedroom, where the window was almost floor to ceiling. I guess they weren't visible from the Avenue. Would have drawn a crowd. Brie, my downstairs neighbor, could also watch the show. She soon became bored with the lack of variety. Man on top, woman on the bottom, get it over with. Don't they do anything else? I didn't see it that way. After seeing them countless times I noticed small variations. And it was fun sex. Lots of tickling and towel snapping. I have a nice pair of opera glasses, and I used them on occasion, but I preferred to see the couple small, across the street and through the trees, almost golden in the afternoon light.

The cat was playing in the hall. I had left the door slightly ajar so that she could push her way back in. I heard a creak and assumed that was Emily, my prize tortoise-shell. Then footsteps, definitely not paws. I grabbed a book from the desk and turned. You can kill somebody with a book if you want to.

He was standing a few steps inside the apartment, me on the other side of the room. Scruffy and obviously crazy. I'm not completely familiar with the pecking order of the street sleepers, but there must be one. There's always a pecking order. This guy was at the bottom. The scent of urine and sweat filled the room. He was familiar. I'd probably stepped over him a hundred times, given or refused change depending on my mood. Reagan let them out. It's a cliché in Berkeley, something you say when you see someone so hopeless that they should be under constant care. Reagan, Prop 13, whatever. America's little Third World.

Sometimes crazy people make their way into the Chandler, but they usually sleep on the stairs. This guy was pretty bold. He looked at me and, I think, smiled.

"Clay Blackburn?" He looked unsteady on his feet.

I stood up and nodded. Made ready to catch him.

"He gave me ten dollars to tell you something. But I can't get it wrong."

"Tell me."

"The drug guy isn't the drug guy." He closed his eyes, thinking hard. "Double trouble. More later." Punctuated with a self-congratulating nod.

"What's that supposed to mean?"

"I dunno. Do you give me something too?"

"Not unless you tell me who sent you."

"Not part of the deal." He looked confused. Me too.

I had a twenty in my pocket. Dug it out and offered it.

"Some guy that Bruce knows. I don't know him."

"What's he look like?"

"Big guy with a beard."

"What color?"

"White guy."

"The beard?"

"Oh yeah. Gray. Gray beard."

"Where'd you meet him?"

"The street." I wasn't going to get my twenty's worth.

"So Santa approaches you and tells you to tell me this. Out of nowhere?" I was losing him. They can't tell what they don't know.

"I'll go now." He put out his hand and I gave him the twenty. Soft touch.

## 14.

Marvin leaned back in his chair and surveyed the post-dinner table. Mussel shells, mostly. Two empty wine bottles, dirty dishes, half bottle of Jameson's. He righted himself, then poured a little more whiskey into a tumbler. Leaned back again. His bicycle pants were a shiny maroon. He was wearing a Chicago Bulls T-shirt, torn at the neck. He had been telling me stories about some adventures in Central America. I believed some of them. When I saw him like this, in his Neil Young drag, drifting on a belly full of good food and wine, it was hard to imagine him doing Marx's work in the jungle.

Between war stories we'd also discussed my case. I wasn't sure that he'd listened, he'd only responded with grunts and nods. But suddenly his eyes showed light and he was focused.

"Saddam!"

I assumed he was onto another story. I waited for the other shoe.

"Just like Saddam! Drugstore Wally has doubles! There are probably scores of Drugstore Wallys, pressing the flesh and giving pep talks. One of your scruffy friends handed you a clue. Jerry isn't just two-faced. He's a different guy."

"Jerry's features are pretty distinct."

"Don't you watch those makeover shows? They knock out your teeth, break your nose, suck out some fat, and you look like Brad Pitt. The docs could turn out a fleet of smarmy CEOs."

## 15.

I hit the streets early and checked all the usual places. Bruce wasn't in People's Park, wasn't in the obvious alleys and doorways. I asked around, nobody knew anything.

I approached a couple of hefty guys with gray beards but got no satisfaction. Mostly I got the bum's rush. Berkeley isn't always the friendliest town. I grabbed a mediocre piece of pizza and hung on the Avenue, asking questions that didn't get answered. The espresso guys, a couple of street vendors, the book clerks. Nope and double nope. I doubled back and sat in Ho Chi Minh Park. A great-looking young man was playing Frisbee with his dog. I watched him with Walt Whitman wonder. The miracle of bare legs. It was getting close to the cocktail hour, or close enough, so I walked up Telegraph, through campus, down to Shattuck Avenue and north to the gourmet ghetto. I wasn't going to César to run into Grace. You don't do that when, after a zipless fuck, you don't get a callback. Or maybe you do.

The bar was full. Usually when it's that crowded I walk out, but I was a little too tired to look for another place. I walked in and I was khaki-deep in blue-staters. It's hard to hate them, but it's also hard to care. I comforted myself with the fact that they wouldn't lynch anybody. There was one stool open at the bar. Well, almost open. I had to ask a business casual type to move her Cody's book bag. The bartender was a young guy, nerd chic with a knockout pair of fashion glasses. He was good too. Caught my eye a few seconds after I'd gotten situated. I ordered a gin and tonic, not bothering to call the label. They use good stuff in their well drinks. I scanned the bar and she was there, at the far end by the bathrooms. Sharing a joke with the guy who fixes my Toyota. He waved hi and she caught my eye and lifted her drink. Got up and came over to me. I liked that a lot. Squeezed in close, inching out Ms. Business Casual. Kissed me full on the lips. Scent of Scotch and perfume. Butterflies.

"What are you up to tonight?"

"I'm on a case." I still can't say this without feeling dumb. Maybe someday I should get a license.

"What do you do when you're on a case?"

"I sit in bars and cafés and talk to people."

"What do you do when you're not on a case?"

"Same thing. But when I'm on a case I drink nicer cocktails. I'm on a retainer."

"Is this a murder case?"

"I'm protecting someone from bodily harm. If you can believe that." This got a chuckle. I'm not quite five foot nine and weigh just under one fifty.

"What are your qualifications for this job?" When she said this she leaned forward and touched my forehead to hers. Oh god.

"I made it to the Golden Gloves semifinals in my hometown."

"Welterweight?"

"You know the weight qualifications. I'm impressed. But I was a lightweight at the time."

"Well, you're no lightweight now." She leaned closer, if that's possible. Sometimes obviousness is a blessing. "Have you had dinner?"

"I don't need dinner right away. Shall we go to the Chandler Apartments?"

Back through campus, down the Avenue, and into the elevator. A second fuck isn't a zipless fuck. Often it is better.

She didn't begin pumping me for information until after, thank god. I told her that these things had to be kept confidential. Something I learned from watching PI shows on TV. Actually I didn't much care about hanging Drugstore Wally out to dry, but I didn't want to let go of any info until I found out who she was working for.

I got up mid-question and went into the kitchen. She followed me and peered into the reefer with me. I pulled out some cheese and a few olives. Half bottle of Tavel rosé. Directed her to the bread. Naked in the kitchen. Something very intimate in that. Two baby steps beyond the zipless. But was she a spy?

I looked her straight in the eyes. Tried not to show another erection. Butterflies again. "Why all the questions?"

"It's all very strange. Book scout, yes. And most book nerds have artistic pretensions, so I get the poetry obsession. Detective doesn't follow. So I'm interested. What's the big deal? Do you think I'm a noir girl? Gonna chase you with a knife?"

"It happens."

A big roll of the eyes. "C'mon. Tell me who you're protecting."

A tongue-in-my-mouth kiss, the kind that makes straight guys feel almost attractive. Luckily, I'm only half straight. I was able to resist spilling the beans.

"Hey, Clay Blackburn, can you do the double fuck?" Another kiss, her tongue cool from the chilled wine. She left a couple of hours later. Not ready to spend the night.

## 16.

Sometimes you see them in doorways. You're not sure if they're dead, sleeping, or in trouble. There's the judgment call where you walk by or you call the police. Cops must get pretty sick of these calls.

No judgment call here. This guy was dead. I was exiting the Chandler on my way to the gym, nice sunny day, students walking by on the way to class. He was on the stoop, blocking the doorway. I stepped over him and touched his face. Cold. Definitely the guy that invaded my living room, even worse for wear. Terrible smell, but not too much worse than when he was alive. I checked his pockets for ID. There wasn't any. I dug the phone out of my gym bag and called the cops. Sat a few feet ahead of him, bottom step, where the air was almost fresh. There wouldn't be much investigation. I guessed that he was shot full of the latest low-end opiate. A little warning?

After the cops left I went upstairs and took a long, hot shower. I had been playing around the edges, spending my advance and having a little fun with the rich guy. Now I was in some real shit, possibly deep shit.

I dressed and put in a call to Marvin. I was going to need a little research, maybe some muscle. I went downstairs and hit the street. The cops were still wrapping things up. They eyed me as I left, but I didn't mind. They eye everybody. Part of their training. I found the Tercel, half block away on Regent. Tore up a parking ticket and headed down to Shattuck. Checked out Bruce's favorite corner. No go. I asked a couple of the street folks if they'd seen him. Blank looks.

Back into the Tercel and down to San Pablo, Caffe Trieste. Parking right out front. Something was going right. I ordered my espresso and found a seat. Two bites into my biscotti, Jocko came in, wearing a maroon shirt and a wide, greenish tie. Light-blue sport coat with kind of matching pants. I motioned him over. He ordered a large orange juice, came over, and sat down. I described the dead guy. Not familiar. No, he hadn't seen Bruce. Not for days. He had seen Larry Sasway's van, though. Up San Pablo, near Solano. Less than an hour ago. I dumped two spoons of sugar into my pinkie lifter and drank it fast. Excused myself and fired up the old Tercel. An illegal U-turn and I was pointed north on San Pablo, up toward Solano.

## 17.

Sometimes fate throws one a fish. I took a right on Solano and the van was there, a few blocks up, parked in front of a Tibetan restaurant, and, miracle of miracles, there was a parking place on the same block. Too bad it was too early for my lunch. I could have gone for a yak burger. As it was, I stayed close to the van, window-shopping and keeping eyes peeled for Larry Sasway.

He left the restaurant carrying a white paper bag decorated with the image of a prayer flag. I decided in a split second to play it tough. Larry's a little guy, with thick glasses and a '50s-style haircut, what used to be called a wiffle. I figured I could take him if I had to. I grabbed his bag.

"I hope this is a burger. I'm hungry!" Clay the bully.

"It's a potato thing. I don't eat meat." Larry gave me a look that could kill, except that it was cockeyed. He grabbed at the bag and I pulled it away, just in time. I know from my boxing days that you can anticipate a guy's next move if you watch his eyes. But Larry's eyes were weird. One seemed too big, due to the glasses. The other looked the wrong way, like Jack Elam. The weird eye slowly looked toward the heavens. A bird? A plane? I followed the eye with both of mine, and he caught me with a chopping left, flush on the chin. I have a tough chin. I didn't go down but it hurt like shit. He grabbed the bag, but it broke and the Tibetan potato thing landed on the sidewalk. I covered up and started my counter, but he ran to the van, around to the driver's side, and got in. I followed. Another fish from the fates. The passenger side was open. I got in and grabbed his keys as he took them from his pocket.

"Okay, Lar, I owe you lunch. But I had to act fast."

"Don't call me Lar. It's just Larry. You're Clay Blackburn, the book guy. What do you have against me? Are you crazy?"

"Larry, with all due respect you're the guy that claims that Saul Bellow drove the getaway car after Gore Vidal shot Kennedy. I'm crazy?"

"Vidal was a decoy. Tennessee Williams fired the fatal shot. Why did you take my potato thing?"

"I'm a little rattled. Somebody was murdered and left on my stoop. And my pal Bruce is missing. I figured I'd get your attention. Then you sucker punched me."

A sly smile. "I've been using that eye fake since second grade. Buy me another potato thing and I'll point you to Bruce. Who got killed?"

"Don't know who got killed." I described the dead guy and got a quizzical look, although all of Larry's looks are slightly quizzical. "Lead me to Bruce and it's potatoes for you."

"He's been hanging out with a guy called Terry. Find Terry and you'll find Bruce."

"I hear you've been hanging with Terry."

"They didn't take me seriously. I have real information. There's big trouble ahead. I need to form a posse to take on the quality lit gang. They've killed so many."

"Aren't they getting a little old? Or dead? Sontag's not going to shoot anyone."

One eye looked to God, the other at the traffic. "They have young followers! Steinke! Lethem! Eggers! Heidi what's-her-name! I'm going to have to repaint my van."

"Before you get started on that, could you tell me a little about Terry?"

Rolled his eyes. Every which way. "He's obsessed with the chain stores. He didn't put down my theories. But he didn't listen either. I thought he was listening at first."

"Does he have an address?"

"He used to have a place on Ashby, above Alcatel Liquors. I don't know if he's still there."

"What's he look like?"

"Do I get my potato thing soon?"

"Sure. What's he look like?"

"Bushy gray beard. Kind of athletic. Tan."

I gave Larry a few dollars for a Tibetan lunch and drove across town.

## 18.

Somebody told me that Lucia Berlin once lived there. It's a solid brick building, slightly down at the heels. The liquor store on the ground floor has been there for many years. Surprisingly good wine selection, considering the neighborhood. No Terry listed on what was left of a directory. I rang all five buzzers. No answer. I went into the store and bought a bottle of something called Lungarotti Rubesco, from a place called Torgiano. It wasn't too expensive and I liked the label. The clerk was a great-looking tough girl with short, very black hair. No color in her tattoos. The straight stuff.

"I was supposed to meet a guy named Terry but he didn't show. White guy, gray beard, tan. Have you seen him?"

She smiled, and the smile said, this jerk's a cop, he gets nothing from me. "He comes around sometimes but I haven't seen him today."

"I'm not a cop or a bounty hunter or a repo man. I just want to say hello." I gave her one of my cards, the one with a phone number.

"Are you a detective?"

"I'm a poet."

She let out a healthy, hooting laugh. She had crinkly blue eyes and a nice, Brigitte Bardot–type mouth. "There used to be a poet living upstairs. She was nice. But she didn't have a business card."

"We're coming up in the world."

"All right, poet. I'll give you a little hint. Terry has a dog. Don't know how he slips that past the landlord. Nice-looking black Lab. Don't look for him across the street at the Petco. Terry hates chain stores. He could be at Redhound, up on College. Or he could be out at the dog park, or at the Marina, walking Ezra. That's the Lab.

Hey"—here she squinted at the card—"Clay ... Blackburn? I think I have a friend you'd like. He's a poet. Do you do boys?"

"Depends. Feel free to show him the card." I left her laughing. Great laugh.

## 19.

It was one of those days when everybody looks great, just enough sun, tattoo and belly button weather, gym shorts to the café, so I wasn't surprised that the woman working at Redhound was a knockout. I waded through two poodles and a mutt with a drooling problem, went past the toy section, and asked my questions. Terry's description did register, but she hadn't seen him.

Next stop Berkeley Marina. I was on a parking run that was truly historic. I found a place down by the water, facing the Golden Gate. Had to fight the temptation to roll down the windows and just sit in the car for a few hours, waiting for sunset. I made myself exit the car and walked toward the part of the park that is reserved for dog walking. Frisbees were flying and dogs were everywhere. A nice wholesome scene. No gray-bearded men with black Labs, however. I walked around for a while. Had a nice conversation with a Jack Russell. Found a bench facing the water and caught some sun. This detective stuff is hard work. I was almost asleep when I felt a wet nose on my arm. A black Lab, but not the right black Lab. The owner was an attractive, slightly hip-looking woman, say, forty. Reeking of "professional." Nerve.com fodder. I smiled and returned to my reverie. That dog had no idea that he was a red herring.

After a while I felt a strong need for a catfish burger. I went back to the car. As I got in I saw a black Lab jump into an old VW Rabbit. A man with a gray beard walked around to the driver's side, got in, and drove off. How the fuck did I miss him?

I pulled out and got behind the Rabbit. I was tailing an out-of-date car in my out-of-date car. Who would win? I stayed back. Easy to be inconspicuous in a gray Toyota. He took a right on Sixth, passed the Creative Arts building, then a left on Dwight Way. All the way up Dwight. He slowed as he got closer to my apartment. Looking for parking? Looking for me.

I went up a block, right on Regent, down toward Ho Chi Minh Park. Found a place a couple of blocks from home. As I walked back to Dwight I spotted his car, parked outside Bongo Burger. Fucker got a better spot than me. Didn't see him on the street, so I assumed he'd be on the stoop. I was right. I braced myself for I-don't-know-what when he approached me. He shook my hand.

"I'm Terry Olson. Figured you'd be looking for me. Are you a hit man?"

"No. I think I'm supposed to find you, though. Were you threatening Drugstore Wally?"

"Hey, that's a good nickname. But Wally's not Wally."

I invited him upstairs. He asked for a bubbly water. I motioned him to the couch and poured him the drink. He looked a little like Dr. John. The face was a little too young and feminine, didn't match the beard and the booming voice. That stretched plastic-surgery look.

"Wally's me, Wally's everybody. Wally's the working man and woman, the down and out. He's anybody who needs a job!"

Shit. Another crazy guy. "We all know he's a smarmy bastard, Terry. But is Wally Wally in the real sense? Or are you speaking metaphorically?"

"Wally isn't Wally at all. In any sense of the word, Wally is not Wally."

I've lived in Berkeley for close to twenty years. Street folks, philosophy majors, aging radicals … life in Berkeley can be one long version of "Who's on First?" Being a poet I sort of like the game. Linguistic juggling is part of what I do. There was, however, a job to be done. I could turn this nut over to Wally, real or otherwise, collect the rest of my pay, and take a little trip down to Baja. Sun and sand, that's what I needed. My Spanish is terrible, but I probably communicate better down there. I was losing the plot up here.

"Terry, did you threaten to kill Wally?"

"The real Wally?"

"Any Wally. Any at all. Disney, Matthau, some guy up the street. Did you send threatening letters to a Wally?"

"Nobody did. That's a ruse. They just wanted to get to me. I'm going to expose them the right way. I'm a whistleblower, like Silkwood. Were you followed?"

Not that I'd noticed, but I'm still not very good on that point. Need more practice there. "Maybe. That would make sense. They follow me to you, and my job is over."

"I'm in disguise! And I'm in Berkeley! You're a traitor. Those people are pigs. I thought you were old Berkeley!" He lunged at me and I sidestepped. He was nimble, didn't fall down. He swung and I caught arm, same side of the face that caught that last punch. I was going to be sore for days. I was pissed so I countered hard. Too hard. A nasty thunk, pain in my knuckles. I think I broke his eardrum. He went down, grabbing his face. "I'll get you for this. Whose side are you on? Bruce said you're a poet. I came to you to reason with you. I think you're a lackey for the chains."

That did hurt. I never shop the chains. "Okay, Terry, I'm listening. But stop the Wally-Wally. Make it plain, okay?"

"I worked for the real Wally in Arkadelphia, when he opened his third store. Store manager. No benefits but the pay wasn't too bad, for Arkadelphia. He was around a lot then, micromanaging. We got to be pretty friendly. This was before the books came out, before the lectures. When the *Win Friends and Influence People* bit took off, he disappeared. Bigger fish to fry."

He became animated and his voice got deeper, more Wally-like.

"Before anyone knew it there were stores everywhere. I was pissed. I thought, as a veteran employee, that he could do something for me. At least make me a district manager. I wrote him a letter. Two days later one of his people came to the store. They pointed out that I look a little like Wally. I was confused, of course. Who cares? So they offer me twice what a district manager makes to be a double. You know, to fool would-be assassins. Except that it took a little nip and tuck, a little something around the eyes. Surgery! Good benefits, though. And I got to fly business class."

It was a crazy story but I'd heard worse. "Sounds like an, um, okay job. If that's what you like. Why are you on the outs with him?"

"Wally and his people decided that it would be more democratic if we made the same as the associates in the stores. We were paid the same as a senior cashier, which was quite a pay cut. No benefits to speak of. Of course, there was always the possibility of working your way up the ladder. We were in the security division, so technically we could be part of the Spirit of '76 crew. They make real money. But that's a long shot when you're fifty and you've had your face altered to look like a famous snake oil salesman."

"So what happened?"

"I up and quit. But they wouldn't let me. Wouldn't look good. I'd signed a series of waivers that included a gag order. Why not? I liked the idea of working in security. Maybe they were afraid I'd go on *Nightline* or something. Who knows."

"So you grew a beard and went on the lam."

"And stopped using the sunlamp. Wally's pretty tan. Now I'm in deep shit, though. The Spirit of '76 crew will murder me for sure."

"What makes you think they'd go that far?"

"They'll go as far as they need to go. Who would question that? Didn't they kill Party Joe?"

"Party Joe?"

"The guy they left on your stoop. Everybody knows about that. I heard it from Julia Vinograd. I feel like I killed him. I shouldn't have gotten him involved. I didn't think they'd go that far but they did. Guess I'm next."

I was beginning to feel the heat. If this nutty story was true, I probably had a cadre of private cops waiting on the stoop of the Chandler. I went over to the window. Wilmer! Somehow I'd missed him. Is there a school for private detectives? I needed to take a class on detecting a tail. He was right there, across the street, in front of the Krishna Copy Center.

I pulled Terry over to the window, but not too close. "You know that guy?"

"He worked at the center."

"The center?"

"The place where they fixed my face. I thought he was the janitor. Guess he got bumped up to security. Probably made more sweeping floors."

"How much security do they have?"

"A private army. Don't you know? You lefties are so naive. They own the world. I'm small potatoes to them. They probably only have a couple of Spirit of '76 people in town, along with a phony Wally."

"I've met Wally."

"Not the real Wally. He's probably down in Palos Verdes. He has a nice house down there."

"Is that where the center is?"

"The center's on Katella, out in Anaheim. Corporate headquarters is in Orange County."

My head was swimming. I wanted to avoid a showdown, give myself some time to think. "I think you need a shave."

"No I don't. Besides, my face hurts."

I pulled him into the bathroom. Pulled out some scissors and a razor. "Maybe we can get you out of here incognito. Old Horst isn't so smart. Maybe we can smuggle you out. Do you have a place to stay?"

"I'm at the French Hotel till the money runs out."

"If they don't grab you on the way out, go there. I'll contact you."

It took him a while to shave. Heavy beard. I found him a pair of cutoffs and a loud Hawaiian shirt left over from one of my Baja trips. Flip-flops and a Moe's book bag for his old clothes. He looked like George Hamilton crossed with the poet Peter Gizzi, on holiday in Honolulu. Hide in plain sight.

"I look goofy."

"It's a goofy neighborhood."

I waited five minutes and looked out the window. Horst was still waiting. Ten minutes later Terry called from the French Hotel. He didn't think he'd been followed. But how was he to know?

## 20.

I put in a call to Snorinda and left a message with Haystacks. Have Wally call me on my cell phone. Then I turned off my cell phone. I needed to check in, but I didn't want to talk to them just yet.

I needed Marvin's help. He had access to all kinds of information. He's a Renaissance man for our times. Computer nerd, hacker, soldier of fortune, poet and critic, proud owner of an Econoline van. Everything a book scout/detective could want.

He said he'd drop everything when I told him I was making risotto. I told him to give me a couple of hours. Dinner at eight. I drove down to Berkeley Bowl and got lucky with the lines. Fennel looked good, and there was some broccoli romanesco. Cute, and good tasting. Hit the cheese counter for Gorgonzola and Romano. Decided against adding meat. The cheese and the stock would make it rich enough. Made my way up to the cashier. Only five people ahead of me. Two women were making out, front of the line. Berkeley!

The town was being good to me. Parking right out front. No dead bodies on the stoop. I shared the elevator with Dina from Amoeba Music, always a nice occurrence. The cat was pissed off. Had I forgotten her morning feeding? Didn't think so. Fed her again just in case. Then I zapped the frozen chicken stock and assembled the ingredients. I'd have everything ready for stirring when Marvin arrived. In the time it takes to stir the risotto he can usually down two cocktails. I needed to soften him up. I opened the Lungarotti Rubesco for a breathing. Figured it would need all the help it could get.

Marvin arrived, Kramer-like, on a bicycle. Didn't feel like parking the van. The bike rolled into my writing desk as he tried to dismount. When he picked up the cat she immediately started purring. It always amazes me that animals like Marvin. He's so floppy and clumsy, yet somehow they aren't spooked.

He was, as usual, wearing bicycle pants and a sweatshirt. Today both were sort-of-green, if that's a color. Hard to believe that he can beat people up. I've seen him do it and he's fierce.

He grabbed one of my Ikea folding chairs from the dining room table and brought it into the kitchen. As always, he would hold court while I cooked dinner. I didn't mind this at all.

"I have Boodles," I said. "Would you like a martini?"

"Let's drink it straight. Do you have lime?"

"Of course. Go to it. I've got to stir this thing."

He poured a couple of doubles and we were off. He was just back from NYC, where he'd spotted the guy who had us thrown out of a Galway Kinnell reading last summer. We were drinking Tunisian red in a North African place on Sixth Street and decided, just for giggles, to go see Kinnell at the 92nd Street Y. Marvin sprung for a cab uptown and before I knew it we were seated down front. Marvin holds many strings.

Galway came out in a white suit, which gave us a fit of the giggles. I blame the Tunisian stuff. It's considered terribly rude to giggle at the 92nd Street Y. That's a serious place. He came on all sonorous, like

William Shatner playing a great poet. We started repeating his lines, softly at first, then louder. He'd boom out, "The dead shall be raised incorruptible," and we'd parrot it back to him. He didn't seem to notice, but the guy in back of us was steamed. He's somebody you see at readings in NYC, probably a poet himself. Who isn't? The final straw was the line "The fishmarket closed, the fishes gone into flesh," delivered with all the flair of a John Carradine. We stood up and blasted the line right back at old Galway, who still didn't notice. The guy in back of us found someone in authority and we were shown the door.

Marvin was doing a great Kinnell as we recalled the incident. I stopped stirring long enough to pick up my glass and toast him. I asked him what he'd been doing in New York but he clammed up. Lefty stuff. Still a few anarchists in the old town. I wondered how they afford the rents.

The stirring was over and we adjourned to the table. I quickly dressed some greens and poured the wine. It wasn't bad. Score one for Alcatel Liquors. Marvin sniffed and tasted, then nodded. Then he dug into the rice and nodded some more.

I brought him up to speed regarding the Jerry Wally case. I tried to keep the story amusing. Crazy Bruce, the potato thing, it was all just a lark. Would he mind helping out? For Terry? He seemed like an okay guy.

"What have you found out about the homeless guy?"

"Not much yet."

"Might tell you something."

"Good point. I'd hate to do it but maybe I should call the cops."

Marvin shot me a look. He enjoys characterizing me as a babe in the woods. "Cops won't know shit. They never do. Call that transgender person. You know, the fed."

I had always thought of Bailey Dao as a woman, but I let that go. Maybe Marvin knew something that I didn't. She did in fact work for the FBI, out of the local office. Agent Dao had gotten me out of a jam and I had done her a few favors. I couldn't remember who owed whom.

"I'll give Bailey a call. Are you on board?"

"With conditions. First, don't let Dao know I'm involved. I have to keep my low profile. Why add to my FBI file? Second, I get to carry my gun."

"I hate those things."

"Fuck that. It's time to shed those bourgeois liberal ideas about gun control. Guns are as American as cherry pie. What's for dessert?"

"Dates baked in filo with a cinnamon cream sauce," I said. "So wear the gun. But don't use it unless the situation is dire."

"I understand the rules of engagement. My own rule is: Shoot anybody to the right of Howard Dean and proceed from there, but I'll go a little easy, just for you. And there's one more condition."

"Whatever you say. I need the help."

"You have to tell me. Have you done the double with Tallulah?"

"You mean Grace."

"Well?"

"I don't usually kiss and tell."

"Bullshit."

"Yes, on the second night. Actually it was early in the morning, after the Scotch had worn off."

"She's dangerous, you know." Said with a smile and a nod.

"She does ask questions."

"Probably works for Drugstore Wally."

"I'm not so sure. Maybe she's just curious."

"She acts like a noir character, which means she likes to think of herself as a femme fatale. She's right out of James M. Cain. She's the kind of woman that would convince you to kill your wife, if you had one."

"I think it's all for show."

"Don't be so sure. If it walks like a duck and quacks like a duck, sometimes it's a duck."

## 21.

I felt better with Marvin backing me up. I was worried about gunplay, though. I'd managed to avoid shootouts in my short career as a "private asshole." Guns put little holes in people. Makes me squeamish. Also, it's harder to keep a low profile when you're spraying the area, any area, with bullets. My motto is, no license, no publicity, no cops. With the exception of Bailey Dao.

Marvin left before eleven. Said he had to do some work later. I asked him to keep an eye on the French Hotel. He said he would.

Haystacks had left a message on my cell. The boss wanted to see me ASAP. Decided it was too late to do anything about that. I cleaned up the kitchen and poured myself a small Scotch. Picked up a copy of Edward Dorn's *Gunslinger*, possibly my all-time favorite book. I've read it cover to cover more than once. Now I use it as a sort of *I Ching*. I let it fall open and I read a few lines to see what the Gunslinger has to say. I sat on the couch. Put my Scotch on the table, next to the stereo. The cat jumped up and took a sniff. Scampered. Not quite the perfect companion. If only she drank Scotch! I wouldn't need friends. I folded my legs and sat the book on my lap. I have many editions of the poem. This was a newish one, from Duke University. Cloth, nice heft to it. I coaxed the book open, somewhere in the middle:

> Cool dry,
> Shall come the results of inquiry
> out of the larks throat
> oh people of the coming stage
> out of the larks throat
> loom the hoodoos

A lark? Or a duck? And the phone rang, just like that. Her voice seemed even smokier than remembered.

"Hello, Clay Blackburn. This is a booty call."

That particular phrase had never been applied to me. I liked it. "I'm home. Nursing a glass of Glenfiddich. Will that do?"

"You're not drunk, are you?"

"Not especially. A little wine with dinner. Does it matter?"

"Want you at your best. I want that thing."

"Thing?"

"Up, down, and up again. Without exiting. You know."

"The incredible double fuck?"

"Is that what you call it?"

"Your first time?"

"Don't flatter yourself. It's rare but not unheard of. And I do have a thing for young boys. It comes pretty natural to them. Actually, old man, you're an exception for me."

"Maybe you should hurry on over before I forget what I like about you. My memory's not what it used to be. Where are you?"

"Look out the window."

She was across the street, in front of the skateboard shop. She was wearing jeans and a men's sport coat. I waved and she waved back. Opened the coat. Predictably, she was naked under the coat. Sometimes predictable isn't so bad.

I met her halfway down the stairs. I noticed that she didn't have a purse or overnight bag. Strange for "booty calls." We embraced and I felt some bulk in her coat pocket. Guess that was her overnight bag. Then I wasn't noticing anything, and we were on the old futon.

I have never done the double with such ease. Had I been twenty, I could have done a triple. I wonder who holds the record. Some porn star, no doubt. Sometimes everything is perfect. London poet Jules Mann once described a woman that she had met briefly in an airport. Her perfect sexual match. And she knew it, though it was never consummated. She probably still keeps that woman in her sex memory, years later. The poet Patrick Dunagan calls this the Tadzio effect. A perfect lust that you would follow to your death.

She wasn't on the beach, down by the water, and she wasn't waiting to pick up her baggage. I was on top of her and we were fucking and fucking.

And then I was sitting up, leaning against the wall. She was in my arms, in front of me. No blankets left on the bed. Cigarette time but I don't smoke much anymore. I said to myself, I will count to ten and she will ask me a question about the case. If Marvin is right. Ten came and went and I thought, Ha! Marvin is wrong. At about twenty she began to nibble at the edges.

"You lead a strange life, Clay."

God. That voice. "Not many book scouts around anymore, I guess."

"I don't mean that. The detective stuff. Tell me some thrilling stories about the case you're working on."

"This case is vexing me. Mostly I don't understand why Drugstore Wally is hiring amateurs. Am I so small-time that I only rate three amateur employees? Where's the Spirit of '76 bunch?"

"What three employees?"

"There's the guy we call Horst, Wilmer's his real name. Haystacks the butler. And you. You're a real pro in some areas, dear, but you're a terrible spy."

She flew out of bed and stood up. Fixed me with a good stare. I admired her flair for the dramatic. I hadn't dropped the blinds, and the streetlights on Dwight provided the perfect light. She stood so straight that she seemed to bend backward, and the light hit her shoulders hard but barely lit her face. God.

I rolled onto my stomach to avoid changing the subject. "Where'd he find you guys? He can't be paying much." She started to cry. No sobbing, though. Her jaw was fixed tight and her eyes were still on me, albeit teary.

"Listen, prick. I was an English major. I had a shit job in one of his stores. Owlsblight, Wisconsin. Ever heard of that town? Had to move there because my aunt owned an apartment building. Cheap rent. I was an assistant manager. Nights, weekends, not enough pay to ever get out. Then the meat cutters went union. Two days after the union election Wally closed the store. Pretty much put the town out of business. I applied for a job at the Drugs and More in New Cheapside, a twenty-mile commute. I was home, waiting for the call, and a couple of people from Spirit of '76 offered me a 'special assignment.' If this works out, I'll get a middle management spot. Full health benefits. What could I do? But I can't do this anymore. I like you, and I like Berkeley. God, you can read! And you don't weigh three hundred pounds, and you don't wear an owl hat."

"Owl hat?"

"The local high school team, the Owlsblight Owls. They're a big deal up there. God, I hate men. But you're kind of different."

"You seem pretty sophisticated for an Owlsblight girl."

"I write a blog. And I did my thesis on Thomas Hardy."

And you throw a good fuck, I wanted to say but didn't. Mind on the job.

"Do you know about Wilmer?"

"No, but they said they'd be following me, for my protection. I took it as a threat. They can be pretty pushy."

"What would it take for me to hire you as a double agent?"

"A middle management job doesn't buy much loyalty. I mostly came down here to get out of Owlsblight. They flew me down business class! If you could find me an affordable rent in the Bay Area, maybe a job in a bookstore, I'd probably come around. And maybe a couple more dates, to see where that leads, and dinner at Chez Panisse, downstairs."

"I can't afford downstairs, and affordable rents are hard to come by. What if I promise to do my best?"

"And the dates?"

"You're on. We'll start this week. I'm going to a reading Friday. Would you like to join me?"

"Beats anything that's going on in Wisconsin. Why not?"

## 22.

Charles Bernstein was reading in the city. Heady stuff but it might impress her. Or not. I could check the calendars, find something else. I'd have a couple of days to cool off and think before seeing her. Grace would come by at about five p.m. I had a vague plan for putting the squeeze on Wilmer if he followed me again.

I had some time to kill. I was planning a trip to the roof for a little sun when the phone rang. My phone is hooked up to the front door. Ring my number and the phone rings. A strange system, but useful. Turn off the phone and, voilà, nobody home. This time I picked up, and it was Bailey Dao. I buzzed her in.

I opened the door and she strode into the middle of the room. FBI training. See as much as you can without a warrant. She is very tall. Mystery-eth. Once described herself as African Filipina with an Irish jaw. Left arm a sleeve of tattoos by Don Ed Hardy. Marvelous work, sailors and crosses and hearts. Jet-black hair, cropped short. A force of nature. It is a good thing that we are no longer allowed to describe people as noble savages. And yet ...

She kissed me full on the lips. I was shocked. I usually got a stiff, official handshake. "Hello, Ms. Dao. How's life with the feds?"

"They cut me loose. Yours was the last call before they turned off my voicemail."

"That's quite a surprise."

"They wanted me to state my gender. Or restate. Or something. I told them it's none of their business. Besides, I'm in a state of flux right now. I could answer that question a couple of different ways. Like that has anything to do with my job! These neocons will be the death of all of us."

"What will you do for a living?"

"I'm working your side of the street now. Going to get a license and everything." She reached into her jeans and brought out a card. I hadn't noticed before, but her clothes were more casual. No more cheap business suits.

Silhouette of a woman with a gun. Bailey Dao, Private Investigator. "Looks good," I said. "But the gun may be heavy-handed. Mostly we spy on people. For that it helps to have a low profile."

"Don't worry, that's my joke card. Got another one for real clients. So, are we partners on this case?"

"I'm flattered that you'd ask, but I still work with Marvin. I was hoping to hit you up for some inside information, but it seems you're no longer on the inside."

"I'm still dating Agent Lazari, so I can get into files, stuff like that."

Was Lazari male or female? Couldn't remember, decided not to ask.

"Are you on a retainer?" she asked. She was going to want money.

"Barely making expenses."

"By expenses you mean Negronis made with the best gin, high-end restaurants, cases of Tavel ..."

"Yeah. Like I said. Expenses."

"I'll see what I can do, then we'll negotiate."

I didn't like the sound of that but I went for it anyway. She's good at what she does. I filled her in on all the details. She tried to tousle my hair, but it was more of a rub since I keep my hair very short. Then another peck on the lips and she was on her way.

## 23.

I phoned the French Hotel. He wasn't in his room. I called the café in what passes for a lobby and described Terry. Not there. I called Marvin's cell.

"He's in the Elephant Pharmacy buying St. John's Wort. I'm just out of earshot, stocking up on shaving supplies. There's a sale."

Marvin shaves every third or fourth day and when he does he goes first class.

"Why don't you hop in your little car and meet us here? We'll probably be checking out in ten. We can go over to César's for a drinky-poo."

"Why not." The Elephant Pharmacy is a hippie-chain corner drugstore. Herbs, chair massage, nutrition classes. Disgusting, but the prices are pretty good and the clerks are cute, in a New Agey sort of way.

I drove the Tercel into the lot and got a space first thing. Uncanny. The gods were with me. The automatic doors opened and I was hit with a wave of patchouli and sage. Not exactly perfume, Scotch, and cigarettes. I tried not to inhale too deeply. Marvin and Terry were at the checkout. Perfect timing. I could taste the Negronis.

"Drinky-poos!" This from Marvin, with a little too much volume. So much enthusiasm for a man his age. Terry looked a little scared. It's hard to know how to take Marvin at first.

I knew when we left the store that there was trouble. We cut left toward the Econoline, parked next to the Tercel. Three guys and a woman exited a black Taurus. They'd found a space too. Amazing. The woman looked like Hilary Swank in thug drag. Probably a yuppie, I thought. Until she kicked me in the knee. Caught us all off guard.

I countered with a lame right that she blocked. Marvin opened the van and pushed Terry in. Meanwhile I took another one for the team, a chopping left from one of her friends. Marvin fished around in his sweatshirt, where was that gun? But he was a little slow and they all drew. We were fucked. Terry was hustled into the Taurus and we were left looking like fools.

Marvin wanted to follow them but I had what I thought was a better idea. We barreled up 24 and under the tunnel. We got to the house in Snorinda in about fifteen minutes, record time.

I could hobble up to the house but I couldn't kick the door. Marvin rolled his eyes and did it himself. It was a tough door. Didn't budge. Marvin fished out the gun. I backed off and covered my ears. I hate those things. He shot the knob, well, the door really, off. Someday he'll do this and I'll catch the ricochet.

"Marvin, you fucker! There are easier ways to do that."

"But this is the fastest, gimpy." He pushed the door open. Empty house. No furniture, no Franz Kline. No bottles at the bar. We checked.

The place was easy to search. Bare floors. Not much else. We walked in the walk-ins and we checked the cupboards. Lots of shrugs. Went out into the yard. Nice yard. Marvin sat on the grass and pulled out his pipe.

"Do you think this is the right time for that?"

"Helps me think. Did you call Dao?"

"A couple of times." He offered me the pipe. I don't smoke much, but my knee hurt like shit. Not the first time I'd taken a hit there. I took the pipe.

## 24.

I spent the rest of the day climbing various phone trees, trying to reach Jerry Wally at Jerry's Drugs and More. Bailey Dao left a message. She was on the case. Hope she didn't expect payment. I was now working against my employer. Not very lucrative, but more comfortable, at least for me. Marvin loved it. The revolution and all. He didn't do this stuff for the money. He made enough at his day job. He was involved in this for, as he said, the pure fuck of it. Wanted to get himself a CEO.

I needed the kind of information that you can't get from a Google search, and all I could do was wait. I went downstairs and around the corner to BayKing for a donut. I checked out the poetry section at Moe's. Decided to do some book scouting. What else was there to do?

I've been a book bum since I dropped out of college, twenty-some years ago. I've worked in chain stores, in one-man operations, and everything in between. I owned a store in Santa Cruz called Campion's, out on Soquel Avenue near the movie theater. I've scouted books all along. The Goodwill, estate sales, whatever. At this point I don't know what else I'd do. I sort of take it for granted that the detective thing will dry out. I'm not inclined to do it forever.

I went home to the Chandler, up the antique elevator to the fourth floor. Said hi to the cat and went into the kitchen. There's a false bottom in one of the cupboards. I pulled out my stash of bills. Not that many. I'd been living well. I grabbed off a few twenties.

The Tercel was pretty close by. More good luck. I pointed it toward San Pablo, left toward Emeryville. There's an especially trashy little secondhand store down there. Proprietor's a real character. Bob Kelly. Slim Pickens type, and there's always a friend with him, shooting the shit. Today's pal looked like Mississippi John Hurt. If you stopped to count his wrinkles, you'd be held up for hours. For some reason I was tempted to do just that.

"Clay Blackburn, poet detective. I've got books for you." He motioned to his book section, a scuffed-up old pine bookcase. I nodded hello and went to the case. Bibles! I can always turn over bibles. I picked out seven, all except the one that was stolen from a hotel room. They were in good shape. Bibles seldom look read.

"The word of the Lord, yes sir." John Hurt nodded, looked serious.

"Five bucks per, Clay. These are nice. Leather!" He grabbed one from me and smelled it. "Rich Corinthian leather." Said with a phony accent. A phlegmy laugh from John Hurt.

I'd be lucky to make three apiece in today's book economy. "Ten for the stack, Bob. I can't get much for those."

"Tell you what. You go across the street to the Black Muslim's and get us a couple of muffins, then to the market for a couple of Millers. Good combination. That and the ten buys you a stack of good books."

I took the deal. Went across the street and bought muffins from the polite young man in white shirt and skinny tie. I was in the liquor store when the phone rang. Grace.

"It's Friday. What time are you picking me up?"

I'd forgotten, but it was only two thirty. Plenty of time to get to the reading.

"I'll see you in three hours."

"What does one wear to a poetry reading?"

"Is this your first?"

"I saw Robert Pinsky in college."

"Then it is your first. Wear whatever you like, nobody pays attention."

"Thanks, Clay."

"To your clothes, I mean. You'll get plenty of attention. I've never met a poet who wasn't on the sniff."

I bought the Millers, crossed the street, and made the deal. Put my copies of the good book in the shopping bag. They had heft, smelled good, meant good reading to somebody, somewhere. Best of all, there was one non-bible in the bunch, a boxed edition of *The History of Tom Jones*. Still, these books would bring in chicken feed. I'd have to find another way to make a living. A detective's license? Hard to imagine. Maybe with Dao as a front...

I had a little less than three hours to kill. I pulled out the cell, left messages with Bailey and Marvin. I would have followed up on some leads but I couldn't think of any. Besides, I had that copy of *Tom Jones*. I drove down to the Marina, past the Trader Vic's, past the Watergate Apartments, and found a parking place facing the Golden Gate. A cool wind was kicking up so I stayed in the car. I rescued *Tom Jones* from beneath the bibles. That Wesleyan University Press edition, edited by Battestin and Bowers, is the one I know best, although I've read the book a few times, including once on a plane to Dalian, China, in a lurid pocket edition from the '60s.

I decided to use the book the way I use *Gunslinger*, the way others use the *I Ching*. Art is my religion. Why not? Does all the same things that God does and is a lot less destructive... "I was second to none of the Company in any acts of Debauchery; nay, I soon distinguished myself so notably in all Riots and Disorders... as I have addicted myself more and more to loose pleasure..." For the sheer fuck of it. This from Marvin, or a Marvin-like voice in my head, not from Henry Fielding, though it could be, in spirit.

I had distinguished myself in all riots and disorders, but I was still nibbling around this case. I once lit a cop car on fire, with Marvin's help. We were able to get away, and when we were at a safe distance we stopped for a drink. About two-thirds of the way into my Negroni I had an attack of the postmodern heebie-jeebies. How on earth would this help the revolution? What revolution? Could any good come of this? I turned to Marvin with my questions, but before I could open my mouth he said, "For the fuck of it. For the sheer fuck of it."

I got out of the car and felt the cool, no, cold, breeze. Litter was flying around, Candlestick Park–style. Sometimes I hate the wind off the bay, but it does keep things clean. I walked along the water, covering my left ear against the wind. I began to tear up a little, which seemed dumb but then it didn't. I'd been nibbling around. It was time to get to the bottom of this rather absurd mystery. Time to throw caution to the, um, wind. Wreak a little havoc on some CEO. For the sheer fuck of it.

For now, though, I was almost late for a date. Grace lived close, so I was within minutes of being on time.

## 25.

Walking with Grace out to the car, I felt a mixture of intense lust and, I'll admit it, male pride. Dressed down and debaubled, in poetry-reading black, straight-stuff perfect, the toughness of her walk and her demeanor took front and center.

"We could just go to the Chandler. Forget the reading."

"You're being too obvious, Clay. We'll do the reading first."

I reached into my pocket and turned off my phone, got into the Tercel, and we were off. No distractions tonight. I'd decided to pull a switch. The Charles Bernstein talk at SF State just wouldn't do it, even though it was the event of the poetry season. Something having to do with Olson and Heidegger, as seen through the ever-expanding ether of the post-poet permafrost of a warming globe. Heady stuff, but not very sexy. Decided instead to stay in the East Bay. Michael Swindle at Book Zoo, very boho. Grace didn't mind either way, was possibly relieved. Bernstein is a snore. As I drove up Telegraph we talked a little about books and current events, and for some unknown reason, Beethoven's late quartets. I'd never thought of those pieces as sexy. I do now.

I liked the way her mouth looked when she formed certain words. I liked the third tattoo up from the elbow, though I couldn't quite make out what it was. It was a light blue. Her skin was very white. Once, waiting for the light at Ashby, I looked at her collarbone against the black of her T-shirt and half closed my eyes as if I were protecting them from glare. For this I got a confused look and, "Are you all right?"

"I'm smitten."

"God. Poets."

I parked at the Chandler and we walked back to the strange little alcove of a mall, somebody's mid-'70s idea of a themed shopping center, the theme long forgotten. There were remnants of a palm-laden South Sea shack look, but only remnants. The anchor business was, and still is, a fondue place. Good god.

Book Zoo is all the way in the back of the semi-covered building. Closet-sized, but stuffed with weird and interesting books. Swindle, the guest of honor, was drinking a beer in the doorway.

"How's the tour?"

"Low-budget fun. But I'm starting to miss New Orleans."

Nice drawl, I thought. I'd read a couple of his pieces in the *Village Voice*, figured he'd do a fun reading. I looked around him into the store. Erik, the proprietor, was opening bottles of Two-Buck Chuck, nothing but the best. Leonard Cohen's first album was, I swear, playing on a turntable next to the register. Berkeley.

There are a few of these places left. Maybe they'll survive the mid-sized independents, since the overhead is low and the proceeds only need to feed a couple of mouths. I went over a mental list of these strange little places. Austin, Boulder, Boston. I hear there's one in Brooklyn. Places where I've done readings or sold a few books to pay for gas and lunch.

We walked in and found a place on the carpet, all eyes on Grace. We leaned on a shelf of old John D. MacDonald pulp. America's greatest gift to literature, next to Jackie Susann. Grace moved left and I shifted right and our sides were touching.

The audience arrived, tattooed and scruffy, save for a few Berkeley lit types. Barry Gifford, John McBride, Julia Vinograd. The under-the-radar crowd. Erik brought us wine before starting the show with a rambling introduction. Swindle, sitting in a well-worn easy chair, seemed to be dozing. He woke up and read stories about life in the Deep South: NASCAR, hound dogs, much drinking. Aside from the drinking it was news from another planet. The Berkeley kids took it all in and laughed at the right time. There was a smoke/drink break, then another and another. The stories went on. I looked for signs of boredom from Grace, but she seemed happily involved. I was impressed.

Swindle finished his last story, something having to do with the Zapatistas, and a Patti Smith record came on. A turntable!

I paid my respects to the reader and his friends, anxious to get Grace back to the Chandler for some post-reading nookie. We hit the street, giggling, our sides touching, finishing off the last of our wine.

Top of the world, the pure laser of lust pushing at our extremities. Even the streetlamps pumped out a flattering light. A black Land Rover rolled by, real slow, windows down, playing, of all things, a Steely Dan song, "Babylon Sisters." I felt a little defensive, for a second. Hadn't I seen that car before? With that guy driving? But then the feeling passed and I was back in the moment. Go for the cotton candy.

The breeze had died away, leaving a very warm night. If we get more than a week like this in a year, we're lucky. Thought about warm parts of the world that I'd been to, Mexico, Sicily, Honolulu. People half dressed on the Avenue, drinking and hanging out on the little triangle park across from the Chandler. It would be noisy in the apartment tonight, but who needs sleep.

We were half undressed by the time the elevator reached the fourth floor. Made the front door, fed the cat, fast. Fell onto the couch. Everything moist and matted, hot-weather sex. Somehow down on the floor when we finally got down to fucking, background music coming from the triangle, some hip-hop thing. Up the hill, then down again like a roller coaster, that roller coaster feeling in the groin, then up again ... the double fuck, then down again, going down. Then a conga, somebody in the park. Made us giggle.

"How do you sleep here?"

"It gets real quiet around three a.m. Besides, I don't need much sleep."

I'm usually real good at subtly turning off the phone. Nothing subtle about tonight's entrance. It rang, I didn't get it. I'd turned my cell off before the reading. They'd call back. We were close, relaxing. Fuck the phone. It rang again. I rolled over, got off the floor, and picked up.

Bailey Dao. "Hey, fucker. Don't ever turn off the cell when we're working on a case. That's completely unprofessional."

"So I'm only semi-pro. What's up?"

"The cops have Terry's body. I'm at the Emeryville Marina. Get here fast, but park at the Chinese restaurant and walk out to the pier. Stay clear of the cops. They're going to question you at some point, but let's not rush it. Let me handle things."

A control freak, and she is bigger than me. Some partner. I dressed, reluctantly, and left Grace to sleep in my bed.

## 26.

I walked down Dwight to the car. The bagpipe guy was on the triangle, inflating the bag in preparation for another rendition of "Amazing Grace." He was late this night. His usual routine involves marching down the street to Caffe Med and ordering a coffee. It was past midnight, the Med was closed. The wind hadn't come back but the fog was in, and "Amazing Grace" felt especially soulful to me, for the obvious reason.

I found the Tercel and it sounded pretty rough. Time for a new muffler, perhaps a tune-up. Put it in gear and pointed toward Emeryville, past warehouses, high-crime districts, and live-work yuppie hutches. The marina was almost fogged in. I parked in the lot of the giant dim sum house at the water's edge. Walked toward the blinking red lights. I didn't really hide, but I stayed behind some bushes. I spotted Bailey Dao and she answered my wave.

Bailey crossed over to the bay side of the break. She was wearing a black turtleneck, extra long, and black jeans that had been tailored. One red streak in her short, very black hair. She's the kind of presence that makes you forget to breathe, sometimes for a couple of breaths. She looked at me the way I imagine she would look at a bug, but I took no offense. She'd probably learned that at the FBI school.

"They didn't weight him down much. Assuming they're pros, they probably wanted him to be discovered."

"They're trying to keep a lid on some folks."

"Why?"

"Something to do with plastic surgery."

"Using doubles as bodyguards? That would be a minor scandal. This is some serious damage control."

I was stumped. "You're the fed. What do you think?"

"We need to talk to your ex-cashier."

"I've talked to her."

"Between humps. Try it with your clothes on."

"Jealous?"

"You're not my type. I kind of like your partner, though."

A couple of detectives came over, flashlights flashing. In case there's some question, they really do wear cheap suits. Bailey gave me a look that said, Let me do the talking. And so I did. I nodded, smiled, shucked and jived. After a few questions they seemed satisfied that I was an idiot and flashed their way back to the car.

Bailey shooed me away and I got into the Tercel.

## 27.

I was barely out of the Emeryville Marina, Watergate Apartments and Holiday Inn to my left, when the cell rang. Bailey. "Wait for me at your place. I'll ask a few more questions, then I'll be at your door."

Entering my place I noticed a piece of paper on the floor. Nice note from Grace. She felt like sleeping at home, took a cab.

It was late, almost early, when Bailey marched into my apartment. I have some Xmas lights around my dining area. That was all the light I needed, mixed with the streetlight, almost at window level. The cat was sacked out on the couch. Bailey startled her and she ran like hell. Bailey didn't notice. She went straight into my closet and fished out a white T. Took off her black shirt and wiped off the sweat. Small but decidedly female breasts. A solid wall of muscle, beautiful brown. Sunbather? She hesitated while I gawked but she didn't smile. Put my T-shirt on. Too small, but in a good way.

"Do you mind, partner?"

"Not at all, but I didn't know we were that close."

"We can talk about that later. Let's get Marvin over here and put our heads together."

"Marvin will be sleeping."

"Somebody just got murdered. He can wake up for that."

Marvin picked up halfway through his message,

"Fuck you, I'm tired. I bought books today. Remember book scouting? A stack of Harry Potters from some dumb kid, possibly stolen, and three boxes of lit. So who got murdered?"

Good long silence on the phone. He'd be right over.

It wasn't quite early enough to call it morning drinking, so I pulled out a bottle of Campo Azul and poured myself a shot. I offered the bottle and a glass to Bailey. She took a pull off the bottle before pouring herself a generous shot. "J. Edgar Hoover used to drink this stuff."

"Really?" I was pretty sleepy.

She shook her head and snorted. "You're a putz, Clay. But I like saving your ass. What happened to your boyfriend?"

"Dino's down in Columbia, I think."

"A walking bag of shit, but attractive." I just nodded. Couldn't really disagree. But there are many lonely nights when I think about Dino Centro.

The phone broke my reverie. Marvin was downstairs. I buzzed him in and opened his door. Heard his hard clomp on the stairs. There wasn't going to be much subtlety in the room, unless I counted myself.

He nodded to Bailey Dao, but it wasn't a respectful nod. She offered him the bottle and he softened his look a bit. Took a healthy swig and offered his hand. They eyed each other, up and down, then shook. Marvin was wearing plaid pajama bottoms and a long leather jacket, no shirt. Hiking boots. He caught us looking, countered with, "A sweet disorder in the dress kindles in clothes a wantonness." Then he opened his coat to reveal a shoulder holster. Oh god. "So are we doing this for the revolution or did somebody hire us?"

"I figured I'd have to do some pro bono work at first, make my reputation." This from Bailey, her eyes on Marvin. "If I solve this, I'll have some cachet with the police. Wally paid you something, didn't he?" she asked me.

"Yes, and he owes me some more, but I doubt I'll be able to collect. He wanted me to lead him to some people and I did. I'm expendable. I feel responsible for Terry, though. Don't you, Marvin?"

He opened his coat again. His pj's weren't very well secured. "I say we find Wally and shake him down for back wages. Then we put a bullet in his head."

"No way," Bailey said. "I'll lose my new license." As she said this it occurred to me that I'd never seen a detective's license. "First we shake him down for your money, then we blow his operation wide open. Let Walgreens take over the market. The publicity will get us lots of work. When I finish this sex change I'll be the new Philip fucking Marlowe."

Bailey Dao was quite the careerist. I was worried about all that publicity. I didn't need the scrutiny. Could lead to an audit. Book scouts hate audits.

"Okay, I won't blow him away, but I'll scare the shit out of him. Fucking capitalist."

"We'll put him behind bars and get rich in the process." Bailey killed the tequila. I went into the kitchen and found some more.

## 28.

Grace to be born and live as variously as possible. Amazing Grace. Tattoos and perfume. The double fuck. The double fuck! Who said I can't question someone that I'm sleeping with. She practically climbs into your mouth when she kisses you. Cool and dry shall come the results of inquiry. The double fuck! The place where the tattoos end on the upper arm, then the shoulder and the back of the neck, that Louise Brooks hairline.

They had stayed till about ten a.m., I'd slept till three, and now I was cleaning up and not quite calling Grace, putting it off the way you put off nibbling the last piece of icing on your plate. Too many questions could drive her away, or maybe not. Indecisiveness like that often gets me through dish doing and sweeping.

Cool and dry come the results of inquiry. I called Grace and left a message, juiced up the cell phone, and took to the Avenue. I was going to make my rounds, scout some books (I was running low on cash), and hopefully run into Bruce. I was pretty sure that there was more information in that rearranged head, if I could just break the code. I poked around Shakespeare & Co., then Moe's. No gaping holes in the shelves. Elliott and Laura were at the buying counter, tough hombres. It would be difficult to sell my wares, if I found some wares. I checked out the bestseller tables at Cody's to see what New York was foisting on us, then walked up Haste to the Tercel. Every good scouting day must start with espresso. I drove down to San Pablo, found a great parking place, and got in a rather long line at the Trieste. Scanned the room for Maser, White, or Jocko. No go. Not a book dealer in sight. All out hunting treasures, I supposed.

I found a table near the window and sat down with a second-hand sports page. I saw him crossing Dwight, weaving as usual, that huge knot on his forehead. Too tan from living outside. Head recently shaved. He crossed against the light, dodging cars. Surprising agile.

I waved, and he recognized me. He stopped at the door. Had he been eighty-sixed? Probably just expected to be. The Trieste is a classy place. Not especially unfriendly, but some things go without saying. I got up and met him at the door.

"You've been looking for me."

"I was worried about you."

He bowed his head. I felt that guilt that you feel on city streets, if you get out to the street, if you feel guilt. "Can I come in for coffee?" He didn't smell especially bad, but he looked pretty well worn. I wondered what the baristas would think.

"Sure, Bruce. I'll buy."

"You go up to the bar, okay?"

I ordered a double espresso. Not a second look from the barista. I felt good about the place. With a second thought I grabbed a pastry.

He downed the pastry in two chews, the coffee in a gulp.

"I have information, Clay."

"What's up?"

He was getting pretty wound up. He held the edge of the table and swayed. His face reddened. He worked his mouth without saying anything.

"Take it easy, Bruce." I put my hand on his shoulder.

"Can you spare some cash?"

I pulled out a ten. Detective work is expensive. He took it, looked at it with disdain.

"I need a hotel room and a shower. I got kicked out of my halfway house, I'm sleeping on cardboard."

"What do you know?"

"I know a lot."

"I'm not exactly rich right now." God. I was negotiating with a homeless person.

"I can tell you a lot if you take me to the pink motel on MacArthur and put me up for two nights." He nodded, too hard. "It will be worth it."

I'd already led a murderer to one victim. I wasn't going to do it again.

"Okay, here's the deal," I said. "You tell me everything you can. Then you wait here. I'll go to the ATM and get you some cash. Then you take a cab to the Holiday Inn Express on University. Nobody will find you there."

He let out a guffaw. "I'm homeless. They won't let me in."

"I'll meet you there and check in. Then I'll hand off the key. You stay there till I come get you."

"Like a secret agent!"

"Just like. Now, what do you want to tell me?"

"They beat up Larry pretty bad but I don't know why."

"Who?"

Long pause. This was going to be a puzzle. I looked into his eyes. I imagined for a second that I could see through to the back of his head. Big white chunks of ambiguity sandwiched between red sections of unimaginable pain. He was reliving the beating. "I was outside Bongo eating a falafel." He drifted back into his head for a full minute. "You know where Joji's lot is?"

"I live on that block."

"Oh yeah. I forget things."

"It's okay, Bruce. Tell me more."

"I saw Larry's van, parked in the lot. That's illegal, Clay. Joji gets real mad if you park there. I thought I could maybe get something to smoke from Larry. Sometimes he gives me stuff. I heard them talking, so I hid behind Joji's shack. They were asking where Terry was. They were hitting Larry. It sounded terrible."

"Who were they?"

He screwed up his mouth, then he went kind of buggy-eyed. I waited. He was feeling the punches. "The guy was British." He spit the words out. Did he not like Brits? "The girl was pretty. I only saw her from the back, but she was pretty."

"What did the Brit look like?"

"He was big."

"When did all this happen?"

A blank look. Bruce had little sense of time. "It was at night."

I bought him a second coffee and crossed the street to an ATM.

## 29.

I took a snaky back route to University, parked the car blocks away, took a little walk, entered the back door of an art store, came out the front. No evidence that I was being followed. Found an alley, came out on University near the hotel.

I found the office and registered at the Holiday Inn. Paid two days in advance, cash. Gave them a phony license number. Went out to the sidewalk. Out of habit, or something, Bruce was spare-changing pedestrians.

"I need a little something for dinner."

I gave him twenty dollars. "I'll call a pizza place and have them deliver. Pay them with this. Don't leave the room. Just take it easy."

"Will they beat me up?"

"Only if they find you. Stay put."

I took out my cell and called Extreme Pizza on Shattuck. Was Bruce a vegetarian? To be safe I ordered a medium with mushrooms and peppers and a couple of cans of Coke.

If Grace is the woman who beat up Larry, I'll die, I thought, then I caught myself. Detectives can't be sentimental. Can they? How would I know. I put in a call to her, one to Bailey, and one to Marvin. Nobody home, anywhere. I pointed the Tercel down University, took a right on San Pablo, then a right on Solano, up to the Tibetan place. No van, no Larry. Decided to scout some books till something broke.

I hit a couple of secondhand stores on University. Only a couple of things, but it felt good to be scouting. I was born to root around old books. All those words, all those sentences, some of them great. Even the bad ones are amusing. Especially the bad ones! Old pulp, self-published poetry, somebody's first novel.

Lots of words, lots of books, but nothing I could sell. I gathered up some pocket books. I could trade them at Moe's, maybe sell the trade slip to Julia Vinograd or one of the café intellectuals at the Med. I'd have to start going farther afield to get books. More trips down to San Jose, even LA. Ugh. Have to sell more business books online. This isn't why I got into the book business.

I drove down to Telegraph, did the deed, and did in fact sell the trade slip to Julia for half value. She offered to sell me her latest book of poetry, but I already had a copy. "That Larry guy with the kooky van is looking for you. He's parked in the lot at Brennan's. Says he'll be there all day. Gore Vidal didn't kill JFK. Did he?"

I downed my pinkie lifter and went back out to the Tercel. Back down University to Fourth Street. I was getting tired of driving.

Brennan's has been on that spot for as long as anyone can remember. I've never been in an Irish bar with more square footage. It's Chinese owned, but there's always a token bartender, pasty skinned and often a redhead. There are sandwiches, carved hofbrau-style from big scary roasts. Not many places left like this in California.

## 30.

I ordered an Irish coffee. I was on a caffeine bender. The alcohol would help calm me a bit. I nodded to Barry Gifford, who was at the other end of the bar, talking to a man with slicked-back hair. Sadly, I was beyond eavesdropping range. They were probably discussing a movie deal.

The bar was dark. As my eyes got used to the light I realized that the scraggly-looking guy in the far corner was Marvin. With Larry! Why hadn't I noticed their vans? I paid for my coffee and went back to join them.

"Cuba's not what it used to be, but you'll do okay. All my old friends are gone. Only people I see there now are Fidel and his flaky brother. All dead, or sellouts. Or both."

"Do you think the glitterati will find me there?"

"No reason to look, Larry. Besides, your biggest problem now is Wally."

"You don't know what you're talking about. Updike's out to get me. He could get a visa."

"No chance. Fidel hates Updike."

"Can I take the van?"

"Larry! Dig this, Cuba's an island. You can't drive there."

Larry slumped in his chair, stuck out his lower lip, then noticed me. Frowned. I put my hand on Marvin's shoulder. He turned and smiled. I noticed that he was still wearing a shoulder holster.

"Clay Blackburn, I beat you to your clue. What do you think of that. Beat out you and your G-girl. Or is it G-boy? Larry here is on the lam. Seems he was privy to some info regarding Terry and Drugstore Wally. Going to spill the frijoles if we get him safe passage. Right?"

Larry nodded. "Don't try and hit me, Clay."

I wanted the info, but I couldn't afford to send a stool pigeon to Cuba. What was Marvin thinking?

"We need to get Larry to a safe place, so he can talk. Then we need to get him on a plane. Okay, Clay?" This from Marvin, with a wink and a nod. I decided to play along.

"Where are the vans?"

"Larry's is in a safe place, and mine is down at the Marina. We were being followed."

"Me too."

"Big black SUV."

"Yeah, I noticed it too," I lied.

"There were at least three in the parking lot." He nodded toward Gifford. "One belongs to them. Do you think they're in on it?"

Larry looked at us with contempt. "Barry isn't part of the conspiracy." Rolled his eyes.

We needed a new ride. I decided to call around. Maybe somebody could pick us up, or maybe a cab. Pulled out the cell. There was a message from Bailey. I'd turned it off at Moe's because the buyers hate it when you take calls at the counter. Forgot to turn it back on. I called her back and she picked up. I explained the situation. "Hold tight and I'll think of something."

And so we ordered a second round. The bar began to fill up, working-class types and serious drunks. And the mayor. I noticed him at a table near the door, talking to John McBride. Despite the representation of Berkeley celebs, Brennan's seems far from Berkeley. I imagined myself in the Barbary Coast, circa 1919. That stale beer smell, people gnawing on turkey wings. Only thing missing was cigarette smoke. Marvin regaled us with his tales of not-so-old Havana, and of trips back with suitcases full of cigars and rum. I could feel the hot sun reflecting off an Edsel, could smell the gas fumes and the cigar smoke. What was I doing in the US?

God help me, my cell phone plays "London Calling." I'm sorry, Joe Strummer, wherever you are. I couldn't help myself. It played the tune for Bailey Dao, trans detective.

"Two cars. The lead car is an old VW Fastback. You guys get in and the second car will run interference. Wait five minutes and get out, to the front door. Got it?"

We downed our coffee and hit the sidewalk as the cars pulled up. The second was an old Econoline, flat black, similar to Marvin's. We piled into the Fastback, Bailey at the wheel. This was no ordinary

VW. We were dodging cars and running lights, down to the Marina, around and back up University, right on Sixth Street. I assume the van was blocking the black SUV, or causing a diversion, or something. Bailey slowed down and we took a joyride around town, finally ending up at the Holiday Inn Express.

"I had it rebuilt. Great little car," she explained as she tore through the parking lot. She made a sharp left into an alley and parked the car. Illegal, but harder to spot. She was wearing a powder-blue business suit, set off by the yellow, hip-hoppy running shoes.

I knocked twice and Bruce cracked the door, then let us in.

"I'm sorry I ate all the pizza." He and Larry gave each other the once-over twice.

"Don't worry about that. We're going to put our heads together and solve this mystery." I hoped. I looked around the room, realized that I was the closest one to sanity. A rare occasion. I began with Larry.

"Who beat you up? And why?"

"An English guy and a woman with short dark hair."

"What did they want?"

"Terry was a double. They said they'd kill me if I told. And they told me not to get near you. That you're good as dead."

Bruce nodded, so hard that I absentmindedly rubbed my neck. "Terry wasn't Terry. No, no. Terry was Terry, but he was made to look like somebody else. I told you that, Clay. You owe me money."

"How do you know this stuff?"

Bruce went all buggy-eyed. "Larry's father owns the building! And he won't even give me any pot!" He gave Larry a look that could kill, if it wasn't so comically cockeyed. "Trust fund baby!"

I exchanged looks with Marvin, then with Bailey. We had ourselves a client.

"I don't usually offer to help out capitalists, but I'll make an exception for you."

"They won't kill me if I don't tell."

"Too many people know. Someone will squeal, and you'll get blamed. Then they'll come after you. Besides, you're not supposed to be talking to Clay here. This conversation could get you killed." Marvin was laying it on thick.

"What are you going to do about it?"

"We'll chase 'em outta Berkeley."

I didn't buy it, but Larry did. Six hundred a day plus expenses, split three ways. Wouldn't make us rich but it would pay the rent. Bailey smiled her noble savage smile, leaned back, and closed her eyes. Rewriting her résumé.

"I'll be broke within a week."

Bruce looked at the ground, shook his head. He seemed to have some secret knowledge of Larry's bank account.

Marvin gave me the stink eye. He was going for a two-week contract and he knew I was getting soft. I decided to stop him. "Okay, Larry, give us a week. After that we renegotiate."

## 31.

Time to call in a few favors. I called a friend in Inverness, a few miles from Point Reyes. Billy Loy. He had two cabins. He lived in one, on a little rise, and he rented the next-door cabin to tourists. He had a shotgun and a redneck mentality. If anybody tried to trespass, or if his tourist-tenants got out of line, out came the gun. I offered to rent the cabin but he said no go. I could have it for free for a week. I explained that a nut and homeless person would be living there, and offered to leave a deposit.

"I've been renting to lawyers and financial types all year. They're boring and they're slobs. I'll bet they don't treat their 'live-work spaces' the way they treat my cabins. A couple of loonies will be a relief. Hope they smoke the pot!"

Bailey came up with a plan involving two cars, alternate routes, and a nice lunch at a winery, where we got some funny looks. Guess we looked pretty Berkeley. Not many homeless people among the vineyards. Or transsexuals in three-piece Efrem Zimbalist Jr. suits (Bailey's outfit of the day). Throw in a Neil Young look-alike and you have a great group. Larry, the craziest of the lot, looks like a stockbroker. I can fit in anywhere. At least until I start throwing Dr. Pepper cans.

Three nice bottles of pinot for four is a perfect amount if you're driving. Shortens the road without too much impairment. Bruce put on a good show, swirling, sniffing, and practically gargling. His conclusion: not as much fun as smoking crack, but okay if somebody else is paying. We toasted Larry.

We took the narrow roads to the cabin with that special deftness that a partially liquid lunch inspires. We learned that Larry had a great singing voice. He'd adapted some of John Updike's dreadful poems, singing them Gilbert and Sullivan–style.

"I respect those guys, assassins that they are. And I don't just do the big boys. Listen to this!" He lowered his voice and his cadence became more bluesy. A few verses into the song I recognized a passage from the avant-garde classic *The Bell Clerk's Tears Kept Flowing* by Stephen Rodefer. I was impressed.

"I was a Language poet after the surrealists kicked me out. No, check that. It was after Ron Padgett cut me in Gem Spa. Wouldn't even say hello. Berrigan, Clark, Notley ... minor leaguers, really. A few heists here and there. Although I hear that Dick Gallup was a Soviet agent. But that's hearsay. Not worth repainting the van. Did you know that Amiri Baraka used to rob banks? He's calmed down a bit."

And he went on like that for a long, long time. Finally Marvin had the presence of mind to ask for another song. "Do you know anything by Basil Bunting?"

He sang a song about a bull, and before we knew it we were at the cabin. There was a great-smelling breeze coming up from Tomales Bay. I could almost taste the oysters. What a great hideout. Did we really need to solve this case?

Billy Loy came down from his place and met us with the keys. He was carrying an Oakland A's carry-on bag. We entered the cabin, one big living room and attached kitchen, a couple of small bedrooms and a bathroom. Big windows looking out at the trees. Woodstove, lots of books. We smiled. Billy smiled.

He opened the bag. "Who needs guns?" I hate guns, have never used one. I've done all right with a brain and my fists. I decided to swallow my disapproval. Guns might be a good idea. We were, after all, fighting a drugstore chain.

"Glocks for all! Got 'em from this guy who runs a speed lab. They can't be traced. But please, be careful. Don't shoot up the place unless you have to. I get two-fifty a night in high season." He gave me a look. "We're even after this, Clay."

"Even. Thanks, Billy."

## 32.

Bruce looked longingly at Marvin's Glock. We wouldn't let him have one. Larry grabbed a gun, saying, "I paid for this microphone!" We watched as he loaded the gun. He knew what he was doing. Straight as he looks, it doesn't take a health care professional to know he's crazy. He looked to the ceiling (and the floor). "Lock and load!"

Marvin showed me how to load my gun, though I protested. I wouldn't use it. Well, just in case.

It was still light, and warm. Late summer breeze and the scent of a forest fire, but off in the distance. I took a walk down to the bay with Marvin. He brought out his pipe as we sat on the beach.

"Who do you trust, Clay?"

"Bailey's okay. We have a good history."

He made a face. "She's a bit much, but I trust her."

"Bruce would go through hell for us, but he's likely to say the wrong thing."

"Well, yeah, the nuts. We'll hide them as best we can ..."

"Larry's the money source. We're obligated to protect him."

"My only obligation is to bring down capitalism." He took a nice long hit, let it out, then a hooting laugh.

"We also have to pay for stuff," I said, pointing to his pipe.

"Point well taken. We'll hit him up for a big advance. Case he gets killed. And do you trust your girlfriend?"

"She hasn't answered my calls. I have to believe she's one of Wally's goons." My heart sank. The zipless fuck that wasn't.

Marvin put away the pipe. He put his hand on my shoulder. We were facing east, and the sun was getting low behind us. It hit the water on the shallow bay, bounced around the trees, glanced off the cars down the road. There were browns and golds, but the dominant color was orange. I thought of how terrible orange is, and life.

## 33.

Marvin's eyes got wide, wide as they could considering his marijuana intake. "Oysters! Johnson's will be closed!"

We raced up the path to the cabin. Bailey was drinking a glass of wine on the porch. We got the keys to the Fastback and took off down the coast. Johnson's Oyster Farm is a ramshackle clump of old houses, hugging the oyster beds. We made our way past the dogs and cats that congregate under the NO DOGS ALLOWED sign. Four dozen small, unshucked. Then back in the car and down to town. Bread, salad makings, many bottles of white wine. A serious situation calls for a serious meal.

We sent Larry up to get Billy and we arranged dinner. Bruce grabbed the shucker and proceeded to shuck, fast. "I used to do this for a living in New Orleans." Our secret lives.

You know you're in for a good meal when a couple of bottles are gone before you sit down. I was tipsy before I touched an oyster. They were perfect, and when they are, they are the perfect food. The wine was cold and clean. We had Tabasco and limes, but mostly we downed the oysters naked, followed by several good gulps of sauvignon blanc.

When the oysters were gone we picked at the salad and the bread. When you've been through a few bizarre event turns you learn how to enjoy those moments of relaxation. Things got quiet, and I knew we were in for some interesting after-dinner conversation. Billy Loy must have sensed it too. He jumped up, ran out the door, and came back with two bottles of absinthe plus paraphernalia and a big chunk of hashish.

For a second I thought it was a bad idea. Shouldn't we have a guard? Weren't we being followed? I decided not to mention it. Marvin was a soldier of fortune and Bailey Dao was ex-FBI. If they were willing to chance it, so was I. I also worried that Larry or Bruce might not handle it well. But what the hell. They couldn't get any crazier than they already were.

I hadn't had the hash/absinthe combination in years. It was in Barcelona, back room of a bar, a night that revived my bisexual interests, after a too-long hiatus.

"If someone's chasing you down the street with a knife, you just run," Marvin was saying. "You don't turn around and shout, 'Give it up! I was a track star at Mineola Prep.' You go on your nerve. That's the best part of doing what we do. Something clicks and you just move. There's freedom in that. It's outside all the rules. A sweet moment of anarchy."

I'd missed the setup to his speech, but it didn't matter. Everything was humming along.

"Yes! You're the thing you're doing, you're not yourself. Look hard enough at something and you forget that you're going to die." This from Bailey, then a dramatic nod from Marvin. They were bonding, the lawman and the train robber. Same skills, same attitude.

I didn't comment. I was a rookie compared to these two. A book scout/poet who dabbled in crime solving. I downed the rest of my drink, got up, and wobbled out to the porch. I spread my arms and let the air sober me up a bit, not too much. There was a nice pile of dry wood at the far end of the porch. It took me at least three hours to pick up some wood. Looking across the porch at the dark and the trees, I was about half an inch from an epiphany. As I waited for it to come, across the porch rail I noticed movement in the trees. I stood straight, listened hard, tried to focus. But my focus didn't last and there was no more sound. My epiphany disappeared, or was lost on me, like Kerouac's *Satori in Paris*.

I marched inside and built a wood fire. Quite an accomplishment, considering my level of inebriation. I heard murmurs, then everyone moved toward the stove. Nobody said much then.

After a time that I couldn't measure I decided to get up and go to the bedroom. Billy had put out sleeping bags and, I guess, gone back to his place. Everyone except Bailey was passed out in the bags, next to the fire. I tried one bedroom. Empty. I fell into a bottom bunk and passed out.

## 34.

Half awake, the air smelled good. Too good. Perfume? For a second I didn't know where I was. Not the Chandler Apartments, I was facing the wrong way. Rome. Yes, Rome. The small bed. No, not Rome, the air smelled too good. Boulder.

That unmistakable, Tallulah-esque voice. "Just lie there. I'll do everything." The bag slipped away from the bed and I saw her sitting next to me. She'd somehow snuck in and taken off her clothes. Skin so pale it glowed. I looked up at the window. Too small. "Don't ask questions yet." Waking up to a blow job trumps all questions.

I gave it up too quick, then listened to the crickets. I could feel the questions out there, not quite in my brain, circling. Give me a few more seconds, I thought. She was on top of me, but the questions won. No double this morning.

"I pretty much walked right in. You're all passed out cold. Some detectives."

"We're poets first. You know, a life of sensation ..."

"Could get you killed. I'm here to warn you."

"Aren't you with them?"

She spread her arms. "Do I look like a Spirit of '76 type?"

"You look feminine, marvelous, and tough."

"Poets."

"Didn't you beat on poor Larry?"

"I convinced them to let him go. Told them he was harmless."

"Why do they listen to you?"

"I've been working for them."

"Are you working for them now?"

"Yes and no. I'm cashing their checks, but I'm on your side. That's why I'm here. They didn't follow me, but eventually they'll catch up with you. They made you a top priority. A bunch of security goons are driving up from Orange County. You need to move fast."

"Move where?"

"Um. I guess that's up to you." She got up and dressed, almost silently. Dumb bad pop songs played in my brain. She slipped out through the living room, carrying her shoes.

## 35.

I turned on as many lights as I could find. There was much grumbling, but nobody went for their guns. Some detectives.

They sat, bleary-eyed, still drunk, and listened to my plan. Then they nodded. I have no idea if they understood. They must get it, I told myself. These are intelligent people.

I started the coffee. They understood that. We had bought bagels, eggs, juice. I put together a quick breakfast. Always prepared, I brought out the Ramos gin fizz makings. Hair of the dog. I mixed, blended, tasted, doled out the drinks to the hangover sufferers. Just one. We had work to do.

I sent Bruce, drinks in hand, up to the big house to roust Billy. He returned with Billy and two empty glasses.

"That stuff's tasty! So, you want me to guard these two hombres while you cross the Orange Curtain into enemy territory."

"Look out, Anaheim. We'll take Mickey Mouse if we have to."

"I'll need to hire a coupla guys from the speed factory. They won't come cheap."

We all looked at Larry.

"I'm not made of money," he said. "You'll bleed me dry."

"He's made of money. He owns the building." Bruce was getting riled.

"What building?" These nuts were getting on my nerves.

"The Chandler Apartments, Clay. He owns your building." He jumped up and pointed, vaguely, toward Berkeley. "And the UC Theatre building, and Black Oak Books, and that Hawaiian bar on University."

I felt a little funny in the stomach. Was Larry my landlord?

I looked at Larry. He looked sheepish.

"I'll pay for the goons."

The Fastback and Marvin's van were too noticeable, and the Tercel would have trouble with the grades. We decided that a rental car would come under the expenses part of our contract. We called around and found a hotel near SFO where we could leave our car long-term when we took the rental. Bailey dropped us off at SFO to throw off our trackers. We walked around the airport, grabbed a hotel van, and met Bailey in the parking lot. Walked to the rental car place.

They gave us a Buick. I didn't know they still made them. It was square as hell. Marvin liked that. "We're undercover." Put Neil Young and a transsexual giant in a midsize and you still have a circus. But I didn't say anything. I let him enjoy feeling mainstream.

"We're going down 101."

"C'mon, Marvin. Five's faster."

"A good soldier of fortune always spends his expense account. Besides, it'll be easier to throw them off our trail. They won't expect us to stay at the Miramar."

I looked at Bailey. She was a pro. Surely, an FBI agent wouldn't do something that silly.

"The pool there is great," she said. "Best to be well rested for a showdown. I could use a nice swim."

## 36.

Down past SFO, then beyond to San Jose, the industrial parks and the smog. Eyes open, looking for clones in black SUVs. Unfortunately that describes at least half the population of central California. Perhaps they were all following the rented Buick. The air was warmer than it was hot. We were in Steinbeck country, carpets of crops on either side.

We came to one of those Carl's or Denny's two-sided stops, got off at the Denny's. As we hit the off-ramp I noticed a big yellow Hummer in front of the Carl's. Hard not to notice. There was no reason for me to suspect Spirit of '76, but I did. A real hunch! Maybe I am a detective.

"Let's park at Denny's and sneak over to Carl's. Check out that Hummer."

Head shaking and eye rolling, then "Why not?"

We walked through the underpass and snuck behind the trash bins, trying to look inconspicuous. They stayed back and I looked in the window. It was Haystacks, Wilmer, and Wally. I remembered the words of the nuts: Wally isn't Wally. Were they headed back to the Bay Area? Were they "following" us, staying a little ahead to throw us off?

"There's one Wally and one Haystacks, eating big messy burgers."

Marvin pulled out a switchblade. I remembered the knife. We each bought one in Mazatlán, then smuggled them through security, for fun. "Those big tires slash just as easily as small ones."

Again it was me, the guy who can pass. Just another white guy admiring the patriotic car. I walked around to the back tires, smiling with appreciation. What a machine! The sun was really hot. I wished I had a hat. I popped the blade when the coast looked clear. Those big tires are really thick, but vulnerable. I got the two on the passenger side and came around. Two tragically fat kids, boy and girl, waddled by drinking Cokes the size of their heads. Dad lagged behind, with an even bigger Coke. Big, pink, and round. They passed by me. I got the front driver's side, just a little poke before I saw another family exit the Carl's. Lost my nerve and retreated to the bins.

"Marvin went to Denny's for burgers. Guess we'll eat in the car." Bailey had donned an A's cap. I wondered where she'd gotten it. We walked back to Denny's and waited in the car. Then we were on the road, burgers and fries in a blue Buick. I love this country.

We were climbing the pass outside of Santa Barbara. The Buick was chugging along. I was driving. Marvin was sacked out in the back seat.

"Did you see that?"

"Another yellow Hummer."

"There are lots on the road now."

"Another portly guy with a beard. Just like your description."

"Bailey, are your eyes that good?"

"You can't be blind in the FBI."

Going in the opposite direction. Maybe we had them fooled. I thought about Larry and Bruce, back at the cabin. I hoped that Billy Loy's boys had Glocks galore.

## 37.

We were sweating the traffic jam at State Street. We'd agreed on open windows, no air-conditioning, and the hot air was beautiful, a real novelty for Bay Area types. We noticed another Hummer but couldn't make out the driver. Darkened windows. Maybe it was Arnold. I remembered the days when Santa Barbara had a bohemian enclave, before the rents went apeshit. Surfers, beach bums, people passing through. Good times, back then. Just rich people now.

Ah, the Miramar. Just down-at-the-heels enough. There's nothing like room service by the pool at the Miramar Hotel.

We rented a two-bedroom cabana by the train tracks. Thank you, Larry. We dumped our stuff and I let my mind wander over my favorite Miramar story: Warren Zevon was having a nervous breakdown. Writer's block, drug problems, fame problems, whatever. He was holed up in a cabana. His hero, Ross Macdonald, came to visit.

Zevon confessed that writing was no longer fun. Macdonald raised one eyebrow, waited (I imagine) a couple of beats, said, "Fun?"

"Fun?" had become another part of my secret language, shared only with Marvin. At some part in our stay here one of us would repeat the phrase. We were both waiting for the right time.

Bailey Dao undressed for the pool. Marvin and I wanted to watch, made no pretense. Bailey didn't throw us out. As I said, her breasts were still woman-like, though small. She could never get away with going topless at the pool. This wasn't the South of France. She has the most beautiful pair of shoulders I've ever seen. Quite masculine, helped along with steroids and hormones, I imagine. Her stomach and her legs also seemed masculine, or maybe in between. Her hands were man-sized yet feminine. Her face wasn't male or female, it was Bailey Dao. Impossible to place.

Six foot six, wearing men's boxer briefs, searching in her small carry-on. She pulled out a one-piece bathing suit, bright red, and disappeared into the bathroom. Marvin exhaled, then me. I wondered why she had brought her bathing suit. Did she know we'd stop at a pool when we went up to Inverness?

"I thought we'd go to the beach at Point Reyes," anticipating my question, emerging from the bathroom, ready for the pool. She grabbed one of the hotel-issue towels, went outside. "Meet you at the deep end."

"I used to think I was totally straight," Marvin said. "I'd make an exception for Bailey."

"Let's not get our hopes up."

I changed into a pair of shorts that I kept in the car. Marvin pulled a pair of sweats out of his old gas mask bag. He opened up his switchblade and cut off the legs. Tried them on in front of the full-length mirror, nodding and strutting. He looked like shit, but in an in-your-face way.

I grabbed the cell phone and we went out to the pool. Bailey had already been in. She was dripping wet on the lounge chair, eyeing a room service menu.

I got comfortable and we ordered some drinks. Dialed the cabin. Bruce answered the phone. "Hummers are cool, Clay. I drove down to the lighthouse. They are a durable vehicle. Sometimes I missed the road but it didn't matter."

"Let's go back to square one. You have a Hummer?"

Long, goofy laugh. "We do now. Want to speak to Billy?" He passed the phone. An old Dylan song was playing in the background. I couldn't quite place it.

"They came in like gangbusters and my boys Glocked 'em. I didn't want to have to kill them, but these speed freaks think fast. Hell, they do everything fast."

My mind was reeling. They must have fixed those tires pronto. "Are they dead?"

"Door nails." I heard hooting and laughing in the background.

"The bodies?"

"Iced 'em down and sent 'em back to Monte Rio. Folks are friendlier over there. Wrap 'em up and throw 'em in the woods. Or send 'em downriver like Lincoln Logs."

"What about the Hummer?"

"Got a buyer who won't talk much. Don't worry, Clay. I know about this stuff. But first I'm going to let Bruce drive it over to Bolinas. We're having dinner and drinks with Joanne Kyger. She'll get a hoot outta this."

"What did they look like?"

"Laurel and Hardy. Didn't give 'em time to say much. They missed, my guys didn't."

The Negronis came as I was relating the news to my poolmates.

"We may have them bamboozled," Bailey said. "They'll send more people up north, and we'll slip into their territory."

"Bamboozled? Where'd you get that from?" Marvin had taken to teasing Bailey. Was he flirting?

"I hate to burst the bubble," I said, "but we don't know exactly where they are. Orange County's pretty big. Anaheim isn't, but still..."

Marvin gave me a "poor Clay" look. Babe in the woods. "I'm going to go into town and buy a laptop. Forgot to bring mine. A few emails, a few calls, a little research, and we'll be knocking on Wally's door."

I remembered the Dylan song that they were playing in Inverness, but I didn't bother to explain my chuckle. Marvin put out his hand and I handed him the keys to the Buick. He jumped up and went back to the cabana. He was back in a couple of minutes but he hadn't changed. He waved a credit card and went off to find a Best Buy. I wondered what the Santa Barbara sales crew would think when he plunked it down, said, "I'll take that one, no service contract."

Bailey waved a sleepy goodbye and fell into a nap. I walked down past the railroad tracks that run between the cabanas and the beach. I got a Coke from the machine and sat on the sand. Beyond the oil wells the poisons were working their magic on the sunset. I watched the pinks, the greens, and the deep grays.

# 38.

"Don't worry about directions," Marvin said. "We'll stay in one of those tacky motels near Disneyland. A rental car in a motel. Can't get more anonymous than that. And I have a contact. Worked with him in Angola, way back when. He's pissed off at the Wally bunch. Seems they cheated him out of his health care. It's stupid to get cheapskate with a soldier of fortune."

We were getting ready to go to one of the little Mexican places south of town. I could taste the Pacifico. Marvin was set up with the laptop, taking advantage of the wi-fi. He had a phone in his ear and was leaning back with his eyes closed, rocking a little. Our information guru.

"He'll meet us at the motel and clue us in to the security system. Once we get inside we'll … what will we do, Clay?"

I didn't answer because I didn't know what to say. We decided to come up with something over dinner.

The city smelled like salt and money for a few miles, and then it smelled like salt and frying tortillas. We found a small place a few steps from the ocean. There was a mix of off-duty waiters, gardeners, and slumming Santa Barbarans.

Over plates of beans and rice we came up with a plan. If we could blackmail Wally into leaving us alone, especially Larry, we'd done our job. Discussing this, we realized that we were in a David vs. Goliath situation. We had to make him believe that killing us would be too much trouble. But first we had to find him.

Once satisfied that our plan wasn't too goofy we ordered a full bottle of Campo Azul and lifted a few. I noticed a change in Bailey's countenance. She was smiling more, responding to Marvin's rough jokes, just generally loosening up. A good thing, I thought. Soon we'd be storming capitalism together. We'd fare better as comrades.

We drove back to the Miramar with the windows down, probably weaving. The air was perfect, and as we passed the pool I caught a telepathic jolt. Marvin was thinking what I was thinking. Was Bailey? The lights were off, except those in the pool. They probably kept those on for effect, or possibly to keep drunks and sleepwalkers from falling in. I took off my shirt and struggled with my pants. Had to sit on a lounge chair to finish stripping. That Campo Azul is strong stuff. Marvin did the same. Bailey stayed standing. She threw off her clothes in what seemed like a single motion.

We didn't want to splash too much. Wanted to have a good swim before getting thrown out. I slipped in and pushed off, floating, I believed, in total silence. There was a tequila time warp, seconds or minutes, who cares. I was sitting on the step on the shallow side and I heard them giggling on the other side of the pool. Giggling, hard breathing, harder breathing. I wondered what was going on. I mean, I knew what was going on. I wondered about the mechanics.

## 39.

We were at Malibu. Everybody was jolly, if a bit hung over. Blasting, beautiful midmorning. Welcome to LA. "Oddly green halos surround summer love, my skeleton has gone on vacation." This from Marvin, quoting my poem "frm zuma to venice." I was flattered, and Bailey, who had no idea those were my words, was charmed.

Way down the coast, the slow way to go but pleasant, Redondo Beach, San Pedro, Long Beach, lots of water on the passenger side. My passengers had their heads out the windows, smelling the air like golden retrievers.

I turned the Buick east when I had to, and a couple of traffic jams later we were over by Angel Stadium. We found a business suite place with a shopping mall facade and checked in. We were watching a Dodger game on a big-screen TV when our contact arrived.

He was as white, male, and square-jawed as a man could be. Must have been a steroid case. Nobody has that much time to work out. Was he a cartoon? He looked like that Russian guy in the Rocky movie. Didn't introduce himself.

"Wallys are due in three places in the greater LA area today. There's another Wally in a meeting in Charlotte, North Carolina, but he's not your guy." A steady look toward Marvin, who looked steadily back. No blinking allowed at this level. "You owe me big time, Marvin."

"I thought you owed me."

"Not anymore. Wally's guys aren't especially good, but there's lots of them. He's a safety-in-numbers employer. They find out, they'll swarm me like ants. Bastards."

"Okay, I owe you. You have my number. Which Wally is our Wally."

"He's at the complex on Katella. Staff meeting, mostly sales people. Two bodyguards, security at the doors, but spread pretty thin. Not expecting trouble. He does this sort of thing all the time. Likes to think he's a hands-on manager. And his doubles sideline is heating up. Some pretty important copies are coming off the assembly line. Sometimes Wally switches up, uses one of his copies at meetings, but when he does I hear about it." He unzipped the front pocket of his orange windbreaker. Pulled out three badges and a parking sticker. Stars and stripes, '76 PRIORITY, in script, across Old Glory. And a piece of paper. Directions.

He left us with a raised eyebrow and a "Have fun." Had he heard the Ross Macdonald story?

We went over our plan. Larry's information, along with the address of the complex, would be emailed to various papers and websites. We hoped to add a few pictures when we got inside. Should be enough to get the thugs to back off, maybe stop the operation. Good for Bailey's résumé, even if the stories never got written. Word would get around that we were ace detectives. What the hell, the book business is dead. Dao, Clarke, and Blackburn Detective Agency. Or maybe that should be alphabetical.

Marvin put up an ideological argument for gutting Wally like a trout. We shook our heads. At least one bullet in his midsection? For the people? Again we said no. We loaded our Glocks. Marvin caught my squeamish look. "One bullet is worth a thousand bulletins!" Out the door and into the Buick.

## 40.

We breezed through parking security, thanks to the sticker. Walked, as directed, around rather than through the metal detector. Security's prerogative. Just one guard at our door. He saw our guns and gave up with a shrug. No health insurance?

I was to do the talking. Marvin was disqualified. Too much commie rhetoric. I'd beat Bailey at the coin toss. Nice dramatic entrance, guns drawn, a chair kicked over for effect.

"No guns, no phones!" But someone had tripped an alarm, or something. Two guards followed us in. Bailey turned, a beautiful swivel. The red streak in her hair was in front of her face, then it wasn't, flaring back with the pivot. She crouched, gunslinger-style, steadied herself, *splut*, one down, a small woman with very short hair. Bailey continued her crouch, got off the second shot, *splut*, through the head of a young Asian guy with slicked-back hair.

Small-caliber guns make little holes in people, but the holes soon get bigger and the life force, or whatever you call it, seeps out pretty fast. They weren't dead before they hit the floor, but they soon would be.

"Jesus, you're fast." Marvin was in love.

We turned to the cowering execs.

Marvin's cell rang. His jaw dropped as he listened. He looked with disdain at the suits, who were in a bunch on the linoleum. "They pulled a switcheroo. Wrong fucking Wally. He's across the street. He'll be in a meeting there for the rest of the day."

We needed to get a look at the operation, find out where they turned people into doubles. Needed pictures of operating rooms. Wanted to scare a couple of doctors too. But mostly we needed to get to Wally.

Marvin addressed the phony Wally. "We're terrorists. If you finger us, you will die. There are thousands of us, pouring over the borders."

"Anything you say. I'm just a double. This is just a training session. Don't hurt us. We're not who we are."

We marched out, flashing our badges. "There's been a shooting. Don't go in there. Sit tight and wait for the authorities." Nobody seemed anxious to investigate.

We kept on marching and looking serious. Marvin took directions on the cell and we followed. Another generic building, low-slung with lots of chrome and tinted windows. Again we flashed our badges. So far we were getting away with murder.

We were in a hospital, or some kind of medical facility. We followed Marvin. We were passed in the hall by two Dick Cheneys! They smiled, gave a little wave. Bailey looked over my shoulder, caught my eye. This was a bigger operation than we'd thought. Government contracts. No wonder they had to kill Terry. Couldn't afford a loose cannon.

We walked into a room the size of a high school auditorium. It was about half full of well-dressed, familiar-looking people. There was a huge poster of Wally on one wall, cult-of-personality-style. I thought I recognized the governor of Illinois, but I couldn't remember his name.

"We need to lose ourselves in the crowd, for now." Marvin had a plan. God knows what it was. He pointed to the pocket that held the cell phone and gave a confident nod. Inside information. He pulled off his security badge and so did we. "You're a diplomat, and you're the daughter of the president of Quebecistan, a former Soviet satellite."

"And who are you?" Bailey was amused, not at all nervous.

"I'm Tom Waits."

"You look more like Neil Young." I, on the other hand, was sweating like a pig, feeling nauseated.

"With a haircut I look like Lee Marvin."

"No you don't."

Wally entered the room. The security didn't look too tough. A couple of Haystackses and a couple of Wilmers. No obvious artillery. Wally felt safe in his inner sanctum.

There were some small differences between this Wally and that first Wally that I'd met in the suburbs. A little smaller, a little pudgier. When Wally made Wallys he romanticized a bit. Who wouldn't?

He briskly stepped up to the mic, fronting his huge picture. This made him look smaller. The wizard, out from behind the curtain.

"Welcome, graduates!" A nice round of applause. "I understand that you've been through a lot. Nips, tucks, voice lessons, new clothes, the like. Now you're at the end of the rainbow. A secure job, health care, the American dream!" More applause. Two rows up a Barbie doll type was clapping and hopping, her perfect hair rising and falling, catching the light. "Soon you will be handed your orders, taken to your cars, and to your new posts. Some of you will be flying away. I am, however, disappointed to give you the sad news that we can no longer afford to fly you business class." The crowd didn't quite turn ugly, but the collective body language changed. There was a groan. "I know, my friends. Taxes, government regulations, and the like have cut into profits. We all have to give a little."

I wondered how government regulations could cut into an illegal enterprise. Then I wasn't wondering anymore. I noticed that Marvin had maneuvered himself to the edge of the stage. Bailey was at the other end. I understood. We were going to grab Wally as he left. I'd watch Wally, then break left or right, depending.

As he exited, stage left, Bailey pulled out her security badge and followed him. I did the same, pushing a senator and a star first baseman in the process. I saw Marvin crossing the stage, bringing up the rear of Wally's entourage, Glock half drawn.

When I drew my gun my pocket turned inside out. Swift. I only vaguely remembered how to get the safety off.

We exited a side door. A parking lot was full of yellow Hummers and black SUVs. Must look pretty from the air, I thought. Checkerboard.

Bailey gave me a look that said, Say something, and I commenced to bullshitting. As a poet, I've trained for it my entire adult life. "These guys are imposters!"

"Of course they are, I pay them to be imposters. Who the fuck are you?"

"They're spies for the FBI."

"Ridiculous. I paid them off."

This wasn't going to be easy. "Okay, we're imposters. And we're going to shoot you with these really hip guns if you don't let us take you for a drive in one of these big dumb cars. We just want to talk a little business."

I eyed the Haystackses and the Wilmers. They were backing away, hands up. Their health plans probably weren't that good. With little prodding a Haystacks handed over the keys to an Escalade.

I'd never been in one. Posh. Of course I'd never buy one, though after all, even Mayakovsky once owned a Bugatti. The lure of great wheels!

Marvin drove. We got on the freeway and headed north, toward LA. Bailey gave me that "you do the talking" look and I launched into our plan.

"Okay, Wally, here's the deal. Terry gathered lots of info and he spilled the beans to a couple of Berkeley characters."

A roll of the eyes. "Berkeley. You guys don't deserve to be in America."

"Be that as it may, the beans, if I may extend the metaphor, have been removed from the scrambled brains of our Berkeley friends and respilled into a bunch of emails. You don't have a license to change people into public figures. Bad publicity, Wally. Very bad. And you could go to prison. There must be laws involved."

I saw him fidget. That bean metaphor wouldn't make it in a poetry workshop, but Wally was a businessman. "Martha Stewart did fine after going to jail."

"Small potatoes. Are all your doctors licensed?"

More fidgeting. Maybe I had him. I felt a sneaking suspicion that this Wally wasn't Wally either. Let it go. "In another couple of months I'll have all that worked out. We just need to buy a few more politicians. After all, they use our services too." A light came on in his eyes. The asshole thought he was at another seminar! "This is a great opportunity. I can let you in on the ground floor. Everybody needs a double. And it provides great jobs. When we work out the legal bugs we'll have double centers in every Jerry's Drugs and More. You can sit at the counter, order up a copy of yourself, fill in some forms, leave a video of yourself, and come back in a week and pick yourself up."

I was surprised by his honesty. The beans were everywhere. "We could blow your operation before it gets started."

He was sweating. That Rotary Club facade was coming down. I watched his face grow mean. Willy Loman without the tragic side. Did we have him cornered?

"What do you want?"

"Stay out of Berkeley and leave us alone. That's all. We'll keep the evidence on file. Even if you buy your way into this scam, murder can get you into trouble. Homicide cops are harder to buy. One of them will want to make a name by frying your ass." I didn't know that, but it sounded good. "And no Jerry's Drugs in the East Bay. San Francisco can fend for itself."

He sat for a while, looking out the window. We passed through Long Beach, through Torrance. It was a beautiful LA day, low on the haze and not too hot. Marvin was having fun driving up the 405 in this rolling house. Bailey was silent in the passenger seat. As Torrance became southwest LA, I looked over at Wally. That blank George Bush look was back on his face. Were the little wheels turning, or was he enjoying the ride?

Bailey turned in her seat. "Wally, here comes Compton. If you don't go our way with this, we're going to take this off-ramp and drop you off down there. And we may also shoot you in the leg. For fun."

A nice hoot from Marvin. He was definitely in love.

"Okay, okay. I hate Berkeley anyway. And Oakland. We'll open in Dublin and put you all out of business. You have your deal. It's not that important. Now take me back to Orange County. I don't like it here." Wally was beat. Could we trust him?

More laughter, then, from Marvin, "We're doing you a favor! Wally, I give you Compton."

We got off in Compton and dropped him off. Gave him cab fare. CEOs never carry cash. Called a taxi. Left him on a corner in front of a beautiful stucco bungalow. If things got tough, he could always use his credit cards to buy the block.

## 41.

Back on the 405 going the other way, south to LAX, through much traffic to the long-term lot. Parked the tank and took the jitney to the Southwest terminal. I found the rental car desk and explained that, due to a terrible emergency, I had to leave the Buick in Orange County. The clerk, a little blond guy with a movie star haircut, emoted sympathy and then charged us a ridiculous pickup charge. Expenses.

We got our tickets, smuggled the Glocks through security, bought an *LA Times*, and settled in. I called Inverness to check on our little private asylum.

Bruce again. "I wrote a poem. Joanne says I'm a real poet. A poet in a Hummer!"

I mulled that one over for a few seconds. Had a vision of John Ashbery driving one. Mary Oliver? I don't think Al Young would drive one, even if he is California's poet laureate. Maybe Arnold should offer him one.

Billy Loy took the phone. "No visits from your friends. Somebody's coming to pick up the Hummer tonight. Larry wants the take, to cover expenses. I told him that half should go to me and the speed freaks. He can split the other half with Bruce. Sound fair?"

"Sounds fair to me. But you're the boss up there, Billy."

"Ten-four."

## 42.

I was deep into a story about Lewis MacAdams's attempts to save the LA River. Marvin and Bailey were sharing an order of fries from Burger King. For some reason (PI instincts?) we all looked up at the same time. Wilmer, or some reasonable facsimile. He was skulking behind some pay phones. Built to skulk!

"I'll pull a Sitting Bull and lead him to someplace quiet. Get ready to pull an ambush." We scanned the terminal. No Haystacks. There was a guy who looked a lot like Charlton Heston. A clone?

I once worked an airport security job at LAX. I checked IDs, looked at the X-ray, got bored. Most of the employees were ex-felons with doctored résumés. Their knowledge of weapons was firsthand, but they had little invested in enforcing the law. The airlines and the security companies didn't give a shit. They'd hire anybody that would work cheap. Probably still do. This was late '70s, early '80s. Drugs of choice: a mix of diet pills and pot. We had a great smoking spot. A little plot of lawn between American Airlines and the international terminal. There was even a tree, for shade. And it was near the least-used private restroom in the airport, for those who preferred the kind of drug that requires a syringe.

I nonchalantly walked out the power doors and down the sidewalk. Just getting some air, no big deal. Wilmer followed at a safe distance. He was pretty good at being nondescript. Guess that's why they mass-produced him. He was wearing a creased pair of light khakis and a blue knit shirt, the kind that has a little alligator on the breast. I didn't get close enough to see the alligator.

I took a discreet look over my shoulder, got the lay of the land. No Hestons, no Haystackses as far as I could see. The crowds thinned as I approached my secret spot.

I was approached on my left by a guy who looked like the sheriff from *In the Heat of the Night*. I was trying to think of the actor's name when he grabbed at me. The element of surprise almost worked, but not quite. I dodged right and caught him on the neck, just below his rather impressive left jowl. My second punch was to the solar plexus. Archie Moore, my old boxing teacher, would be proud. He didn't go down, but he was temporarily out of commission.

I walked briskly toward the bathroom, as planned. They would follow me in, corner me, and Bailey and Marvin would ... shoot them in the back? I hoped not, but Marvin was unpredictable sometimes.

Incredible adrenaline rush as I stood, half crouched, in front of the trough. I always had to pee right before the fight. Nerves. Thought about taking advantage of the urinal, didn't have the time.

This Wilmer wasn't at all like the one we dangled out the window. Intense eyes, stretched face with no expression. Loosey-goosey stance, hands held just high enough. Wiry, probably quick.

"I've got backup." He did that little neck move that fighters do when they loosen up. Shrugged his shoulders.

"Me too." I gave him my best stink eye. Sonny Liston, all the way. Where the fuck was Marvin?

I didn't notice the kind of bulge that a gun makes. Mine was back in my carry-on. Not that I'd use it. The real world melted away. I concentrated on the matchup. I was only a fair Golden Gloves amateur, but I liked it. And it's why I'm a poet! Somebody told me about A.J. Liebling. After reading *The Sweet Science* I turned to books and writing. This explains my boyish good looks. I got out before I collected too many scars.

He swung hard, missing with a couple of rights that were so clumsy I thought they might be feints, designed to draw some counterreaction. He smiled, shrugged. I started to smile back. My lips were barely curved upward when he got me with a high left hook.

It wasn't a crashing knockdown, the kind that leaves you limp, like a wet hat, or jerky, like a new-caught fish. Most painful part was when my ass, then an elbow, hit the hard, slippery tile.

It was a sit-down-and-think-it-over knockdown. To my surprise he let me do just that. Wasn't he sent to kill me? I looked around, got my bearings. Rod Steiger (I remembered his name. Thanks to the punch?) was still outside, presumably doubled over.

I got up. He danced around. Gave me a few seconds. I covered up and feinted, he bounced away. I was outclassed, I had to stall. In the stalls! I smiled at the joke in my head.

"Something funny, poet?"

"We're all a little crazy. Are they paying you full benefits?"

"Except for the business class thing."

"You guys need a union."

"Fuck that."

I caught him with a little jab that shouldn't have scored. Bad peripheral vision? The last guy I fought had nothing but peripheral vision. I moved left and caught his temple. Hard on the hand, but it made him flinch. I moved left, then right. He stared straight ahead. I caught some blows on the shoulder. They smarted but did no damage. Still no Marvin, no Bailey, no sheriff, no Heston.

There was a goofball fighter in LA, Windmill White. Almost won the light heavyweight championship. He had a weird series of windups, overhead punches, bolo punches. One of his moves was to come around his opponent and tap him on the back. I danced around Wilmer. He turned his head, but he couldn't quite see me. I hit him with the hardest kidney punch I could muster.

"Fowl!"

"This is a street fight, idiot." He was rolling around on the tiles. He hooked his right arm on the trough. I think he expected me to go to a neutral corner. I braced myself, got good balance, and kicked him in the head, hard. He slid back down. He wasn't completely out, but he wouldn't be going anywhere soon.

Bailey Dao entered the men's room as I was leaving. Sniffed and made a face.

"They smell bad, Bailey. Sure you want to be a man?"

"I'm my own sex, Clay. I have invented a sex. I'll explain it to you sometime. The guy with the chiseled face is dead. Drew on us, wouldn't drop his gun. Marvin dropped him. We couldn't pry the gun from his hand, so we threw him, and the gun, in a dumpster. Maybe he wanted it that way. That fat guy limped away. This part of the airport sure is deserted. Where's Homeland Security?"

"Probably watching a ball game in the lounge. But we should move before the seventh inning stretch."

## 43.

We needed to make a statement. Needed to do something that would scare Wally off, or at least make him believe that we weren't worth the risk. We decided to hold on to the damning info a little longer. We'd take Wilmer back to Orange County and dump him at headquarters.

Wilmer was quite dazed. He took us to his black SUV and gave us the keys. Marvin insisted on driving. I got on the cell and, somehow, convinced Southwest that my travel companions had taken sick with food poisoning and that I was taking them home. We were issued a voucher for another flight.

"I'm dumping the Econoline and getting one of these. They're no easier to drive, but feel the comfort!"

"Doesn't suit your lumpen style."

"Don't worry about that. We'll get Larry to paint a Che portrait across one side, Malcolm X on the other. A commie-mobile."

I was in the back seat. My Glock was in my lap, but Wilmer wasn't going anywhere. I played with the gun. It was cool and light, with a sexy shape. Guns and SUVs, a slippery slope. Once you get on that streetcar named desire ...

Marvin decided to change lanes. Every lane, all at once. Many honks. He sped up, did it again. I looked around for cops. He put on the radio and by some miracle found a station that was playing Coltrane. Turned it up loud. Nice ride!

We almost took flight as we rounded the off-ramp. Then down Katella to the headquarters. We circled the lot. There was a guard shack and a wooden gate at the exit. Marvin stepped on the gas, yelled, "Four-wheel drive!" And we snapped the gate, but it had a line of those "don't back up" tire spikes. Four blowouts. Bailey socked Marvin on the shoulder.

"You fucked up our ride, dickhead."

"It's okay. There's the Buick!"

The rental place hadn't picked it up. I'd palmed the keys. I'd have to call them and do some fast talking. Expenses.

We pulled up next to the Buick. Two rent-a-cops followed us, on foot. Guarding a parking lot was below Spirit of '76. We pulled our guns and their hands went up.

"You guys have cell phones?" They stared at Bailey, nodded.

"Drop 'em, and your walkie-talkies and your guns."

"They won't give us guns."

"Okay. Take the rest of the day off." And off they went.

We drove off, leaving Wilmer holding a note: Dear Wally, we see your guys again and we blow the whistle.

## 44.

Dead of winter, Berkeley-style. It was cold and clear early in the day, wind off the bay, no hint of smog. Dark and cloudy by five. I walked around the corner with a small bag of books. Nice-looking stuff. Leather, Franklin Library. A Joyce, a Hemingway, *Tom Jones*, John Dos Passos, Willa Cather. Christmas stock.

The book thieves were swarming like vultures. New buyer at the Moe's counter. Slowdown John, Senior Scabarino, Bob Dark, Woofman, a tall guy in a slick suit who steals tech books. They mingled with the ex-cons, street folks, and '60s vets in front of Caffe Med. I decided to go over for a cup of coffee, just to check out the scene. I nodded to Julia Vinograd, ordered a pinkie lifter, and took a seat by the window. The light was bad, the room was drafty, the coffee so-so. Home sweet home. It started to rain a little, just enough for the sidewalk party to move under the eaves.

An especially dodgy fellow stood outside the window and watched me drink my coffee. Acid victim, lost his mind in the revolution. Wild eyes, stringy hair. Showing some age now. How did he last this long?

Three months, no sign of the Wally squad. Also, sadly, no sign of Grace. Wally'd gotten himself in some trouble in Wichita. Bribed a couple of local officials. A tough DA brought one of his minions up on charges. No conviction. Marvin and I had talked about spilling the beans then but decided against it. Eventually the investigation would lead back to us and the case would be blown. A bisexual poet, an anarchist soldier of fortune, a transsexual ex-FBI agent. Bad witnesses.

And so we sat on the information. Larry and Bruce had started a beautiful friendship. They went to Italy for the winter, guests of Kathleen Fraser. Thanks to his start at Joanne Kyger's, Bruce had begun a career as a poet.

MBC Investigations did get some jobs, nothing involving CEOs, fistfights, or plastic surgery. Take some pictures, interview some suspects, drink martinis at César. Expenses. A pretty good gig. I did as much scouting as I could, but the books were thin and prices were low. In the words of Jimmy Buffet, my occupational hazard is that my occupation's just not around. I'd been Amazoned.

Skootch Leroux is a leggy book thief with a bit of a drug problem. Her look is disheveled, but not quite the worse for wear. I watched her cross the street with a small stack of art books, covered in clear plastic. Her ass, in tight black jeans, was a masterpiece, a miracle. A fuzzy thrift store sweater didn't cover the tattoo on her lower back, a bird of some kind. Long black hair, moist from the sprinkle.

I decided to watch the fun. I covered my Franklins as best I could and crossed over to Moe's. Skootch was wiggling, dancing, leaning across the counter.

The fresh-faced young buyer looked, almost leering, but not quite. Who could blame him? He smiled at her, then at me. He wasn't that green. The thieves would have to find another fence.

"I'm an artist, but I'm through with these. I'm sick of Klee and Kandinsky."

I was impressed that she'd pronounced Klee right. Berkeley has a well-educated criminal underground.

"Tired of the K's, I guess. Do you want cash or trade for these?"

"I wish I could take trade. I love books. But I need money for my brushes." Nice little flip of the hair.

Good thing I'm not a book buyer. I'd have given her all the money in the cash register.

"Sorry. We can't use these." He had round horn-rimmed glasses, kind of Harry Potterish. No wonder the thieves thought he was fresh meat. He looked too sweet for Telegraph.

## 45.

He gave me a good price for the Franklins, but not too good. We chatted for a while and I went in for a browse. I wanted some new poetry. They have a great selection. I thought about Robert Lowell for a second, though I'm not a big fan. Read a few lines, then put it back. I wasn't feeling East Coast neurotic. Almost fell asleep with quandariness. Lorca's too sad, and I was feeling a little sad. It occurred to me that I had been lonely since our big caper. This surprised me, because I'm not usually prone to loneliness. The pain of the passing of the last romance had snuck up on me as winter came on.

I opted for a little Micah Ballard pamphlet, all gothic and spooky. The Keats of New Orleans.

Out into the night. Telegraph Avenue, empty and cold in that end-of-the-year way, everything closed except one bookstore, one café, and Fred's Market. Wet copies of the *Express* lining the gutters, street folks hiding under anything that would stop the rain. My heart as desolate as a staircase. As the poet said.

Around the corner and up the stairs, feed the cat, put on some Townes Van Zandt. High, low, and in between. A shot of the best whiskey in the house, Oban. Settle in and read some poems.

The phone rang. The voice of Tallulah Bankhead, back from the dead. My pounding heart. Stay cool, Clay.

"It's fucking wet down here!" She was at the door. I buzzed her in and collected myself as she came up the stairs. I timed her entrance, opening the door before she could knock.

And it was her. Her-her. Grace and Grace. Grace twice. The short straight black hair, light light skin, sexiest mouth(s) I'd ever seen. I noticed that one was slightly taller. Which one was Grace?

"Move aside and let us in. We're quite wet." I recognized her as the real Grace. Well, the Grace I'd known.

But I was still confused. "Grace? Is it you?"

"What's left of me. This is Mina. We were discontinued."

"Fired?"

"Whatever. Somewhere there's a rich woman that looks like us. Guess she didn't pay up for her doubles. Or something."

What could I do? I went for the Oban. When life throws one a fish, one finds a frying pan and chops up the herbs. I probably should have asked some questions. They could be working for Drugstore Wally.

But I didn't have questions. I had the answer to everything, the pot of gold at the end of the (double) rainbow. I poured the drinks and settled in for an incredible double fuck.

# Mayakovsky's Bugatti

*This world isn't well equipped for enchantment.*
*We steal delight from the time we have here.*
*Existence is iffy*
*it's quite easy to die.*
*To live high and right*
*is harder by far.*
—Vladimir Mayakovsky

# 1.

Marvin always got there early, so the lights were on when I came in. On nice days the front door was left open while he swept the store, opened the safe, counted the money, and warmed up the register. It was several years out of date but we backed it up with a laptop so we could meet and beat Amazon prices on used books and do special orders through jobbers and distributors. There were five members in the collective, three hardcore book nerds and two people with kitchen experience to run the café. At first the book guys were comical at making coffees but we quickly got up to speed. The food service people were also literary types so they took to bookselling okay, and actually sometimes were better at pointing customers to good books. Still enthusiastic.

Marvin and I had been scouting books for at least thirty years between us. Book scouting: finding sellable books in piles of unsellable books, at estate sales, secondhand shops, garage sales, then selling them online or to secondhand bookstores. Scouting had paid the bills for a good long stretch, but changes in the biz moved us into other things, other adventures. Change is good, except when it isn't. Okay now, our other "jobs" seem a little hard to believe but here we are. We're lefties, anarchist types, and our ideological quirks lead us down strange roads. I work as an unlicensed "detective," finding people, finding stuff, doing research for radical journalists, whatever comes along. Marvin is ... a soldier of fortune, mostly for the losing side, so the money isn't great, but he does get to travel and he has an expert's knowledge of guns and other arms, has great contacts, and can smell a cop a block away.

Almost on a whim we started a bookstore in the front room of a cavernous old building, in what used to be called North Oakland but now is referred to as Temescal, replete with those chamber-of-commerce-style banners advertising street fairs and neighborhood improvements. The building was being bought by a group of radical types, a collective of collectives, in a run-down defunct bowling alley with terrible lighting and plumbing. We had lots of good books to sell, but with fewer used bookstores in the Bay Area we couldn't wholesale to our satisfaction, so we went retail. A young bookseller named Chad Recife was involved with the Emma Goldman Group, the people who were trying to buy the old bowling alley. Chad was a low-down wheeler-dealer with grifter tendencies but also irresistible, and in Marvin's estimation a "good commie," high praise from him.

Chad set up the deal and, we found later, somehow greased the wheels so that we could bypass the strict set of interviews and vettings that would have come before the collectives voted us in or out. We were in, even though at least half of the eight collectives were against any kind of retail space, "radical" or not. We couldn't avoid being questioned on that note and took great pains to explain the difference between radical commerce and capitalism. Chad was excellent at this sort of thing and spoke, no, sang and danced, at the open meeting, quoting all the lefty heavies, from Marx to Silvia Federici, spreading his arms and looking to the heavens, then not so subtly reminding them that we could come up with some mortgage payments. Articulate (and entertaining) as he was, it was Marvin who closed the deal. They trusted him, he'd been very visible on the front lines, had fought for them, gone to jail for them, slugged cops, perhaps even killed. These meetings had strict verbal codes, signs, and stances, coming out of the Occupy movement a few years before, that had to be adhered to, unless you were Marvin. He'd been in Central America, he'd been in the Balkans, he'd been in Seattle.

"We can make you some money and get some bodies in here. This is looking too much like some white Marxist social club. We'll bring in people from the neighborhood, all factions, with their wallets. Now hurry up and vote."

And so we closed our expensive storage spaces and moved books in, then covered them with tarps and painted the place, took stuff to the dump, tore down the old shoe rental space, sold some copper pipes that we didn't need, hooked up a great-looking old espresso machine, talked to coffee and book sales reps, built shelves. We had gone through our nut just making the place ready, started a crowdfunding site, a "worker-owned welcoming space for the Emma Goldman Group and community," an "intellectual meeting place" with no wi-fi on weekends, to promote debate and camaraderie. I wrote the text, mostly quoting Chad as he sat across from me at a long table in what was to be the café.

My part of the initial investment had come from one of those other jobs, the detective type, a real Travis McGee deal involving stolen ancient Roman trinkets. Recovering the antiquities took some doing. I even had to call on my old boxing skills—Golden Gloves as a boy. I did the job, got paid handsomely, and bought paint, shelving, and an old cash register and paid for part of the espresso machine. Also a month's rent's worth of dinner at Chez Panisse downstairs for Marvin (he loves old-school Berkeley) because he helped out, and a case of cat food. The glamorous life of a book scout/detective.

Welcome to the commie clubhouse! The collectives included a gang of tech rebels, a hippie-style soup kitchen, a theater group, and a free school that specializes in Marxist thought, with a little experimental poetry and a couple of dead languages thrown in. We were the retail outliers, handling the filthy lucre that mostly kept the lights on, and the building's front lines, putting up with all the shit that comes in from the street to obstruct the workers' paradise. And yet there was some glimpse of paradise in it all, the light coming from our love of books—not just the ideas but the scent and the feel and the dust. Who had bought this one and did they read it, and why did they? And then, breaking the reverie yet not tamping down the excitement, what can we get for this thing? Marvin, what's it worth? Clay, have you seen this? Supply and demand at the street food level.

## 2.

It was still bare bones but it mostly looked like a store, more like a store than a café because there were so few tables. We had found two tall ones for a stand-up espresso bar and one unpainted picnic table with benches, a real wood-sliver danger. We had folding chairs for readings but we didn't unfold them for everyday use. Lots of floor space for browsing and chatting. The place had a good feel, partly due to some big splashy mural-type paintings gifted to us by a guy who wouldn't give us his name but whose graffiti locals would recognize. He dropped off the art and left and we never saw him again. We had framed some pages from *The Black Panther* newspaper, found in the building when we were cleaning up. Great graphics. And a blown-up portrait of Emma Goldman, hand-colored by the staff. Just enough lefty chic to satisfy our audience but nothing to put off the techie types who would keep us afloat with their Google dollars. Piss-elegant, as Marvin liked to say.

Marvin had started up the coffee machine and the scent covered up the hippie-grub smells from the kitchen downstairs. I pumped a double coffee and took one of the vegan croissants, just delivered by a local off-the-books chef. The café was a "donation" space because we weren't legal to run food service yet. It was working out well enough. We were close to getting a business license and the proper insurance to run a bookstore.

Marvin was up in the front corner shelving critical theory. A grunt and a wave. Mr. Laconic, at least until he feels like unloading with a speech. Patti O'Hara and Percy were still out. Percy and Patti, the café people, had come in early and gone out shopping. Marvin pointed to the farthest corner of the store, the corner I hadn't noticed yet, and there I spied Dino Centro. O Dino Centro. Always trouble, always worth it on some level and not worth it on others. Not-so-petty criminal, sometime love of my life. I suddenly became aware it had been a couple of years. I wondered how much thinner my hair was. Dino was ageless, northern Italian dirty blond, blue eyes. "Hello, hello, dear Clay," kiss on the lips that brushed lightly and lingered.

A little smarmy. Crisp white Brooks Brothers and tailored jeans. White Feiyues, no socks. Very out of place in Emma Goldman's house, but didn't know it or didn't care. I resisted, at first, hesitated before asking him what he wanted. Didn't seem like good manners, and anyway I wanted to just stand there and look at him for a few minutes.

"Dear Clay. Have I seen you since I left that little apartment on College Avenue?"

We both knew he had, a late-night visit to my place on Dwight Way, and I had a vision of us standing in front of an open window looking down at the denizens of Telegraph Avenue, then looking at each other.

"Oh, I remember," he said. "South Berkeley." Teasing me.

"Take a walk?"

People hanging out by the door, playing stoop games, smoking and passing a bottle. Real urban, except that they were surrounded by wealthy "workers" and baby carriages. A clash of cultures, but for that moment nobody cared, and I didn't care because I just wanted to see the sun play on Dino's hair.

"I have something for you. I'd call it a caper. A little outside your comfort zone but you'll be well compensated. I know you need the money. The"—short snobby pause—"commie café can't be making much. Is it true that you give things away?" Dino had a bit of the capitalist in him.

"The books are selling and they usually throw down a couple of bucks for an espresso."

"You could do better but that's your business. This will fund your socialist experiment, with a little left over to fix the convertible."

I'd bought another vintage Miata. The top was a little porous. I have a strange, sentimental attachment to those cars. I wondered how Dino knew about the top.

"They all leak, Clay. Some sort of manufacturing fuckup. Next time get a Fiat. Or with what I can do for you, put a down payment on a real sports car. I can sell you my Triumph, low interest."

I was intrigued and ready for an adventure. Bookselling is always interesting, but starting a business, even (or maybe especially) a workers' collective, was boring me to smithereens. The meetings, the insurance, the plumbing and painting. Love's vessel crashes on the rocks of the day-to-day. As the poet said.

"Who do you trust to do this kind of work? I know, Marvin. But we need a crew."

"Anyone from the bookstore. That's why we're together in this."

"Things could be rough-and-tumble. I know you're quite capable. Marvin doesn't like me but he's a superstar in his category. He'll love this job too. What about the others?"

I'd already had a couple of adventures with Patti. She was tougher than I could ever be. Chad? I was under Chad's spell at the time, thought he could probably handle anything. Percy was trustworthy but may not be interested in our shenanigans. At any rate they wouldn't go running to the cops, if this was that kind of job. I thought of Bailey Dao, a defrocked FBI agent who I had worked with. We had been out of touch but I could poke around.

"Okay, Dino, why don't you spell it out and I'll either have a good laugh or start making plans."

Dino brushed my hand as we walked toward that place where Shattuck intersects with Telegraph. The brush could almost be an accident, but I knew it wasn't. I was, of course, intrigued. With all of it. A caper? A couple of nights with Dino? We needed either a bar or a café but I couldn't quite decide which.

"Do you know this place?" he asked. I didn't. Looked like a space for serious day drinkers. Very film noir. I liked that. Dino leaned into me, steering me into the dank. I wanted a Negroni made with Boodles gin but it wasn't that kind of place. I can't drink cheap stuff. I know, bad commie. Quickly it occurred to me that I was with Dino, who would even turn up his nose at Glenfiddich. I don't think he knew that "blended" exists.

But this is the Bay Area, where the top shelf is always the top shelf. Still, I didn't want to be a snob. I started to order a well drink, but Dino made the bartender climb up the back bar for a double dose of Blanton's.

"Bourbon? I didn't think you drank American."

"It's good, Clay. God bless this wonderful country." And, glass aloft, "Long may it burn."

I happily drank to that, and hoped that Dino was buying.

## 3.

I couldn't afford a second so we made the firsts last. Dino started out by talking up the charms of Piedmont. Piedmont, California, not his home country.

"It's nothing like Piemonte, no. It's a moneyed oasis, if that sort of thing is your taste."

I knew those tastes. I had once rented a room in a cavernous house near the Oakland Rose Garden, on the Piedmont line. It's a clubby little town. We were there illegally, because at the time these houses were zoned as "single family dwellings." The neighbors knew it and lorded that over us. We were quiet working folks, so there wasn't much reason for real complaints. Mostly they hated our old cars, for aesthetic reasons. Also we weren't an all-white household. Made them nervous.

"I lived there once. What happened to that awful mayor? The

guy who said trans people are mentally ill? I think he said some racist shit too."

Dino shrugged, ordered another. Reached over and touched my hand. "My treat. We can split a shot." It came and he took a sip, handed me the glass. I drank from the same side, my lips touching where he'd drunk. A small thrill, but a thrill.

"The mayor resigned after the expected fauxpology. He's living in Georgia. The whole town's gone subtle. There are these little moneyed areas around NorCal. You know them. I'm not talking about the Marina District. I'm not saying, 'Let's hit Diane Feinstein's place.'"

"Hit?"

"In a manner of speaking. More like a little touch. A laptop, a wallet, a stray phone. Little toys. Too insignificant for the cops to care much, and easily replaceable if you have the means."

I laughed, a little too loud. "Muggings? Not you, Dino. And I can't imagine you breaking a car window. What are you talking about?"

"I have been trained as a cat burglar! For fun and profit, Clay. You'd love it. I know you're an adrenaline junkie. Remember trading blow jobs in front of that FBI agent?"

It was in fact my fondest memory, though I do wish we'd shot that guy. It occurred to me that Dino was kind of catlike, light and lithe and hard to figure.

"I worked with a woman in Milan, Felicia Hardy, though she goes by many names. I was in love with her, in my fashion. We zigzagged Italy and parts of eastern Europe. Felicia taught me to ignore the big score. You can live well on trinkets and petty cash, you can quickly use a credit card and discard the evidence. We lived in nice hotels and we ate well. Thanks to her skills and teaching, I stayed in cashmere and champagne."

"Are you offering to train me?"

"And others. A crew that hits the upscale white ghettos. If more than two do it, the cops suspect a crime spree rather than random thievery. If we all split up and are careful, we can continue for as long as we like. It isn't even like stealing! It's a kind of gift culture. We lighten up their lives. A cultural trade-off. A giveaway."

Keeping a bookstore alive isn't easy, and for all my complaints about the Emma Goldmans I liked the work they did. We could possibly fund their whole operation. I knew Marvin would love it, although he seems a little clumsy for cat burglaring. Are there Rottweiler burglars?

"Do you see yourself as a Fagin?"

"Hardly. You're all too smart and sophisticated. I don't associate with grubby little boys. I like bigger boys that clean up nice."

"I'm intrigued. I'll run this much by the others and set up a meeting. Marvin will jump, Patti will probably say yes. Not sure about the others."

"But you and I know they can be trusted. Commies tend to avoid cops. They make excellent thieves!"

## 4.

The bookstore, actually the entire building, had no heat. We needed to look into that. Also, we hadn't named the store, and we needed to work out a DBA and get a business license. We did find a nice big couch, only slightly used, and placed it near the entrance. We were sitting, shooting-gallery-style, shivering, and discussing business.

"Let's not make it too left wing. Not Commune Books and certainly not The Commons. Those terms have lost all meaning. Let's name it after somebody." Patti was taking the lead. It's fun to name things when they aren't really things. Bands, lit mags, imaginary pets. When it's real it's harder, more permanent.

"The doors are open and we're taking in cash. It's past time for a name." I was ready to vote yes for anything. I really didn't give a shit.

"Red Emma's is taken, so not that. Pick your favorite hero and go for it." Marvin's body language said he also wanted to get it over with.

Chad, for once, wasn't talking. He was, I suppose, praying. He was always praying. Then, finally, "Let's go all in. Let's pick something that messes with the local techies without them even knowing it. I go with Meinhof, or maybe her full name, Ulrike Meinhof's."

We all admired the Baader-Meinhof bunch, but the name did seem a little outré, even for us. Calling it Baader-Meinhof would be too obvious, but maybe if we buried it a little …

"Cut the first name. Meinhof's could be a deli, for all the squares know."

I liked Marvin's use of the word "square." He often said it. Who doesn't love beatniks?

I loosened up a bit around that decision, and together we felt that shared excitement that happens when a collaboration is working. Meinhof's.

## 5.

The general meetings were marathons. Each collective was to send two reps, second Thursday of the month. Public invited, with a general discussion of just about everything following.

We were getting more pushback from the Emma Goldmans. We had come up with a price list for the café and we were plowing ahead on getting the proper insurance and licensing. The donation idea for the café was a bust. Donations didn't cover costs. We gave out breakfasts to people in need, but judging by the look of some of our "customers," we were being cheated. The Cadillac stroller crowd, as Marvin called them, proved to be especially rapacious, but I suppose it is difficult to raise a child if you're only making $100K and you live in Rockridge. One tattooed hipster complained about the coffee (a little weak) and asked if it was free trade. Marvin chased her out with, "Fuck you, and fuck your little baby bauble." The only thing worse than a paying customer is a nonpaying customer. The failure of communism. Of course we couldn't put it that way to the Emmas, just as they were getting more comfortable with commerce.

We decided to form a phalanx of particulars and attend the next meeting en masse, to show how much we cared. We met in Meinhof's, which was originally the front room bar and shoe rental area of the bowling alley. For some reason Marvin wore one of those T-shirts that look like a tuxedo. I didn't know they still made those.

"They don't. I bought several when they came out. Through the years they've gone more out of style. Everybody hates them now."

The others were in anarchist drag, black on black, equally useless as signifiers in this post-signifier world. I had dug out my La Commune T-shirt, A WORKER OWNED BOOKSTORE AND CAFE, long out of business, another glorious failure. I used to drink free coffee there, although it was always a little weak.

We did a semi-ironic group hug and entered the auditorium, once the bowling lanes. Marvin had dubbed it the "great hall of the people," and it was huge. We had helped with (and paid for) the removal of the lanes. Someone had brought in some old folding chairs. People drifted in. The mic offered feedback. There was a projector showing a laptop screen. A crowd that could be pegged as East Bay, except that they were mostly white, and young. I liked, even loved them for their fire and for their hardheadedness, but I was put off by their lack of humor and their hubris.

We started on time, nearly. Someone was appointed moderator. This didn't take as long as one would expect. Nobody wanted to do it, really. We all sank back into our folding chairs. A guy named Devon, hippie type, took it on just as the schedule appeared on the screen. Seems we were last on the docket, after the Inner Strength Church of Fruitvale.

And the games began. Someone was always getting banned, sometimes for life and sometimes pending some sort of hearing. We could all be party to the hearing, but dates never seemed to be set at the general meetings. Somebody would ask for clarification. It was "coming soon." It was all open and loving, lots of "transparency." When you hear the word "transparent" keep your hands on your wallet. Marvin said that to me once. I caught his eye and smiled.

As with any cavernous unlocked building there were squatters. Devon announced that there could be no overnighting. He did this every week. Someone named Stevie was banned, again, for making unwanted sexual advances and for burning candles in the basement. Somebody suggested buying some nonburning candle-type lights. This was voted on. I wanted to act out, but they were so sincere I refrained from joking. In cahoots with Marvin, I once had a reputation for giggling at Language poets, but those days were behind me. I was a businessman. Check that. A worker, part of a worker-owned bookstore. We waited our turn.

The boredom was broken a bit when Stevie entered and demanded a hearing, right then and there. He was "talked down," then very gently given the heave-ho. Heave-ho. Did they use that term at Occupy? They certainly wouldn't use the more accurate "bum's rush."

I wondered if we could find another cheap lease for the bookstore.

Put our Emma Goldman days behind us. But that thought set off "death of communism" ruminating and feelings of depression. I tried telling myself that the least interesting parts of the revolution could be the most illuminating, then I laughed out loud. Nobody noticed. They were discussing poor Stevie, who, though most definitely a victim of capitalism, didn't give a shit about that. He wanted a blanket in the basement.

I thought we were up next and felt a little anxious but we weren't. I'd forgotten about the Inner Strength Church of Fruitvale. The reverend got up, not quite protocol because people mostly spoke sitting down. Looks were exchanged. She gave a good, if scripted speech. They had been moved out of their building, not quite evicted, but repairs were needed that made the church uninhabitable. They feared a landlord scam, that they wouldn't be invited back and the church would go condo. They went through examples, that church on Shattuck, another just above San Pablo. I wondered about church building ownership. Who holds these deeds?

The Inner Strength folks asked for one of the small office spaces on the second floor above the former lanes, and Sunday mornings in the big room for services. I exchanged a smile with Marvin. They'd have to walk through the bookstore to get to church. Customers. And they seemed like a shoo-in to join the Emmas. Queer-friendly, multicultural, steadfast leaders since the early days of the civil rights movement. So very Oakland.

A woman I would have thought to be very Rockridge (Oakland parlance for "not poor") was first up with a question.

"This is not a religious organization. I don't want the Emmas to be thought of as Christians." And here you can insert your favorite Marxist critique of the opiate of the masses.

Then similar remarks from a white guy with dreadlocks. Eye rolls from Marvin, as atheist as the next commie, but I knew what he was thinking. I did my best to shush him, then felt bad. Not our fight, but the ideological bullshit was hard to take.

The minister sat, a tight smile, like she knew the score. She smelled racism, we could tell. I remembered one of Marvin's mini-lectures on shared/not shared ideology: "Figure out who's got your back, then stop asking questions."

The moderator thanked the minister and the others from the congregation. They were excused. Their application would be discussed at the next meeting. Don't call us, we'll call you.

And so by the time we were up we were a little miffed at the Emma Goldmans, and our attitude probably showed. Patti started speaking for us, seated, trying to look sincere and speaking slow and clear. I have watched her break a man's nose with her beautifully tooled deep-blue boots, but here she was playing another part, perfectly. I was grateful that we had saved Chad for later.

"We would like permission to padlock the bookstore portion of the front room. At this point we can only stay open for about six hours a day, and our stock isn't protected after closing time. People come and go at all hours."

A person named Kyle spoke next. They were part of the dance collective, levelheaded, possibly not political enough for some of the group. "Makes sense. Maybe we should talk about locking individual collectives, or installing lockers."

We knew bringing up locks would be controversial, but what could we do? We had spent much of our nut on books, coffee, cups, plates, the espresso machine. I could see my retail comrades sink down in their seats.

The meeting was interrupted by a little comic relief. It was the hand rubbing again. Somebody's nervous habit, and it was some sort of irritant for another of the Emmas, a trigger that, um, triggered a discussion of hand rubbing and the sounds that it makes. Two people walked out, and a guy in a wheelchair wheeled into the middle of our big circle and said, "Could everybody please calm down!"

I was sitting two chairs down from an old-timer, Lucas, who I had known in younger days, had seen at demonstrations for a good chunk of my adult life. He had prepared food for the soup kitchens, done jail time, helped out with the Panther breakfasts, one of those Bay Area radical résumés. He motioned to me, and I leaned forward and toward him.

"I'm not sure I like what I'm hearing."

All I could do was nod. I was in a gray area between two ideologies, or perhaps just two styles.

We were cut off, almost mid-argument, because it was getting late and people were tired. There would be a vote on locks and keys at the next meeting. To us it meant another week of stolen books. We made a deal to rent a big walk-in closet on the second floor. It was big enough to house our most valuable books, a not-too-portable safe, and an old filing cabinet. The "office."

## 6.

"This is a strange bastardization of ideology." Dino smiled, knowing he'd said a mouthful. He'd been hanging around, sore-thumb-like, drawing strange looks from the other denizens. He dressed too well and laughed in the wrong places, at the wrong lines, which made me laugh. He had once said to me, "You and I take nothing seriously." I had tried to disagree.

We were sitting at the picnic table, drinking a nice bottle of Montepulciano supplied by Dino. Marvin took a sip, said, "It's not like that. Every generation puts a different spin on it. It's mostly just language. The urge to rebel is always there, for some."

The table felt a little crowded. The Meinhof's Books brain trust. Patti seemed to be drifting, but Percy and Chad were focused on something.

"I had a talk with Dino and I think I'm in." Percy.

Dino raised his glass. "Then it's agreed. I've spoken with all of you privately and you know what to expect. But I don't want to step on your bookstore project. We'll agree on a time for your, um, education. I would like to get started soon if we can."

So much for the bookstore meeting. There would be time to talk about markups, window design, paying invoices. We were going to be petty thieves for the revolution!

"I said I'm in, on one condition. We set a percentage to be given away. If I wanted to get rich, I'd be doing something else." Percy was usually the poorest of the group, and the most generous.

Marvin had obviously been thinking about it. "Half to the Emmas."

I didn't really mean to groan but I did.

"It's a mostly good operation, and none are perfect. And, face it, money buys influence. We can get the church back in, for example."

"Okay, Marvin. What happens to the rest of the loot?" Next to

Dino I was probably the most skeptical of the bunch. Always looking for the grift.

"We make our expenses, we pay ourselves minimum wage, we build up a small nut. After that we give it all away."

"That's pretty vague."

"Jesus, Clay, give him time. You think I'm going to steal it?" Patti was awake. Soon we'd be at odds, like those cute couples in rom-coms. It was shtick. We were old friends.

"When we see the take we can work that out. I'm thinking, some play on the Rolling Jubilee." We sank down, as much as we could on a bench, and waited for Chad's sermon. "We put out feelers, we poll the community, we pass the cash at an open meeting! Let the people see the money go where it needs to go! Feed the people!"

"Hold on," Marvin said. "This is hot money, Chad. We'll give it on the sly, totally anonymous. Remember that old TV show?"

Nobody remembered so Marvin filled us in. "Some rich asshole who was never on camera passed a million bucks to someone in need. Only his assistant could be identified."

Nods all around. Then Dino squirmed.

"I will be teaching you the ropes and doing advance work, and though I support your altruistic intentions I really can't make ends meet on minimum wage. I'd like to charge fifty percent for my labor."

Marvin stood up, almost tripping as he freed himself from the bench. "I honor your labor but not quite to that extent." Then, looking at the rest of us, "Twenty percent."

Again, nods all around. Dino said he'd have to eat and sleep on it, all the time looking at me. He loved obvious flirtations. I once was embarrassed by them, but by this time I just took it as a hint to cancel any other plans I had for the evening.

# 7.

We adjourned and I paired off with Dino. It was around nine p.m., late-dinner time. I was set up, grocery-wise, so Dino agreed to follow me down to Telegraph and Dwight.

The Chandler Apartments, yes, a fitting name for a detective's place. Possibly how I got the idea. A stolid old apartment building where I lived for many years. Built in the '20s, with an ornate facade, with a tenant mix of rent-control hangers-on and grad students. I beat him there and found good parking, waited in the lobby, and we took the antique elevator to the fourth floor.

I had a view of the parklet on Dwight Way and from my kitchen I could see down Telegraph toward Oakland, a constant view of the South Berkeley open-air asylum. Mostly, those days, I saw cranes, the beginnings of a construction boom. Big-box apartments, built to accommodate increased enrollment at Cal and the influx of tech workers who came, from where I don't know, to appreciate the joys of Bay Area life.

My place was old but well kept, decorated with framed commie posters from Italy, my only tourist trinkets. I knew Dino coveted one in particular, a drawing of a hand holding a white rose, PARTITO RADICALE, white on red. Simply drawn, or at least it seemed that way at first, until it grew on you.

"I won't make an offer on this because you won't sell, but let me know if you tire of it."

I had acquired it at a communist festival years before, when I was young enough to think the revolution was weeks away, with the workers' paradise right behind. Early fall in Pisa, accompanied by the attorney for Partito Radicale, who had carte blanche to free posters, even the big full-color ones they were selling to fund their activities. We walked the park, stopping every few booths for politicking, listening to old Dylan songs sung with an accent, then back up the hill to a party at his rebuilt old barn. High living inside the party circle. Mayakovsky's Bugatti.

I'd taken my cues from Partito Radicale, always living to the best of my abilities between lefty actions. There was a time when a book scout could live high in Berkeley, mostly thanks to rent control. Seems like an age ago. Things have gone so far south.

But at this point the wolf was far from the door, and Dino, O Dino, was drinking a Negroni made with Boodles and Campari and Carpano Antica, mixed in a Prohibition-era shaker, a regift from the poet Garrett Caples, through John Yau.

It's a studio but a large one with very big windows and hardwood floors. Dino stood in the middle of the sleeping and sitting area, looking out the window to a kind of middle distance, holding the coupe just right. Reached into his seersucker jacket, pulled out a pack of unfiltered Gauloises, and in one move sat down the glass, took off the jacket and tossed it on the bed, still holding the blue pack, held it higher, giving me the eyebrows-up questioning look that Italians seem to do so well (see: Giancarlo Giannini), as if to say, Are these still all right inside? I nodded and he put down the drink, pulled a lighter from his pants pocket, and lit up. He offered me one but I was off tobacco, though I still enjoy the smell.

"Can I get a little background on your life as a petty thief?"

"You just have to be quick, because the only way to be quiet is to be quick."

"That's a little vague, although I suppose those could be words to live by."

"They are and I'm not being vague. If you enter someone else's home, eventually you are going to trip on something. Common sense. So I was taught to get in, make a grab, and get out. Small electronics, jewelry, cash. Like any, as you say, petty thief. But it isn't petty when it's smart."

"Does it really add up?"

"It really adds up. I'll show you soon."

And the conversation drifted to other things, a Melville retrospective at PFA, a poet's archives that went to Stanford, a new young painter that Dino liked, like Clemente but not as spiritual. I had made what Marvin called the Sam Spade dinner, rare steak and a sliced tomato salad, produce from a friend's backyard. In honor of Dino I opened a bottle of Barolo. We started with pasta with garlic and butter in place of the baked potato, and I added basil and fresh mozzarella to the tomatoes. Italian wine too. Would sex have been better on an empty stomach? But we weren't really ready, hadn't seen each other in a long time. The conversation went late and we ran through the bottle and some grappa. He and the poet Andrew Schelling are my only grappa-loving friends, besides Marvin.

I didn't think about it until coffee the next morning but spending the entire night really wasn't something we'd done, how nice that it didn't feel awkward.

He got up a little after me. Didn't say anything until the second espresso. "Are you busy today, Clay?"

I wasn't set to cover at the store that day. I had hoped to do some scouting but really didn't want to. The books had been crap and the stores weren't paying much these days. Sometimes you do things because you are used to doing them, or because it feels like exercise. "I could have the day free, if you like."

"Very good. Let's steal laptops. But only the most expensive kind, and only out of big houses." With a smile I've seen before, a little cockeyed, eyes buggy. The most beautiful man in the world turns into Peter Lorre.

I figured he was joking.

"We'll use my car. It's parked down Dwight. Get dressed, and put on a nice clean shirt. Think Cary Grant. We are more than petty thieves."

I went with a light-blue oxford button-down and black jeans, but stayed with the Apikas I'd bought in Beijing. I have a weakness for kung fu shoes.

## 8.

Midmorning we took off in his vintage red Triumph.

"Surely we can't go cat burglarizing in this, Dino. And in broad daylight?"

"Who says 'broad daylight' anymore? You are funny, Clay."

"Well?"

"Lots of old farts have cars like this. It won't be noticed in Piedmont. And daylight's fine. They're out jogging or buying things."

We went into the hills but not too far up. Dino doesn't like those little roads with only one escape route. We parked in one of the daylight-deserted upper-class suburban neighborhoods. Dino led me up the street to a place I assume he'd been watching. We knocked on the front door, no answer. He walked the length of the big porch and tipped an earthen pot, spied the plant. "Madagascar palm. Expensive and hard to care for." I hadn't heard of those but it was an interesting plant. He reached under and picked up a key and blew off some dirt. Opened the door just like that.

"How long were you casing the place?"

"Just say 'watching.' 'Casing' is yardbird speak, or something out of a bad movie. I drove by a few times and kept my eyes peeled."

"'Eyes peeled'? Isn't that yardbird talk?"

He ignored me. We entered a room with one of those McManse cathedral ceilings. This wasn't one of the sweet old Victorians that you see in the Bay Area. Probably built in place of a torn-down, only slightly upscale tract home. Tacky. The furniture in the front room looked expensive, possibly made to order by some artisan who'd lucked onto a family of suckers. As we toured the house the furnishings got cheaper, mostly Ikea. Fucking nouveau riche. At the very least they could have gone to Fenton MacLaren. They make nice stuff.

Dino pulled a pair of gloves from his seersucker. "Don't touch anything. Just watch." He had a light touch, sifting through drawers and picking up laptops, a nicely designed electronic piece that I took to be a speaker. I was later told that it was a Gold Phantom Premier ("titanium tweeter!") and could be turned over pronto for at least a thousand bucks.

"Learn to recognize expensive and light. And we never 'toss' a home. We show respect, even to people with taste like this," he said while looking at a print advertising a Monet show at the Orange County Museum of Art. I followed him around as he scooped up trinkets. Somebody liked watches. He left two and scooped up one: "Hublot, blue titanium. I'm seeing a theme. Such obvious idiots but somebody here has taste and likes titanium. Or maybe they just like the sound of the word."

We went out the front door. No alarms, to my surprise.

"Lots of people don't bother with them, but I know what to do when we run into one. Don't worry."

# 9.

My shift at Meinhof's was about to begin. Two guys were eating hippie slop at one of the tables. I couldn't throw them out even though they bothered me. They were comrades. Also lumpen but we were to tolerate lumpen. I pulled down the protective canvas covers that we had devised to protect the books from thieves. They didn't work, except maybe as a reminder to those with a conscience. The guys made a move toward helping me, then sat down. It's okay. To each according, I guess. Maybe they had bad backs.

Marvin came in, though it wasn't his shift. He was carrying a white bag. There was a bakery down the street that I liked.

"Chocolate chip, mostly chocolate."

"Thanks, Marvin. What brings you here on a day off?"

"Do you know where your boyfriend is fencing the trinkets?"

"Not my boyfriend. We agreed not to ask. Better if we don't know."

"I have my doubts about Dino. He gathers up the loot and comes back with money, which is good, but I think he's nicking more off the top. And he's ... iffy."

"You always have had doubts. But the money does come back. You routinely deal with iffy people. Gunrunners and such. All lucre's filthy. I think I'm quoting you here. And who said money is the mother's milk of politics?"

"Jesse Unruh, but he was probably quoting somebody too. You've worked with Dino before. What's he like?"

"At times he can be a Mr. Norris type, a little shady. Mostly he's okay. Find out who has your back and stop asking questions. He's worth the gamble."

## 10.

Patti had been away for months, or maybe a couple of years, returning to Berkeley just as we were coming together to start Meinhof's. She's one of those friends—you can be apart for years but when reunited good conversation comes back at once.

I needed a more intimate evening with her, because we'd wasted too much talk on the business of opening a store, and then on the crazy idea of being cat burglars. That one gave us some shared laughs.

My studio apartment in the Chandler had a great kitchen, surprising in a small apartment. I put it to good use. This night I was making a fairly simple pasta with pancetta and garlic, saltimbocca, salad, and lots of the thin, dry Orvieto that seemed to be my most recent wine of choice.

Patti arrived and we started with the Negronis. I've gone through all the fancy recipes since, but back then I was making the classic drink, and I'm back to that now. Sometimes the old ways are the best ways: Boodles or Plymouth, Campari, Noilly Prat this time. I could figure that Patti hadn't had one since our last night together, wouldn't drink them as a matter of habit like me, but would appreciate the gesture and love the drink.

"Nice, thanks. When did you start drinking these?"

She hadn't heard my "first Negroni" story, or maybe she had and was leading me on, seeing if there were multiple versions, or perhaps she just wanted to break the ice after so much time.

"Haven't I told you?"

"If you did, it was late and I'd had a few of these. Who remembers?"

"Okay, so I was taking the train from Rome to Pisa, sharing a compartment with two priests from Chicago. The Cubs were in the playoffs, so we started talking baseball, then politics—they were Dorothy Day types—and of course the charms of Italy. They were good-looking, young, perhaps 'together' in some way. It was really warm in the compartment..."

"I didn't ask for a sex story. Were they drinking Negronis?"

"At some point they mentioned a bar in Pisa that made a 'charming little cocktail' called a Negroni. They had a flirty argument about the recipe. One said it had a spray of orange juice, the other 'just a thin slice for looks.' We decided to hit that bar soon as the train pulled in. It was a long, liquid evening. I almost converted. Or maybe they almost deconverted. A magical drink, they kept saying."

Patti picked up the pitcher with a questioning look. I proceeded to build our second.

And on and on like always, the spell only broken a couple of times to discuss the Emmas and Meinhof's, and then sometime after midnight when she made mention of "Dino's capers."

"Is he going to take the money and run?"

"You don't trust him?" Laughing in spite of myself, and Patti laughing too.

"He's the most charming crook I've ever met but that's not necessarily a good thing. You're wrapped around his ... little finger."

"Or something."

"Or something." And then she left off, and then there was some shared knowledge that our hearts were beating in time, and I took closer notice of Patti, the bangs and the almost artificial green in her eyes. Long ago I asked. No, they are not contacts.

## 11.

There was a house, squeezed between two apartment boxes, that had that early-California Spanish look, except that it was stucco, and boy did they get stucco—as the poet said—because the light was blocked by the apartments on each side and a McMansion at its backside. Just made for the tech rich, and according to Dino, they love places like that because you can pick one up for under two mil, say you live in Piedmont, and fit all the toys in. Who looks outside anyway?

Easy break-in, though I didn't, at that point, understand Dino's technique. No alarm, a slide-through-the-window deal, and there we were. Dino loaded stuff into his Avalanche duffel, retro brown leather, very smart. He found a stash of Apple watches, different designs, right on top of the underwear drawer. A watch for every day of the week? These people have more money than God.

Face it, stealing from the rich is sexy as hell. A poet once told me, as we were checking out the shelves at SPD, that the revolution could only succeed if it became sexy again, that this generation of agitators needed a Che, or some other sex godix, to lead the way. The light streaks in Dino's hair, the back of his neck just showing above the collar of his Napoli shirt, made of some bamboo material that added an extra layer of scent. Expensively well groomed, setting up an arousal partly fueled by guilt, how can a Marxist ... but then, again, Mayakovsky drove a Bugatti. And, as was our habit now, we found the bedroom (people like this have amazing beds) and, carefully, dry-humping at first before finishing discreetly (no stains), had a nice little ride.

All in a day's work now. We returned to Meinhof's with a duffel full of baubles.

## 12.

Where did I read that he drove a Bugatti? Perhaps it was in one of his letters to Lili Brik? That he was sent to Paris to spread the good word and went just a little crazy, good clothes, White Russian girlfriend, fast cars? Or maybe I'm confusing this with, say, *Silk Stockings* or some other anticommunist propaganda. Mayakovsky played by an aging Peter Lorre? Hardly. No, he really did drive his Bugatti through Paris. Was it the same Bugatti that killed Isadora Duncan? Don't think so, but I can't be sure.

"Isn't there some way of tracking the stolen watches?" We were back at the store, Marvin peering into the duffel.

"Anything done can be undone. I know a guy, as they say in the movies." Dino, in control. Marvin, not too sure. I was lost in poetic reverie, not caring for the time being.

"I must be going. I'll move these and come back in a couple of days with the cash. I've got things to do." Dino, all business.

The store was pretty empty, just one guy in the back by the PM Press section. Marvin put on some Steely Dan. Don't know why he listens to that shit. To look at him you'd expect scruffy singer-songwriters, perhaps because he dresses like Neil Young and sports a similar (lack of) hairstyle.

"Is Dino going loose cannon on us?"

"Don't think so."

"He's in it for the money. I don't like that."

"Mother's milk of politics."

The customer came up with some Paul Goodman. Made my day. Almost nobody reads him but I insist on keeping his books on the shelves. Caught Marvin's eye and we smiled in unison.

## 13.

Things were rolling, maybe even snowballing, at least for the bookstore/cat thief enterprise. The café was having permit trouble and was becoming a money pit. We needed a new fridge, better plumbing, more electrical outlets. We were still operating the café as a free place, taking suggested donations for espressos and vegan donuts. We were under the radar, so far, but nervous. We couldn't afford any form of government poking around. We discussed dumping the food service idea but our coffee and donuts were too popular. Our egos wouldn't allow it.

I was dunking a donut in a triple espresso, shooting the shit, and occasionally selling a book. Somebody came in, with a flourish, too well dressed and a little too confident to be liked. It took me a few minutes to recognize Astor Ratcliffe, world-famous chef, third generation in a line that formed behind Alice Waters. I think he once worked for her, but what famous chef hadn't? He went to our tiny Food Writing shelf and picked out some Liebling, in that nifty North Point edition, the one with an intro by James Salter.

"How are the donuts?"

"They taste like rubber, but no animals were harmed in the—"

"Oh jeez."

"But our coffee is amazing. Italian all the way. Not a hint of Seattle."

"A double, please. Do you have real milk?"

"Of course. Double cap?" And I made him a good one. "Slumming, Mr. Ratcliffe?"

"I lent the Liebling to one of my staff. I keep one on my desk at all times. And I wanted to invite you to dinner at Pomo Langpo. Bring your scruffy friend, but not the others."

I was a little nonplussed. I'd never met the guy. Maybe Marvin knew him?

"What's the occasion?"

"I like the space. Slumming, yes, but there's a lot to be said for the slums. They are a rich stew. I think maybe we can work something out. I like that you've involved Dino Centro too. He has a less, um, communistic view of business."

And he's beautiful, I thought, slipping back into reverie.

## 14.

Pomo Langpo. Vaguely Native American? Or perhaps a reference to postmodernism. Postmodern cuisine? But aren't we a few posts past postmodern, even in cuisine culture? And Langpo, as in the fad that passed through the poetry world a few decades ago? But how would Mr. Ratcliffe know about that obscure movement in mostly West Coast lit? The restaurant was causing a major sensation, multi-starred reviews, celebs smoking on the sidewalk, waiting for a table. Astor Ratcliffe was a household name, if your household happened to be in Temescal, Rockridge, Noe Valley, the Mission, or any other formerly affordable neighborhood. He had been interviewed everywhere. Had he made it big during the Clinton years, he would have been invited to the White House. When he was discovered shopping at the Ferry Building he was mobbed by foodies chanting, "Vanilla hots, vanilla hots!" in reference to one of his signature sauces.

Mr. Ratcliffe hadn't just whipped up a couple of new sauces. He had invented a culture. He claimed that the Langpo was a lost tribe, once centered in Brazil, or was it Ecuador? Astor kept it all vague, to "protect those survivors who hold the secret recipes." All this with a wink and a nod, or maybe not. Maybe these people did exist? Food writers would pry, but he would go all Bob Dylan interview on them, regaling them with bad puns, various origin tales, presumably anything that came off the top of his head and would pull the wool.

I wore white and Marvin wore tweed. I have one of those Tom Wolfe ice cream suits. It went well with the kung fu shoes and an A's cap. Marvin was resplendent in the tweed jacket, a golden paisley shirt, bicycle pants, and wingtips. Hair tied back, samurai-style. In deference to the weather I went into the kitchen and built him a tall, icy Boodles and tonic. Astor had told us to forgo the line (Langpo took no reservations), so we had time to drink in my apartment.

"Nice jacket, Marvin."

"Once belonged to Frank O'Hara. Tony Towle gave it to me."

We went out in Marvin's borrowed car, a 1977 Fiat 500, even tinier than the new Chrysler cuties. It was once bought on the gray market by an owner of the old Black Oak Books, one of the "Bobs," and since had been bought/passed around the bookseller world. It currently belonged to an ex-buyer at Moe's Books, bought before an anti-union drive drove her out of that job. She was still a good commie despite losing the book gig, and freely lent the car out. It was a very bright red, repainted over the years. Perfect for this kind of outing.

Pomo Langpo was at Shattuck and Vine, in a building that had formerly housed a failed bookstore. Perhaps because of the address, the joint was immediately popular with the literati. Even before the boffo reviews made a table difficult to come by, the likes of Chabon, Rupi Kaur, and Ishmael Reed had stopped by (presumably not together) to order pitchers of the frozen rose punch and douse their fish with vanilla hots. Once the bankrupt bookshop had proudly displayed photographs of the authors who had given readings. Shrewd old Astor bought the pictures from the ex-owners and stored them in the stockroom. A famous writer would stop by for lunch and before the cocktails had arrived their photo would be hanging near the booth. The "pix trick," as it came to be called, soon became the talk of what Marvin called the "glamor profession."

## 15.

Late-spring nights in Berkeley are okay but rarely outstanding. It's a little too cold for crisp white shirts, half unbuttoned, cropped tops, and bare shoulders. When there is an exceptionally hot night the town moves outside, giving the lie to its "roll up the sidewalks" rep. This night was perfect, as warm as LA and not as poisoned. There was a long line in front of the restaurant waiting for the last seating. We shed our jackets as we cut the line. Is that Michael Lewis or Michael Pollan? Can't tell them apart sometimes. Alice was by the front door, schmoozing the bouncer. She gave us a quick nod (knows Marvin) before turning to walk, presumably, to her own place. The bouncer looked great, unbuttoned shirt, washboard chest! But does the bitch know what to do with it, as Dino likes to say. I gave him the perfunctory once-over twice.

We were waved in with a flourish.

"Oh jeez, who let the book scouts in." This from Andy Ross, formerly of Cody's Books, long defunct. Marvin flipped him the bird.

The once-picture windows were covered with heavy tapestries, kind of like a medieval version of Azteciana, with some sort of text, a mix of pictograph and Sanskrit-like lettering. We were directed to a low table. Pillows on the floor—orientalist? The light was low, and despite the openness of the big room there was very little noise. I noticed tapestries buffering the ceiling. No open kitchen, no banging pots. Quiet as a cathedral, and the place smelled great, spices and herbs, and a definite hit of vanilla.

A server approached our rock slab of a table, a shimmering beauty in a tunic, floating above all gender considerations, far above being classified as a lowly human. Where did this mystery-eth godix come from? Was Pomo Langpo a place that people "came from"? We ordered the punch because everyone seemed to. Like Vinho Verde but not as sweet, very light and with some rose extract though not enough to be pukey. We downed our carafe, fast, then ordered a second.

The silence was broken by an Alice Coltrane piece, nice choice. Someone came out of the kitchen, said, "Mingle! Your amuse-bouche is at the bar, and the next punch is free!" It took an amateur yoga stretch for me to crane my neck, watching the watchers watch. I noticed him at the bar, half hidden behind a saguaro. I wondered how they kept it alive, inside and in Berkeley. He was also wearing a white suit. Don't you hate when that happens? The only two white suits in all of Berkeley.

Server came by with more wine. "There's something for everyone at the bar." I asked if we could get a proper cocktail, was told there was only the local wine.

And, in unison with Marvin, "Wine from Berkeley?"

"Just for tonight you are not in Berkeley. We are aswim in Pomo Langpo."

Aswim? I was a little tired of it all, but Marvin was amused.

"What's the capital of Pomo Langpo?"

"Unpronounceable."

I picked up my glass, got up, crossed the room. Wet kiss from Dino.

"Nice suit, Clay, but not your style. You're too white for it. You look like Tom Wolfe." And Dino was right. He seemed perfectly at ease in his ice cream suit. "How did you get in?"

"Marvin knows everybody. You?"

"I know everybody too. I'm a famous cat burglar. Gives the place a mid-twentieth-century feel, like a Hitchcock film. Mr. Ratcliffe is attracted to criminal chic. I drink here every night, hit the amuse-bouche, and leave before the main course, unless they're serving the oxtail. I'll be staying for dinner tonight. Join you?"

The amuse-bouche was a peapod filled with minced raw oysters, with a dribbling sauce served in an eyedropper. The sauce was a take on the famous vanilla hots, but I later learned that it wasn't the classic. More black peppery. Not bad. I picked up another for myself and one for Marvin, who had stayed seated. He held out his hand for Dino, an ironic gesture. I wondered if Dino would kiss it, but they had a normal shake.

A bell rang. It was dinner. The food was laid out rijsttafel-style. Clay pots with a clear tasty broth, flatbread with herbs, a bright-red rice dish, a mystery meat on skewers (Marvin guessed goat), vegetables cut to look like other vegetables, huge unpeeled shrimp, the size you never see in Northern California, probably up from Mexico. Tables full, the staff came out with trays of those cheap squirt bottles that usually hold ketchup. The crowd began the chant. "Vanilla hots! Vanilla hots!"

I tried a squirt on my shrimp. Life changing. I didn't actually taste the heat, I got it through my skin. No, I intuited it, felt it as an epiphany. These weren't your normal serranos. Something was going on. I looked over at Marvin, smiling and nodding, then at Dino, looking same. I added another squirt.

Orders of slow-cooked oxtail, in a sauce that was more cuminy but still had an undertone of vanilla. Our squirt bottles were a little stopped up. "Fuck that," Marvin said as he removed the screw top and soaked every plate with the sauce.

And we were off. Later I had some memory of "coming on." Remember that phrase? "We'll be sweating like pigs from all the peppers! Drink more of this," and Dino refilled our glasses with the cold rosy cocktail.

I was halfway through a lobster tail, though I didn't know how it got there. The roasted garlic and parsley garnish was moving around the plate on its own. It was an old mushroom-type feeling, but different too. Euphoric, and pretty clean. Mixing nicely with alcohol and food, unlike other psychedelics. No wonder this place was so popular.

A nice high, but I was a little worried. In the detective game you are often subjected to the old Mickey Finn. I was once fed a brownie that had more than the usual dispensary-level brownie filling. Almost blew that case.

Surprise dosing can be pleasant, though. The poet Keith Abbott once told me a story of flying from SFO to a reading in Boulder, or maybe it was Iowa City, with Andrei Codrescu. A friend had given them something "for the flight" that they assumed was a sedative. High above America they realized that they had been dosed heavily with LSD. I suppose there are lots of us who have lived through something like that. Marvin calls it a "magic punch bowl" incident.

As I was drifting through dosage memories Marvin leaned over, one elbow brushing an oyster shell. "Magic punch bowl!"

The table was beginning to levitate as the coffee was served. It was late, but the place was still pretty full. A kind of Spanish guitar thing was playing, or was it live? I looked around, no musicians. The lights were even lower, I think. I looked over at Dino. Everything melted away except him. This often happened to me, drugs or no drugs. The coffee, boiled Turkish-style, tasted of vanilla. Uh-oh. I experienced a telescoping effect. Dino's eyes, Dino's lips. Beatific smile. Was my smile beatific? The blond streaks in his hair seemed to catch fire. A halo for Saint Dino, patron to thieves, and for the descendants of Robin Hood.

Interrupted by a server. "The chef will be out to see you shortly."

# 16.

Astor Ratcliffe approached our table but didn't get too close. Having gotten our attention, he motioned for us to rise. He was wearing the traditional double-breasted chef coat, but it was tinted a beautiful blue. I think. Or was it white, and was I just seeing it as a beautiful blue? I hadn't seen that shade, ever.

We were led back, then upstairs to his "office," but his office looked like your hippie great-aunt's Haight Street pad, circa 1968, drapes right out of Pier 1 Imports, or perhaps the Akron. "Indian" prints covered the walls. "I know, ridiculous, but a previous tenant decorated, and it kind of grew on me. I wasn't even born in the '60s, or the '70s for that matter, so it seems exotic." We didn't know how to respond, and so we didn't. I wasn't even sure where the floor was, or if I was standing on it.

"Ah yes, the hots. You must have been liberal with the sauce. Too much can overwhelm other flavors. But how much is too much? After all, Clay, as a poet you know how it is. The road of excess ..."

"Leads to a big hangover." Marvin.

"My hot sauce burns clean! You will wake up refreshed, craving eggs and bacon."

My addled attention zeroed in on his eyebrows and silver swept-back hair. Was he trying to look like Alain Ducasse? Except for the dangling earring. Can't imagine Ducasse with one of those. It was a little like a Calder, a thingy within a thingy that moved with his head. In my inebriated state I thought of flicking it, but I (barely) held back.

"Can I cut to the chase? The grand hall of that old bowling alley would be perfect for Bugatti, my next restaurant. I have several new ways to market vanilla hots, and this super-distressed place is perfect."

"Grand hall? It's a fucking bowling alley." Marvin wasn't going to get along with this guy. "And for all its problems it aspires to be an anarchist space."

"Perfect! If you haven't noticed, we're selling, along with inventive food, a new form of psychedelic. We're not talking about depressed charter members of the bourgeoisie microdosing their cares away. This stuff is new, the latest chance to see God. These Occupy types will eat it up. Hipster pop culture influencers won't quite get it. Their time has passed. Scruffy is the new black."

Occurred to me that Dino would love this con as much as Marvin hated it. I was a little miffed at the obviousness of Astor's spiel, but not uninterested. Was his thinking upside-down or cutting-edge? Could it pay expenses for the building?

"Are you offering to lease the space?" Dino was interested.

"Not ours to lease. It's a co-op." My lust buddy and my best friend were about to get into it. Not the first time.

"Bugatti will pay for the building, and there will be enough for Meinhof's to fund a small revolution or a large bookstore."

Everything I saw took on a blue tint. The vanilla hots? I wondered why he was calling his new restaurant Bugatti. Wasn't I just thinking about a Bugatti? No, something to do with Mayakovsky. I think. I'd never seen that shade of blue. It wasn't really a color. Something more.

Next thing I knew we had left the restaurant. It must have gotten late. That block of Shattuck was deserted, but Marvin suggested we walk over to César and have a nightcap.

César, since defunct, had been old Berkeley since the days when "gourmet ghetto" was a term still in use. We ordered a bottle of Tavel, not that we needed it in our psycho-retro-hippie-high state, but Dino said that a little taste of Liebling's favorite wine would take us out of the '60s—not an easy task in Berkeley, even sans drugs. And isn't it strange, considering the way the town has been rebuilt in the image of a million-room tech dorm? The place is ruined, and yet, and yet, the ghosts remain. Isn't that Ginsberg's cottage? Is Angela Davis in town? There's a slight scent of the old revolution, still.

Manchego cheese, a little more wine. The place was half empty. Was it late? I was, as they say, rolling.

"If we can convince the Emma Goldmans to lease the hall, we can clean up." Too up front, Dino. Marvin will jump on this.

And so he did, and we argued through another bottle of Tavel, drawing attention from the patrons. I played middle child as much as I could—we could put the money to good use, like Allen Ginsberg's Gap ad. But the blue! I had never seen that shade, ever, and now the table was blue, even the Tavel, or maybe the glass? When I blinked the blue came at me, hard, but not in any way threatening. I got in the last word, I think: "We can't go forward without the other Meinhofs."

## 17.

I got home late, but reasonably late. The cat was angry, so I put down some food. I wanted to hear some music, then didn't, then did. What to play? Alice Coltrane ended my quandary, the spiritual stuff. I don't really get it but that doesn't mute my appreciation.

Mostly the hots had worn off. I felt a little down, but in a romantic poet way. It came as a gentle buzz, not harsh like a speed crash. When I closed my eyes I could still see the blue, lighting up the insides of my lids. I had a huge Franz Kline poster that had a bit of blue in it. Sort of cobalt. Was that the blue? I crossed the studio apartment and got up close, looked at the Kline, then blinked and blinked again. Not quite the blue. I thought about writing but I couldn't really write about blue, because that is played out. I mean, do I reference the blues? Decided that, beyond casual conversation, I wouldn't, at least at first, reveal the secrets of my eyelids. I was curious, though, was everybody seeing blue? A color that couldn't be found in nature? Or could it? Curiosity would drive me to conversation, but I wouldn't include it in a poem. At least for now, the blue and its blueness would only be hinted at, and mostly remain internal.

## 18.

As predicted, the day had begun with bacon and eggs, at Mama's on Broadway, and all were bright-eyed and ready to get back to running a radical bookstore.

There's the everyday stuff that can be boring, even destructive, *love's vessel beached* ... , but then the same activities can serve as a caesura, a time-out, a rest. We were ordering up books from PM Press, good solid revolutionary fodder for the lefty heads. A little Kropotkin, a little Angela Davis, pour some coffee, back to the laptop. Nice music on, more Alice Coltrane because once she gets in your head ... It was all a lead-up to the general meeting, an evening that could easily be overthought had we not kept busy.

But first, the lock-and-key controversy needed to be dealt with. Once philosophy creeps in, problem-solving takes a back seat, but there was hope on the horizon, in the person of Glue, possibly not their given name, but there was probably real symbolism in it. Glue seemed to pull things together and cement them. Glue was ... grounded? Or that was their reputation.

"I know a few things about lasers, and I know people who know more, and we can set you up for a sort of laser field. You close up shop, you turn it on. If someone walks into your store and trips the laser, it sets off a gentle, humming alarm. We elect a laser monitor. There's always someone in the building, even late. When the alarm goes off, they check it out."

Marvin and Dino were both intrigued. Chad, who had been pricing used books at the other end of the counter, drifted over. "With the front door locked, the lasers protecting the bookstore space, we'd only need someone to volunteer to monitor the situation. Problem solved." He clapped his hands and looked heavenward. I wondered if someday he would develop neck and back problems.

So it was set, Meinhof's was to be protected by laser beams. I thought of those old caper movies where the thieves lower themselves onto the floor of the museum, grab the golden chalice, then slither like reptiles, dodging the beams and escaping. Those old movies were an early sex fantasy for me, watching them on TV as puberty invaded my body. Since then, the thought of someone in tight black clothes doing any sort of slithering can drive me up the wall.

Chad asked me out for lunch, which meant that I would pay, so we left Marvin to mind the store until Patti arrived late afternoon. She was driving Lyft mornings to make her rent.

We walked over to a "street taco" place on Telegraph. Another food truck had gone brick and mortar, replacing recipes with higher-end ingredients that, thankfully, tasted the same. I ordered two cabeza. Chad went with vegetarian. Sometimes, especially in the

Bay Area, that is an affectation, but I think Chad was truly appalled that animals are killed for food. Likewise, my choice of taco could be seen as self-conscious—why not just get beef? My order, though, was sincere. I like strong flavors.

"Marvin called a meeting that includes dinner. What's that all about?"

I knew, but didn't know that Marvin had included dinner. Probably meant I'd be cooking, to help butter up our comrades.

"I'm cooking for the meeting?"

"Tonight at your place." A sudden intense look from Chad.

"It's about Astor's plans to sublet the big room. You've heard about that?"

"I don't like Astor."

Chad was a bullshitter but he was also pure of heart. Can that happen? Did that make him a good liar? Or was it that he wasn't a bullshitter, that everything he said was sincere? I felt a quandary coming on.

"Not many people like Astor, but he runs a tight ship and his food tastes great." I blinked and the blue was still there. Actually, I would admit to myself later that I blinked in order to see the blue, to be reassured by it.

"I don't like it. Fine dining in the big room? The Emmas will never go for it."

Money talks, dear Chad. I thought it but didn't say it because at that moment he went all angelic on me, a look that could melt a glacier. Preachers. Jeez. We finished our tacos and went back to work.

## 19.

It was strawberry season and quite warm. I made a cold strawberry soup to start us off. It's really just the berries, cream, a little orange juice, a little yogurt, some mint leaves from the back alley. Shots of vodka, straight from the freezer, to cut the sweetness. Baked some quickie biscuits from a YouTube recipe.

Marvin, as usual, started the show as we finished the soup. He had more details, including financial terms that really would cover repairs on the building, insurance, taxes, with lots left over.

Patti was skeptical but didn't immediately say no. "We're getting into lawyer territory. We need an ironclad agreement. Astor is a small business owner. So many of them are scumbags."

"Isn't that what we are?" Dino, cutting through the bullshit.

"A collective isn't a small business, exactly."

"The government would see us as business partners."

"We have a different mission."

And from Chad, "We do! We're a collective and part of a collective of collectives. We're educating people. We aren't an overgrown gift shop, like Moe's or Barnes and Noble. We're doing good work. It isn't at all about profit. We're making minimum wage, except for you, Dino."

"I'm keeping your project alive because you need help. Bookstores don't generally survive on their own."

And it was true, bucks from our pilfering project paid a big chunk of the bills and could fund the work that would allow us to make necessary building repairs.

Patti swung over to Dino's side. "I think we should push for Astor. Meinhof's is doing fine, but the Emmas need the bucks, and look at the work they do. Food distribution, legal aid, child care. If they go away, the old bowling alley will soon be a fifteen-story techie condo."

Smiles from Dino, for Patti and also for the eggplant tower and the grilled asparagus. I had allowed some time between courses so that we could switch over from fruit and vodka to a nice lightish red and the vegetables. No vegans this night, so the eggplant was covered in cheese. This would please Marvin, who is opposed to plant-based meals.

Percy, to my surprise, was in from the start. "Get the money! We can fund a nice chunk of East Bay radicalism, and we can up our café game. We could even make sandwiches."

That last point put it over. We were going to convince the Emmas to lease great-hall time to Astor's Bugatti. Sandwiches!

## 20.

We had asked Astor to stay away from the public meeting. The Emmas would take one look at him and back off. He wore ascots, without (or maybe with) irony. Either way, he was not part of their subculture. Once, before they moved into the building, there was a long-winded argument over where to meet. McDonald's was thought to be more "working class," but it was an evil corporation. The local café was full of bourgeois types. They had once met over iced tea at a local Thai place but the proprietors hated them because they took up tables and refused to order food. Fine dining (except perhaps on the sly) was frowned upon.

 The Meinhofs were sitting in a circled group of folding chairs, middle of the great hall. We were going over our arguments as people filed in. It looked to be a full house. Word was out that something was up. Astor walked, no, strode, no, half jogged into the room. No ascot, but still piss-elegant in a full-length black leather jacket and a sky-blue beret. "Jeez, who the fuck…" This from Marvin.

 The bowling alley, cheaply refloored and stripped of its drop ceiling tiles, resembles an airplane hangar or an overgrown high school gym. The acoustics are terrible, but two huge speakers, punk band castoffs, could fill the room with a booming sound between bouts of feedback. I had turned in my chair to see Astor enter, prompted by Dino. To my field of vision Astor seemed bigger than life, his bereted head fronting the high arched ceiling, light from one of the newly excavated skylights giving him a backlit halo, as false as a halo can be, given what I'd always heard about him. Still, it looked good, if a little corny.

 He pulled up a folding chair and sat with us.

 "Do we have a plan?"

 Marvin beat us to the eye-roll punch and so spoke first. "Something along the lines of 'We paid for this microphone.'"

 "Wouldn't that be considered an ideological broadside?"

 "Astor, we're commies but we're still American, and in the US nobody has a soul. We have bank accounts, or not. It doesn't talk, it swears."

 The meeting came to order, or at least some sort of order. Chairs in a circle, people cross-talking, somebody slicing a couple of mangos, so perfectly that I felt a little jealous. I always fuck that up somehow. The mango circles the room, the screen shows an agenda. For some reason the beginning of a Creeley poem came to mind: *The bell rings. It is Ted.* Hard to stay focused on these things. I'd rather be home reading *The Finger*, that piece to Zukofsky, or maybe one of those New Directions gray covers where he goes on about death. Being a poet is a curse, if you mean to get things done.

Shelley from the Anarchist Hackers chaired this night, a blessing for us because they are somewhat literate and, unlike the other radical techies, they care about books. A little intro for first-timers (the place was still filling up with new faces), then some old business. The radical Black church had begged off, "not the best fit." My eyes met Patti's. She was pissed, but shrugged it off.

I was thinking about Wanda Coleman for some reason, but I couldn't fully recall even a line of her work. People were talking, blah blah, about another banning, someone was lighting candles again. *Wind giving presence to fragments.* Where did that line come from? And then it was our turn to speak.

Percy, as a café worker, started things off with a rather bland (planned it that way) rundown of the things a restaurant may need to move into the space, followed by praising Astor's relation to his workers, the profit-sharing plan that almost but not quite amounted to "worker-owned." All well put, but I wondered what Percy's stake was. He veered left, I guess, but mostly I think he wanted a stable barista gig.

The white guy with dreadlocks, newish, but always vocal, shot down the entire proposal, calling it a capitalist food court and taking a couple of swipes at Meinhof's. The phrase I remember, and kind of liked, was "shopping mall with pretensions." This was red meat to the purists. If this were a horror movie, their collective glares would burn out our hearts.

I kept my mouth shut and waited for Marvin and Chad, our big guns. I looked over at Dino, who sat low in his chair, thinking what I was thinking.

They started in together, a sort of call and response between God and Money, two old friends.

"Filthy lucre, right?" Marvin said. "Up to now the money's come from a couple of trust funds, a City of Oakland grant, crowdfunding, and generous donations from the Meinhof group. We paid the PG&E bill. Not especially pure but you can't prepare free food without gas and electricity. It's all about the money. Astor"—looking over, getting a solemn head nod from the chef—"will keep us afloat so we can do good work."

Chad waited a couple of beats, and in a mild voice of unassuming authority, calmed yet excited the gathering. He paused again, then, folding his hands (he has beautiful hands) in front of his chest, looked to the rafters. "Fate has laid a hand on us!" I feared that he would overplay his own hand, but he bowed his head and showed an aspect of deep humility. Corny, but things that seem corny can melt away when Chad gets going. "Forty-two million people in this country experience food insecurity! This goes beyond ideology. We can funnel Astor's resources into every food bank in the Bay Area. We can fund our own food project. Where people are hungry the end justifies the means!" And getting back to his radical Christian roots, "The fishes and the loaves!"

The speech continued for a bit, but he ran out of gas and bowed his head again. I remembered that old James Brown shtick and fantasized covering him with a cape and walking him offstage.

Back to Marvin. "We'll keep the restaurateur honest. Let's put together a committee. We can make this work."

It was getting late, and, as always, the meeting broke up before we could take a vote. I had been counting the house, happy that the people from the sex workers legal defense were in attendance. We backed them when they wanted to join the Emmas. They owed us. The Forever Light poetry chapbook group was also a shoo-in. They'd published me once, and we always stocked their books at Meinhof's.

Damn. The clock had run out. No vote this night. Did this happen every time?

## 21.

I was out with Marvin, buying books from a storage locker in El Sobrante. Dino and Chad were up in Montclair, "foraging." Wednesday afternoon, too warm for book browsing so no customers. We came in first, tired from the buy, tired from loading the van. Percy drinking iced coffee and Patti at the register reading an illustrated edition of Kropotkin. Living the good life.

Patti got up and helped us get the boxes inside. Nice enough books, mostly solid modern lit, a few volumes of poetry, some popular science from years past that would fill a dollar table. Got them cheap because the woman who rented the locker was tired of paying the storage bill. She had fantasies of starting a little bookstore but never quite got there.

Boxes unloaded, van parked, we stopped at the nearest convenience store for beer. Intellectual working-class heroes.

We were drinking at the coffee bar, talking about the books, when we were interrupted by, I thought, a customer. Nice looking, though a little better groomed than I usually go for. I very slowly zeroed in on recognition. Different hair maybe. Shorter. Marvin got her name first, so I didn't have to search my brain.

"Brianna, hello. Long time." I thought I remembered that she had always been friendly.

"Really long. Good to see you. Don't mean to be rude, but I'm here, well, kind of, on business. I need Clay's detective expertise."

I'd never heard it described as expertise and I rose to the flattery. "Well, shucks. What do you need?"

"Are you currently working on a case?"

More flattery. I never called them cases. Jobs, pains in the whatever, but not really cases. "Nope. Writing poems and wrangling books. The usual."

"Have you heard about all those petty thefts up in the hills?"

"Something."

"A couple of places were broken into in my neighborhood, so the crime wave is reaching the flats." Brianna had a house a few doors up from the Popeye's on San Pablo, kind of old-school Berkeley. I vaguely remembered it as a little dowdy but spacious. "Cops don't give a shit if you lose a laptop, a phone, a set of earbuds. I can't afford to lose my stuff. My neighbors are in the same boat."

I wanted to say, "I didn't do it, we only do the Robin Hood thing," but I couldn't, and I was pissed to think that some other cat burglar was hitting the scruffy semi-middle class. Was Dino moonlighting?

"What would you charge to poke around, hit the streets, set up a stakeout, whatever the fuck it is you people do?"

Nice edge. Memories were coming back to me. Brianna could be a little, um, difficult. I don't have a set rate. Mostly I do a Travis McGee thing, taking part of what I salvage. I channeled Marlowe, came up with something off the top. "Three hundred a day plus expenses usually. But you're talking about petty theft. Why hire an op?"

"I'll pay the price. It's for the neighborhood. We can't have people losing their stuff. Besides, it's creepy, people breaking and entering."

I didn't buy it. Something was definitely hinky. I wouldn't pay myself half that. And to retrieve earbuds? But one does have a lifestyle, and even with a discount these dinners that feature the hots could get expensive.

I switched from Marlowe to Rockford. "I'll have a look around, but no promises. I am kind of busy."

"I know, Clay. Poetry is awfully time consuming. You're hired." We shook, and I liked the feel of her hand. We swapped phone numbers, standing close. She had a deep, Demi Moore kind of voice. I go for that.

I watched her walk away, then caught an iconic Marvin eye roll. "Back to your old bisexual tricks. Dino and Brianna. Both great looking and completely untrustworthy. Total tools." Mayakovsky's Bugatti with a sexual slant.

## 22.

"Are you freelancing, Dino?"

"I don't go near the flats, except to have lunch at Bartavelle."

"The MO is similar." I didn't know that for sure but it seemed like a believable gaslight.

"Modus operandi? Are you back to sleuthing?"

"I am back to sleuthing. Trying to catch a cat burglar."

"Nothing in that neighborhood would suit me. They use cheap phones and laptops. I'd be lucky to get away with a dated Roku box. Must be another cat. Dear Clay, do you see me as a tabby, a Persian? Or one of those black or gray and white cats that look like they are masked?"

I went with "cool cat," hoping a little flattery would get him back to my apartment, but he had another engagement. I wasn't convinced that he was too snobbish for the flats. Scruffy middle class has come up in the world. Houses there are of the million-dollar variety now, and probably chock-full of techy toys. To Dino, "all for one" was a part-time job.

## 23.

Exited Meinhof's, leaving Dino to a macchiato, an Apple watch, Series 7, and an expensive-looking Bluetooth speaker. I found the Miata parked on Shattuck and took off for the flats of Berkeley. My memories of Brianna were vague, quick hellos at a poetry reading, or sitting at a table with four or five guests. There was one strange conversation in the lobby of the Chandler Apartments, me entering and her exiting someone's (don't know whose) apartment, where she declared that there were no male bisexuals, that they (we) were all faking it to interest women. Don't remember where that conversation went—just a postage stamp of a memory that flew by as I was waiting at the red light at Ashby.

She had a '50s box of a house, white picket fence, probably not ironic because who would go that far with it. Previous tenant, I'd guess. I crossed the small lawn and knocked.

Marvin has a speech about this. If it had a name, I'd call it Fucking Against Type. When Mayakovsky was sick with lust and tenderness, did he ask if they were red or white or even fascist? Or did he take them for a ride in his slick Italian car? Marvin's affair with an FBI agent came to my mind, but then my mind went animal as she opened the door. Such a cliché! Down, Clay. She was wearing an anklet, something I like, probably because I saw *Double Indemnity* on TV when I was twelve.

"Clay Blackburn, obscure poet and famous book scout. Come right in." Hair falling, just long enough to obscure the left eye, oh the obviousness of it all! We, all of us, were born to eat, fuck, and die, but that isn't always a comfortable fact, especially for those who fancy themselves "deep."

"And ace private asshole."

"So I hear." With a look straight from Martha Vickers. Dangerous fun.

"I gather this is some sort of neighborhood-watching situation. Do you want me to stand watch?"

I eyeballed the old house. It had that slightly sunken look that these Berkeley baby-boom-era houses sometimes have. There was a smell that wasn't quite musty—pre-must? Nice furniture, worn but well chosen. The walls were painted whimsical colors, the hardwood floor had just enough age. Rich buyers would love that.

"It's actually more than that. The house was tossed a couple of days ago. Do you say 'tossed'? Or is that just mystery novel lingo."

"Works. What was taken?"

"Small stuff, a Chromebook and a couple of speakers. The mess bothered me more. They went through drawers, closets, pulled up rugs."

"What do you think they wanted?"

"How the fuck would I know? It's just a house full of house stuff. I live fairly simply. People have been losing cameras, watches, and laptops, but mine aren't worth that much. There's nothing that would warrant a further search. At least I don't think so." But she was lying. I knew the tells without even knowing her tells.

I remembered her car, a little red Fit. Her clothes were obviously well chosen, possibly expensive in a low-key way.

"I forget. What is it you do?" I remembered as I asked.

"I co-own Hard Bop."

Hard Bop was a little record store on San Pablo, just past Gilman. I liked the place, went in once in a while, but had never seen her there. Hmm. Jazz nut. Maybe it wouldn't be fucking against type.

"I haven't seen you there."

"Come in on the weekends. I'm not around much during the week. I do most of the buying, keep the books. It's a collective. Barely pays the rent but it's fun."

Okay, still a little girly-girl for me, but she was getting more interesting. "I'm still not sure how I can help you. Thieves often leave a mess. They look for cash, jewelry, small electronics. They almost never get caught."

"Something more is going on here. I want you to run these guys down. Get them off my back." Quick pivot. "I don't feel safe. If they come in when I'm around, I will shoot them. You don't want that, do you?"

Made no sense. "You'll have to give me more. Is somebody singling you out? I thought this was a neighborhood problem."

"I didn't know what to say."

Of a sudden I was bored. "Cut to the chase." A little too pointed, like when you are losing patience with someone and then you feel a little guilty for it.

She moved to a low-slung bookshelf, good heavy lumber. She grabbed it and pulled. I moved forward to help her but she waved me off. And then, a floor safe! The look of it excited me. It was flush with the floor, so you wouldn't notice. She pulled a book from the shelf, rapped the floor twice, and a handle popped up just enough for her to pull. She dialed it open, stuck her hand in. "I'm going to trust you, Clay. Doing it on instinct and semi-solid hearsay. My only fallback, if you prove me wrong, is to tell you that I will pull your guts out with my bare hands." And with this she pulled a coin from the hole, held it between finger and thumb, okay-style.

I didn't know what the fuck it was but I know a MacGuffin when I see it, and judging by the glint in her eyes and her body language, this was big shit MacGuffin.

"I don't collect old coins. What is it?"

"I'm going to tell you, but first I need to remind you—"

"That you will gut me, shoot me, then throw me in the bay?" Somehow, the thought of that excited me.

"I'm not joking. I spend lots of time at the range, and I'm certain I could take you one on one."

Her glint was gone, and I was getting bored with this setup. "Tell me more or throw me out. I'm considering lunch at Flacos. I'm hungry."

She didn't hesitate. She struck me as the type that never hesitated about anything. "This is a nearly pristine Eid Mar Denarius of Brutus. Big bucks. Turn this into modern cash and you're set for a while."

"How long?"

"Say, a couple of years in Monte Carlo, top-shelf housing. Or a lifetime in El Cerrito. Two lifetimes in Stockton."

"A droll stroll up Mount Moola, as the poet said."

"Huh?"

"Where'd you get the relic?"

Sly smile, and I couldn't quite get a read when she said, "Took it off a dead boyfriend." Really?

## 24.

Extra-spicy lunch at Flacos while I thought about the difficulties. Yes, I took the job, then I excused myself to ponder with a couple of vegan tacos.

I wondered if Brianna had the floor safe installed just to house the coin. Who has a floor safe? So small and compact, just right for a really expensive Brutus nickel.

Another cat burglar in Berkeley? They would have to be good to find the location of the safe and open it.

Why did she trust me? Maybe because it's a stretch to imagine me as a high-class thief. I don't own a tux, don't look like Robert Wagner at all.

I was deep into taco number two when Chad came in and ordered a Tamal Poblano, extra hot.

"Okay if I join you?"

"Of course. What are you doing in Berkeley?"

"Best vegan Mexican in the Bay Area. You?"

"Best …"

"You aren't vegan."

"Good is good. Got nothing against vegetables."

Oh damn, but it's Chad. We would have to say grace. I napkinned and bowed, put my semi-greasy hands together.

"Oh heavenly deity, bless this food and watch over those less fortunate. In the name of all, hear our prayer."

Short. He must be hungry. And no gender assignment to the deity. Good call.

"And what are you up to today?"

I wasn't sure I wanted to tell him, and wasn't sure why I wasn't sure. I couldn't imagine him going out on his own as a burglar, and he would button up about it if I asked him to. Still, I went with my hunch and made something up.

"Going up to Moe's to say a quick hello to John Wong, maybe buy an art book. I've been thinking a lot about Clyfford Still. Just hanging out in town."

"I heard that Brianna was in the store. Doesn't she live around here?"

Damn that Chad. "I think she does. It was nice to see her at Meinhof's. She bought a couple of books and had a coffee."

"Weren't you two involved?"

"No." And with that he left off, and we talked, in hushed tones as they say, about the store's finances, about the money split with Dino and the Emmas, about vanilla-flavored psychedelics, and about God of course, but thankfully not too much. He bragged to me that he had become a crackerjack cat burglar, and I wondered about him, just a little. Was he hitting the flats? How could I not feel a little paranoid? We live in paranoid times.

We finished and we walked in the direction of my car. I remembered that he hadn't really told me why he was in Berkeley. Oakland to Berkeley for fake meat, beans, and rice? Who in Oakland comes to Berkeley for a taco? I decided to let it go because I couldn't think of a subtle way to bring it up.

## 25.

An anti-Emmas faction had entered the social media world. Having a "techie orientalist" pop-up on-site wasn't appreciated by the anti-orientalist, anti-techie crew. I thought of myself as part of that bunch but had trouble taking Astor's absurdist theater as anything but that, or maybe it was the filthy lucre that was being funneled into various unofficial philanthropic projects. His last big check went to an abolitionist group, anonymously, but probably not really because people tend to find out how the money flows. Despite the flood of (probably warranted) criticism, we helped Astor set up a pop-up vanilla hots extravaganza, one that would begin at Meinhof's and move into the great hall. The bookstore would be refitted by his designers, and we would serve "donation" cocktails, with donations starting at fifteen bucks. The Emmas had allowed it as a one-off, then probably had regretted that, given the criticism from the more-radical-than-thou crowd.

Astor, thankfully, had muted the pseudo-eth portion of the decor. It still felt somewhat strange to the visitor, but dumbed down (or smartened up) so as not to be as offensive. The designers had gone all in with lefty chic, probably because they figured that nobody would get the references—extra large strategically torn posters from Baader-Meinhof Komplex, lent to us from someone at PM Press. Most of the Emmas, somehow, were on board with Astor's plan, though everyone felt squishy about it. Mother's milk.

It was one big seating, nine thirty, late dinner, "deep into the night," as the invite said. An invitation allowed parties to text in their reservations.

With about an hour to go we opened the store, display tables stacked with popular foodie books, books on sustainable this or that, books on decorating. The anarchist material was discreetly moved to the back shelves. We were ready to suck up the mother's milk in order to sustain the revolution. Or something. The place was crowded, even that early, with khaki and pastel types browsing the tables and small-talking. Not a decent fuck in the entire generation. As the poet said. They dropped good dough on coffee-table food porn, they asked when the bar would be open.

Presently Astor appeared in white chef's drag, the type he probably almost never wore, black being more the style these days, the toque blanche so tall you would need an escalator to scale it. He tried to jump on the bar and lost his balance, but somehow not his toque. Hat pins? The second jump was successful, thanks to a boost from Patti, who was at the bar. Astor let out a bellow worthy of a prizefight announcer.

"It is the cocktail hour! First one is on Meinhof's Books!" I shot a look at Patti. Were we covering the cost? She shook her head, Fuck no!

I had only once before seen a bar rush of that intensity, at closing time in a working-class bar in Limerick. The grabs for amuse-bouches nearly became a food fight. It was a wonton filled with chanterelle pâté, lightly sauced with what some were now calling V-hots.

A woman with a roving eye and a jeweled cane pushed her way to the bar. "Where are the squirty bottles!"

Patti, who seldom does, looked terrified. "Chef will be sending those out with the first course. This is the amuse-bouche!"

"We are not amused. Gimme the hots." Leaning forward, menacing look.

She was restrained by ex-mayor Libby Schaaf! Her date?

And so went the cocktail course. It was our first glimpse of hots withdrawal. I wondered what we were getting ourselves into.

Marvin arrived. Where had he been? We needed more bartenders. He vaulted himself up and landed behind the bar. We were running low on glasses. He found a package of those red tosser cups and handed them around. Went to the fridge and pulled out two liter-sized carafes. "Drink up, comrades! More where this came from!"

And so they did, and the party began to roar. We were worried about stolen books, but needlessly: These people weren't readers and the picture books had already sold out. We also ran out of the frozen rose punch and the appetizers. I went into the great hall to fetch something that would keep the crowd happy until dinner.

Astor was barking orders, the tall toque still standing, ridiculously, atop his head—something out of Dr. Suess. He spied me and trotted over.

"Go to the back of the kitchen and talk to your commie friends. They are getting in my way."

Devon was with a character named Gemmie, or Gimmie, I never could get it right. They were mid-kitchen. Chad was there, trying to ease them out of the way of what looked like offal as it flew from sharp knives.

"We thought this would be some little pop-up, not a capitalist food fest. This is not in the spirit of what we agreed to." Devon had a hair-flipping tic. I hadn't seen that since my teen years in Redondo Beach.

"We're also a little surprised, but it's too late to stop now." Chad was slipping into deep lies, familiar territory. We were using Astor's script, including his edits.

"I can't stand you book people." Gemmie/Gimmie picked up an oxtail and flung it, hard. It thonked the wall. "I am vegan. This is gross."

More fast talking from Chad. Maybe that's what worked, or maybe they just got tired. We left the kitchen for Astor to work his magic as they were hustled out the door.

## 26.

Bugatti's was the pop-up to beat all pop-ups. Course after course, covered in hard sauce with squirt bottles for the heavy imbibers. The evening ended near orgy, and probably inspired after-party orgies all over the East Bay. The V-hots was flowing. The Meinhofs stayed in the bookstore as the others enjoyed themselves. We kept the glasses full, then Marvin went to the kitchen for a squirt bottle and some pasta with a thick red sauce, bread, and Gorgonzola. He also grabbed a couple of bottles of red because he was tired of "that rose stuff."

"We're going to get kicked out of the Emmas' place, I fear. This isn't their scene." Chad looked a little guilty.

Marvin knows not of guilt. "We're bankrolling the place. How many free breakfasts? How many hours of free online time for the LeftyTech group? Between Astor's Food and Drug and Dino's suave swiper capers we're scaling Mount Moola, and the bucks are going where they should. It's a messy world, Chad."

"Aren't you afraid of getting caught?"

"I was once left for dead in Mozambique, where there was a price on my head. I was afraid of getting caught there and then. Not now. A little petty theft? And Astor's drug may not even be illegal. You think too much."

Dino came in from the main room. I had been so busy tending bar that I had forgotten that he was in the restaurant. I remembered quickly when he entered the bookstore. He was wearing a well-fitted gray suit. Where did he get his clothes?

"There's an interesting conversation in the main room about cultural appropriation. Is it possible to steal from a culture that never existed? There was talk of some sort of protest between courses. They wanted to get some V-hots before deciding on a course of action."

I had a pretty good bottle of rye, Bulleit, for special customers. I scooped up some ice and poured him a double. "The whole thing is pretty smarmy, but I can't imagine anyone being hurt by it."

"Smarmy. You overuse that word. It's possible to watch out for number one and save some spillover for those in need."

"A trickle-down theory of Marxism?"

He saluted me with his glass of whiskey and went back to join the party.

# 27.

No action was taken to show solidarity with the nonexistent people of Langpo. The food had been sped to the great hall from Astor's kitchens, piping and perfect. Roasts were pulled from the ovens at just the right time, sides were cooked on burners, steam-table-style. It was very traditional, and an insult to vegans at first, but none of it was real. As the plated food was brought out Astor stood on a table that almost capsized and announced, "No animals were harmed in the making of these roasts! Eat 'em and weep, carnivores! Waitstaff, bring out the vanilla magic!" A roar of approval from the crowd.

Someone brought the Meinhof's staff plates of "meat" with various starches, root vegetables that were sculpted and roasted. Some resembled rodents, crustaceans, and beings from the bug world. Funny old Astor!

I decided to get drunk, a rarity for me outside my apartment since I'd become a private asshole. You know, fear of the Mickey Finn.

I was deep into the rye and V-hots when Dino came to me with a dessert. I have no idea what it was. Some kind of cake. There was a memory gap, and then I was back at the Chandler Apartments with Dino. I guess my comrades cleaned up and closed the joint.

## 28.

We were having breakfast and I was drinking lots of water. Phone buzzed. Brianna. "Meet me at Hard Bop. Right away."

Said my goodbyes and went downstairs. Where was the Mazda? I know I didn't drive home. Thank you, Dino, assuming he was driving. Practically out front, semi-legal space. How did I miss it! In the Miata and down to San Pablo, right turn toward the dreaded El Cerrito, but not all the way to the Berkeley line.

Hard Bop was a sweet little store, a kind of miniature version of the disappeared hippie/punk record stores of years past. For me, it was a comfortable place to go when Amoeba left me dizzy with possibilities. There was a clerk at the register, straight out of central casting. Blindfold him, throw him in a plane, put him in front of a register in Berlin, Copenhagen, Tokyo, or even Beijing, and he could do the job.

An obscure Coltrane/Pharoah Sanders live album was playing, a little loud. He looked at me, reeking of attitude. I liked him right off.

"Brianna sent for me."

He liked that. "The boss is in the back room. You have been allowed safe passage." The boss? I thought they were a collective.

I squeezed around a stack of boxes and entered a walk-in-closet-sized office. Another throwback—the cramped offices of small retail, where the sausage is made.

"I hired you to protect my stuff! The coin is gone! I know where you were last night when my place was trashed. Partying with the vanilla people. Someone found the safe and somehow opened it."

"I didn't promise around-the-clock protection. There are security companies for that. Was the alarm on?"

"Of course, but somehow they got through. The safe was open and empty." Brianna must have been upset but somehow kept her cool.

"How much insurance were you carrying?"

"Minimal house insurance. I didn't want anyone to know I had the thing."

"It's hot?"

"Somewhat warm, I guess."

"What does that mean?"

"It means no cops. Round up your detective friends and find the thing."

"My cut?"

"I'm not ready to sell, so I can't pay you a percentage, but I will renegotiate our previous deal. Twenty K up front, double it if you find the coin."

"Plus expenses."

"Up to a grand."

"Doesn't even cover premium coach to New York. Up it to three bozos, and I will supply receipts."

"Bribes?"

"I'll invoice you for those."

Discussions of money are, sad to say, sexy. Sorry, Mr. Marx. I imagined fucking her, covered in hundred-dollar bills. Forgive me, dear reader. The lock of hair over one eye, the love of jazz. The anklet and a strong scent of large bills. Jesus Christ would have signed on with Lucifer for that.

"Clay, if you told anyone about my"—lowers voice—"floor safe, you know I will kill you."

"Not even Marvin knows. And certainly not Dino." This may have been a lie. I was severely juiced the night before. When I write my memoir one possible title will be *Anything for Dino*.

She asked me to turn around while she went through some drawers. I assume she opened a safe or a lockbox. "Okay, you can look." Slapped a stack of hundreds on the desk. No sex today. Just money.

On the way out I spied a nice of copy of *Money Jungle*. I only had it on CD. Seemed appropriate, so I bought it.

## 29.

And so I entered the Chandler Apartments, at the corner of Dwight and Telegraph, balancing high atop Mount Moola but possibly feeling responsible for the theft of a "somewhat warm" Roman coin. I was anxious to talk to Dino. Dino, who lights up even the stars, whose spit turns to pearls. Dino! Let's put a hold on metaphors and speak in facts. Did you steal the Eid Mar?

Dino was getting dressed, half listening, or making like he was. "I've never even seen an Eid Mar, except in auction catalogs. Whose was it?"

I'd said too much. He makes me stupid. "Just something I heard."

"Tell me more!"

"Later."

He turned, quickly, and was out the door.

My phone buzzed.

Chad called to say that a cop had come around asking about the store and the building, supposedly to warn us that there had been lots of breaking and entering around town, lots of petty theft. Obviously feeling things out. They wanted to look around the place. Chad told them that only the bookstore was open to the public but that with a warrant they would be welcome. He offered to sell them a copy of *Fight Like Hell* by Kim Kelly because "I know you folks are pro-union." They demurred and left, promising to "visit often."

They may have been on to something, but, you know, cops. The men (and women) in blue. Evil, but not too smart. Although in nature blueness refiningly enhances beauty, as if imparting a special virtue of its own—sky, birds, certain aspects of bodies of water—nothing is so pure that it cannot be perverted, and the blue uniform, when clothing a cop, emits a type of visual stench that poisons even those examples of the beauty of that color.

I was sure that Dino had done a good job with the flow of possible evidence, and that it was in the hands of greedy bargain hunters. I knew from our tutorials that we had left no fingerprints or DNA trails. I was a little surprised that the cops were bothering, unless they had gotten wind of the coin and wanted it for themselves. Their visit to Meinhof's couldn't have had anything to do with crime fighting.

I got on the email thread and called a meeting of the Meinhofs. Seemed like a good time to discuss damage control.

## 30.

We closed up early, slow weekday. We turned on the laser alarm and took our places behind the bar, a "safe area" free of the beams. Percy brought beers, Trumer, and handed them around. He had become the backbone of the business, taking care of details and making friends with the regulars. Quiet leader type. Good fellow, well met. He declined the cat burglar training, electing to keep things running. We didn't suspect that he wasn't all in. He helped with Dino's crazy drop-off plans, wrapping iPhones and laptops in old bags and leaving them on park benches, in trash cans, wherever asked. Needless to say, Dino collected all the cash.

"You called this meeting, Clay, so you're the chair, but before we get started I'm going to suggest that we come up with an exit strategy. Not for the store or café, but at some point we will need to cool it as cat thieves."

I had been thinking the same. Things were getting too complicated. "I think we should let things cool for a few weeks, then talk about it."

Marvin nodded in agreement, but Chad shook it off. "We need to make a few more scores. We've got too much going. We gave ten grand to Glide, we hired a bunch of lawyers to defend demonstrators at People's Park, we are making donations all over the city, and we're funding three small presses. Can't stop the flow now."

According to Marvin, "We have enough in reserve to take a few months away from burglary."

Patti agreed. "We have stacks of bucks sitting in credit unions, we have cash buried everywhere. I say we lay off and pay down. If the cops are around, maybe the IRS will take notice."

"We've been careful about that. Don't worry. We can change locations. We haven't touched Marin." Dino the gambler.

I saw my chance. "I have a client who lost a very expensive item. Help me find it. I'll split the fee, and if we find this coin we can make a little more. It can float us while we lie low."

Lots of questions. I filled them in but not completely. Neighborhood, "a rare coin" without too much description, a burglary.

In an ad hoc way I put myself in charge. Not very democratic, but that could come later. I know, that's what they all say, but history will absolve me! Like fuck it will, but I needed to get the job done.

## 31.

Okay, so I spent the following night at Brianna's, and it was really pleasant. She was a little businessy for me, I'll admit, but also well read, fun to cook with, and the jazz collection! It was her idea that we would pull together the world's best risotto, a corn and basil job, with Gorgonzola and pecorino. A substantial first course, followed by grilled summer vegetables. For once it was summer in the Bay Area, nearly blasting. She had a great kitchen that opened to the yard, door and windows open, light clothing. Vinho Verde, one tall empty bottle and another getting to the end. Talk of books and film, of a recent trip to Big Sur, "Expensive and a tourist trap but what can you do? Those cliffs, and the bakery!"

When small talk wound down I took on the coin issue. "Are you recovering from the shock of being robbed?"

"No, I am not. I'm taking a stress vacation, thanks to the food, wine, and company. I'm pissed, hurt, feel violated, all of it. Can you find my coin, Clay?"

I was a little too happy that she had included my company with dinner and drinks. I did like her, and was beginning to respond warmly, the way I usually respond to flattery. Marvin's rule: Two types of people. Those who respond to flattery and those who respond to intimidation.

As they say, things progressed. Was I still fucking against type? Or had I misread her type? Time would tell, or so I thought. If the attraction is there, if the house is comfortable, if the conversation is good, it's best to let those other thoughts go. Let all thoughts go. And so I ignored all caution, even though I know that sex can at times act as its own Mickey Finn.

## 32.

Next morning it was back at the Chandler, hello to the cat, get to work on some poems. I almost forgot a date with Marvin, to do a book buy up in Montclair. The store was thin on stock and someone up there had a room full of novels, French, mostly in translation.

And so I made arrangements, and Marvin picked me up in his Econoline, at least twenty years old, lots of miles and terrible on gas but, oddly, clean inside and out. He treated that van like an old friend. I hopped in, said hi. As ever, he was wearing sweatpants and an ironic shirt. This one was probably collectible, a Virtual Moe's T-shirt, vintage 1998 or thereabouts, manufactured to advertise the famous old bookstore's online catalog. Hippie-style graphics, true to Telegraph Avenue. I wouldn't mind owning one.

Beautiful warm day, great old house. Montclair, land of bazillion-dollar homes. Yet, somehow, it still has some charm. There are a couple of old-style lunch places, a good café, a surprisingly nice feel to the little downtown.

The owners had already moved or died. We didn't ask. The agent, or perhaps relative, wasn't very forthcoming about their circumstances. We were shown through many rooms, empty except for the books, shelved loosely by subject. French novels, French literary theory, even the cookbooks pointed to a Francophile. We looked, we categorized, we quietly discussed prices. We researched a few items on our phones, but not too much. We had an idea of their worth, enough to make an offer.

"We can't go more than eight hundred for these. And we can only take about twenty-five boxes. Will that work?"

"Fine." Not a conversationalist. And so we paid, boxed, and loaded the Camus and the Baudrillard, leaving most of the Balzac, except for a great copy of *Lost Illusions*, Folio Society, but nice Folio Society, not the usual schlock illustrations. Classy. Probably not a great translation, but I wanted it. Marvin knew and handed it over.

Lunch was at a little Mexican place, the kind they used to call Sonora-style. Maybe they still do. Lots of sauce and cheese. Guilty pleasure Mexican American. I brought him up to speed on all aspects of the Brianna affair.

"Fucking against type will end all wars!" From Marvin, who gets paid to fight in wars. "Any leads on this coin? And how much is it worth? I won't tell the others."

"Enough to buy one of the smaller houses down the street." And as I write this I imagine him whistling, '40s-movie-style, but he never whistles, or exclaims. I probably got a slow, thoughtful nod.

"Any leads?"

"Just got started."

## 33.

We unloaded and did a little pricing, but we were tired and working in slow motion. Patti was there and the place was pretty empty. I left her to it and went home for a long, hot shower. I was at that place in life when the horrible tremendousness of youth was about to depart. The boat was ready! My leg muscles, apparently, had already departed and were fording a burning river. I needed that shower. As I write now, the boat is nearly to the cold side of the river, but back then all I needed was a shower, a Tylenol, and a shot of Boodles over ice with a slice of lime. Jeans, black Vans, and a button-down oxford, ready to go. The part of me that remained youthful went downstairs, found the Miata, and pointed it toward Brianna's place.

I saw the cops, the ambulance, the fire truck, as I turned a corner toward her house. Were they at her place? Couldn't tell but I pulled up to the next block anyway. I have no truck with cops. When I was twenty I worked at LAX, baggage service. We shared a break room with cops from Venice Division. They were, by far, the most disgusting human beings I had, and have, ever met. Racist, violent, surly, whiny. You haven't heard whining till you've had to listen to a cop. Absolute scum, and every interaction I've had since then proves the rule. And so I drove away, just at the speed limit. I'd need to ask around, find out what happened.

I felt a little shaky as I drove. It took a few blocks before it fully dawned on me that the cops would have to be at Brianna's house. She once had a million-dollar coin in a made-to-order floor safe. Someone had swiped it. She was into some deep shit. Maybe they had stolen something more? Maybe she had decided to call the police after all? But no, there were too many cops, and the BFD was also there. I drove on automatic pilot, almost sideswiping a Tesla at one point. Oh well, good riddance to bad rubbish, as my grandma used to say. Why do those cars exist?

I made it to Meinhof's, got a parking place out front for once.

Marvin was working the desk with Chad. "Brianna's been murdered." Marvin had an in with the BPD, god knows how or why.

Reader, have you ever had someone die on you at an early point in the relationship? Not necessarily a romantic connection, could be anyone you are "just getting started" with. It sets up a Janis Joplin/John Keats feeling. Too soon! Sentimental, not a shallow kind, but also not the bottomless forever grief that comes from a deeper love, and it's followed by a kind of guilt feeling, like when you cry at a funeral though you didn't know the corpse that well, like, Do I have the right?

"You don't look so good. How well did you know Brianna? Let's go for a walk." Marvin has seen more bodies than a smiling mortician, but that hasn't turned him completely cold.

"Are you ready to hear some details?"

"Okay. I'm shocked. I was just getting to know her."

"She drowned in a bucket of vanilla hots. I wasn't given any details beyond that."

We had to laugh. The laughs that come out of you when you know they shouldn't. Drowned in hots?

"My source had to hang up fast. That's all the intel I have. It must have been gallons!"

# 34.

It looked like *Berkeleyside* was handed a snow job by the BPD. There was a note about a "possible" homicide, street address, date, and a quote from Officer Giff Hartnet: "We are pursuing an investigation with great vigor." Whenever someone says "vigor," or "vigah," I think of JFK, who often used the word. Officer Hartnet had a strange vocabulary.

I wasn't sure where to go from there. If I got involved in a murder investigation, I could bring the pigs down on me. Not that I haven't done that before. I would have to be cagey. Needed to think things through.

Sometimes, most times, drugs just make me stupid. That can be relaxing, but it's no help when doing whodunit work. As a very young man I would down a couple of black beauties in order to think and write poetry, but at that point in life I had lost my taste for speed. I did have a "complimentary" (it left the pop-up in Marvin's old coat) squirt bottle of the hots. Maybe it would help me focus.

I made what I call the detective's special, because they seem to live on red meat. I dug out a cast-iron grill, the kind that leaves grill marks. Got it nice and hot. The galley kitchen filled with smoke. I had one steak, good size, that I had warmed to room temperature. A few minutes on each side. Pulled it off and threw some asparagus on the same pan. While the steak was setting up and the veggies were warming I opened a bottle of Masciarelli Montepulciano d'Abruzzo. Good and good for you. Dinner!

The cat jumped on the table to watch the show. I cut her a piece and put it on a napkin. Then I doused the meal in vanilla hots. Better than A.1. sauce!

I was back on the couch, listening to that copy of *Money Jungle*, nibbling a bar of Puchero chocolate. Expensive, but you know, Mayakovsky. The blue came to me slowly, as if a light came from above, down from the ceiling, to drench the room. When I closed my eyes the color changed only slightly, but that was the real V-hots blue, the one that brought things into focus. After what seemed like a long wait my thoughts came to a point, and I thought about Dino, but then those thoughts turned inside out, and I somehow was shown that Dino was the one, that he had the coin, or had access to the coin. Did he kill Brianna, after the theft? Or did someone else kill her, thinking the coin was still in the house? I couldn't grasp the facts that led me to this, but I knew I would, and although this was disturbing, the blue wouldn't let me take it as a negative thing. It was just what was, just another fact.

## 35.

Cops are cops, and you should never let TV copaganda trick you into thinking otherwise. Reader, this is to be the primary takeaway from my story, not just this particular chunk of narrative, but my complete works. Everything else is secondary, or possibly food for thought, or just a good tale. It would be impossible to remove sadism from the cop trade. But we can't live without them? Maybe that remains to be seen, as humanity either evolves or devolves.

Doesn't mean they are smart. Often they are dumb. Best plan for non-cops, when around them, is to dummy up, nod and smile, and listen deeply. Don't be (too) scared! They will often trip themselves up.

And officer so-and-so told officer number 2, who told a guy who works at Amoeba Music, that Brianna was hit "upside the head" (cop's words) with the proverbial "blunt object," though not hard enough to kill her. Probably died by drowning. Just information, probably not much help to me. I don't know shit about forensics and I've never had to care. Cop didn't mention an open safe, meaning the murderer either didn't know about the safe or had some other reason for entering. Of course, if they did open it up they wouldn't have found anything. Cop line was that they had no suspects, still investigating. No mention, at least to the record clerk, that there was a robbery. They would do their cop best to find the killer. Berkeley isn't Oakland, where there are more murders than slaughtered pigs at Clove and Hoof, to the point where overheard gunshots are as boring as Muzak. Berkeley cops could have enough time to get in the way. I would have to go deep cover and keep Marvin in the background. They know his face and reputation.

I had to pump Dino for information. If he had any, he would slide around it, lie a little, whatever he needed to do. I am deeply in love but not blind, exactly. Rather than waiting for him to slip up I would have to listen, put everything he said into a metaphorical centrifuge, and examine the loose bits of misinformation for possible content. I would take him out, then rope-a-dope him into the Chandler, then pretty much the same as always—food, drink, sex, conversation—except that this talk involved theft and possible murder. Not that I suspected him of actually swinging the blunt object—at least I don't think so?—but he could possibly know who, why, and where the MacGuffin could be hiding.

My landline, hooked to the front door, rang. It was Dino. We had decided to go out to dinner a little early. Another warm night, so we sat outside at Passione in West Berkeley. He drove, top down. You don't get to do that very often in the Bay Area. He found parking out front, as he always does, and this time it was even legal. Rigatoni Amatriciana after the Aperol spritz, then seared duck breast over white polenta. Bottle of barbera. Tough conversations call for a higher level of intake.

The spritz portion of dinner was given over to car talk. He loves his Triumph. What's the Euro, smarmy version of a gearhead? Do they talk grease and motors over sparkling wine? Mixed in with conversation about art, film, and philosophy? Probably not, but this gearhead does. The handsome Roman (we asked) waiter brought the wine. It was solid, good, just right, closely followed by a version of pasta that brought me back to Via del Corso, a semitouristy place, sure, but they knew their stuff. In the sensuality of the moment, sitting across from him, I considered dropping the whole thing—fuck murder, fuck thievery, can't we hover above that? But no, duty called.

Dino, refilling our glasses, "We're thinking of the same trattoria. I'd bet my life." I nod, he smiles, says, "You want to talk about something more serious, so let's get it done before the next course."

"You know about the coin."

"The coin is famous, and not just among numismatists. At any gathering of thieves the subject comes up, along with certain diamonds and stamps."

"Gatherings? Like, at the local pub? Or perhaps at the Ritz bar? I didn't know it was a club."

"You joke, but as with any shared skill, people get together to compare notes, tell stories, share trade secrets."

"In tuxedos?"

"That's a stereotype, but it is a nice one. I look great in a tux! So would you."

Cutting to the chase is boring, but, "Do you know where the coin is? Any idea who killed Brianna?"

"I really don't know, but I could help you find out. Are you asking for my help? I could possibly see clear, if we could come up with an agreeable split. I know a certain party who could afford to buy."

"There was a murder."

"We could solve that too, as a sort of side project."

"But currently you have no information."

"I could speculate, based on my experience, but what good is a wild surmise before the duck has arrived? We'll finish this beautiful meal, have a coffee, take a nice stroll, drive, top down, to the Chandler Apartments, and shake on it. So to speak."

What the fuck. I refilled our glasses and waited for the duck.

As the night progressed very little information was passed, but the duck was quite good.

## 36.

"You're a detective, right? Not just a bookseller, and god forbid, not just a poet. Is anyone just a poet these days? How do you detect, and what do you charge? Are you listening?"

I hadn't had a chance to say hello, or hello, Astor, as we do when we remember somebody's name. "I do some detective-type work, sometimes. What's up?"

"Do you have a license?"

"Fuck no. I'm an anarchist. And a poet."

"I'm short on hots. Someone has stolen several gallons. I have a pop-up in Point Reyes, and the main store is low on supply."

"Fell off the back of a truck?"

"Well, yes."

My little joke turned out to be a good guess.

"It does have a half-life. It remains edible, but if it isn't served fresh, the, um, effects of the, um ..."

"Drug. It is a drug."

"After a fashion. Is Châteauneuf-du-Pape a drug?"

"Get off the semantics. Sometimes drugs taste good. Just the facts, Astor." I was doing a pretty good Joe Friday. Maybe there was a payday here, or a lead on who drowned Brianna.

"The drug can become unpredictable. The stuff, um, the sauce, comes by van from a redwood glen near Big Sur. It's the only place where the secret herbs are grown and blended. I have a trusted driver. Or had."

I offered up my price list and he went for it.

"Okay, Astor, let's start with the five W's and an H. Who, what, where, when, why, how."

"Delivery usually comes to the Shattuck location midmorning. They never showed."

"Driver?"

"We keep names out of it. They deliver the sauce and we pay up."

"Sounds more and more like a drug deal."

"Call it what you will. It isn't technically illegal, yet, but I have elected to remain discreet. It's only a matter of time before the DEA will get wind, and then we'll have to pay off the cops. I hate the thought of those idiots coming into my restaurants."

"So a van comes from somewhere near Big Sur, but you don't know the driver. Have you been to the farm, or plant, or whatever is down there?"

"Of course. For quality control. But blindfolded, always blindfolded."

I didn't believe him but I let that go. It was a small-money operation, but anyone with a brain could see it getting bigger. I understood his discretion.

"Who received the package?"

"Several packages, five-gallon containers. They unload the van and come back to my office. I pay in cash."

"How much?"

"Won't tell you."

"No biggie. So you were missing a delivery?"

"I wasn't sure at first because there's no clear schedule. It had been at least a week, so I checked inventory. Very low. I have a text number. No answer. So can you do it? Help me find the hots?"

"We take half the take. That's a lot of hots. You can buy our cut back from us. If you don't want to give me a wholesale figure, I'll just come up with something. Let's say five thousand plus expenses. Does that sound fair?" I had no idea what was fair.

"That's a little steep. Half that, and I will leave you with one container. I know you like the stuff. Not for resale! I have exclusive rights. But you could host some spectacular parties."

"Three thousand and you comp me and a guest at your restaurants whenever we show up."

"Done. Now get to work."

## 37.

Am I the only unlicensed detective in the East Bay? The jobs were coming hard and fast. Related? Possibly, but how does a coin tie in with a shipment of drug-laced sauce? Not exactly the existential question, but this is the stuff that private assholes deal with. Every day job makes me wish I could be a full-time poet, like Bob Hass or Jorie Graham, but teaching poetry and placing poems in *The New Yorker* must be some really boring shit. And so I go on, dredging the bottom of the artsy/foodie/commie barrel for clues and such.

But not this day, where I was happily ensconced at the front counter of Meinhof's, buying and selling used books, frothing coffee drinks, and shooting the shit with Patti.

"Hey, fuck buddy! Make this guy a cap with the phony milk product, low foam." Patti doesn't self-censor.

"Soon as I find a copy of *No Gods No Masters*. Wasn't it on the hold shelf?"

That act of relishing the work at hand, if the work at hand is at all worthy, small sparks of joy lighting up the day-to-day. Sometimes that happens, especially in an environment free of bosses. Rare, for most.

The book found, the almond milk steamed and added, the customers drifting out into the stacks. Alone, or kind of alone, with a dear friend.

Patti lowers her voice. "The knuckleheads took a bridge loan to buy this place. It's coming due in a couple of months. They owe around half a million."

I hadn't been paying attention. We had discussed possible exit strategies but hadn't come up with one. For all of our complaining we loved the old building and the philosophy that had brought us together. The decision to buy had been made before we were voted into the collective, so we had accepted it.

"The Meinhof gang can't come up with more than our small payments. We'd have to sell hundreds of hot phones and laptops. We're too small-time."

I thought about the coin but I wasn't ready to say more than I had. I'd had my own selfish dreams around the Brutus and I wasn't quite ready to give them up. A farmhouse in Tuscany, an apartment in Rome, something along those lines. The chances were slim that I could recover it, but I wanted to linger on the street of dreams for as long as possible.

We were pricing books and chatting, and occasionally bumping into each other behind the small counter. A few bumps into the shift and the friction turned up the temp. I got the what-are-you-doing-tonight questions and we agreed to takeout and a movie at her place, a live-work, old style, from before that became real estate hype. She was actually loft sitting for an artist who was traveling, teaching art in Beijing. The space was self-consciously scruffy but the furniture was nice and the stove was chef quality. This artist was doing okay. It was off Fruitvale, an old paint factory, I think. The building was surrounded by real industry. The air was bad but a couple of heavy-duty purifiers kept the loft comfortable. I wondered aloud if Patti was paying the PG&E bill.

"I'm splitting it with Andi. They're really generous now that they've struck it rich."

I looked around the room at Andi's work, massive pieces of soiled rope interspersed with glass balls and driftwood, an ironic comment on nautical decor, at least at first glance. A longer look discerned an aesthetic strategy that was quite beautiful.

I gave Patti my pocket art review. I thought I was being insightful, almost Schjeldahl-like, but she answered with a shrug that said, Well, I guess so. "Let's dig into these tamales. Is Tecate okay?"

I eat, we eat. I drink, we drink. A little mezcal after the meal. I tell myself that I'm not going to tell her all I know about the coin. Then something hits me and I almost tell her. I don't but then I do. "I'm working on a new case. It's kind of complicated."

"Ooh. I love it when you talk like a detective."

"Fuck you, and listen up. This one is interesting." I paused, deciding what to edit out. Looked over. She was still interested. I didn't know until that moment that I wanted her in on this. Needed her eye for detail. Patti may have an artistic sensibility but she is definitely not a poet. Fewer flights of fancy.

"I've heard about the missing vanilla hots," she said. "Astor came by the store right after he discovered they were missing."

"Brianna was drowned in the stuff." I had wanted to tell her everything about the coin but got temporarily waylaid.

"I've heard about the murder too, but not how. The sauce was a murder weapon?"

"Seems so. It gets more complicated. Can I trust you to be discreet?"

"More than you can trust yourself. Poets love to blab."

And so I spilled all the beans and asked her if she was in. She answered with a shrug, then, "I'll stick to the cat burglar gig, thank you. But keep me in the loop. One never knows, do one."

## 38.

Astor was granted a second pop-up, part of what was to be billed as a series. The Emmas mostly hated the idea but they needed the bucks. The food and drug orgy wouldn't pay the loan but it would cover some operating costs while things, hopefully, were worked out.

As a show of respect Astor agreed to completely forgo the cultural appropriation of the nonexistent culture, with the exception of one very large hanging tapestry, rolled down from the high ceiling. It was a bizarre collection of nymphlike beauties of all genders doing what looked like a folk dance. You would expect the style to be neoclassical but it wasn't like that, it looked more urban '80s, Basquiat-like, or perhaps '90s Mission District.

Marvin and me, standing against the wall of the great hall of the people, watching Astor's assistants try to hang the thing. It wasn't easy. As it unfurled we both caught sight of the blue. The background, somehow, had captured the color that lit up the backs of our eyelids on VH (emerging slang for hots) nights.

Marvin nodded, pulling a face that seemed pure stoner, à la Cheech Marin, and I wondered if he was serious or just mugging. Either way, I got it and wondered how old Astor, or his artists, had found a way to duplicate that seemingly unduplicatable hue. And, looking past the dumb subject matter and the derivative style, I was temporarily changed, and thought of the message tattooed on my arm, a translation of a line by Giuseppe Ungaretti, ENORMITY ILLUMINES ME.

And so we watched the late-afternoon comings and goings as the latest Bugatti dinner party was assembled. Business was slow at Meinhof's but would pick up as the diners arrived. Astor had invented a new drink, a smoothie thing. We had a line of blenders, chopped fruit, ice, and illegal (Cuban) rum ready to go. Chad had set up the usual mainstream book tables and had hid the anarchist lit. We were ready to have a party and make some money.

Somehow, crazy Astor had found a Bus Station Loonies cover band, or were they the real Loonies? Anyway, it set the tone. I wouldn't have expected that type of music to pair with rum drinks, but it somehow was perfect. The guests arrived, a little more urban than the previous bunch. Had Astor salted the crowd with "characters"? After all, these affairs were mostly performance, with a little food thrown in.

After a while we could spot the ringers. The foodies and techies were the ones doing the double takes. The Astor plants were dancing and singing along with "Everyday Bullshit" and "Playing Silly Buggers." The punk music sounded like home to me and Marvin. Even Chad was bouncing along, manning the blenders and assembling the amuse-bouche. There was a paneer-like cheese but it didn't taste like paneer, more like vanilla, wrapped in a form of phyllo. Busy! No wonder restaurant workers are partial to up drugs. Bring on the blue!

Cocktails were consumed and the guests, at last, moved into the great hall. It was just me, Marvin, Patti, and Chad. Patti put her head down on the bar to show her exhaustion. We chuckled, nodded, we get it.

We sat out dinner, waiting in the bar for the end of the meal and to our workday. People stopped for drinks on the way out but we decided that the bar was closed. Food service work is hard work.

I was knocked out yet wired, a feeling that is familiar to night workers.

"Anyone for a quick snack at the Chandler?"

No takers at first, then Chad raised his hand, meekly, like, Do you want to hang out alone with me? Actually I did, partly to get an idea where he was going with our little enterprise, but also to get a bead on him. We'd known each other for a while, but except for his mini-sermons and some book buying I knew him least among the Meinhofs.

"Sinaloa is open late," I said. "We can walk down Telegraph, get some tacos, and come back for beer and tequila."

"But I'm driving."

"My couch pulls out. Very comfortable. Or you can wait out the alcohol and leave in the wee hours."

And so we were off, in his car, a serviceable Toyota from the early aughts. I had come in Marvin's car. Chad double-parked in front of Sinaloa, I ran in, vegetarian for him, al pastor for me. Then back around the block, where a parking spot was waiting for us on Dwight. Chance is the fool's word for fate, as the poet said.

I watched him eating as we warmed up to conversation. He had asked me to say grace, and, as always, I blessed the workers who grew, made, and served the food. As if my blessing mattered. I called his taco basic veggie, and he set me straight, describing the beans, pickled carrots, and pico de gallo as works of art.

He had turned down the volume on his intensity, or maybe he was just tired. I had come to regard his life as a performance, forgetting (or not caring) that he too was forced into living the day-to-day. Poets and preachers share fears of that torture.

Relaxed, his features softened. I started to like him. I had been unaware that I hadn't liked him before, and my own softening was a pleasing feeling. Disliking is hard work.

Nice brown eyes, hair longish and combed back, Billy Graham-style. It was a warm night so he had shrugged off his Salvation Army suit jacket and untied the tie. I had once assumed that his dress was ironic but came to realize it was a serious uniform. He was thin, very thin, but there was a strength in his wrists and his hands.

"What do you know about Robin Hood?"

Strange question, but I liked it. "When I was a kid I saw all the old movies, and read and reread the Howard Pyle edition. I've read into the old poems. Haven't really studied them. Why do you ask?"

"Are we like the merry band? Or at least part of a tradition? Am I Friar Tuck?"

"You'd have to gain some weight first, but I get what you're saying. Some of us thrill to the idea of redistributing wealth by force. I have to admit, it gets me off."

"Me too. I wrestle with it. What would Jesus say?"

"He probably wouldn't kill anyone. But we wouldn't either. Would we?"

"We're into something that could result in violence."

"The bible is full of violence."

"It ends in peace. Well, sort of. I want to be as New Testament as possible."

"A little Blakean lamb with the gift of gab. And a second job as a thief."

That got a laugh, a good one, not the salesperson laugh that he used for the Emmas. I realized, for the first time, that I felt an attraction, but it didn't come as a surprise. The terribleness of youth was near departure, but it hadn't quite happened. Erotic energy was everywhere for me, real, imagined, who cares. My life's goal was to scare the horses.

"I've become quite the thief, thanks to Dino Centro."

"Rewarding work."

"Can I trust you?"

Possibly, I thought to myself, but I pushed things ahead with, "Of course."

"I've been doing a little freelance work."

"Lining your pockets?" Only half joking.

"Funding a couple of churches."

"Where are you working?"

"The flats, mostly. And no, I don't have the coin."

I let that sit for a couple of seconds, then, "Go on."

"I've hit a couple of places in Brianna's neighborhood. I've seen some things. Strange coincidence, but I did see something over there, one night when I was casing a place down the street."

I raised my eyebrows. He dummied up. Did I seem too interested?

"I'll get around to telling you." Then, eyes closed, back to preacher mode, "'Christ have mercy on his soul / for he was a good outlaw / and did poor men much good.' Hey, Clay, I'm tired. Don't bother to pull out the couch. I'll just crash on it as is."

I eyeballed the empty beers. We had finished dinner off with a shot of above-average tequila. It came in a beautiful, Picasso-like bottle that somehow seemed to improve the taste. Maybe the drinks did him in. We hadn't sufficiently dosed up on VH to stay up all night. Or maybe he backed off on spilling some beans, last minute. I didn't ask him to share the bed. Didn't seem like the thing to do, somehow.

## 39.

I waited out on Dwight Way, early, and Marvin came by in the van. The buy was over the bridge, Russian Hill. Where would we park? But it seemed worth the hunt. At least twenty boxes of mid-last-century small-press poetry. Beatniks! We could have breakfast down the hill at the Trieste to put us in the mood.

And there was breakfast, then up the hill to an incredibly close parking space. We were met by a real estate person, apparently this was an estate sale. We were surprised that we didn't know the seller since most of these collectors are known to us. The real estate person let us alone to do our work, no kibitzing, always a blessing.

We had carte blanche to offer on any book in the house. The agent didn't seem to know or care about what was on the shelves. We did notice some holes in the collection, evidence that Jeff Maser had gotten there first and had picked off the really expensive stuff. Moe's hadn't been called. If they had, most of the books would be gone. So, low-hanging fruit. We had fun picking out the Burroughs, Di Prima, McClure, Ginsberg. We traded anecdotes, some repeated, about our meetings with them—the readings, parties, first encounters with certain poems. *I have just realized that the stakes are myself / I have no other...* and before we knew it we were trading lines across somebody's living room.

Some of my best conversations have happened during book buys, that unstated appreciation of plainly relished daily work. On this day we let the poetry carry us.

We offered a grand for about twenty boxes. Nothing rare, but lots of good solid poetry and fiction, with a little anarchist literature thrown in. Easy deal. No dickering, no whining about supposed rarities. Cut the check and out of there. Down the hill to Mario's for an eggplant sandwich. View of Washington Square park, looking out the window at the church, moderately okay glass of Montepulciano, red sauce eggplant, lots of cheese, café Vov, and a walk in the park. Unseasonably warm, but then there is no real warm season, so the weather was a gift. We sat under a tree. Weekday, so no big crowd. Some guy and his girlfriend, shirtless and bikinied, pleasant.

"And how is your complicated life?" From Marvin, and I realized that we had been somewhat out of touch, even while working close. Sometimes the business you love can block deeper communication.

"You know Brianna's dead. And you've heard about the coin. I have no moral obligation to follow up on that."

"Then don't."

"Can't let it go."

"For Brianna? Or the money the coin can bring?"

"Not real interested in the bucks."

"You always say that, but we do like flying business class. And there's keeping up the Miata, and the Allbirds. How many pairs?"

"Just two. The blue suede shoes are Samuel Hubbard. They're for the opera."

"So it's not for the money, because you dress like Charlie Chaplin."

"Not as the Tramp. Maybe in his personal life. But no, it's not the money. Coins bore me. If I want to look at something that old, I'll think about a trip to Rome."

"Were you in love with Brianna?"

"I barely knew her."

"When has that stopped you. How well do you know Dino? Just occurred to me. Are you doing this for Dino? To impress him with shiny things?"

"Interesting idea, but no."

"Brianna employed you. Loyalty to a client? Or maybe you thought of yourselves as partners, of a sort. Your Miles Archer?"

"You're a little warm, come to think of it. I mean, as much as I have an idea myself."

"What do you know about the murder?"

"She was drowned in a vat of VH and the place had been tossed, but the coin was missing before that."

"And the killer didn't know. Unless he/she had another motive, which is doubtful. Too coincidental."

"You're right. It had to be the MacGuffin."

"Interesting. Okay, I'm in."

"In. We can work together on this."

"What's it got to do with the revolution? Your commitment is—"

"To leading a good life and fucking with authority. I'll find a way to fit this into my philosophy."

Right, Marvin. Money talks to everyone. Commies listen to it too.

I walked over to an Italian bakery and bought a few cookies while Marvin guarded our shady place. When I came back he had drifted off. I woke him up and showed him the bag.

"Is Dino a suspect?"

"Not as far as I know. The cops haven't called him in."

"Fuck the police. Do you consider him a suspect?"

"The vat of VH wouldn't have been his style. He'd sneak in and toss the place without being noticed. Still, I didn't want to say no. Dino is full of mystery."

"If we had one of those big boards like on cop shows, I may pin up his picture."

"Anyone else?"

"Chad's been doing a little cat work, funding a church or two."

"And like most of his ilk he likes to play fast and loose with the shalt nots. Pin him to the board."

And one has eaten and one walks, back to the van, another lucky parking place, Green Street.

## 40.

The eager note on my front door said, "Call me. Call when you get in!" Signed Astor, with (of course) a flourish. But how did he get through the lobby and upstairs to my place? And why didn't he text?

"One of your neighbors let me in. I'm a little paranoid about electronic communication."

"Whatever you say. What's up?"

"I would like you and Dino to come by for a late dinner tomorrow night."

"What's the occasion?"

"Talk soon." End of call.

Text from Dino. "Dinner tomorrow night. Any idea?"

"Nope."

Astor's place was in North Berkeley, off Solano. Nice old Victorian, but not ostentatious. The sinking foundations, aged paint, and overgrown gardens of the Berkeley Bourgeoisie, but the house had to be worth two million. Sprawling, two big porches, backyard. I picked up Dino from his long-term Airbnb houseboat rental in the Berkeley yacht harbor and headed north.

I thought of "The Yachts" by W.C. Williams, so I recited it in the car, or at least what I could remember: *contend in a sea which the land partly encloses / shielding them from the too-heavy blows* ...

"Does not apply. It's a houseboat. Not cheap, but hardly a yacht. And I've never been shielded. I only look like a capitalist pig when compared to you and your friends. Find a new metaphor, or stick with cat burglar. I dress well, speaking of metaphor, but it's a scruffy existence."

"Why do it?"

"One must eat. I like to eat well. I like being freelance. There is no such thing as a good boss."

Of course I got it. It was my life too. I did once work as a book buyer in a big scholarly bookstore. I liked the work, and even though I felt somewhat trapped by the hours and the rules, commerce interested me. I left because the boss was an idiot who didn't share my love of books. As I walked out the door for the last time she called me an intellectual snob. I took that as a compliment.

Parking out front. I was on a winning streak. Astor had a door knocker that could possibly be antique. No bell, far as I could tell, so I used the knocker. It had a nice heavy feel to it.

Astor at the door in Mario Batali drag. That surprised me, given Batali's fall from grace. Hair pulled back and ponytailed, a vest-like fleecy thing, baggy shorts, and kitchen clogs. Waved us into a lived-in front room. The furniture was worn, but just right, and the hardwood floors were polished. Walked through a hallway. Old-fashioned kitchen/dining room setup, not the open jobs that people prefer now. He said, "Sit," and so we did, and he brought out a plate of fried anchovies, olives, and a loaf. The wine was Languedoc. He poured and we toasted "to the good life." The wine was good in a dialed-down way. He went over to a stereo and turned on some music. Paul Desmond, "Funny Valentine." Chamber music jazz. I wondered if it was making a comeback. I have a soft spot for that Brubeck shit because it challenges me in surprising ways. Sneaks up on you.

The fish was so just-right that I didn't feel like talking straight away. Breading, salt. The second bottle was cold and semi-bubbly. After several of the little fishes I looked over at Dino, but he was in some kind of food-loving reverie. Astor was back in the kitchen. "Drink and eat up! I have something nice for you," voice raised over sautéing sounds. Desmond started in on a stringed-up version of "Almost Like Somebody in Love," a favorite standard of mine, although my favorite version, oddly enough, is by Björk.

A Moroccan-style salad came out, the kind with cuminy carrots, and a plate of especially tiny kefta, like little brown marbles.

"We can pick at these before the tagine," and he pulled the bottle out of the ice bucket and poured, then sat down.

This was all very nice, and I planned to eat and drink anything put in front of me, but one thing that poets, book scouts, and detectives have in common is an intense curiosity. I am all three. "What's the occasion?"

"Business, I'll admit, but let's enjoy the food and the company first."

Dino raised his glass, mouth too full to comment, then swallowed as a Nina Simone version of "Falling in Love Again," also with strings, came out of the speakers. Not my favorite Simone, but tasteful, possibly the theme of the evening, but for Astor's outfit.

"If we're going there, could you cue up some Clifford Brown or Charlie Parker?" Bravo, Dino.

Astor pulled out his phone and obeyed, punched up Brown and Max Roach and the violins, then rose to fetch the couscous. The tagine was chicken with prunes, straightforward and "Paris-style." I believed him. Having never been to Tangier I had nothing to compare it to, excepting a North African blowout in Paris. It was perfect. Seems Astor doesn't fuck too much with the food when he's cooking at home, but he makes no mistakes.

A look at Dino got the same response, Delicious, but then raised eyebrows that said, Where are the hots? Perhaps he doesn't serve them at home.

"What's New?" came on, brightest gem of the American songbook. Brown's is the best outside Sinatra.

"I didn't know you as a jazz cat, Astor." First thing I'd said since the first course.

"So nice that you said 'cat,' since our resident cat burglar is in the house." He chuckled, then made a move that said, Hold on to your wallets. Dino pretended not to hear.

The Clifford Brown wound down as we shoveled in the chicken and the couscous. The wine had changed to a funky red, like those Tunisian bottles you might pick up if it's your second month in France and you would like something a little less sophisticated. I had a memory of drinking some out of the bottle, down by the Seine, with a writer friend, down and out in Paris except for that sweet hotel room in the Marais. Down and out is relative. What wine and food can do.

Turkish coffee, of course, and those Moroccan sweets that resemble Turkish delight, then a plate of roasted fruits with cinnamon, served with a gravy boat full of … crème anglaise! Vanilla custard! VH in eggy, sugary cream!

I took a small portion, showing some respect for the Mickey Finn rule. Too delicious, so I ladled more sauce.

The blue hit me quickly but not too hard. A gentle come-on, aided by the wine. I became aware of conversation but couldn't quite get the drift, at least not at first.

"But cat burglars steal small things. Clay, what do you think?"

Astor switched up the music. Sinatra and Jobim. Hadn't heard that in a while.

"Come at me again, guys."

"Fifteen five-gallon pails full of industrial-strength VH. Are you looking for it? You are supposed to be working for me."

"Not yet."

"You were hired to look. But surely you've heard something."

I wouldn't admit it if I had.

Dino looked uncharacteristically worried. "So big and bulky. But what would they be worth?"

Astor looked flustered. Astor flustered, Dino worried. I sobered up fast. "I don't just sell this stuff at the restaurant, you know. I'm wholesaling, and I'm thinking of packaging it in frozen dinners. That many vats could bring in at least forty grand. When I hired you I had no idea that we were missing so much sauce. Listen, you don't have to deliver them, just find them. I can send people out to fetch. I've read John D. MacDonald too. You're getting the Travis McGee deal. Half the stuff, or the cash equivalent. I can't have people stealing my sauce. What if they suss out the formula? They need to be stopped. I need to make an example of them."

I figured Dino would try to negotiate up, considering the size of the heist, but he poured more drinks all around (a bottle of arak had appeared) and toasted. I guess we were detecting partners, among other things.

There was one small detail I wanted to discuss. "Astor, what do you know about Brianna's murder?"

"Nothing, except that the VH was worth thousands and now it's ruined or tossed out. A terrible waste. There are better ways to commit murder."

Things were getting complicated.

## 41.

The Meinhofs were assisting with the coin caper, and now Dino was working with me to solve the mystery of the vanilla hots. Marvin was, as always, everywhere and anywhere, a mentor and most trusted friend. My life was a Venn diagram of overlapping collectives, interests, and possible motives. I needed to get down to business but my head was spinning. Decided to take a heavy dose of blue, go out into nature, hippie-style, and figure things out, catch the drift, get the picture, read the plot, grok it, and, having done that, punch myself in the face with my fist, grab the bull by the horns, and face the situation.

I know of a cabin in Olema, an off-the-books cash-only rental. Not cheap, but with no Airbnb-style mystery charges, affordable. It practically fronts a trail, not too challenging, the kind that I could negotiate while ablaze on blue. Ablaze! I was getting comfortable with the new talk around the drug. There was "sauced," of course, but also the oddly poetic "moored." I'd also heard "have a nip of Astor" but hadn't had the occasion to use it. The hots being illegal now, blue slang has entered the public language, gone from new to hipsterish to passé. It was evolving then, in those heady days, post-Occupy, pre-Trump, pre-pandemic.

The cabin had a vacancy that night and the next. I lucked out. Asked a neighbor to feed the cat, packed a duffel, hit Berkeley Bowl on the way out for provisions. I had transferred two squirt bottles to a Moe's Books water thermos and took small nips of Astor along the way, just a little dose that hit me as I crossed the Richmond Bridge. It was a beautiful bright day, warm but not too, and the water became a brighter blue as I passed San Quentin, making even that monument to suffering seem benign. Over and up, around and out to West Marin. The air got hot, then cool as I got closer to the coast. Blue sky but not *the* blue, that blue was coloring the wispy clouds.

Pulled into the cabin, got situated, put on a pair of boots that I had bought at the suggestion of the poet Michael McClure. Taking drugs and taking in nature. What kind of mammal am I, Michael? Do I roar or hunker down? Hunt, or sit and appreciate.

A large glug from the VH jug, a couple of apples, and a Snickers bar to be eaten early, before melting. But would I melt before the candy? I hadn't taken this big a dose, and not out in nature. The path was beginning to wind but I could follow along. The trees made a nice canopy, the path was well worn. Tourist hiking but I didn't care. Still trees, still birds, still those strange rustlings in the undergrowth, and air that smelled like air.

A clearing, probably less than a mile in, but I was getting beyond those kinds of considerations. Nice DIY bench, probably not '30s CCC vintage, looked like someone carved a downed tree from the last storm. I ate the candy and an apple, downed more hots that I'd diluted with water. Decided to roust myself and walk to the next bench, farther in so that I wouldn't encounter fellow walkers.

There was a good one, set back and facing what was probably once a babbling brook, long dried after years of drought. Comfortable, and I could sit with my back to the path.

I held my hand in front of my face to gauge the power of the blue. It appeared, behind a scrim, just brighter than the scrim, like a lantern in the fog. I set about to define the blue, but the blue wouldn't allow me the luxury of precise thinking. Sky and water when nature is being peaceful, Vishnu, Krishna, and Shiva, the darker the blue the calmer the mind. Kuaneos, darkening, not quite this shade of blue. When the sea roils it turns dark brown, and black. Those places, no, placements, in nature where blueness enhances the beauty of the experience, standing on the wharf on a bright day. Homer doesn't say "blue" but alludes, is the wine-dark sea a shade? Mary in flowing lapis lazuli, baby Jesus in pinkish red, in opposition to modern infant wear, Fra Angelico mixing the blue, this has been going on for a long time. Old hunters wore blue in the years before the Civil War and so the US chose a dark blue for its uniforms. None of these shades matched the blue that appeared behind my eyes. IBM blue? The blue on the screen? Hardly. How depressing that would be.

The scrim gave a bit and I decided to walk back to my cabin while I still had some semblance of eyesight. I had given myself quite a dose.

The blue allowed my mind to wander, and my eyesight was distorted, but I didn't feel inebriated, exactly. The high came from the perception of the color. It just grew out of that. Other thoughts could move around it but they were always filtered through some amplified version of the sea off the coast of Bimini, Crete, or Bali, but then, not quite.

I had, on a whim, bought some blueberries. Blue fruit for the occasion. They stood out on what I'd imagined was a white plate but was now the lighter hue.

One blueberry at a time, and a look at the plate and the trees out the window. The trees refused to go blue. Somehow I respected them for that. They were keeping their distance from the habits of this lower form of sentient being. Good call.

"This is a nice way to pass the time," I said aloud, to myself, before I felt the beginnings of a wild surmise, but it stayed just out of brain range.

## 42.

Back at the Chandler Apartments, well rested after a long sleep at the cabin and a surprisingly traffic-free commute. The surmise still hadn't turned to language, but the little detective's voice in my head told me to check out Hard Bop. Hardly the stuff of wild surmise, but I decided to follow my instincts. Fed the cat, got in the car.

These small shops look like sets for a TV series, and the record nerds are right out of central casting. Every book and record store is a reworking of a '70s situation comedy, though with slightly more intelligent jokes. The owners, the clerks, the various kinds of customers are the regulars and the special guest stars.

I could tell by her slouch that she didn't have a piece of the action. Perhaps Brianna was really the sole owner, and the collective idea was just good publicity. This one was kept employed by her wits, her knowledge of the stock, and because she was able to live at the margins. Retail pays shit. Also, music store work was (still is) mostly a boys' club, so she had to be extra sharp. She was wearing a newsboy cap and a turtleneck shirt that came up too far, to her chin. Black on black. A look that said, I can help you if you really need it.

"I'm a friend of Brianna's. Sorry to hear the news."

Sizing me up. "The store could be sold. Don't know how long we'll be around. Buy now while you can."

"Can I ask a few questions?" Detective mode.

"The sections are marked."

"I can see that. I'd like to ask about Brianna."

"Why?"

"I'm the curious type."

She wasn't flirting, in that meet-cute kind of way. She truly didn't give a fuck about me, or Brianna. "Ask me and I'll answer if I like."

"Was she a good boss?"

"She thought she was. Refused to be called 'boss,' since there's some bullshit profit sharing that nobody sees. I'm twenty-five and I share a room. I'm not talking about a boyfriend or girlfriend. I can't afford my own room. Brianna was civil enough, but I share a room. Get it?"

"Did the staff resent the low pay?"

"Does the pope shit in the Vatican?"

"Was somebody angry enough—"

"If you are a cop, you are eighty-sixed. If you would like to buy the business, talk to somebody else. If you do buy the business, give us a fucking raise."

"I'm not a cop or a buyer."

"Then who the fuck are you?" She moved down the counter, the way you do when you work for the public and encounter a nutjob. Should I tell her?

"I'm helping some people sort things out. The cops won't get it right, so somebody asked me—"

"Game over. Buy something or get out."

"Okay, I'm an unlicensed detective. I'm trying to find a rare coin that is worth a million dollars, and I'd like to know who killed Brianna. Also, I'm looking for some rare Sun Ra records."

I turned to leave, but mid-turn noticed her face soften a little. Was it the Sun Ra reference?

"Don't have much right now. I'll keep my eyes open." Still not flirty. I had no chance there, but the musical connection was working.

"Steve Lacy?"

"We might have something. What is it with him? He doesn't move me."

"It's head music."

"Not for my head. How can you be a detective without a license? What does that mean?"

"Means I try to help people out when asked."

"Okay, I'll bite. There's a guy who works here, Jimmyjames, all one word. Tell him I sent you."

"And you are?"

"I don't give out my name to weirdos who come in from the street. Just describe me to him."

# 43.

Jimmyjames, all one word, wasn't at work that day and the nameless Sun Ra fan didn't know his schedule. I would have to stop by another time.

I went home and put on Steve Lacy's Monk record. Occurs to me now that there is another Steve Lacy, not a jazz guy. Did she think I was referring to him? And was he around then?

I got on the laptop and revised a chapbook's worth of poems. Made a note to ask around for a tiny press that would publish them. Maybe Cedar Sigo or Micah Ballard would do a reading with me at Moe's. The phone, in its wisdom and respect for poetry, refused to buzz until I was finished. The poems were printing, I picked up.

"Marvin here. Come down to the bowling alley. Big score."

Back outside, back in the Miata. I was beginning to feel like a boomerang.

Percy was at the counter when I arrived at Meinhof's. "They're in the nursery." We just called it that. People deposited their kids there sometimes. The room was full of toys.

The full collective, minus Percy, was in the room, sitting on little kid chairs. A comic scene. We sat in a tiny circle, with Dino in the middle.

"Shut the door!" In unison.

I did. I towered over them, sitting in their tiny toy seats. Dino was wearing a wool herringbone suit. It wasn't even that cold out! His legs were up near his head, due to the shortness of the chair. It was perched on his left knee. How could it shine so, given its age? Was that really Brutus's face? They stared at that shiny thing, like apes before a monolith.

"Where did it come from?"

It took them a few seconds. "He won't say." Again together, like a Greek chorus.

Dino turned his rolling eyes to me. "I was waiting for you. It was left in the pocket of this suit. As far as I can tell someone snuck into my closet and left it there."

"Who was in your closet?"

"Therein lies the rub. I have had more than one overnight guest recently. At least two, maybe three since the coin went missing. I'm a little unclear with the timeline."

"I didn't leave the fucking coin!" Patti? She spent the night? Gore Vidal always said that everyone is bisexual, but I thought that was just wishful thinking. Dino sleeps with girls? I did a quick check of the jealousy portion of my brain, figured everything was jake.

"Others may have had access to my closet. A cat burglar, perhaps? It wouldn't be difficult to board my little houseboat."

On Marvin's laugh: It is a guffaw that covers three octaves, and, as the poet said, pulls everyone's lapel and makes them confess to him and to all.

Marvin let go of an especially good laugh. "So that narrows it down to Dino's lovers and every thief with a Cary Grant complex. I love a mystery!"

Chad, a realist among poets, as is true of many preachers, cut through the fog and led us onward to materialism. "If we can fence it fast and move it along, we can come out atop Mount Moola! I could build a church that would rival that papist monstrosity out by Lake Merritt!"

I was trying to read Patti's face. Embarrassed? Perhaps guilty? Could she be the one who took and deposited the coin? I wondered who else Dino had invited in. Maybe I was a little jealous. I had recently spent a night or two with him. What was the timeline? Would the others see me as a suspect?

I decided to play William Powell and hold court over the other suspects. "Let's assume that it wasn't a cat burglar. Dino, tell us who was on your boat over, say, the last week."

He looked over at Patti. He was loving this as much as she wasn't. Then he smiled at me. The others got it. Two down.

There was ... a perfectly placed pause. "Jimmyjames. That's all one word. And Astor."

"Who the fuck is Jimmyjames?" From the chorus, not perfectly synched, but close enough.

"He's a musician. He works over at Hard Bop. I met him at the White Horse." He looked over at me again, said, "It isn't necessarily the better part of valor. Sometimes it's better to just do what you like, Oscar Wilde-style."

Chad spoke fastest. "We can't put it back at the houseboat. I'll take it to a safe place." He grabbed it from Dino's knee. Nobody argued.

## 44.

Somewhere there is a loop, as in, keep me in the loop, but I wasn't being kept in it.

Something good was playing at Hard Bop. I wanted to be a good jazz aficionado and call it, but I couldn't.

"Yusef Lateef." He must have noticed my knitted brow. I nodded like I knew something. He had bushy sideburns and a mod cap, circa 1966. Thick glasses. Nice looking in spite of the affectations. Paisley? Really? But sometimes things work when they shouldn't. He seemed comfortable with it.

"Are you by chance Jimmyjames?"

"Himself." This guy was dripping with affectation.

"I was working for Brianna. I'm trying to find out what happened."

"Who do you work for now?" I should have seen that one coming but didn't.

"Myself. Just a friend."

"Cops were everywhere. They can probably fuck it up on their own."

"They aren't known for their competence. I'm just doing it because she was a friend."

"And because there is a coin knocking around, somewhere, and you'd like to score. I heard from both Brianna and Dino."

Jesus Christ! Loose lips! "My concerns are about three-quarters humanitarian. Do you have the coin?" I know, I knew. But Jimmyjames didn't know that I knew.

"Wouldn't tell you either way. I have an alibi, ask the cops. I wouldn't have killed her anyway. She's just another small business owner, and I'm just another record nerd. Low wage, lunch out of the register, four-day week, all the records I can eat. And I didn't hear about the coin until somebody iced her. No motive."

Iced? Who says that outside of Elmore Leonard? I thought the interview was over. Crossed the little store to have a look at the Mose Allison collection.

"I hear you are close to Astor. Dino won't take me there. Can you possibly get me a table? Or, failing that, a squirt bottle of hots?"

"Am I to take that to mean that you have some information?"

"I don't know shit about this coin except the price. I do think I know who killed her. I'd bet my first pressing of *L.A. Woman* on it, and I'm a huge Doors fan."

Fuck. Now I'd be humming Doors songs all day, and I don't even like them much. And would I have to have dinner with this guy? Excepting me, Dino has terrible taste in men. "Okay, Jimmy. Dinner for two next week."

"It's Jimmyjames, all one word. And I'd also like some to-go sauce."

"A vat of it if you like." Then I remembered the murder weapon. Oops.

"I'll tell you at dinner."

"You will tell me now. Who is it?"

No hesitation. "That smarmy Christian guy you hang with."

Hmm. Chad. Our own Robin Hood? Would Errol Flynn do that? Maybe.

"What led you to this conclusion?"

"Details to come." We traded numbers and set a tentative date.

## 45.

In response to a crime wave in London, eighteenth-century popular writers rewrote the legend of the good thief who took from the rich and gave to the poor. The pure-hearted commie of the fourteenth century was recast as a cruel, low killer. Rich folks didn't take kindly to bandits. Writers and politicians have been inventing crime waves ever since, if not before. As an amateur student of literature, and a lefty, I wanted to believe the original myth. We choose our own.

For me, Chad was just starting to fit in with the early ballads. He was a little strange, but also a leader. I saw through his gift of gab, maybe most did, but we didn't care. We responded to the sincerity that somehow anchored him, like, "he's feeding us a little shit but it's because he loves us." His speeches and his goofy prayers somehow aped the fake Olde English of the kids' Robin Hood novels. No surprise if he came out with a "thy" or a "forsooth." It played into his persona.

Our Robin also killed, but killing Brianna seemed more like the cold-blooded murderers in the 1700s ballads that writers invented as a way to control the masses. If the coin went to the poor, Hood-style, it could buy a lot of dinners, provide a lot of shelter, even buy an old bowling alley that could serve to further the communist experiment. Nice motive. But cold-blooded murder of a small businessperson? Chad? How Christian? Well, Christian soldiers. We choose our own myths.

And so, sitting in Ho Chi Minh Park after a walk around the neighborhood and a burrito from Gordo, I shot Chad a text. I suggested a walk out at the Marina, followed by a beer somewhere or another. He said he'd meet me there.

## 46.

Driving down University Avenue to the Marina, still humming those damn Doors songs, going through my sixth-grade song list, my brain cues up Michael McClure reading "Riders on the Storm" with Ray Manzarek, recorded somewhere in Europe, discovered on YouTube just recently. Okay, that works.

Overcast as I approached the water. Parked real close, for once. Did I accidentally sell my soul to the devil? Detectives in the movies always get good parking, or they park illegally and don't get ticketed. I'll have to try the latter soon.

Minutes later he pulled up beside me. Wouldn't have been like him to go down to the crossroads to get some parking luck, so I put it down to Jesus. He drove an Accord, black and beat. We hugged, as is his habit, and walked down to the water. Not too windy for once, sun getting low, possibly the best view in the Bay Area. Directly across from the Golden Gate. Just behind us, up the hill, the kites were barely airborne in the stillness. I was still hearing McClure reading "Riders on the Storm," wrong weather but the forbidding aspect was fitting. I imagined what we looked like from the street, for some reason. Backlit, or is that frontlit? Staring out to sea, having a tense little talk. A couple of skinny white guys with glasses.

I got right to it.

"Did you take the coin?"

"What makes you think so?"

"A question with a question?"

"Why not?"

"Somebody thinks you did it, and killed Brianna."

"Who thinks so?"

The short answers threw me. He was supposed to be sonorous, dramatic, wordy. Suddenly everyone was speaking film noir. Expected him to say, "I didn't do it, see?" à la Edward G. Robinson.

"Let's play '40s detectives. Where were you on the night of?"

"I'm not a killer, but if I was a killer I'd make sure to have a good reason. I would think and consider, I would do it for the good of humankind. That's the only motive. It's my only motive, whatever I do."

Errol Flynn would toss those lines off better. Chad was a different breed of Robin Hood, but he was ours. He recited his lines with the usual ramped-up sincerity, like a grifter, but then you see beyond the grift, or you think you do, and there's something real hidden in the mush. And of course when you think about what's said, you can put your hand right through it, it's not a real statement of fact, or of anything. But it seems sincere.

"I'm not getting anywhere with this."

"Trust me, Clay." Watery eyes? I don't really remember, or maybe I do.

We walked north, around a bend where the breeze, at least this day, was stronger. I thought he'd open up and talk but he didn't. Eventually I changed the subject. Perhaps dinner with Jimmyjames would bring me closer to the truth.

## 47.

"Hi Astor—looking to have dinner soon in North Berkeley—table for two?" Sent in an email because I didn't feel like talking. Didn't work. He called twenty seconds later.

"Did you find my VH?"

"Zeroing in on it." A good detective knows where to place a lie.

"I fear that 'zero' is the operative word."

"I'm meeting with a source soon. I can have something for you when I show up for dinner, say, Wednesday?"

"I'm bleeding hots. I think it's an inside job. I'd fire my entire staff, but if I do the Wobblies will get on my ass, and I'll lose our deal with the Emmas. I need that space! I'm not pulling enough out of Pomo. People are ordering one appetizer and flooding it with sauce. That's not the point. This is supposed to be fine dining!"

"I promise to order lots of dishes."

"I always comp you."

"I'll pay the bill, and I'll order the foie gras."

"It's off the menu. We were picketed. Order a hanger steak. It's not really steak, but the 'frites' are carved out of filet mignon, breaded, and fried in goose fat. It's a dish that loves the sauce."

"Table by the window?"

"I guess you're handsome enough. Is your date presentable?"

"I think so. He looks like Kenneth Koch circa 1968."

"Who?"

"Sideburns and a corduroy cap. Some will find it cute. It won't drive away the sidewalk trade."

"Okay, and come armed with some information. I need to find the hots!"

## 48.

I took a Lyft and so did he, to avoid driving while sauced. We met at César for a pre-dinner Negroni. Too crowded to have a conversation, but there would be time. Nice, convivial bar feeling to start the evening. Whenever possible, combine business with pleasure. As the poet said. Or maybe as all poets have said. Jimmyjames looked folk-rock sporty in one of those satin-like warmup jackets, Roger McGuinn glasses, straight jeans, and flashy boots. The cap was vintage Montreal Expos, red and white, blue bill, worst logo in the history of baseball. Was that supposed to be an *M*? I had gone with blue oxford, tweed, jeans, and brown dress shoes. Rusty Staub/Roger McGuinn out on a date with his English professor, with me as prof, wearing my homage to Jonathan Lethem.

I decided he was kind of my type since I like goofy, but I wouldn't go there. All business tonight.

As promised, a table by the window. The scene was no longer cutting-edge, even though the place was crowded. It seemed a little too comfortable for the more avant feeders. Restaurant fads come too quickly for me to keep up. I prefer lived-in places that hang around, like Le Bateau Ivre on Telegraph. No matter, the food was good and, far as I know, Drunken Boat has never offered drugs.

We ordered the "steak." I think it was fashioned out of some mushroom and beet mixture. The "frites" were amazing, deep-fried yet somehow rare in the middle. Goose fat! We passed on the rose beverage and ordered a bottle of Tempranillo, some Kermit Lynch choice, always reliable, although the bookseller John McBride once confided in me that "Kermit's tastebuds are shot." Can't remember the second part of that quote. Maybe Kermit had minions with decent buds, or perhaps John and I were on our second bottle, most likely at a Moe's Books Christmas party, trading lies.

This Temp was pretty good with the meaty fries. We dipped them in a new generation of hots, spicier and not as vanillaed. Imagine an extra fancy A.1. sauce, just vinegar-and-salty enough, not as sweet. Would be equally as good on fried fish.

We were talking about loft jazz, ignoring the elephant in the room. I was interested in the New York Art Quartet and their collabs with Amiri Baraka. Were there recordings, other than "Black Dada Nihilismus"?

"I don't think there's anything else around. There must have been tapes. I'll look into it." I think I impressed him with my knowledge of the genre, though it isn't that deep. I usually get a little fuzzy after Albert Ayler. Or maybe he's enough to satisfy.

"I'm not an expert but I'd like to be."

"When I want that sound I mostly put on Ornette, but I have to know all the names to keep my job. I play a game with customers. They need to stump me to show their knowledge, but they need to know that I know some stuff." And, shrugging, "It's a living, I guess."

If you carry an American passport, have a place to live, maybe even drive a car, you are part of the grift. Your soul was taken away at birth, but the perks are the best on the planet. I was hearing Marvin's voice in my head.

"You seem to know a little something." Hoping a little flattery would get me closer to the intel.

Smile and a nod. "I know things that you want to know."

"How is dinner?"

"Great and possibly expensive. Second bottle of wine?"

This was going to cost me. I would need to bear down on finding Astor's stash or risk going broke. I ordered another bottle.

"And something dark chocolate?"

Astor had done away with cute dessert names. I ordered the one called "chocolate." It was a series of lumps on a big plate. They were all chocolate, in varying degrees of sweet and bitter. Two shot glasses of a sweet VH to sauce the bonbons. Great with red wine.

He was a little drunk, but I was holding my own, thanks to the heavy meal. There's something about opening a second bottle. It sets up expectations. Lowered voices, deeper communication, sex, secrets revealed ... I was hoping to hear some secrets.

"I came back from my break. We heard shouting from the office, then hysterical shrieks. Stuff being thrown. It was great! This never happens in record stores! The Christian came out, looking red in the face, and beat a retreat. Brianna came out like there was nothing wrong."

"That's it? An argument with the victim? That happens in every dumb PBS murder mystery. Is that all you got? That's a sixty-five-dollar bottle of wine. I thought you had evidence."

"There's more but it will cost you an Armagnac."

Shit. That thing that book scouts, detectives, and poets have in common. Curiosity. We will risk it all for a juicy bit of gossip. I ordered, in warmed snifters with a twist.

"She was on her phone in the back. I was in and out of the office. She didn't try to hide it. Don't know who she was talking to. She said she was afraid that Chad was crazier than he seemed. She said, 'What if he kills me?'"

That didn't look so good.

"Did you tell this to the cops?"

"No. I'm not going to help them solve their little mysteries. I mean, who cares? I'm talking to you because I like you." And to show his lack of sincerity he lifted his snifter and shook it at me, as if to say, Buy me another.

I did, but he drank it in near silence. I had overmedicated him. End of first round. Call up a Lyft.

# 49.

Moe's Books is next door to the Chandler Apartments, and there's an alleyway in back where the clerks sometimes take their smoke and coffee breaks, since there is no break room at the store. I occasionally went back there to shoot the breeze. Book scouts and book buyers, same breed. It was also politic for me to get along with these people, since I often sold books to them. I miss those conversations, miss the heady days of the teens, meaning 2013 to around 2016, a time that didn't seem simpler but was.

Trash smells and piss, sometimes a sleeping unhoused person, just Telegraph, just Berkeley, just America. Talk of big book buys, or maybe just gossip, passing the time. That urban situation where you make yourself comfortable where it isn't comfortable.

I went downstairs to get some orange juice across the street at the old Fred's Market. The alley was swarming with cops, dark blue for blocks, squad cars from the park and way down Dwight Way. They ignored me and went about whatever business they were going about. The dark blues were mostly congregating around the entrance to the alley, looking serious because it's all about presenting with these types. Showing tough, standing close, straining to get a look at something. I recognized one of them.

"What's up?"

"Dead guy. Drowned in a big plastic tub of something, maybe sugar water."

I tried to angle forward but the Berkeley Barney Fifes were thick on the ground, like ants on a cupcake.

"Do they know who it is?"

A shrug and a harsh though slightly puzzled look. Trying to place me. This pig had ass eyes. I hate ass eyes.

Angled forward a bit more, stood as tall as I could, but couldn't get a look at the victim. A vat of sugary liquid. Not hard to make an educated guess. I felt a flash of worry. Dino? Astor? One of the Meinhofs? They weren't going to let me hang around. I went up in the direction of Fred's Market, anticipating a "move along now" order or, worse, a set of questions.

"Hey, Fred, do you know anything about it?" We called all the clerks Fred, even though the original Fred had sold the business around the time of the first People's Park demonstrations.

"Don't know a thing but I wish I'd ordered more donuts." Hooting laugh at his own joke. I chuckled politely.

Back up the elevator to the fourth floor, then over to a window that faced the alley, down a hallway and out by the fire escape. I drank my juice and waited, a little back from the window to avoid cop stares.

As if by instinct I crawled out the window and perched on the fire escape just as they were moving the body. It was covered but wasn't in a body bag. My perception, somehow, telescoped down into the depths of the alleyway as the sheet-like covering slipped off the body, and just as the material was caught and replaced by an EMT, I caught a glimpse.

Chad Recife.

## 50.

"But Robbin Hood so gentle was / And bore so brave a minde / If any in distresse did passe / To them he was so kinde." Patti, reading from an old anthology of child's verse, "A True Tale of Robbin Hood," seventeenth century, though the legend goes back another couple of centuries.

Patti and I were at the Chandler, planning one of those typical poet's memorials, to be held at Meinhof's. Mostly we would read Chad's poems and some of our own, but Patti took particular interest in the Robin Hood myth and applied it to Chad's life. I knew she was fond of him, but as much as anyone she saw him as a grifter. She is not the sentimental type, but we all react to death the way we react, often surprising ourselves.

Though unspoken, we had decided to get drunk and weepy. Chad liked beer, especially IPA, so we drank one in his honor though we weren't crazy about IPAs. We switched over to Guinness and shots from a bottle of Writer's Tears.

We had met at a reading. That sentence applies to us, and also to me and Chad, Chad and Patti, also Marvin and the three of us. I met Patti when, seeing her across the room at a Burroughs reading, years ago, I decided I had to meet her. This was in Santa Cruz. She was in school and I had dropped out to go surfing with Kevin Opstedal and to do my drinking at the Catalyst. I got on her bus after the reading. I was living on Seabright but the bus went the other way, out to Natural Bridges. What a great story, to say that we fucked on the beach! We didn't, that night, but certainly hit it off, and we stayed (and have stayed) close, even as she moved to Prague, London, and various versions of hip geographic triangles: SF, Austin, Iowa City, then NYC, New Orleans, Portland, and at some point back to the Bay Area because, as she said, "Nothing's cheap anywhere, may as well settle into Berkeley."

She started out gangly but bulked up, learned to show tough in wifebeaters and dangerous shoes, and now, as I write this, she's salt-and-pepper and sinewy.

"Where did you meet Chad?"

"He tried to chat me up at a reading. I wasn't interested in that but I was interested in him. You've said it, his charm comes from knowing that he's trying too hard to charm you. I fell for the flattery."

"Is he straight? I mean, was he coming on to you?" For lack of a better phrase.

"I don't know what he was except Christian. He made no physical advances, at least not exactly. Or maybe he read me correctly and backed off. He could be pan or asexual for all I know."

"He told me he was married once, but our conversation died out after that. For such a great talker he doesn't reveal much."

"Didn't." And when she said that I felt sadness, for the first time since I'd seen him, for that fraction of a second, as they loaded him up for a ride to the coroner's.

"Right. It takes getting used to when someone dies. How deeply do you think he was involved in all this skulduggery?"

"Great word, Clay. You're either a poet or have watched too many Vincent Price movies."

"Both."

"He was proud of his skill as a thief. He could have had the coin at some point, I guess."

"Someone thought so."

I used those battery-powered candles so I can't say the candles were burning down, but you know what I mean. I was waiting for a clue to drop but all I'd gotten was some biographical information. Was she holding out? I didn't think so. I filed the conversation in a small corner of my brain. The talked turned to sex, and how VH enhances the experience, but people always say that when drugs are new. Death, grief, can be an aphrodisiac, like in the movies when, zombies approaching, two teens stop for a few minutes to fuck like bunnies. It's an older stimulant but can also enhance the experience.

## 51.

I wasn't acting like a detective, even though I was spending money earned, or not earned, by detecting. My sort of grieving was turning real with each murder. Chad was a friend, of sorts, and someone I saw almost daily. That thing that happens—you see them in the old familiar places. There he is, reading at the counter, chatting up someone from the poets collective, putting in some shelving time.

I shook myself several times in the days following the murder, until finally something clicked, and I went out into the world to do what all good detectives do, which is to thrash around and make yourself obnoxious until something gives.

Drowned in V-hots! A message for sure, and an expensive one. Couldn't quite wrap my brain around that. Where's the motive? I needed to go to the source, ask some questions.

Midmorning and I needed a walk. Down to Shattuck, then north to the restaurant. Went into the Cheese Board for a scone and coffee, then crossed over to Astor's place. The crew was cleaning up when I knocked. The worker recognized me and let me in.

"Is the boss in?"

"Hi, Clay. Chef is in his office. I think he spent the night there." And, leaning forward, "He may be a bit cranky."

I crossed the room and went upstairs. Cranky doesn't scare me. Knocked hard, to establish my seriousness—though I wasn't sure how serious I really was.

"I haven't slept much." Definitely looking the worse for wear, but still sporting a peach scarf over a silk shirt.

"The questions won't be hard. Well, not too hard."

He waved me in and sat at his desk. Looking closer, I noticed how rumpled he was.

"Drowned in hots. Somebody must hate you. And they can't be poor. Otherwise they would have sold those vats of sauce. Any ideas? A competitor, perhaps?"

"I have no viable competitors. Would you call this a ritual murder?"

"Or at least a repeat performance."

"I have no enemies!"

I certainly didn't buy that. "I think you do, and I'd guess you're next." I didn't really know that but I needed to push him a little. It worked. He did a double take that was worthy of a bad comedian. For a moment, I saw him swimming in Buddy Hackett's gene pool.

"Someone has been pushing me to sell the recipe, but they haven't really shown themselves."

"Why didn't you tell me that? I'm supposed to be working for you."

"They weren't very assertive, just an email or two. And they didn't make any threats. Lots of people ask me how it is made."

"Who knows the recipe?"

"Just me. The folks at the plant have a partial, and I add the active ingredient myself. I drive down to the plant late at night, add the stuff, and stamp the vats when I've juiced them up."

"But the people down at the factory know it's being done."

"Of course."

"Could there have been a leak? And could the secret go out to, say, Chad? Or Brianna?"

"I follow you, but I don't know."

He didn't, far as I knew, know about the missing coin, so I didn't fill him in. There had to be a connection. The recipe and the coin set up a double MacGuffin situation, which in turn gave way to a series of buy-and-swap scenarios, with enough total worth to provide motive, but the story had too many holes. I needed to poke around some more.

Somebody killed Brianna to get the coin, and killed Chad to get … the recipe? The coin? I thought of Dino, trying to be fair, but if Dino killed to get the coin, would he hang around with it? Wouldn't he be playing at his favorite casino, atop Mont Parnes in Greece? Or perhaps he'd take it on the lam to Gibraltar, where it is illegal to feed the monkeys but he just wouldn't care, would probably feed them caviar. For a second I surmised that he'd stayed to spend more time with me. I could nearly rule Dino out but not quite, because Dino was capable of almost anything. A bad boy's bad boy! Thinking about him, I felt pangs of deep lust. Decided to text him.

"Dinner?"

"Yes, but no VH tonight. Chez? We can probably get in upstairs. I'll call them."

I hadn't been to Chez Panisse in some time. I was happy for the suggestion. I was getting tired of state-of-the-art eateries. Ready for the tried and true. Rumor had Dino once romantically involved with Alice, so our table upstairs was assured. Within minutes a text said, "Table at 7:45."

## 52.

The skate would be cooked very plain, with some high-grade olive oil and fresh herbs. The gentleman at the table next to ours was an unhappy mansplainer. This is why I prefer the café, though calling it a café isn't really accurate. Informal, but not a café. I liked that the tables were close together. The better to eavesdrop.

"It's supposed to be served with browned butter."

The server nodded, playing it close to the vest. "We think it works well this way. The skate's flavor comes through without being overpowered."

"I'll have the butternut squash ravioli with browned butter, but I wish you could switch the sauces."

No answer from the server. Dino leaned over to me. "He should have asked, more seriously, if the chef could trade sauces. Eventually the waitperson would blow. I could feel the anger from across the way."

We both ordered the skate, with a bottle of Forlorn Hope Semillon.

"But hopefully it springs eternal." This from Dino. I wasn't quite sure what he was talking about, or maybe I was.

"Forlorn hope can spring eternal too. It's just a little ... forlorn."

It came to the table just right. Didn't taste forlorn.

"Chin-chin, Clay. Every meal a banquet." The Peter Lorre eye-bug, but said with tired irony.

"Shall we lead off talking about murder and the coin? Or flirt around a little, talk about art, politics, the dangerous intensity of the lives we've chosen, our forlorn and broken hopes ..."

"We've been close for years but I still don't know when you are joking. Maybe it's my European upbringing. Different sense of humor? But then, I've always thought of you as having a darker sense of humor than most Americans, who are as deep as a koi pond at some orientalist city park in Cincinnati."

"Cheap shot! There are some very deep Americans out there."

"Now I know you are joking."

"I would like to know who slipped you the Brutus."

And now, full-on Peter Lorre: "I know nothing about that, dear Clay. One moment you put your hand in a side pocket and feel nothing. You hang up the jacket, you go about your business. Another time, you put your hand in the same pocket and there is a million-dollar coin there. But the Brutus is lost again. Chad snatched it, and I suppose the killer knew that." Spread his hands, then reached for the bottle, refilled our glasses.

The skate arrived, perfectly cooked, a dribble of fragrant and fruity olive oil dripping over the sides of the wing, pooling. Silence for a while, as we appreciated the fish, the tiny boiled potatoes, the rabe.

I would have countered with my best Bogart, but I can't do Bogart, never could. Went, reluctantly, with straightforward Clay Blackburn, private eye.

"We have two bodies, one is a good friend. Drowned in vats of the hottest drug on the street. We have the Brutus coin, worth a million dollars. And I am having dinner with a professional thief. All things connected?"

"All things are connected. Whatever befalls the earth befalls the sons of the earth. Chief Seattle, I think."

Was that a clue? Should I ask? Dino was talking in circles. "I know that speech, Dino. What are you getting at?"

"Let's go on as before, for now. Take some trinkets, sell some books, steal from the rich, give to the poor, eat and live well. Mayakovsky's Bugatti, as you like to say."

"I'm losing patience. I'm afraid there could be another murder. I was fond of Chad."

"Me too, up to a point." Pouring out the rest of the wine. "Coffee? Dessert?"

We split a Paris-Brest, perfect choux, coffee, and cognac the way I like it, in a warmed snifter with a twist.

And so, as it stood, and for all I knew at the time, I went home with a murderer, but that wouldn't have been a first. I'd been a private asshole for some time by then. Goes with the territory.

# 53.

The idea that the VH-induced blue vision was a visualization of the life force, a kind of transubstantiation (sauce to color yet still a sauce) taking place in the eyeballs (though some will say it is only symbolic), was first verbalized by crazy old Astor, while downing espressos at Meinhof's.

It was Bay Area blustery outside, but sunny. You put on a nice sweater or a hoodie, then remove it several times during the day. My memory of that day turns on that, weather as madeleine, Astor looking windblown, striding up to the counter and rapping it, half joking, or maybe not, and getting a quick double, pumped by Marvin, but with an eye roll. There's a story that Artaud, after living abroad, came straight from traveling, valise in hand, found a chair at his favorite café, and proceeded to hold court before going home. Astor was that type, going straight to a café or his restaurant, his public presence more important than unpacking.

"Come here, Clay. Is Patti about? I've told this to Dino and he only half got it, but half is better than none. Half full, right? And Dino is an optimist." Then, looking at Marvin, "You won't understand, but on that point we understand each other."

Astor was "on something," as we used to say. Perhaps the hots? And lots of coffee? Hard to imagine him on speed or some legacy psychedelic. I wonder how much he experimented with his own stuff. "You'll all be skeptical. I haven't given this much weight to the importance of a food, or rather a drug, since I read Liebling on cassoulet."

I hadn't considered cassoulet a drug, although I have had some great ones. I made a mental note to reread Liebling. Astor was our Leary, and his pronouncements, over time, had come to be taken seriously, as if he were some kind of sorcerer, or even a haruspex, reading and seeing the future in a once-living being, whether animal or exotic herb. Perhaps that is the connection to Liebling's work on the cassoulet, since the best of them contain cheap cuts of meat. Entrails?

"Jesus fucking god, Astor. What are you talking about?" Marvin had little patience with alchemists in general, none with Astor.

"Funny you should mention Jesus, because when he prayed in the garden and his sweat turned to blood, the process was similar. But then that was red and this is blue, and not so messy."

Patti entered the room at that point, coming in with a couple of rolls of quarters, fetched from our closet safe. She gave me a look. I shrugged. She turned to Marvin, who made the universal sign for crazy, a circling finger pointed at his head.

A couple of customers came out from the philosophy section to give a listen. I recognized them as theoryheads. One was an aging Language poet, the other liked to quote Benjamin, or Ben-ya-meen. Me, I was enjoying the show, relaxed and paying attention. This is why I moved to the Bay Area, where the norm is not the norm.

Astor picked up the sweater that he had thrown on the bar, adjusted his scarf, body language saying, Time to go. Would he elaborate? But elaborate on what? He hadn't really said anything that any of us could understand.

The scarf perfectly wrapped, the sweater carefully donned, the short leather jacket shrugged on and half zipped. His small audience looked at him and each other, trying not to laugh.

"The life force, you goddamn fucking idiots, the life force! The hots are the key. You take the hots and you see it all. It's all there in the blue."

He stepped behind the counter, grabbed a copy of *Function of the Orgasm* that he'd had on hold, and strode out without paying.

The theoryheads drifted back to the stacks. *In the room they come and go.* I could hear them discussing Reich's theories on the color blue, then chuckling.

Me, Patti, and even Marvin leaned on the counter, dumbstruck. After a while Marvin came to, said, "Life force. Sheesh."

# 54.

Dinner with Marvin at the Chandler Apartments.

"This changes the MacGuffin situation," he said. "There is a spiritual element, or a cultish element, that transcends the coin and drug angle, but, fuck, they must be related somehow. Two people drowned in the stuff that contains the key to the meaning of life? Is that it? Or is it the meaning of life? Hunting down fascists in El Salvador was less taxing. I'm going to sell my share in Meinhof's and go back to mercenary work."

Marvin was right. The meaning of life is not your normal MacGuffin, or then maybe it is. "Maybe the MacGuffin is the unobtainable truth."

"Oh jeez, Clay. You're beginning to sound like our demented chef."

I had spent the day preparing the cassoulet. I thought it might help, somehow. As a good commie I didn't believe the life force shit, but my own experimentation with the sauce had brought up a series of epiphanies, I guess you could call them. I felt obligated to go with Liebling.

It takes all day, but it's really just slow-cooked meat and beans. I used chicken, some duck sausage, a couple of wild boar sausages from the Berkeley farmers market, and pork jowls. Soaked beans, browned meats, garlic and bay leaf, black pepper. Cooked for hours in a cast-iron Dutch oven. I have read that there is a special pot that they use in Languedoc or someplace, but my Lodge Dutch oven from Tennessee makes a great cassoulet. They know how to cook meat down there.

Negronis first, then a red from ... Languedoc.

"So we don't use the V-hots on the beans?"

"Flavors wouldn't match up."

"But the point is to discuss the possibility of the blue as the life force, and to decide if it is in fact the cause of murder and mayhem."

"First the beans, to pay homage to Liebling and his theories on cassoulet as a talisman."

"Stew as luck charm?"

"It enters your system and you carry it around."

"Not for long."

"Pretty long. Cassoulet sticks to your ribs."

"This is getting to be a jumbled metaphor. I don't see how boiled sausage can show us the meaning of life, much as I love it. Shouldn't there be a more dramatic passage, like a sacrifice, involved?"

"A pig sacrificed his jowls. And consider the ducks!"

"Your bank account was sacrificed to buy all this meat."

"Mayakovsky's Bugatti. Dig in."

Food takes center stage when it's that good, but the wine and the company and the weather outside, the music that is or isn't on, dictate the way of the evening. My banter with Marvin made humor the ballast as we talked about deeper stuff. For all our joking I was trying to solve a murder.

I made a crème anglaise and whisked in the VH. Poured it over cooked apples. Made some stovetop espresso.

"If I was looking for the meaning of life, I'd go with the stew, followed by a revolution, or at least a general strike. Who needs more?"

"There are probably places where people need to murder for

stew, but I think we're getting off track. Stew isn't the motive here. Did he/she/they kill for the coin? Or the hots recipe? And did they know of Astor's theory of a deeper meaning in the sauce?"

We had eaten our sauced baked apples and we were feeling the blue hue, as the aficionados called it.

His goofy smile told me that his thoughts were elsewhere. "Did he mean to say that the meaning of life is contained in a single shade of blue? Isn't that kind of simplistic?"

Marvin doesn't usually go out on such an esoteric limb, except when discussing Marx. "And is the shade the meaning or does it represent the meaning?"

I'm half Irish Catholic. That wine-is-the-blood-of-Christ shit gives me the creeps. I dummied up, though Marvin still seemed to be looking for an answer.

Finally I went with, "The killer may just be after the money." I knew this would resonate with Marvin. It brought him back to earth.

"Right. The MacGuffin is the money, pure and simple. Drugs and money."

He seemed relieved, and for the rest of the night we got nowhere, and happily. Food, wine, a cutting-edge drug. The poet's little sports car.

## 55.

A color is a thing, or a noun, right? Or not just a noun, but the real thing—the poet Darrell Gray said that. Our perceptions invest it with meaning. Or not. They are their own meaning, true as a brick. I had two survey classes in philosophy, a class in existentialist lit, and some casual (if you can call it that) reading in Western and Eastern philosophy. As a poet, half my friends are Buddhist, or some form of, or can talk the talk. I'm swimming in these kinds of thoughts, though a master of none. Have never been able to hang myself on a spiritual hook, actually avoiding that in favor of "communist," "anarchist," or "syndicalist," at least until I tired of those terms too and took that aspect of life one riot at a time.

So how could a color be, or Be, the meaning of life?

I was up at the Berkeley Rose Garden, a beautiful place. Not currently in full bloom, but there were some flowers. I was to meet

Dino and take a walk but he was late as usual. The garden is tiered. I was sitting near the top looking down at the bushes, mostly pared and bare. Fall air in the Bay Area, cold on top but with some warm undercurrents, especially when the wind stops.

I look across the park and here comes Dino. The bell rings, it is Dino. A bell in my head, as the pleasure principle personified approaches.

He began to speak before he sat down. "In his typically ego-driven way he's gone *coco pazzo*. He's sitting on a gold mine. He needs to patent it and bottle it, sell it as a food. The life force as a color? Who gives a flying fuck. Nobody reads Reich anymore. If he tries to sell it as a drug, Pfizer will take it away from him, and they'll find a way to stiff him too."

"I think he really believes in what he's doing. Sure, there's the grifter angle, but there's also sincerity. That seems to be the prevailing brain stew around here. That 'seems almost true' quality. Elusive."

"I'm sincere too, but I'm not delusional."

Dino's sincerity was debatable. I let that pass.

"Not to change the subject, although within this milieu that's probably impossible. Where is the coin?"

"In a safe place. Burglars know where to hide things."

## 56.

If anyone offers to build a security system based on lasers, with a human or humans in the next room listening for an alarm, you have my permission to beat on that brat with a baseball bat. As the poet said.

Meinhof's was tossed. Books on the floor, couch slashed, rugs rolled up, kitchen area trashed. They took our starting cash, though most of our money was locked up in the office safe. Marvin opened, saw the mess, called us. Apparently our security person was asleep or absent.

"Where is the coin?"

I think he was asking me, but he was facing the bar area, stacked with junk that had been removed from drawers.

"I'm guessing Dino has it."

"Find him and get him here." Marvin had gone into commander

mode. This is probably how he rolled in El Salvador. You can take the mercenary out of the developing country but he'll still be a machine.

Turns out Dino was in the neighborhood. Not sure what I thought about that. Within a few minutes he entered the bookstore, looking suitably shocked.

"Where is the fucking coin, Dino. If you say you hid it here, I will break your collarbone."

And once again, the sexiest man alive turns Peter Lorre. "Do you think I know where it is?"

"Where—"

"If I did, but not saying I do, I wouldn't say. It isn't that I don't trust you all, but the walls have ears."

I couldn't believe he said that, and with such inflection. I suggested we clean up, lock up, and reconvene at the Chandler Apartments.

And in a couple of hours we were crowding my studio apartment. Two on the bed, two on the floor, and Marvin in a kitchen chair.

"Where did that word come from. 'Tossed.'" Percy. Was he stoned? He got up and walked to a shelf near the bathroom, picked out a volume of Mencken, and started to research.

"It isn't going to be in Mencken. It's too obvious, Percy. They picked up our stuff and they tossed it on the floor. Get it?" Patti wasn't one to muck about. A no-bullshit human being.

Dino, still in his leather jacket, white dress shirt underneath, reached into a side pocket. I thought he'd pull out the coin, but it was just one of those oval Russian cigarettes. Marvin proceeded with an eye roll that almost lifted him off the floor. "We are a mugging away from losing at least a million bucks. Apparently cat burglars have brains as small as a cat's."

Dino chuckled, reached into the other side pocket, pulled out a gun. Small, elegant, deadly. A little like Dino. "Nobody mugs Dino Centro. And the coin is currently worth at least three million. You saw it. It's real gold. That's the scarcest one. There are only three left in the world. This is loaded, and if I find the killer and the tosser and the coin stealer, I'll use this."

The coin didn't look like three million dollars, but what do I know. I've never gone much for old coins. Knowing it's so ancient does make it more interesting. Brutus has a kind of Beatle cut and a scruffy beard, the kind that young men like to wear when projecting studied insouciance. You know the look. He's shown in profile, large Adam's apple. Masculine. He was killed soon after the coin was minted, but here he seems happy. After all, he has just killed Caesar. Must have been a thrill.

"Okay, now it's an open forum. Who tossed the store?" Marvin, still in charge.

"Well, we can eliminate Chad!" Percy had to be inebriated in some way. V-hots? I found myself warming to him.

"Percy, Dino just pulled out a gun." But Patti wasn't going to sober him up.

"Well, you don't really toss the stuff. Maybe 'dropped' or even 'flung' could work better."

I'd gotten used to guns. Will save those stories for another time. Went with, "Percy, have you been saucing?"

A shrug, an artificial smile, an implied yes.

Marvin lost patience. "We are missing a piece. Two people killed, and the store, um, flung, or whatever you want to call it. Can we assume they're looking for the coin?"

Not necessarily. The vats of hots as murder weapons suggested something else, though I didn't know what. I said so, and the room got quiet. Things usually move faster for me. I was doing too much thinking. I needed to poke the beast, but I couldn't pick up the who, what, where, when, why, or how. Where was that fucking beast?

Decided to start over, be an asshole, make everybody as nervous as possible. I'd start with Astor.

## 57.

I parked the Miata in front of the restaurant. Not lucky this time. I parked illegally. Let them come after me.

Astor was at a front table with one of his lieutenants. I knocked on the window. He saw me, quickly turning a scowl into a phony smile. That's okay. I prefer a phony smile to a scowl, though just barely. He waved, and his lackey jumped up and opened the door. Lackey was kind of cute. They hire that way in restaurants.

"Clay Blackburn! You have news for me?"

"No, but I do have a few questions."

The scowl was back. "My inventory is disappearing, and I'm paying you to find out what's up."

"Maybe you should tell me more. Give, Astor. You must have suspects in mind. You've been no help at all."

"All I know is that somebody's stealing sauce. Have you talked to Dino? Isn't he a thief?"

"What makes you suspect Dino? This isn't his MO. I'm more interested in your relationship with Chad. I think you know why Chad was killed."

"Ridiculous. I barely knew Chad."

"When did you last see him?"

"A few days before he died. He wanted to do some business."

"Business?"

"He wanted to buy into the restaurant. He wanted a share."

"What did you tell him?"

"Not for sale." Astor was getting antsy. I was getting somewhere, though slowly.

"And what made him think that you might sell?"

"Go out and do some detecting. This is none of your business."

"Just doing my job, Astor."

"I said get out."

I was definitely getting somewhere. "Somebody tossed the bookstore. Any ideas?"

"Why should I have ideas. I'm trying to retrieve many gallons of vanilla sauce. It's expensive. I hired you to find them. The things you speak of have nothing to do with me. Find my fucking sauce!"

"Answering these questions could help you find the hots."

And it went like this, back and forth. Sometimes that's a good way to go. Wear them down. Maybe they say something they shouldn't. But Astor was sly. Eventually he tired of me.

He raised his voice. "Can I get help out here?"

A couple of guys that I can only describe as loogens came out of the office. I didn't know Astor hired bouncers. "Astor, who are these goons?"

It was completely cliché. Early Dan Blocker and late George Foreman. Severely puffed. I felt the adrenaline. Would my Golden Gloves training win out against these two? Each one took double deep breaths, then a couple of steps forward. I kicked Dan Blocker hard, just below the knee but a little inside. Too hard, really. When the adrenaline is flowing ... I grabbed a coffee mug from Astor's side of the table. Caught Foreman flush on the left ear. Cup was empty. No mess. They stepped back and looked at the boss.

"Fuck you, Blackburn. You're fired!"

The keys were in the door. I got out of there fast. Let him have the last word.

# 58.

"He is, after all, a drug dealer. Also a restaurateur, but that's really a front. I don't follow your theory that he's pushing the life force. I'm a poet too, and I love it as metaphor, but there's some cutting-edge mix of chemicals, he or someone he knows discovered the mix, and they're out to make some bucks off it."

Marvin had gone clear-eyed on me, and probably was right, but I wasn't ready to let go. There was something magical in the hots, and in that shade of blue. My poet's soul hated to admit that it was just another drug deal.

We were walking up Telegraph Avenue toward Channing. Coffee at 1951. Best in the neighborhood.

"What do you see when you eat sauce?" He didn't sound sarcastic for once.

"Can't explain."

Back to sarcasm. He started humming the old Who song.

"Do you want to hear this?"

"Sorry."

"Think of all the clichés and phrases that don't quite hit the mark. In the zone, bodhisattva, nirvana, God, apotheosis, bhakti, reverie, epiphany, satori ... just there, just in there." I was surprising myself with this talk. I was sounding like Timothy fucking Leary, yet I didn't care. Even that drug-soaked grifter's cockeyed philosophy made sense to me now. My punk rock friends, if they were still alive, would spit beer in my face. I stopped myself, looked over at Marvin.

We were about to enter the café. He put his arm around me, kissed my cheek. He'd never done that. "Well, if you can get there, spend some time there. Say hello for me."

"Are you saying you get it? Because I'm not sure I do."

"Don't worry about it too much, but remember this. If you stay there too long ... that way lies the booby hatch."

I walked back to the Chandler Apartments. Marvin had something to do, vague about it so I assume it was connected to his soldier of fortune job. Maybe making contact with a revolutionary? I could only guess.

Entered the building and the old elevator. Fourth floor. I wanted to hear some music. Lately I was listening to Ayler or Ornette, but I needed something with a narrative I could more easily follow. Dug up an old Van Morrison album, my third or fourth copy since school. Dropped the needle on "Into the Mystic." Was I turning into a hippie? Again, I ceased caring. I fed the cat, took a shower, found my favorite T-shirt, the one from a book collective in Seattle, BUY A FUCKING BOOK, white on black. Found the squirt bottle, provolone and mortadella on Acme bread, topped with a hots mix that has less vanilla, more pepper, and a little mustard. Great for sandwiches.

Out the window, down at the triangle pocket park, a guy was losing it. I stared out the window as he raved, screaming at his demons. Had I stared too long? Or is this a simplistic and romantic way of explaining the intricacies of the brain? I felt for the guy, but mostly felt curiosity, my personal devil.

I got into these games because I wanted to know stuff. Wanted to know everything. Who took the strigils, who has the coin, how is it that this line of poetry takes the top of your head off? Why does that big painting do the same when it's just blobs of color? What is Albert Ayler getting at, and why does his playing drive me to another dimension? What's in this drug? That it feeds yet threatens to destroy my soul?

The blue seemed to wash down on me from the ceiling. Seemed? And I was in there.

# 59.

Marvin came over for a glass of wine, stayed late, but left when I was about to offer the couch. We had tried a new hots recipe, a chocolate sauce, dark and deep, on vanilla ice cream. It was a little cloying but it worked its magic. We were both stunned enough for me to ask if he was okay to drive. He gave me a look that could kill, then laughed it off. "I once drove through Burma on Kachin ayet, with a price on my head. I'll do okay on Ashby." And I believed him. Why not?

The wine dulled the hots but that was nice in a way. Hots isn't speedy, exactly, but it is a wide-awake drug and it does usually take over. The wine allowed me to slow down and think on things. The blue was there, but it only appeared at the corners at first, coloring the cheap apartment blinds and some of the book spines. This has been going on for a long time, the metaphysical branding of a substance. Many have related one drug or another to the life force, a pathway to the gods, so many that it would be easy to believe they were/are onto something, but I had thrown in my lot with The People, to put it in the most banal way, and I had believed that any move toward spirituality would separate me from the human condition. This didn't seem true of the blue. True blue? Ha! I was on the bed, looking at the ceiling, and it was turning, slowly, from off-white to the color, but I realized that the change came from me, out of me, through my perception. It wasn't from a deity, it came from the ingester (ingestee?), then moved out from me, from anyone who also had ingested. I was the blue, no, we were the blue, we are the life force. Fuck God. I said it out loud, then, as if to hedge my bets, I apologized, not to God, but to Chad's ghost. The poor sap was killed before he could know.

I slept a little, morning broke, I had some toast and lots of coffee. An epiphany, then breakfast, then *The New York Times* online.

And one has eaten and one walks, as the poet said. I walked several blocks to the Miata and drove down to the record store. I had a mystery to solve.

## 60.

You know that old Einstein quote, something like, and then, while eating an apple, you get a brilliant idea. This wasn't quite Einsteinian, and I wasn't eating an apple, I was downshifting into second while approaching a light, looking ahead for parking near Hard Bop. Did the death vats bear Astor's stamp? If they did, they were loaded up with the hots. Otherwise they were just vanilla water and pepper juice. Purely symbolic. I found a somewhat legal space and pulled over. Not flagrant, like something Robert Urich would use, that kind of parking gets expensive. I was a smidge in the red. I called and texted Astor, Dino, Marvin, and a couple of people who had cop connections. Those vats were in evidence lockers, somewhere in Berkeley.

I congratulated myself for making the connection, if a little late, and proceeded up San Pablo to the record store. Jimmyjames was mansplaining Mingus, somehow getting away with it. He noticed me, then turned away. Some greeting, after a dinner that cost over two yards, not counting Armagnac.

Customer gave him a "take the air" look and put back a copy of *Ah Um*. Guess his expert sales job backfired. Took the air herself, shaking her head and muttering.

"Couldn't quite close the deal, I guess."

"Fuck you, Blackburn. I'm not talking to you."

"A blessing and a curse. I need some information but I can't afford another dinner out."

"I'm not interested in drowning in hot sauce. You're a jinx."

Jinx. I hadn't heard that word in a while. J.J. was a throwback, but I couldn't tell how far back.

"At dinner you hinted at something, but you were so obscure that I didn't get the drift of your hint. I'll just throw something out there, and you can nod or not, or we could come up with a code name, like, if I'm on the beam you can say something about Mingus. Seems you're an expert."

"I was smashed. I didn't know what I was saying."

"You are familiar with the plant where the V-hots are produced, aren't you?"

I tried to fashion a look that said I was certain, not just shooting from the hip. To my surprise it worked.

"Used to be Blues and Roots. Same building. I worked there, know the staff."

"Did some hots, as they say, fall off the truck?"

"Oh yeah."

"Were some of the stolen vats shooting blanks, so to speak? Nothing but pepper sauce?"

Furtive look, unnecessary, but letting me know that this was deep-six info. "*Tijuana Moods*, definitely." And then, "Dinner once a month until I say no more. But you can pick the place."

And from me, hoping it wasn't too obscure, or maybe hoping it was, "*Pithecanthropus Erectus*!"

He was smiling when I left the store.

## 61.

I was pinging and ponging, no, pinballing, because rather than going back and forth, I was bouncing off of various people and situations. I was picking up facts, like cat hair off a sweater, but I couldn't ... oh shit, I'm caught in a metaphor. Well, fuck it. Just say I couldn't classify.

Now, when I'm behind the eight ball I go to Blake, but this is now and that was then, and at that time I had been coming out of Dorn and Mina Loy, settling into Prynne. Jeremy Prynne was my *I Ching* at the time. Looking back now, every time I think of Prynne I'm brought back to those times, and to those lines, completely obscure, unreadable except at certain times when, for lack of a better way of putting it, the stars align.

I splayed a chapbook and stepped on it. The line closest to my instep was, I felt, the one. *Bored with fraud rowdy crowds flip coin exchange macaronics like polar bear packs propped on the escalator.* What the? But then, "What the?" is a sane reaction to any mystery. We're trying to find out what the fuck is going on. But macaronics? I had to look it up. Didn't know how it applied, except in a nonliteral way, depending on the definition of language. I decided to let that part of the line go, for now.

Perhaps the coin held some answers. I felt heavy in the heart, because pursuing the meaning of the coin would bring me close to Dino again, and that was always dangerous. I wanted more from him than information, and that often obscured the pursuit of information. An old story. Old and clichéd, but clichés are repeated so often because so often they are truths. I started making dinner plans. Cacio e pepe, perhaps roast a chicken ... I shot him a text.

## 62.

Talk about a Bay Area crowd! Meinhof's was suddenly very hip, thanks to Astor's pop-ups. The locals had traipsed through, bought books, hung out, thought of themselves as radical, or something safer: progressive. A mix of techies, DSA types, *Zyzzyva* writers, SPD poets, landlords, tenant rights activists, book collectors, leftover hots heads waiting for the next pop-up ... seen and seeing.

I was taking over for Marvin, who had another job somewhere, and I was working with Patti, who was sick of these people and threatening to quit the collective. Retail is hell sometimes. Customers can be fierce. Facing a line at the register, I began to worry that I wouldn't have enough energy to make dinner, host dinner, get some info out of Dino.

"Retail sucks." She was watching a techie type leave the building, shooting him in the back with her stare. I perked up a bit, loving the spectacle.

"You tell him off?"

Beginnings of a giggle. "Sure as fuck. Lucky we own the place. A boss would have fired me."

And so it went until closing, but getting a little better because we had decided to laugh it all off. At least they were buying things, though not the books we would have liked them to.

Half hour before official closing we pushed them out. Why not? We owned the fucking place. We counted out the register, put padlocks on the doors even though that hadn't been voted on, then hit the streets.

Rushed home, got a space up on Regent. Fed the cat, heated the oven, dressed a small chicken by stuffing it with orange sections and fresh herbs. Showered and changed, straightened up the apartment, stuck the chicken in the oven. Don't know why but I put on the Beach Boys, *Holland*. I had no idea if Dino liked the Beach Boys, and I'm a little embarrassed that I do. Now, years later, I can remember that night by playing that album. Had he even arrived while it was playing? I think so, and I even think of "Sail On, Sailor" as our song, totally ridiculous because he really wasn't much for popular music. He liked Chopin.

He arrived and I heard the familiar bell. The night felt ominous to me, but there was no reason for him to notice. We'd done this many times. The chicken smelled great. I started building cocktails.

He did sense something. "You seem nervous, Clay."

"I'm not completely comfortable with murder."

"Me either. We only play at being tough guys."

"We're thieving communist detectives. I guess that's tough."

"Speak for yourself. I'm just a thief. And a lover of life."

"Your life."

"Yes. Dear Clay! Are we talking about morals?"

I was talking off the top of my head. I didn't mean for the discussion to begin that way. Where would I go with this? I'd ruminated over this stuff before, lost some sleep, moved on. Fighting for the workers, taking my little bite. Honest graft. Dino only fought for himself. Hypocrisy needn't be considered. It was part of his charm, usually. If he had murdered Chad and Brianna for the coin, his charm would be tarnished, at least with me.

"You and Marvin have killed people. Life is a war. Maybe we're on different sides? It's like a western, the lawman and the outlaw, except that the roles are fluid. It was probably like that in the Old West too."

He could have easily taken me from the track. I'm no Marlowe. If they come on sexy, I follow along. Eventually the work gets done, I guess, but not right away. Or maybe the work doesn't get done, or some other form of work gets done, like, maybe I'll get a poem out of it.

"I'm not going to confirm or deny. The coin went around and it landed with me. It wasn't completely random. Good thieving takes skill. It's work like any other work. Like writing poetry, detecting, wrangling books."

I was flustered, didn't know which way to fall. Just play along, for now.

"We'll sell the coin and you will get your cut. Do some good with it. I'm taking my cut to Malta. I'll get domicile status pronto and won't have to pay out much in taxes. I can fly to other parts of Europe to do a little catting. Why wouldn't that work for you? We'd make an aesthetically appealing team."

The pasta was al dente. I tossed it with the cheese, pepper, and the salty pasta water. Perfect. We had been drinking a nice Barolo, a gift from the poet Amy Spade. We had about finished the bottle, so I opened a bottle of Ruffino Chianti Riserva. Not quite authentic, I know. Romans usually drink white with this pasta. Dino could have remarked on that but he just smiled and nodded.

"If you slip and tell me too much, I'll feel obligated to act."

"Act? Calling the cops is against your code. You wouldn't shoot me. But you don't have to worry about that."

Didn't have to worry. But why not?

We tore through the pasta, drank more wine. I sliced up the chicken, plattered it, spreading the roasted oranges over the pieces. I wondered if he'd spend the night. For a moment that seemed more important than murders, capers, politics. I should know now that it's just a spasm. Like the poet sang. But I'll never learn.

The conversation went away, then drifted back unfocused. I took the plates and brought out the salad. We'd killed the wine.

# 63.

Same place, next night, risotto with a handful of mushrooms from Berkeley Bowl. I needed to get more out of Patti, even if it meant somehow playing her against Dino. I made a full pitcher of Negronis because once they're made it's a sin to let them just sit there. The occasion called for truth serum.

I was stirring, Patti was sitting at the kitchen table, taking in the view of Fred's Market (now gone) and the down-and-out fellows drinking outside his door. I looked at her, and it was almost reverie, or a kind of double reverie because the big green eyes seemed unfocused, and I was focused on the big green eyes. A penny for her thoughts, I guess, or a couple of strong Negronis. I took her in, the loose-fitting look, Mao cap over bangs. Felt a nice pull, then returned my attention to the rice and broth.

"Veggie! You heard."

"That you are sparing the animal kingdom."

"No jokes. I feel better this way."

"Won't it sap your strength? Can you still beat people up? Will you lose fights because you've refused steak?"

"Fuck that. I could easily take you."

Old set of jokes, with the new addition of vegetarianism. We've both been amateur boxers. She spots me at least twenty pounds but she could easily knock me silly. I'd probably like it.

We switched to a zinfandel because I figured it would taste good with the mushrooms. An old friend from the book trade had gifted me a couple of bottles from Lodi. Don't know what brought him to Lodi. Are there any books there? No matter, I flavored the rice with Gorgonzola. Great with the wine. Patti wasn't vegan. Yet.

Best strategy would be to let Patti get ahead of me, wine-wise, but we matched each other glass for glass, and I spoke the truth first. "I was surprised to hear that you and Dino had hooked up."

"Jealous?"

"Always! But Dino does what Dino does. Did you talk about the coin, between breathy sighs?" Breathy sighs, sheesh. I caught myself, a little late, and pulled back. Took a long drink of bubbly water.

"He's fun. Sometimes smarmy can be amusing. He seems more harmless than he is, and he has a great sense of humor. We talked about the coin in historic and aesthetic terms. Left off on the filthy lucre part, but of course that was in the air. Money is the biggest elephant in any room."

"I didn't know he cared about the aesthetics."

"His interest was probably piqued by its worth. He was interested that the inscription was actually Eid Mar, and that 'the Ides of March' is a phrase that still runs through Western culture, even though most people, at least around these parts, don't know what the fuck an 'Ide' is. And so we talked about the look of the coin, the surprisingly pleasing look of the images. He called it a coin without bullshit. The two daggers, the cap—according to him, a hat that was worn by freed slaves. Brutus frees Rome from Caesar. Of course he bit the dust soon after."

The history lesson, passed from Dino through Patti, was interesting. I expected to learn more because Patti was too well read to stop there, but I really needed to move things back over to the caper, or possible caper.

Except we didn't, at least for a matter of hours.

We were in bed and on the way to sleep when she turned toward me and said, "You know he did it."

"Who did what?"

"Dino did it all. That's how he got the coin."

"He told you that?"

"He wouldn't have told me. But think on it."

"I have." And I knew it too, knew it somewhere and somehow but realized it when she said it too.

"What are you going to do about it?"

"Can't prove it and as far as I know the cops don't know much. They seldom do. They mostly solve the easy ones."

"Wouldn't this be a high priority? Because of the coin?" I realized that she was schooling me on detecting but I wasn't surprised.

"They know nothing of the coin. They're probably involved in the hots trade, or would like to be. No reason to rock that boat."

## 64.

Eggs at Tomate on Fifth Street, as ever, no talk of the night before, also our habit, but this was more than a tacit agreement to refrain from boring ourselves with a "what are we doing together" talk. We suspected Dino of murder, even thought of it as a done deal. What does it mean when a lover kills and nobody seems shocked? I was traveling in an interesting milieu. To say the least.

I couldn't keep quiet. "Chad too?"

She shushed me, whispered across the table, leaning forward. "That amoral fucker? He must have had the coin, or was on his way to getting it."

"Why drown him in hots?"

"Lukewarms, from what I hear. No drug in the sauce."

How did she know? Decided, at first, to concentrate on my muffin. No, couldn't do that. Needed to think while chewing. It was a pineapple coconut setup, one of my favorites, but I needed to figure things out. Why was Patti telling me this? Not that it was out of character. We had a friendship without filters, the kind of honesty that "relationships" won't allow. I knew who she liked and hated and why, and who she was fucking. Who was killing whom wasn't that much of a stretch. I guess.

A couple of refills and we were ready to meet the day. We had taken separate cars, mine was closer, so she walked me there. We didn't kiss or even hug goodbye, as usual, but today, to my surprise, I felt the space between us in a more tangible way. Miles of space, a Grand Canyon of it as the realization of what we'd talked about the night before surfaced. Did she feel it too? We turned away at the same time and I got into the car.

## 65.

I couldn't sleep at all, and no amount of VH could summon up the life force. It hadn't happened like this before, just a pretty color and the slightest buzz, like after a half carafe of red wine at a pizza joint. I felt cheated at both ends, no sleep, no lift, no feeling, false or not, that there is limitless potential. I hadn't spoken to Marvin about Dino's guilt, and I put my faith in that, that Marvin would laugh and point the finger elsewhere.

Dino Centro, O Dino Centro, always preceded by that "O" for me, O as in Ode, as in deep romantic thoughts. Bad boy love. But is this still love, now that the first love has finally died, where there were no impossibilities? How bad must a bad boy be before he is ... too? Did Dino Centro (O Dino Centro) kill our Robin Hood?

If he did it, he did it for the money. Of course. My capitalist friend. And yet he kept company with a group of anarchists, or at least anarchist types, allowing us more of a cut with the stolen goods than he needed to. He didn't say much when we passed the wealth over to the Emma Goldmans, seemed amused, maybe bemused, but didn't ridicule.

I tried to think like a detective but couldn't think like a detective. I blamed the hots for clouding my brain. I'd think, Was he in cahoots with the chef? But my mind would fog before I traced connections, and I'd think of O Dino, long conversations, real tenderness. It wasn't just fucking. No. Was it? No. Wasn't just fucking. Was killing Chad part of a double cross? Can't think. Let it go, Clay, think about it tomorrow.

For now I was looking out the window, not as late as I'd thought it was. The traffic triangle, Fred's Market, the skater store, just one touch of moonlight.

*Let us fake out a frontier—a poem somebody could hide in.* Folks coming together to get things done, taking that energy and forcing it out, sharing what they have. To each according... Pretend it's never been attempted, realize it's never been done. Fake a frontier until you make one. Until you can. No gods no masters. A brick poem house, so strong you can't even drive a Bugatti through it.

I wasn't getting anywhere. I walked into the kitchen to make coffee. The life blood of tired men. As the poet said.

## 66.

Why would he kill Chad? I can understand why someone would knock off Brianna, if they thought she still had the coin, not that I condone that kind of killing. Perhaps Chad was part of the coin shuffle. I sat with it, and a double espresso, and looked out my kitchen window at Telegraph Avenue and Dwight Way, midmorning. Students and stragglers, the usual, but not uninteresting. My detective instincts kicked in (I do have some) and I thought of Astor. I needed to talk to Astor.

I raced the Miata to upper Shattuck, or raced it as much as Berkeley's puzzling maze of one-way streets and dead ends allowed. When I'm in the right mood I try to think of the city's "plan" as a kind of spiritual labyrinth. Mostly it's just a pain, but then Berkeley is a perfect pain. I'm not blinded by my affection for the Athens of the East Bay. Love isn't always easy.

I pulled into an illegal space out front. My luck had been good and I had money in the bank. This is how detectives roll.

The restaurant wasn't serving breakfast or lunch, but I figured Astor would be there. He was, and one of the loogens let me in. Dan Blocker. I said hello, suggested that he do something about his underbite. He actually smiled, or I think he did. Pit bulls usually look like they're smiling. I like and trust pit bulls, wasn't so sure about Dan Blocker.

"Did you find out who is stealing my hots mix?"

"Why is that important? It's just the base. Can't be worth much."

"If they can steal the mix, they can get to the good stuff."

"There's more to this."

"Detectives and poets always think that way."

"Why would someone steal your mix, then use it as a murder weapon?"

"Not my problem at all. Dan? Shuffle this guy out. He's no use to me now."

His name was really Dan? Another loogen appeared, like magic, from the back office. They must have communicated on some sort of thug beam. This one was smaller, compact and ready to go. He came across the room, near trot, and I met his momentum with a body block. He wasn't as solid as I might have guessed and went sliding across the well-mopped floor. Fell back and bonked his noggin. A loogen's noggin. The poet part of my brain felt a flush of delight. I pulled my car keys from my jacket (the advantage of having an old car—keys, not a fob) and hit Dan with an uppercut, trunk key facing up. The key entered his nostril and almost tore through. I turned on Astor, who affected a stagey duck.

"Why me? I'm a victim. I was robbed!"

"What about the hired muscle?"

"I'm a genius chef, a passable restaurateur, and a fun person to be with, but yes, I am also a drug dealer. Maybe the drug is legal, so far, but I travel in gray market circles, if only to procure ingredients. I'm vulnerable. After all, as I said, I was robbed."

We weren't getting anywhere, and I couldn't come up with an angle. I wasn't ready to leave so I did a little more fishing.

"Who do you suspect?"

"Dino, Chad, you. You're all a bunch of thieves. I'd probably go with Dino, much as I love the guy. So suave, like an Italian Cary Grant. He'd steal your wallet, then buy you a drink with your credit card. I can appreciate that, but I'd gun that fucker down if he took my VH."

"What about the coin?"

"I never saw it, though I'd love to get my hands on it." He eyed Dan and the wiry thug, who apparently had cracked his elbow when he fell. "Okay, since we're having a serious talk, I did try to get at the coin. I put out feelers, bribed a cop or two with gallon jugs of VH. Do you know how hard it is to run a restaurant? I'm bleeding money. People like the hots, but cannabis is everywhere, about to be legal. There will soon be a pot store on every corner. I'm offering the life force, but there's a better markup on drugs designed to avoid the life force. I know this only vaguely, but Chad had the coin for a minute, and he was planning on putting money down on a church in Fruitvale. But then it was gone."

"He got it from Brianna?"

"I've only heard."

"Where? Hadn't she lost it? Did she get it back? Did he kill her for it?"

"Wouldn't tell you if I knew. Can't get involved in that."

## 67.

Bribed a couple of cops, eh?

I needed to talk to Marvin. It does seem strange, but he likes to hang with cops, and usually comes home with intel. I've often surmised that he has a "thing" for cops and that it goes deeper than info gathering. He was, after all, romantically linked to former FBI agent Bailey Dao.

I texted him, "Meet me at Saijo Persimmon." Within seconds he answered, "K."

Saijo Persimmon was a Tokyo-style listening bar on University, down by the Holiday Inn Express. Hipster orientalism, but with an amazing list of Japanese whiskeys and a wall of rare and imported jazz discs. I feel intimidated by it, never know what to request. I usually go with something semi-esoteric, hoping that the bartender will think I'm a real aficionado trying to downplay my deep knowledge.

"*The Blues and the Abstract Truth*. What whiskey do you suggest?" He put something down, straight up, without asking. Tasted good. Oliver Nelson came up on the very expensive sound system.

Marvin came in and ordered Chichibu something or other. The place was pleasingly empty, with a couple of jazz nuts listening intently to "Stolen Moments." I was happy that they approved of my choice. I hadn't sat and visited with Marvin in a minute or two. We had bought books together and discussed business, but we hadn't seriously shot the shit. We fell into it. There was a good show at BAM/PFA called *Reimagining the Lost Cause That Was European Modernism*, a mouthful, but the examples of failure were exquisite, some miniatures of rich guys three or four centuries ago that somehow foreshadowed techniques and attitudes that came later. We understood the theory but didn't give a fuck, moved by the pallor of the flesh tones and the amazingly tall hats. And PFA was showing *Sebastiane*, we decided to see it again. I love being a bookseller poet thief in Berkeley! So much to see and do. But I had to move things along.

"Any truck with Giff Hartnet? I need some information."

"I've been following along with the plot. Right on top of it."

"That's more than I can say for myself."

"Old Giff is a hots head all the way. For a small percentage of my stash—by the way, you owe me—I heard from him that the cops know nothing of the existence of any coins. They think Brianna was robbed, perhaps because someone thought she had the recipe in her safe. They think Chad was killed for trying to steal either the VH recipe or gallons of the stuff. They suspected Astor but he has a series of tight alibis. He's always at the restaurant, either with kitchen staff or the loogens. They'll testify for him. Clay, it's probably your boyfriend. Perhaps in cahoots with Patti? You do have a way of sleeping with the devil. I mean, who wouldn't go mad for that coin? He really could buy a Bugatti, or move to Gibraltar, buy a closet full of white linen suits. It's worth a couple of million, isn't it?"

"Last one went for over four mil." I knew he knew. I also knew he knew more.

"Would buy a nice place in Gibraltar then. And I hear there's two, a gold and a silver. That's the word on the street."

What street? Certainly not Telegraph Avenue.

He caught my look. "Don't ask. The silver isn't worth as much, but as a pair they would pull in a nice price."

The music had changed. Frantic '20s hot jazz. Bix and the like. The mood changed, but it was okay. I like these bars. Our conversation also changed, to the death of the Oakland A's. Marvin still had season tickets but little hope. "Las Vegas is a shitty town. Nevada is the rock bottom of the union, down there with Florida and Texas. I'd rather live anywhere else."

We stayed for another whiskey and listened to the Hot Sevens. "Potato Head Blues." This time I took the bull by the horns. "So we're both thinking that Dino could have done it."

"Clay, I've been waiting to say this for years, as a joke, but I am sorry to say it now, because it is going to hurt: No shit, Sherlock."

## 68.

I didn't have to bribe cops, talk to record clerks, go on long drugged-out walks in the country, lose sleep, take boring people out for expensive dinners, buy records I didn't need. Just needed to acknowledge that love is blind, that some crooks are charming, sexy, can even be great fucks, wear great clothes, know how to discuss art and literature, drive cool cars, show up with an amazing bottle of wine and kiss you as they enter your place, calling you "dear." This is noir, I've read the book, seen the film. He was Jane Greer, Mitchum, Robert Walker as Bruno. Someone comes along with a very bad character. He seems attractive. Is he really? Yes. Very. He's as attractive as his character is bad. Is it? Yes.

That's what you think of in the city.

I didn't have the proof but I knew. I didn't know who had been with him, helping him. I wanted to find that out. Who could I trust? I wondered if he, or his posse, if there was a posse, would kill me too.

Black widower.

I was alone in the Chandler Apartments, sitting on the bed, my brain a twirly little thing. I thought about a dose of hots but then didn't. I wasn't sure where it might take me. I got up, went to the kitchen, found the Glenfiddich, had a short shot. So this is noir. So much more manageable on a screen or a page. Poured another short one. Just a steadier, getting drunk would be too depressing. At some point I would need to walk or maybe drive.

Back on the bed, looking up at the ceiling. Dino Centro, I think of Dino Centro, O Dino Centro. Please don't poke my eyes out, please don't shoot me. I could take a stabbing, or poison if it could somehow be passed in a kiss, but then it would have to be murder-suicide, and Dino never dies.

## 69.

I would go to Hard Bop, though I wasn't sure why. Follow your nose, Marlowe would say. Well, maybe he wouldn't. I had a hunch or maybe half a hunch, and sometimes you just go on your nerve. The Miata was close by. I unsnapped the top and put it down. Why did I do that? As if some outside force were pushing me along. At least it was a warm day. My old car still played tapes. I had a copy of *A Love Supreme* and put it on loud. Haste, Shattuck, MLK, Dwight, San Pablo. Got thumbs-ups and honks due to the loud jazz. Coltrane fans? Probably stupid to risk being pulled over, after the Glenfiddich, but I'd only had one shot total, and I felt somehow free. Free, knowing that my love, and possibly our friends ... counterintuitive but my brain had stopped twirling and was moving in a straight line. Solving the problem, apparently, was more important than love. Maybe? Or was it too early to tell?

My parking chops failed me and I had to park up a side street. I passed over some crunchy spaces and did a head-first parallel park just ahead of a driveway. I left the car topless, even though I had a copy of *The Making of Americans*, nice early edition, on the back seat. What thief, besides Dino Centro, would think that worth stealing?

The record clerk that would not be named was at the counter. "You looking for Jimmy?"

"You don't use his full name?"

"He doesn't either now. Got sick of that shit."

"What does not change is the will to change."

"Huh?"

"As the poet said."

"Do you enjoy being obscure? At least you have good taste in music, except for your love of Steve Lacy."

I was flattered she remembered, and though not quite smitten, intrigued.

"Is he around?"

"Not working today."

"Maybe you can help." I pulled out my phone and scrolled through pictures until I found one that wasn't obscene. "Does this guy come in here?"

"Fuck yes. That's Dino Centro. Where's his shirt?"

He was about to tie me up with it. "We were going swimming. What does he buy?"

"Nothing. He picks up Jimmy."

Bingo. "Where does he go?"

"How would I know? I don't know what guys do."

"You assume they were doing something?"

"Very chummy."

I felt jealous for a second, then it passed. "How often did this happen?"

"You think I was counting?"

# 70.

So Dino and Jimmyjames, now just Jimmy, were somehow in cahoots. Was that jumping to conclusions? Probably not. Dino is involved where Dino can prosper, and Jimmy wasn't handsome or charming enough to be around just for fun. Well, okay looking but certainly not charming, and Dino valued charm.

Another hunch, or educated guess, took me to Astor's place. They were open for lunch, a scaled-back affair, vegetables and/or protein over polenta, a side or two, with a not-too-generous ladling of vanilla hots, enough for an afternoon blue buzz but not the hours of entertainment promised by the dinner seatings. The place was mostly full but, having spotted Jimmy, I was able to grab the next table over. Before noticing me he called the waitrix over, asked for extra sauce, but was told that portions were limited at lunch. Cranky face. Others heard and a ripple went through the room, followed by a low, then louder, chant: "Bring us the hots!" I watched in amusement as my rose punch was delivered. I expected a smirk from the waitrix but instead got a worried look. They remembered me and nodded, but still worried.

"What's up?" I asked. "They're just hots fans."

"No. They are addicts, and belong to the cult of blue. Yesterday we were able to quiet them down with some squirt bottles but the budget won't allow for that. We're working on a close margin."

"Don't drugs have a great markup?"

Indignant look. "We're a restaurant. Astor is trying to build up his savings to open Bugatti, and his distribution deal on VH hasn't yet materialized."

The chants grew louder. Still no squirt bottles. The tables being closer together during the lunch hours, I was able to reach over and touch Jimmy on the shoulder. "Congrats on the name edit, Jimbo!"

He gave me a good Elvis-style sneer. He was wearing a '70s Donnie Hathaway hat that didn't match his straight white-guy hair. Rhinestones on his jeans jacket. Supposed to be clever?

"Oh hi, Clay Blackburn. I don't answer to Jimbo. Just Jimmy now. Care to join me?"

I was reluctant, but it's all in a day's work. I supposed that he would try to stick me with the check. At least it was only lunch. I grabbed my chair and moved over, caught the busser's eye. My table setting was quickly moved. Astor's crack staff.

I had to lean in to speak. The chants were louder, and a little scary. The hots heads were getting restless. I took my biggest and boldest shot, probably motivated by my love/hate for Dino, wanting to prove that, although a thief, he couldn't be a murderer. If I was wrong I was wrong, but security is a false god. Make sacrifices to it and you are lost. "You took some defanged vanilla hots from the warehouse and drowned two people. Why that MO? Send a message?"

No answer. He scooped up a heavily sauced chunk of braised rutabaga and shoveled it in. At another, more "noir" time that would have been a shot of bourbon. Jimbo was obviously nervous. Bullseye.

"You can't prove anything." Said just like they say it on *Murder, She Wrote*. As if I had anything to prove.

"I'm not the DA, not even a cop. I'm a private asshole. Just looking to satisfy my curiosity. Did you deplete Astor's VH stash? Someone is siphoning off the good stuff. Not the unmixed sauce that you used to drown Chad and Brianna."

"I'm not admitting to anything."

"I'll take a wild guess. Brianna and Chad were nicking sauce and you, working for Astor, sent a message to future crooks." Jimmy flinched. I am a genius of the wild surmise.

"I won't say yes or no, but somebody was, or is, stealing the active ingredients. Probably analyzing and reproducing, or trying to. Isn't that why Astor hired you? Aren't you just as much a suspect?"

I probably was. A smarter police force could view me as a person of interest.

The crowd was getting mean. They were craving the power of blue but Astor was holding out on them. It occurred to me that the lunch sauce was somehow watered down. The white tableware showed a subtle blue tint, not strong enough to fill the soul with wonder. The life force had been stepped on. Such is capitalism. Damn that bottom line.

A snowball-sized piece of rutabaga flew high, then arced down, a perfect noggin shot to the forehead of one of the workers. They signaled the office upstairs. Loogens descending! A volley of bone-in chicken spoiled their shiny suits. Everybody was pissed.

Interrogation over, I slinked my way under our table. Jimmy had joined the food fight, flinging a shrimp at an especially chunky loogen. Easy target. I crawled toward the exit. Somehow I had avoided airborne lunches.

## 71.

He bought a Renault in Paris and shipped it to Lili Brik in Moscow. That is well documented. His version of "I'll buy you a Cadillac, long and shiny and black." Sent to her, instead of a letter. The Bugatti story isn't as well known, and some histories claim that he never learned to drive, but the real deal comes down through generations of radical gossip, more accurate than mainstream history. I heard it from Marvin who got it from an old Wobbly in Santa Cruz, a Russian immigrant who knew somebody who knew somebody. The Isadora Duncan connection is third-hand and gray area but doesn't seem out of the question. Where did that Bugatti go? Who had it first?

When he drove down the narrowest streets in Paris, nearly scraping paint on ancient buildings, the girls could not resist his stare.

We were at Passione, me and Marvin, West Berkeley, but in my mind I was tooling through narrow streets in Paris. Deep reverie, a poet's prerogative. I came to, or at least nearly came to, noticing Marvin's impatient look. We were at a small table in the warmest corner of the place. The weather had turned cold without warning, as it often does in the Bay Area. The pizza came as we finished our second glass of barbera.

"I don't know if it was the same car. I haven't heard that one, but there aren't many Bugattis in this world, probably very few in Paris in the '20s. Nice story. I think I'll pass it around. The current crop of agitators is a little bland, especially with Chad gone. We're short on mythology."

"You know who killed Chad."

"Everybody knows except the cops. Chad was, among other

things, a thief in training. But there's a master thief, a mentor thief. Someone who can slip in, pull out a few baubles, and slip back out."

"But Chad got the coin."

"Chad got the coin and that didn't sit well with the mentor. There was a coin, there was a popular drug, but the mentor didn't have his hands on either."

"He doesn't seem like the murdering type."

"What type is that? How many people have you killed?"

Not as many as Marvin, but I got the drift. If you carry an American passport, you don't have a soul. Did Dino carry a US passport? Probably, but one of many.

"Everybody's been there, Clay, just not to the same extent. The bad lover, and he gets you off but it's unhealthy but that gets you off too, and the drama of saying, or thinking, I can't take this, this person is wrong for me, is evil, is a big pain in the ass, whatever. It's just that, with the ... say the name? With regards to"—chuckling at himself for using the phrase, then repeats it—"with regards to Dino Centro, mentor thief, we are talking murder, perverse murder, people drowned in some vanilla and pepper concoction. Not sure what kind of pepper. Scotch bonnet?"

Until he said the name I could pretend I didn't know, well, just barely but it was something to hang on to. There was no proof, just "everybody knows," not quite a convincing phalanx of particulars, but now Marvin had said it, fingered Dino, and I've seldom known Marvin to be wrong.

He came out of nowhere, taught us how to steal, made us some bucks. He must have known about the coin and the hots before he came back to the States. He didn't just come to be close to me, dammit.

## 72.

We had to go through with the pop-up, despite Astor's fall from grace. The lunchtime swindle, as it was being called, had angered the hots heads, and, something we didn't know previously, an angry hots head is not to be fucked with. When you know the source of the force (to quote the language of the subculture) you want the force. I was feeling a little antsy myself, but since my intake had been moderate I only experienced a slight anxiousness, no worse than the usual existential angst that I get pre-coffee.

We feared another food fight, or worse, if Astor didn't dole out the dose. The beleaguered chef had written instructions delivered by two assistants who also served as directors. The Meinhofs got to it, and soon we had turned the great hall of the people into a whimsical mess, part medieval, part ancient Rome, part graffitied subway car. A truck arrived bearing long tables and black and white tablecloths. Crazy old Astor was pulling out all the stops.

"The hour of my redemption has come!" He arrived as I was smoothing out the tablecloths. Even Dino was at work, setting out plumed hats that served as table ornaments. Neat idea. We stopped to admire Astor's ensemble, a prison-striped muumuu, knee-high boots, and a plumed toque, seemingly designed by Dr. Suess. And the scarf! The size of a boa constrictor, tie-dyed. I hoped he wasn't driving a convertible, thinking of Isadora. That Gertrude Stein line came to mind: "Affectation can be dangerous."

The food was brought in. Steam tables? The tacky kind, like what you see at a catered wedding reception. Smelled like canned soup. If I didn't trust Astor's palate, I'd have been worried.

The stage was set. We went out to the front room to staff the bar. The doors opened. The conversation wasn't as bubbly as previous pop-ups.

We hadn't been shown the amuse-bouche. The trays were brought in barely ahead of the crowd. Marvin removed the lids and let out a good healthy guffaw. "Toilets!"

We gathered around, along with some of the guests. I wondered what they were made of. Curiosity got the best of me. I grabbed one of the perfectly sculpted little WCs, felt it between finger and thumb. It squished a little, maybe marzipan? I gave it a sniff. Cinnamon, chilies, something buttery, and, as a kind of olfactory finish, urine. Light, but not what I'd call subtle. I believe the French call it *pipi de chat*, often a characteristic of fine sauvignon blanc, but this wasn't cat pee. I've cleaned a cat box daily for years. This was more human. I'm not a connoisseur of golden showers, but if you live long enough and you have even normal curiosity, you try different things. And then of course there is the scent of urinals in various places, bars and ball games and bus stations. Proustian, I suppose. I took a bite. The little privy had nice mouthfeel, sweet then roundly saline, then acrid.

The crowd had multiplied as people entered the front room that doubled as the bar. My comrades were pouring the pink drinks, adding sliced lemon and a float of spritz, as directed by the chef. I stood for a few seconds, eyeing the customers, holding half of a mini toilet with (not sure why) lifted pinkie. I came on, my face forced itself into a smile. Fast work! And they caught my look, and as one, cried, "HOTS!" and grabbed at the tiny toilets.

The little beauties came in various colors and, apparently, flavors. A beautiful young woman, alt-girl type, massively frizzy hair and clothes about to fall off, began a dance. "Mine tastes like come!"

Some amuse-bouche! The customers were eating piss, shit, come, puke, and blood, and it was a love fest. It occurred to me that the life force comes in all flavors. The toilets were gone in a few minutes, more appeared, the lights dimmed, and music came on, something a little funky, fitting, given the funkiness of the first course.

People picked up the dance vibe and twirled and stomped into the main dining room, holding as many toilets as they could handle, juggling them, throwing them in the air and catching them in their mouths, playing catch, mixing the red ones, the yellow, the brown, and the off-white with chunks. The morsels must have been massively dosed. We were ripped.

The music changed. A literary reference. That old Badfinger song. "If you want it, here it is, will you walk away from a fool and his money?" *The Magic Christian*. Tonight our greed, our lusting for what had been advertised as the life force, was pushing us into a pool of shit, piss, and blood, so to speak.

Marvin leaned over, put his arm around me, said, "It doesn't matter so much, Clay, tomorrow we'll shake it off. Live to fight another day. All is lost, but all is not lost." He picked up a red one and tossed it in his mouth. As he chewed a dribble of blood—was it real blood?—ran down to his chin, vampire-style.

"But isn't it the death of communism?"

"Humanity is the death of communism, but, oddly enough, communism has a life after death. Figure that one out. No, don't."

A bell rang, the same bell we'd been hearing all along. The chef arrived, wearing his whimsical toque. He jumped up and stood on a table. I didn't know he could be so lithe.

"Welcome to our version of the acid test! You are being treated to the ultimate dose. Well, not exactly treated. Pull out your credit cards. We will come around to collect." They came out wearing T-shirts, COLLECTOR across the back, otherwise crisp and white. Nobody asked for a bill, or about the cost. The ultimate dose!

The staff joined the customers. I found a seat and, somehow, Dino joined me. I could barely see my hand in front of my face but I could sense Dino, and food did appear, I could smell it, wonderful food smells with the funkiest of undercurrents, offal, excrement, sweat, and blood. There were no vegans that night. Everything was dosed, and so not off-limits.

He put his head on my shoulder, then came around and sat on top of me, facing me. We fed each other strange food through our mouths. Everything was blue, I could see his face through the blue scrim, the most beautiful face I'd ever faced. He grabbed something off the plate and jammed it in my mouth and we both laughed. Life force or sewage, it's all the same.

"Shall we take a little walk?" He got up, his hand lingering on my left ear and the back of my neck. I got up too, stumbling. He held me up and we guffawed, but everyone was laughing, and I wondered for a split second why this was happening. What was up the chef's sleeve?

And then I didn't care about that or anything. We walked back through the bookstore, where there was a quieter party going on, and I sensed, by the giggles and the breathing, that an orgy would soon be underway. We went out a side door. The sidewalk was blue, the cars and the surrounding buildings, they vibrated blue. I could feel the force of everyone in the neighborhood, it was too much to take. Dino nodded. "I know. Let's go around back."

And so we did, through a parking lot and back to the loading dock. It glowed blue but was more subtle than at the party. Easier to take. There was an old pleather couch where people went to smoke, but nobody was out there. They were all at Astor's VH orgy, and again I wondered why he was giving them such high doses. Was he just being generous? Perhaps?

We sat on the couch, surrounded by dumpsters and broken-down cardboard. We could hear the music inside, at a pleasant volume. You know how it is when you leave a crazy party, and the air wakes you up a little, and you notice that it's pretty clear, and you can even see a few stars through the gauze of urban sky? And you're with somebody you want to be with? I leaned in and nuzzled around his collar, breathed deeply as he turned into me. It was moderately warm, just barely warm enough for outside sex, but then there was the heat of the moment. Someone may have come out to smoke, I thought I heard someone, but they, I think, respected our privacy and retreated.

Much later I heard my detective self asking, before I had a chance to shut myself up.

"I'm the villain in this narrative, Clay. Can't help myself."

"How much of a villain?"

"Maybe I did all of it, maybe others did some of it. Maybe things just happened to roll my way, or maybe I'm the mastermind."

"I'd like to know."

"I trust you, Clay, but only up to a point. What you got is what you get. I think it is, in a way, a form of love that we share."

I still had trouble figuring him for the murders but I concluded, somehow, that he had the coin, maybe even two coins. He was a magician, in a way, and he would make them appear.

We pulled in, buttoned up, rearranged our clothes. "Come back in for a nightcap?"

"I don't think I have time. I should be at the airport soon, and I have to go home and pack up."

"Where to?"

"I have a few stops, but if you promise not to tell anyone, and I know you do, I'll tell you. I'll end up eventually in Gibraltar and you will possibly hear from me then."

He did it, I thought, he did it all. Dunked them in de-drugged hots until they were dead. But seconds later I thought, No, he couldn't do it. Not his style. He'll sell the coin and live awhile in Gibraltar, but the coin came his way after someone else did the murders.

He took out his phone and ordered a car. I held myself together, telling myself that this wasn't our last kiss, that we always seem to find each other.

"I need to talk to Astor."

"Don't bother. Come see us in Gibraltar."

## 73.

No matter what I told myself, I was deciding on my breakup song, soon as I turned away. Last kisses are seldom remembered. Why is that? I did make a note of this one, and of his last look, getting into the back seat, white shirt, as bright as water glistens from the eyes, as the poet said, but just a little rumpled, no luggage. There are people who always look like they're stepping into a limo, even if it's a Lyft Camry, silver-blue with plastic interior.

I entered the bookstore and walked through to the grand hall of the people. In the aftermath of that last food fight I had expected a *Day of the Locust* scene, given the drug intake. It was the opposite—perhaps also because of the drug intake. How does a heavy dose of the life force manifest itself?

I walked through a slowly undulating mess of bodies and empty plates. Ambient music played. Astor was soothing the crowd, slowly showing them the door. They were hugging him, some were crying, some were laughing, some both. I thought I heard him tell someone that he had a plane to catch. He bowed, looked at the door. We were bathed in the blue but I couldn't tell if it was true. I looked up at the track lights but I'd dosed up too, so I couldn't tell if it was a trick of the filters. Astor was glowing, though, that wasn't an illusion. I waded through the crowd and came up close. He hugged me.

"That was all of it. I'm not making any more. Tonight was a form of redemption for me. I lost boatloads of money. I gave them a nearly lethal dose. I've directed my people to stop making the hots. It couldn't stay legal. Too dangerous. I feel the heat closing in, feel them out there making their moves, setting up their devil-dog stool pigeons. Tonight was our version of the acid test. People will leave here changed forever."

He did a little pirouette, nearly lost his Dr. Seuss–sized toque, blue, or white gone blue because. As he went through the door the hat did fall off, to be picked up and passed around, thrown in the air, caught and dropped, all with a sense of happy play. No riots tonight. That was the last time I saw Astor.

## 74.

Time passes quickly, slowly, then quickly again, hurry up and wait. In the weeks following Dino's escape—if that's what it was—I spent some serious time with Gertrude Stein, *The Making of Americans*, a big long story, though a little tedious. I think that was her point. Everybody's life is everybody's story. I also thought a lot about Marvin's forever war against the rock wall of capitalism. The arc is long, like they say, but also squiggly, and you just never know where it's going and there are no guarantees. Reader, I'm seeing things from a different part of the arc now, still high and dizzying, but, tragically, on the descent. Indulge me, allow me to direct you: If you have a little Marvin in you, keep hurting them, for the sheer fuck of it. Take advantage of the highs by pissing on them (you know who they are) from a higher place. Find your personal Bugatti and drive.

And sometimes, as I broke from Stein's words for a bit, to get some air and avoid the seasickness of language, I thought of Dino Centro, living a refined and sophisticated life in Gibraltar, or so I assumed. Pissing on them, the squares and the marks, from a higher place. I thought of the elegant grifters and how they move through the world. I thought of Dino Centro.

# ACKNOWLEDGMENTS

The Clay Blackburn saga has come slowly. I began writing these books in 2001, and over that period friends, editors, and collaborators have come and (too often) gone. I'm going to forget some, and I suspect that some have forgotten me, but here goes.

Dan Lebowitz read *The Chandler Apartments* in pieces, as it was written. He has a sharp ear for language, and his appreciation of the humor boosted my confidence and helped me keep on track.

Noah Ross read *Mayakovsky's Bugatti* in rough cuts and listened to scattershot ideas over cups of Folgers. I deeply appreciate his patience and encouragement.

Don Ellis and Creative Arts Book Company published *The Chandler Apartments* in 2002. Such an honor to be published by the press that originated the Black Lizard imprint.

PM Press published *The Incredible Double* early in their existence, 2009. I was amused by the concept of an anarchist press publishing genre, then amazed to be in such good company. Thank you, Ramsey, for including me.

Pam Jackson, Carol Jameson, Kimn Nielson, Thomas Ziemer, Colter Jacobsen, and Wade Ostrowski provided encouragement, editorial assistance, proofreading, typing, and good conversation as this collection was being formed.

So many others to thank! In no particular order: Michael McClure, David Meltzer, Julie Rogers, Julianne Leigh, Summer Brenner, Gloria Frym, Anthony Rizzuto, Amy Spade, Jerry Thompson (Thompson), Robert Eliason, Tom Clark, Michael Price, David Ulin, Lissa Fox, Jeff Maser, Eileen Myles, Brent White, Kim McMillon, Ray Davis.

Barry Gifford for suggesting the title.

John Howard for help with the cover.

Jennifer Dunbar Dorn for permission to quote Edward Dorn's *Gunslinger*.

The cranky ghost of Raymond Chandler.

Jonathan Lethem, whose work gave me permission to stretch the concept of genre.

The cats who watched over me as I wrote: Gertrude, Mina Loy, HD, Zelda, Lottie.

And, always and forever, Liz Leger.

# ABOUT THE AUTHORS

Owen Hill is the author of three crime novels, two books of short fiction, and many collections of poetry. He coannotated and edited *The Annotated Big Sleep* (Vintage Crime) and coedited *Berkeley Noir* (Akashic Books). He was a buyer at a secondhand bookstore for many years and is now a union organizer for the Industrial Workers of the World. He lives in Oakland.

Jonathan Lethem is the author of numerous books including *The Fortress of Solitude* and *Motherless Brooklyn*, as well as more recent best sellers *The Feral Detective* and *The Arrest*. Several of his novels have been made into major movies, and his shorter works can often be found in *The New Yorker*, *The Atlantic*, and many other venues. One of the MacArthur "genius" grant winners, Lethem is well known and widely respected for his vivid literary style, sardonic humor, and deep understanding of American culture.

## ABOUT PM PRESS

PM Press is an independent, radical publisher of critically necessary books for our tumultuous times. Our aim is to deliver bold political ideas and vital stories to all walks of life and arm the dreamers to demand the impossible. Founded in 2007 by a small group of people with decades of publishing, media, and organizing experience, we have sold millions of copies of our books, most often one at a time, face to face. We're old enough to know what we're doing and young enough to know what's at stake. Join us to create a better world.

**PM Press**
PO Box 23912
Oakland, CA 94623
www.pmpress.org

**PM Press in Europe**
europe@pmpress.org
www.pmpress.org.uk

# FRIENDS OF PM PRESS

These are indisputably momentous times—the financial system is melting down globally and the Empire is stumbling. Now more than ever there is a vital need for radical ideas.

In the many years since its founding—and on a mere shoestring—PM Press has risen to the formidable challenge of publishing and distributing knowledge and entertainment for the struggles ahead. With hundreds of releases to date, we have published an impressive and stimulating array of literature, art, music, politics, and culture. Using every available medium, we've succeeded in connecting those hungry for ideas and information to those putting them into practice.

*Friends of PM* allows you to directly help impact, amplify, and revitalize the discourse and actions of radical writers, filmmakers, and artists. It provides us with a stable foundation from which we can build upon our early successes and provides a much-needed subsidy for the materials that can't necessarily pay their own way. You can help make that happen—and receive every new title automatically delivered to your door once a month—by joining as a Friend of PM Press. And, we'll throw in a free T-shirt when you sign up.

Here are your options:

- **$30 a month** Get all books and pamphlets plus a 50% discount on all webstore purchases

- **$40 a month** Get all PM Press releases (including CDs and DVDs) plus a 50% discount on all webstore purchases

- **$100 a month** Superstar—Everything plus PM merchandise, free downloads, and a 50% discount on all webstore purchases

For those who can't afford $30 or more a month, we have **Sustainer Rates** at $15, $10, and $5. Sustainers get a free PM Press T-shirt and a 50% discount on all purchases from our website.

Your Visa or Mastercard will be billed once a month, until you tell us to stop. Or until our efforts succeed in bringing the revolution around. Or the financial meltdown of Capital makes plastic redundant. Whichever comes first.

# *The Collapsing Frontier*
Jonathan Lethem

ISBN: 978-1-62963-488-3
 979-8-88744-029-3
$16.00/$24.95   176 pages

This collection compiles his intensely personal thoughts on the most interesting and deplorable topics in post-postmodern America. It moves from original new fiction to insights on popular culture, cult and canonical authors, and problematic people.

Plus...

"David Bowman and the Furry-Girl School of American Fiction" is a personal true adventure, as Lethem tries (with the help of a seeming expert) to elbow his way into literary respectability. "The Collapsing Frontier" and "In Mugwump Four" are fictions mapping ominous new realms. "Calvino's 'Lightness' and the Feral Child of History" is an intimate encounter with a legendary author. In "My Year of Reading Lemmishly" and "Snowden in the Labyrinth" he explores courage, art, and the search for truth, with wildly different results.

*And Featuring:* Our usual Outspoken Interview, in which Lethem reveals the secret subtext of his books, how he spent his MacArthur award money, and how a Toyota he owned was used in the robbery of a fast-food restaurant.

*"Lethem is one of our most perceptive cultural critics, conversant in both the high and low realms, his insights buffeted by his descriptive imagination."*
—*Los Angeles Times Book Review*

*"One of America's greatest storytellers."*
—*Washington Post*

*"Lethem has talent to burn."*
—*Village Voice Literary Supplement*

*"Aside from being one of the most inventive writers on the planet, Lethem is also one of the funniest."*
—*San Francisco Examiner*

# Send My Love and a Molotov Cocktail: Stories of Crime, Love and Rebellion

Edited by Gary Phillips and Andrea Gibbons

ISBN: 978-1-60486-096-2
$19.95   368 pages

An incendiary mixture of genres and voices, this collection of short stories compiles a unique set of work that revolves around riots, revolts, and revolution. From the turbulent days of unionism in the streets of New York City during the Great Depression to a group of old women who meet at their local café to plan a radical act that will change the world forever, these original and once out-of-print stories capture the various ways people rise up to challenge the status quo and change up the relationships of power. Ideal for any fan of noir, science fiction, and revolution and mayhem, this collection includes works from Sara Paretsky, Paco Ignacio Taibo II, Cory Doctorow, Kenneth Wishnia, and Summer Brenner.

**Full list of contributors:**

Summer Brenner
Rick Dakan
Barry Graham
Penny Mickelbury
Gary Phillips
Luis Rodriguez
Benjamin Whitmer
Michael Moorcock
Larry Fondation

Cory Doctorow
Andrea Gibbons
John A. Imani
Sara Paretsky
Kim Stanley Robinson
Paco Ignacio Taibo II
Kenneth Wishnia
Michael Skeet
Tim Wohlforth

## *Jewish Noir*
### Edited by Kenneth Wishnia
ISBN: 978-1-62963-111-0
$17.95   432 pages

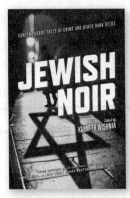

*Jewish Noir* is a unique collection of new stories by Jewish and non-Jewish literary and genre writers, including numerous award-winning authors such as Marge Piercy, Harlan Ellison, S.J. Rozan, Nancy Richler, Moe Prager, Wendy Hornsby, Charles Ardai, and Kenneth Wishnia. The stories explore such issues as the Holocaust and its long-term effects on subsequent generations, anti-Semitism in the mid- and late-twentieth-century United States, and the dark side of the Diaspora (the decline of revolutionary fervor, the passing of generations, the Golden Ghetto, etc.). The stories in this collection also include many "teachable moments" about the history of prejudice, and the contradictions of ethnic identity and assimilation into American society.

Stories include:
- "*A Simkhe*" (A Celebration), first published in Yiddish in the *Forverts* in 1912 by one of the great unsung writers of that era, Yente Serdatsky. This story depicts the disillusionment that sets in among a group of Russian Jewish immigrant radicals after several years in the United States. This is the story's first appearance in English.
- "Trajectories," Marge Piercy's story of the divergent paths taken by two young men from the slums of Cleveland and Detroit in a rapidly changing post-World War II society.
- "Some You Lose," Nancy Richler's empathetic exploration of the emotional and psychological challenges of trying to sum up a man's life in a eulogy.
- "Her Daughter's Bat Mitzvah," Rabbi Adam Fisher's darkly comic profanity-filled monologue in the tradition of Sholem Aleichem, the writer best known as the source material for *Fiddler on the Roof* (minus the profanity, that is).
- "Flowers of Shanghai," S.J. Rozan's compelling tale of hope and despair set in the European refugee community of Japanese-occupied Shanghai during World War II.
- "Yahrzeit Candle," Stephen Jay Schwartz's take on the subtle horrors of the inevitable passing of time.

*"Stirring. Evocative. Penetrating."*
—Elie Wiesel (on Stephen Jay Schwartz's "Yahrzeit Candle")

*"Wishnia presents the world of Ashkenazi Jewry with a keen eye for detail. Wishnia never judges his characters, but creates three-dimensional people who live in a very dangerous world."*
—The Jewish Press on "The Fifth Servant"

# *The Jook*
Gary Phillips

ISBN: 978-1-60486-040-5
$15.95    256 pages

Zelmont Raines has slid a long way since his ability to jook, to outmaneuver his opponents on the field, made him a Super Bowl–winning wide receiver, earning him lucrative endorsement deals and more than his share of female attention. But Zee hasn't always been good at saying no, so a series of missteps involving drugs, a paternity suit or two, legal entanglements, shaky investments and recurring injuries have virtually sidelined his career.

That is until Los Angeles gets a new pro franchise, the Barons, and Zelmont has one last chance at the big time he dearly misses. Just as it seems he might be getting back in the flow, he's enraptured by Wilma Wells, the leggy and brainy lawyer for the team—who has a ruthless game plan all her own. And it's Zelmont who might get jooked.

"Phillips, author of the acclaimed Ivan Monk series, takes elements of Jim Thompson (the ending), black-exploitation flicks (the profanity-fueled dialogue), and Penthouse magazine (the sex is anatomically correct) to create an over-the-top violent caper in which there is no honor, no respect, no love, and plenty of money. Anyone who liked George Pelecanos' King Suckerman is going to love this even-grittier take on many of the same themes."
—Wes Lukowsky, *Booklist*

"Enough gritty gossip, blistering action and trash talk to make real life L.A. seem comparatively wholesome."
—Kirkus Reviews

"Gary Phillips writes tough and gritty parables about life and death on the mean streets—a place where sometimes just surviving is a noble enough cause. His is a voice that should be heard and celebrated. It rings true once again in The Jook, a story where all of Phillips' talents are on display."
—Michael Connelly, author of the Harry Bosch books

# *Pike*
## Benjamin Whitmer

**ISBN: 978-1-60486-089-4**
**$15.95   224 pages**

Douglas Pike is no longer the murderous hustler he was in his youth, but reforming hasn't made him much kinder. He's just living out his life in his Appalachian hometown, working odd jobs with his partner, Rory, hemming in his demons the best he can. And his best seems just good enough until his estranged daughter overdoses and he takes in his twelve-year-old granddaughter, Wendy.

Just as the two are beginning to forge a relationship, Derrick Kreiger, a dirty Cincinnati cop, starts to take an unhealthy interest in the girl. Pike and Rory head to Cincinnati to learn what they can about Derrick and the death of Pike's daughter, and the three men circle, evenly matched predators in a human wilderness of junkie squats, roadhouse bars and homeless Vietnam vet encampments.

"*Without so much as a sideways glance towards gentility,* Pike *is one righteous mutherfucker of a read. I move that we put Whitmer's balls in a vise and keep slowly notching up the torque until he's willing to divulge the secret of how he managed to hit such a perfect stride his first time out of the blocks.*"
—Ward Churchill

"*Benjamin Whitmer's* Pike *captures the grime and the rage of my not-so-fair city with disturbing precision. The words don't just tell a story here, they scream, bleed, and burst into flames.* Pike, *like its eponymous main character, is a vicious punisher that doesn't mince words or take prisoners, and no one walks away unscathed. This one's going to haunt me for quite some time.*"
—Nathan Singer

"*This is what noir is, what it can be when it stops playing nice—blunt force drama stripped down to the bone, then made to dance across the page.*"
—Stephen Graham Jones